WHERE THE PRETTY THINGS ROT

HENRY SNIDER

WHERE THE PRETTY THINGS ROT

POLYMATH
— PRESS —

Aurora, CO

Where the Pretty Things Rot by Henry Snider

This book is a work of fiction. All incidents, events, characters, names, businesses, places, and other entities depicted are either fictitious or are used fictitiously.

Publication histories of the stories included are provided on the facing page.

Published by Polymath Press, a trade name of Polymath Enterprises, LLC. Please direct all inquiries to Polymath Press, P. O. Box 461870, Aurora, CO 80046-1870, online at www.polymathpress.com, or via email to editor@polymathpress.com.

First edition

October, 2025

ISBN (trade paperback): 978-1-961827-16-5
ISBN (eBook): 978-1-961827-17-2
Library of Congress Control Number: 2025946896

"The Clown" first appeared in *The Best of the Horror Society 2013*, edited by Carson Buckingham, The Horror Society Press, 2013

"Sandcastles" first appeared in *Canopic Jars—Tales of Mummies and Mummification*, edited by Gregory L. Norris, Great Old Ones Publishing, 2013

"Someone to Watch Over Me" first appeared in *Summer Thrills*, edited by Dorothy Davies, Static Movement, 2012

"Taste" first appeared in *Once Bitten ~ Never Die*, edited by Jessica A. Weiss, Wicked East Press, 2011

"Singed" first appeared in *Full Metal Horror 2*, edited by Adam Bennett and Sam M. Phillips, Zombie Pirate Publishing, 2019

"Room Service" first appeared in *Sick Cruising*, Notch Publishing, 2020

"Lunar Descent" first appeared in *A-Z of Horror: L is for Lycans*, Red Cape Publishing, 2021

"Songbird" first appeared in *Solitude*, edited by Zach Friday, DBND Publishing, 2020

"Fellowship" first appeared in *Ultimate Angels—Tales of Winged Warriors*, edited by Elizabeth LaFond, 2012

"1865" first appeared on episode 121 of *Library of the Living Dead* podcast, Library of the Living Dead, 2011

"The Vessel" first appeared in *Help! Wanted: Tales of on-the-Job Terror*, edited by Peter Giglio, Evil Jester Press, 2011

"Trophies" first appeared in *Ghost Stories For Starless Nights*, edited by Zach Friday and Nate Vice, DBND Publishing, 2020

"A Murder of Crows" first appeared in *Anthology: Year One*, edited by Mark Wholley, Shroud Publishing, 2012

"Skewed Perceptions" first appeared in *Darkness Wired*, edited by C.S. Olson, Notch Publishing House, 2019

Other Polymath Press titles featuring Henry Snider

In the Woods: A Fiction Foundry Anthology
edited by Robert Lewis (November, 2023)

Forthcoming Books by Henry Snider

Drive-In Feature (Coming in 2026)

For my family.

CONTENTS

AUTHOR'S NOTE

Collected within these pages are sixteen stories – some new, some previously-published—but all with themes as dark as my favorite kind of chocolate.

One of the most frustrating questions for an author is, "Where do you get your ideas?" It's not that we don't know—often we do. It has more to do with confessing that writers—hell, creative people in general—daydream constantly. We don't sit and produce word vomit on command...well...most of us don't. Ideas fill our heads constantly. It could be from seeing someone in a fit of road rage on their way to work, or just as simple as that uncomfortable knot in your stomach when you pass too close to a shadow-filled alley. Some come from bets—such as this collection's opening story, *The Clown* (*you can find more on the bet after the story*). Essentially, daydreams and experiences plant the seeds of what become art.

I do want to take a moment and acknowledge that some of the stories carry subject matter involving eyes. This was pointed out by my editor. In hindsight (*pun totally intended and abused for your pleasure*), the reason leads back to a car accident my wife Hollie and I were in during the late 2000s. I was struck essentially blind for months and deaf in one ear. It left me unable to focus my eyes for more than a second or two. After months of nausea medication, specialists shrugging their shoulders, and my family's immense patience, my vision stabilized. Life returned to normal, but my writing had a few changes while my subconscious worked out the trauma. Now vision jokes are the cringe-filled norm in our household.

I've done my best to share what planted the initial seeds that ultimately grew into the stories you now hold in your hand. I hope you enjoy the "behind the scenes" as much as I did living them.

Fair warning, these snippets do contain spoilers, so read the story first.

- Henry

THE CLOWN

Smells of rancid popcorn permeated the air, leaving a buttery film no one wanted. Lisa Welsley leaned forward, resting elbows on knees, and studied each street performer along the boardwalk. Geeks walked past—each offering a different take on their iron stomach—the last of whom bit the end off of a bottle and pierced his cheek in the process. Blood strained through his grizzled beard, changing the color from dishwater blond to burnt amber.

"Thon-of-a-bith," the geek managed to the jovial laughter of those who succeeded where he failed. He dislodged the green glass and shook his head as a wet dog would, spraying bloody spittle across the wooden boardwalk and peppering Lisa's white sneakers.

"Asshole," she muttered.

Barkers shouted out insults and challenges to passersby, daring them to prove their worth at various games of chance. A wisp of cotton candy escaped its machine to be carried away by the night breeze. Lisa watched it, transfixed by the pink fluff as it danced over the rail, lifting higher before it disappeared beyond the shine of the lights. Her gaze returned to the rather tasteless striptease performed outside of one tent that offered more patch than substance. She counted over half a dozen cracks and holes along the side of the clapboard and canvas structure, some clearly made by those too cheap to pay for their extracurricular activities. An involuntary shiver coursed through her as one of the patrons stopped in the entrance, stared back at her and smiled a Cheshire cat grin before entering.

"I'm fifteen, you sick prick," she muttered to herself.

Then the clown appeared again.

Decked out in classic clown attire, and barely three feet tall, the entertainer wound through the crowd, over-sized red plastic sunglasses bobbing with each exaggerated step. A couple, obviously on vacation, tried to get the small character's attention for a photograph but only succeeded in running into locals as the little black and white comedian darted between legs and navigated strollers with practiced ease. Lisa moved from her vantage point and trotted after the green-haired performer.

The clown threaded the masses to the burlesque tent's entrance and looked back. It scanned the crowd as if searching for someone. Lisa ducked down, pulled the red ball cap low and continued to close in on the small form. As she closed in, the clown focused on her. It backed up the two risers, stepped behind the show's barker and peeked, to the catcalling amusement of all, from between the tall man's legs and waved a flyer emphatically at everyone.

"Shit," Lisa mumbled.

"Right here, right here!" The barker called out and tapped his cane against the clown's backside. "We have them short and tall, thick and thin, dry and…well…." He used the tip of the cane to lift the side of a dancer's robe and flashed a length of ghost-white hip where panties, if there were any, would have rested. She smacked the cane away in mock modesty and resumed her gyrating pre-show actions.

Lisa stood at the front of the crowd, a solitary Eve in a mob of eager Adams. She and the clown stared at each other, mere steps apart. The teen's hand went out, palm up, in an attempt to coax her small quarry down from the current perch.

Suddenly the clown pushed the barker from his stoop. The man staggered and waved the cane as he fought to regain balance. Lisa instinctively reached out, caught the man and tried her best to steady his skeletal form. He recovered, stood upright, then grabbed her by the hand and pulled the teen two steps onto the makeshift stage.

Shock and embarrassment flushed Lisa's face red. She stared at the clown who looked up from less than two feet away. White cake makeup covered exposed flesh where costume did not, though now smears showed hints of the brown skin below. Heavy forehead wrinkles marked where the semi-bald wig began. Cheeks sat sallow below the giant sunglasses, giving the impression of malnutrition hidden by layers of flaking white makeup. A sudden jerk on her jean jacket twisted Lisa around to face the barker.

"See here, one and all." He let go and she staggered down one step. "Even this pretty little doe wants to see Dante's Delights." The barker towered over Lisa, breath stinking of soured fish and chips. "You *do* want to see what we have to offer inside, don't you?" He stood upright quickly and the sudden change in focus left Lisa dizzy. The clown squatted, slid over the riser's corner and disappeared down the short alley, illuminated by scattered beams of light spilling from the girlie show's tent. The showman pressed the handle of his bird's head cane against Lisa's chest.

"Hey!" A smack at the cane but only succeeded in hooking it into her t-shirt's collar. Balance gone, Lisa performed her own stumbling act, similar to that of the barker's a moment before. The cane's beak ensnared both shirt and bra before it ripped free leaving the teen to land hard on the ground. Ocean air bit at the newly exposed skin and she scrambled to cover herself amidst the throng of onlookers.

"I...sorry..." the barker began before hearing the assembled crowd cheer and whoop at the sudden flash of nipple. What began a second before as concern hardened once more to a money-driven game face. "See that, folks? Women can't even keep their clothes on *just standing* in front of my fine establishment." A volley of lewd suggestions erupted from the crowd, things so sick Lisa couldn't fully fathom. The showman continued and drew the crowd's attention back to the dancer he'd previously taunted by pointing at the woman and offering a mock-shocked expression. Lisa took the opportunity to backpedal to the riser's edge and followed the clown into the alley.

Two steps into the alley Lisa stopped. A few beams of light shot out at different angles and offered sparse illumination by which to navigate the narrow passage. Garbage bags and other bound refuse littered the ground. A stink no better than the barker's breath hung in the air.

At the far end of the alley stood the clown's silhouette, outlined perfectly against a gray night. The clown didn't move.

Lisa took the opportunity to pull a bobby pin from under her hat and threaded it through the torn portion of her shirt. She bent the metal over, anchoring the collar to the tattered front once more.

"There's no place to go." Her voice echoed louder than intended. "Just come on. Please?" A forced smile played across her face. "Come with me."

The clown's head cocked to one side then shook side to side with an automated slowness and waved the flyer up and down as if it were a bird's wing.

"Heh. I'll go with you, sweetness."

Lisa looked down to the nearest bundle and recognized it as a bum taking advantage of one of the holes in the dance hall wall. The way he hunched as he glared over one shoulder left no question of his current activity.

Instinct screamed for Lisa to turn and run into the relative safety of the boardwalk crowd...but that led away from the clown. She couldn't do that.

"Piss off!" She closed in on the clown in two self-assured steps.

The bum's hand shot out and grasped her calf. "Aww. Don't be like that."

His hand felt disgustingly warm and she thanked the stars above that she chose to wear jeans tonight instead of shorts despite the warm weather. Lisa kicked free and the bum tumbled. Rather than look back, she continued toward the shadowed form at the far end of the alley. The bum rustled to right himself as the distance between teen and clown grew short.

Ten feet.

Seven.

Lisa reached out again. "Don't be scared."

Five.

The clown took off with surprising speed, darted to the left then shimmied along the narrow space between the rear of a tent and the pier's rail. With no desire to lose what little distance she'd gained in the last few minutes, Lisa squeezed behind the shop and followed her pint-sized leader.

"Heyyyyyyy…" the bum said from right behind her. "You don't wanna go that way. The railing's rotted. You best come with me."

A hand brushed against Lisa's ponytail. She scooted faster, then sprinted a handful of steps before daring a look back. The bum still stood at the alley's threshold, arm still outstretched toward her. All the lectures her mother gave about being safe and treating every solitary location as the ideal place for a rapist to take advantage surfaced. The man's hair, now visible, hung in sweaty clumps and offered no hint of showers past.

Her chest hurt.

At first Lisa attributed it to the cane head, but it really hadn't impacted hard. This was something else. Her breath hitched. Inhaling required a conscious effort. Lisa leaned on the rail to steady herself, felt the rotten wood lean, then crack and threaten to give way.

Panic. I'm having a panic attack.

The clown—*her* clown—stopped at the end of the next tent, head swiveling from side to side to scan each possible path: the walkway along the backs of the structures, the alley back out to the boardwalk proper, or the barred ladder to the beach below. The clown's gaze focused on the latter.

Finally, a break. "Don't move. That ladder's dangerous."

The clown took a step towards the single metal bar that blocked access to the ladder, jerking movements appearing like a little dance, daring Lisa to speed up.

"I mean it." Lisa took two more steps. Behind her, the bum called out something, but whatever he said ended up stolen by the ocean breeze. Lisa reached forward, only grasping air as the clown shot underneath the metal bar and worked the rungs with practiced agility.

Lisa dove. Half her body slid under the bar and out into space before she reached down and grabbed the clown's black and white striped shoulder. A rung broke and the clown fell out into open air, turning a comical half cartwheel as gravity laid claim to the tiny entertainer.

"No!"

The figure shrank in size until she was sure the clown would disappear entirely.

Then the clown struck water.

A gray poof in an otherwise black sea showed the impact.

Lisa squinted and tried to make out the clown in the blackness.

Nothing…then lighter pinpricks moved in the dark as the clown fought hard against the ocean's pull and half swam under the boardwalk.

"Damn it," she breathed. "Not again." A half-dozen splinters bit into her belly, each doing its own part to keep the teen on the pier. Lisa freed herself from the anchored splinters and followed down the latter, careful to test each rung before putting her full weight on it. Repeated glances down offered little hope to pinpoint which way the clown went. Gray caps from waves striking pillars reflected little light.

Ten minutes of careful descent brought her to the final rung. Still the distance to the waterline looked dangerous. The rung groaned… cracked, then sent her splashing into icy water.

Lisa bobbed, gasping to the surface, only to have a wave steal the breath and knock her into the pillar she'd just climbed down.

She grabbed at the wooden beam and leaned against it while she struggled to stay afloat. Seawater fell from her mouth with each coughing exhale.

"No…more," she said around deep heaves for breath.

Parallel blades of light streaked the sand and offered soft illumination from the myriad of activities a few dozen feet above. Trash, netted by an ever-present length of seaweed, blanketed an otherwise beige surface of sand. There, among all the other forgotten debris crawled the clown. Moving in slow motion, one hand reached out, the clown pulled itself forward, then stretched out the opposite hand to mimic the first.

Lisa followed, kicking her way through the black water. She took a moment to study the small form.

Soaked fabric clung to the clown and showed a figure significantly smaller than the wire-assisted barrel waistline proclaimed. Oversized sunglasses, now dislodged, hung loose around the costume's collar.

Lisa kicked out hard, catching the small form in the hip.

It jerked away.

"No…more," she repeated.

A second kick rolled the clown onto its back, revealing a handful of blonde locks peeking out from the wig. Locks of hair the same shade as Lisa's. Cake makeup washed away by the ocean left leathery skin exposed. Shriveled sockets stared up at her from a face dead two years this past Halloween.

"Iiiiiiaaaahhhh…" the mouth worked, "…wuh…wuh…."

Lisa kicked out a third time and caught her little sister in the ribs and exploded a word from the child's corpse.

"Wuhon't," the child barked.

Another sneakered blow rolled the small corpse onto its side. "Won't what?" She kicked again and one toe painfully struck the child's pelvis. The impact rolled the clown onto her belly again. Her toe throbbed. "Tell?" Lisa knelt. "Is that what you were going to say, Carrie? That you're not going to tell?"

Lisa stood and backed two steps. Adrenaline kicked in. "Of course you're going to tell, Carrie. You *always* tell."

Carrie reached brittle hands out and pulled herself another foot away from her big sister.

"You told about me and Ted in the shower." Lisa stepped forward again, rolled the clown-corpse onto her back with a foot before straddling her. "You told about me sneaking out." She smacked Carrie across the face. White makeup sloughed off along with some of the skin that held it in place. Slitted leathery skin, stretched drum-taught across empty sockets, stared up at the teen. "You told about my suspension." Another smack loosened the bald wig further, exposing a deep depression just above the left ear.

One of Carrie's arms raised to hold off the attack.

Lisa knocked it away.

"You *tell*, Carrie. That's what you do." Lisa emphasized each of the last four words by thunking a finger hollowly against the corpse's forehead.

"Iaaahhhhhhh," Carrie said.

Lisa adjusted her position and let both knees rest on the girl's chest. She felt the corpse struggle to inhale, just as it had every month for the last two years. Her knees dug in and a rib cracked. Lisa's little sister struggled harder, heels kicked into the sand, digging for purchase.

Carrie's reached up, grabbing at Lisa in an effort to dislodge her.

"No more!" Lisa brought both hands down, smashing them into the clown's face. Bone buckled and the child's skull bloomed open to the night air as Lisa's fists broke into the husk of young corpse's face.

Carrie's kicks stopped.

"No more," Lisa repeated, voice no more than a whisper, pulling her hands—one dripping blood—from Carrie's body. She sat with her little sister for a time and watched the waves splash against water-soaked pillars. An hour later found Lisa covered in sand and sitting atop a small rise on the beach. Her hand, now clotted, but open and raw, showed a new train track pattern of teeth marks that carved a vicious half-moon into the palm. The scarred remains of similar wounds peppered up and down her arm.

One of the flyers, showing a cherubic little girl, emblazoned with, "HAVE YOU SEEN ME?" blew free from the nearby seaweed and disappeared into the night.

"You won't tell this time, Carrie. I won't let you."

Behind the story...

"The Clown" actually came from a bet. My wife, Hollie, has coulrophobia—the fear of clowns. For clarity, we're not talking about not liking them. We're talking about absolute terror at even seeing one. It took over 25 years to convince her to watch Stephen King's *It* miniseries with Tim Curry. By the end of the second half, she was green enough to have had food poisoning.

A better example might be when we went to Zak Bagans' Haunted Museum in Las Vegas, Nevada. The tour was fantastic, akin to being inside a giant, albeit morbid, cabinet of curiosities. Each room offered one dark piece of history after another...that is until we got to the attic. Now, this attic is a long room lined with—you guessed it—clown statues along the entire hallway and lit by strobe lights. At the end it turned right, then left where attendees would exit through a doorway and continue the tour. With no way to go back, Hollie just started screaming. Now, understand, Hollie's a tomboy. I can count the number of times she's lost control on one hand and still have three fingers free. This is *not* typical. She just closed her eyes and screamed while I followed behind her, gripping her shoulders and guided her down the hallway as fast as I could. Mid-way along there was one person in a clown suit ready to do the fun "jump scare." He took one look, put his hands up and waved us on. As I mentioned, the hallway was only lit by strobes. When I reached the end of the hall I slowed down to see where I needed to guide Hollie next.

What we didn't know at the time was that the museum had a famous little person, whose name eludes me at the time of writing this, performing as one of the clowns. This individual climbed out of an over-sized air vent positioned on the floor right in front of us. So—of course—this was the instant Hollie chose to open her eyes. Her foot went up and I had just enough time to turn Hollie away from the tiny clown and guide her around the first of two corners.

That's right, folks, my wife nearly curb-stomped a little person.

But it's not over.

I guided her around the second wall and right where the exit is there's a third clown performer who jumped out, not more than two feet in front of Hollie. Her fist lined up… and I shoved my lovely wife into the hall right before she got an assault charge. About an hour later, we're leaving the museum's gift shop and the clowns are having a break in the parking lot. They look over at her and all start talking about the crazy lady who wanted to kill them. Hollie took one look at them and went right back into fight or flight mode and was ready to finish what she tried to start.

Although you can't take photos inside the museum, we have a few from outside and a couple of the clowns in the parking lot.

When I say, "Hollie has coulrophobia," I *mean it.*

Now, about this bet for "The Clown." Please note that bet actually took place before the Zak Bagans Museum incident.

Hollie and I were talking about that there had to be a clown somewhere that she didn't hate. She stuck with variations of, "Nope," and "They only convey one emotion. They're all evil." This went back and forth for a few days before I bet her I could find a clown she didn't hate. Her only condition was that animals didn't count because people force them into the outfits and animals are always cute.

Fair enough.

I wrote "The Clown" over one weekend to make a point. What surprised me is that while writing it I discovered myself really starting to care for Carrie and hate her sister. I finished the story, took a deep breath, printed it, then handed it over to Hollie.

She looked at the title and cut me a "You will pay for making me read this" stare before reading "the Clown." After setting the last page down she flipped me a very unladylike bird and left the room with the story. An hour later she dropped the pages in my lap with red editorial marks adorning every page.

I've never been told I won…or lost.

But, I've gotta admit, being flipped that bird felt pretty damned good.

SANDCASTLES

The Utah wind whipped against the car's right side, threatening to force it into the neighboring lane. Teri overcorrected and felt the vibration strips bordering the shoulder. A second jerk of the wheel pulled the car back between painted lines.

"Damn it," she muttered and stole a glance at the passenger seat. Melanie didn't show any signs of waking up. Her wife stayed neatly curled as if a cat in a warm ray of sunshine, dark curls masking naturally caramel-colored skin.

Her wife.

The thought rolled through Teri's mind like a freight train. Not even married a week and the two had settled on a cross-country adventure for their honeymoon. They flew four hours to Los Angeles and rented a car so the landscape would be new from day one. Angry urban lifestyles had given way to equally angry suburbanites as they tore through the land of actors, aspiring actors, and would-never-be actors. That first day came to a close and the second was nearly half-gone before the couple happened across someone who wasn't hoping to make it on the big screen…or little screen for that matter.

Teri leaned her head from side to side, stretching tense neck muscles.

A semi blasted past them doing at least ninety, and the car shuddered in its wake.

"Damn it," she repeated and adjusted her glasses. A bit of blonde hair escaped her scrunchy and tickled the front of her face. She pulled the band and chucked it onto the passenger floorboard where two others lay discarded. Hair fell around her shoulders wicking the sweat from her neck.

"You gotta get a new curse," Melanie mumbled, then shifted and stretched her legs out.

"Sorry. Didn't mean to wake you."

"Well…" she said through a yawn as she rubbed sleep from her eyes, "you wouldn't have if you didn't keep thumping my head against the window."

"Sorry." Teri gripped the wheel a little harder. "It's this damned wind. It keeps tossing us all over the place." She blew at the free strands of hair, trying to get them away from her lips before giving up and tucking the cluster behind one ear.

"You know, we could have stayed another day in Salt Lake City and rested up a bit more."

"Pass."

"Oh, it wasn't *that* bad."

"Once we were on the outskirts it wasn't that bad, but the hotel… and right across from the compound."

"Teri, it was the Latter-Day Saints, and no one said a single negative word to us the entire time we were there."

"It wasn't what they *said*. It was the men." Teri's grip went from tight to white-knuckled. "You know what I mean."

"What?" She smirked and crinkled her nose. "Seeing two beautiful people in love?"

"No. The men seeing us as if we were two porn stars about to go at it any moment."

"Well, after the dancing last night—"

"Stop it," Teri said. A smile played at the corners of her mouth.

"And that trick you did when we got back to our room."

The smile wouldn't be refused and grew. "I mean it." Her grip on the wheel eased a tad.

"Listen, Em, most men are just going to do that. They can't help it. Besides, I think I can keep the assholes at bay for you."

Em. Short for emerald, the dark green of Teri's eyes. The perfect name to be whispered in her ear where no one else could hear. A name given to her.

The perfect name.

"I know." Teri reached over and squeezed Melanie's leg. "You did take care of the 'Boy Wonders' at the club, didn't you?"

"Yuppers."

In fact, she did. Last night, they enjoyed an evening of dinner and dancing up until around ten. That's when Steven and Cal cornered them at the bar and offered to buy them drinks. Melanie politely refused the offer when one—Teri couldn't remember which was Steven and which was Cal—noticed their wedding rings and said he was sure it would be okay to steal a dance or two until the girls' husbands showed up. Without missing a beat, Mel replied that they were on *their* honeymoon, then snatched Teri by the hand and whisked her back to the dance floor before the statement sank in with the would-be Romeos.

Melanie massaged her scalp vigorously, trying to wake up before reaching into the back seat, and pulled a bottled water from the cooler. "Want one?"

"Still on my soda."

"Munchies?"

"Nope."

"Shit."

"Uhhh…cute, Mels."

"No. Check out the rear-view."

Teri glanced at the rear-view mirror and saw the razor-straight stretch of interstate behind them disappearing into a dusty beige landscape. "Looks dusty."

"Dusty, hell."

Teri gave a second look. The shifting beige background went from the ground to so high in the sky it disappeared out of sight at the top of the back window. She checked the side mirror. Same thing. "How big is this thing?"

Mel stayed turned around in the seat looking from left to right.

"It goes as far as I can see both north and south."

Teri waited for the wind pounding against the side of the car to ease, then craned her head to look over her left shoulder. A wall of dust and debris pushed from the west, swallowing everything in its path. "Christ. How far back is it?"

A canary-yellow SUV shot past going the opposite direction and straight toward the dust storm. "Tell you in a sec." She felt Melanie tapping her fingers on the driver's seat as seconds became minutes.

One....

Three....

Five....

"Almost six minutes behind us," she blurted out. "That storm's so dense the Hummer was there one second then gone the next."

"Guess we're going the right direction then, huh?"

"Creepy." She was still turned around and staring out the back window.

"With all this wind, I'd be a lot happier if you'd turn around and buckle up."

"Don't wanna be a widow before the honeymoon's over?"

"There are times...."

Melanie slid around clutching a bag of Cheetos and a water. She dumped both onto the seat between them and locked her safety belt in place. "Better?"

"Much."

They peaked a small rise and noticed cars coming the opposite direction flashing their lights. The distant sound of horns overshadowed their music playing. Ahead of them, maybe five miles away, twinkling reflections of cars jammed bumper to bumper met their eyes.

Melanie slapped the dash. "A traffic jam?" She tore the Cheetos bag open without looking down.

"Out here?" Teri added.

The multi-colored line of traffic went as far as they could see, disappearing over a rise ten or so miles ahead.

Melanie pointed to a sign as they shot past. "There!"

"What?"

"An exit coming up in a mile."

"But we don't know where it goes."

Melanie motioned to the road ahead. "The evil we know, or the evil we don't?"

Teri looked around at the landscape. Ground so dry even scrub brush refused to grow met her gaze in every direction. She glanced at the fuel gauge—three quarters of a tank. Butterflies danced in her stomach at the thought of being stranded in such desolate territory. "I don't—"

"There it is. Take it."

"I—"

"Em, just do it!" Melanie jabbed an orange-stained finger in the exit's direction for emphasis.

Teri rolled her eyes and sighed but flicked on the turn signal. She had to brake hard because the off ramp was shorter than expected, and the car went from sixty to fifteen in a short span before skidding to a dusty halt in front of the stop sign. There was no on-ramp across the road, only a crevasse serving as the final resting place for old tumbleweeds. A left turn would take them under the interstate on a single-lane access barely big enough for a car to navigate. Shadows contrasted sharply in the midday sun, making the underpass appear darker to the naked eye. Their other option bore little in the way of promise. To the right, a dust-encrusted blacktop ended a dozen or so yards from where the car sat. Granted, the road continued, but appeared to become more washboard than actual road before vanishing over the rise a quarter-mile away.

Teri sat and stared first at the underpass and then to the rough stretch of road before settling on Melanie. "Well?"

"Well what?" She took a long drink from the bottle of water.

"Which way, oh great adventurer?"

"No idea."

Teri reached over, popped open the glove box, and grabbed the last remaining scrunchie. She fumbled with it, pulling the sweaty mane off the back of her neck again. "No one's come down after us. Maybe I can back up."

"And wait who knows how long before traffic gets moving again? I think not."

The air hung heavy in the rental car with Teri struggling not to lose her temper and Melanie obliviously content to follow her Zen approach to the situation.

Teri looked at Melanie then straight out the front of the car. "What did it say?"

"Hmmm?"

Words came from Teri's mouth both slow and quiet. "The sign for this exit. What did it say?"

"Free beer." Melanie sat a little straighter when the comment fell flat. "Sorry, Em. I didn't mean to…." The words trailed off.

Teri continued to stare out the windshield for nearly a full minute when she said, "I know. I'm just hot, tired, and not really looking forward to any of the options before us right now."

Wind buffeted the car, rocking it from right rear to left front.

"I don't remember what it said. I just caught sight of the thing as we went by." She furrowed her brow and pinched the bridge of her nose with a forefinger and thumb. "I *think* it said something about a rest stop."

Teri chanced a look over her shoulder. "You'd think with a sandstorm coming there'd be a line of cars coming down here after us."

"There weren't that many behind us." She stuck a thumb out to the right. "I doubt the rest stop's that way."

"Good. I don't think my back could handle that."

"So," Melanie said with a renewed grin, "our adventure takes us to the left?"

Another sigh escaped her. "To the left," she agreed.

Her wife leaned over and stole a quick kiss, leaving a Cheeto-encrusted orange print on the side of Teri's mouth.

"Keep eating those and I'm going to start calling you Chester."

"Chester?" Her eyes lit up. "Oh, the cheetah. Cool. I can be Chester the cheesy Arabian lesbian cheetah."

"Quite the name. Sounds right up your alley."

"Halloween's just a few months away."

Another gust of wind hit the car, causing them both to crane their necks and look out the rear window. The sky still shone blue, but the onset of the storm was evident. Air pressure increased, and they both yawned in an effort to get their ears to pop.

Teri turned left. "Pillow talk later."

Melanie sat back and stared at her. "Pillow talk? After three years, your pillow talk's still about as Disney as it comes."

Teri cut her a look and stuck out her tongue.

The bridge loomed overhead. Two slices of shade and then the road curved left and out of sight. Sand peppered the car along the driver's side, leaving residue a darker hue of orange than Melanie's kiss. She stepped on the gas. Shade engulfed the vehicle, and the bridge shielded them from the worst of Mother Nature's assault. Both women looked at the narrow access. Graffiti covered the concrete where the hill's slope met the underside of the structure. All of the writing and artwork was too small to make out and lacked the general soft-cornered touch that spray paint offered.

"Creepy," Teri breathed. She strained to make out some of what marred the slate-gray surface. Words and drawings stayed just out of focus. Her eyes watered, causing images to blur into ant-trails and deny her any sense of enlightenment.

A low rumble filled the car as the wind whipped up ahead of them. Dirt, tumbleweeds, and loose clumps of weeds whipped past at crazy speeds.

"Em," Melanie said while gripping the car's door handle, "we better get moving. Looks like the storm's about here."

Teri stepped on the gas and moved the car into the channel between the bridges. "Only fifty feet. Only fifty feet," she repeated. The car rocked as they left the relative safety of the underpass. "Come on." She stepped harder on the gas pedal and felt the slip on the sand.

"Easy," Melanie said, raising her voice to be heard over the gale.

Fifty feet fell to thirty, then to ten. Just as quickly as the wind assaulted them, it blew past as Teri stopped the car once again, this time directly beneath the road.

Melanie grasped the door handle and slid her flip-flops on. "Will you look at that," she said, staring at a new batch of graffiti up high on the concrete.

Teri clicked the lock button just before her wife pulled on the handle and was rewarded with a motherly look.

"Come on, Em. Let me out. I wanna see. I mean look at all this graffiti...in the middle of nowhere!" She grinned. "Aren't you at least a little bit interested what people had to say out here…under a bridge? It could be like some kind of prophetic poetry."

"Not as interested as you might think."

"It could be prophetic."

"It's probably a limerick about a man and his horse."

"Let me out," Melanie said playfully. "Let a girl have some fun."

"You could have fun at a funeral."

Her smile broadened. "Depends on the funeral. Five minutes. I promise."

"How about we get to the rest stop and you can look at all the urban hieroglyphics you want after this blows over?"

"Deal!"

"And," Teri added, "you drive the next leg."

"But it's so *boring*!" She stressed the last word in such a salute to teenage years past that they broke into laughter.

"That's the deal. Better take it before I add a foot rub in for good measure."

"Fine," Melanie relented. "But hurry up. I've got to pee."

Teri urged the car from their relative safety and back into the storm. She followed the road around to the left. The car faced back in the direction they'd come and the coming storm's full fury slid into view. The virtual wall of wind was nearly upon them. Good-sized pieces of sand pitted the glass as each second passed.

"Em, go." Melanie gripped Teri's shoulder hard. "Go! Go, go, go!"

Teri stomped on the gas, spinning the tires as they raced toward the cluster of brown-painted structures just ahead. Something swung across the middle of the road. She hit the brakes just as quickly, but not fast enough to stop short of the heavy-duty chain barring the road. Headlights shattered and the hood popped free of the clasp, only to have the wind jerk the plate of metal up, straining the hinges and blocking any view of what was about to hit.

"CLOSED," the sign read before the hood blocked it from view.

"No," Teri whispered.

"Back!" Melanie went from gripping her shoulder to smacking it repeatedly. "Back under the bridge!"

Teri put the car in reverse and backed as quickly as she dared. Bright blue sky fell to an angry orange then darkened. The underpass appeared as little more than a mirage through dust-coated windows. She felt the tires spin, not from speed but from the gale urging the car faster.

She heard herself say, "We're not going to make it."

Melanie reached in front of Teri, grabbed the wheel, and jerked it counterclockwise. The car's rear end turned toward the bridge, then the wind caught the front of the car and continued the spin as tires lost their grip. The newlyweds screamed as the vehicle turned in a slow 180, mercifully ending overall in the direction of the underpass. Tires gripped pavement again and Teri put the car in drive and, looking through the narrow gap under the raised hood, pulled the last few feet, retreating back beneath the interstate.

A minute passed and neither said a word.

Then, Melanie grabbed the door handle again.

"No!"

"Em, we have to get the hood down before the engine clogs with dirt!"

"Don't…please!"

Melanie reached out and gently ran her fingers down Teri's jawline. "Have to."

Before Teri could object a second time, she watched Melanie slam all her weight against the door.

Nothing happened.

Another slam.

Metal groaned, and the door pulled out of her hands.

"Mels!"

Teri reached out and felt her fingers drag along Melanie's t-shirt as she forced her way free of the car. Her door whipped closed with the finality of a kettle drum. Wind forced Melanie against the hood of the car, her head striking the open hood's edge. Red joined the orange hue, muddying an area half the size of a softball in the second before dust clotted the wound. Teri scampered across the seat to the passenger side of the car, less than two feet from the woman who'd been at her side since they'd met at the coffee shop just a few short years ago.

"Melanie!" Teri's scream sounded little more than a whisper.

Clumped hair whipped around the woman's face, dirt clotting

both eyes and crusting them shut in seconds. Still, Melanie managed to stay on her feet with hands gripping the hood for balance. Her face turned in Teri's direction as she pressed down on the hood. It resisted, bobbing down briefly before popping up again.

She watched as Melanie pushed down on the hood again, this time locking both arms and pushing down with all her might. Metal bobbed down a second time. Peppered red patterns appeared on her arms and shoulders.

Teri bit her lip. "Just come back," she pleaded to no one…to *anyone* who might answer the prayer.

Wind caught again, thrusting Melanie across the top of the Buick and onto the road. Teri grabbed the driver's door handle and pushed with everything she had. The door refused to budge.

Teri saw Melanie struggle to her knees, a crimson gash already scabbed across her forehead, her mane of black hair now sporting deep dust-orange highlights. Blood crusted below both eyes, telling of her mistake opening them. "Mels!"

A silent scream came from her wife as she sat back on her haunches. White teeth went first red with blood then orange, and layers of sand, dirt, and clay worked to clog the woman's airway. The peppered areas on her skin grew as blowing dust blasted layers of skin off.

She smacked against the door rhythmically—first the door, then the door glass, then again against the door.

The roar's volume deafened all other sounds.

Melanie reached out with one hand toward the car when the wind knocked her over and rolled her up the slope to the bottom of the bridge. Fingers grew bloody as she scrabbled to find a grip along the wall of graffiti-strewn concrete.

Teri pushed her way back to the passenger side of the car to follow her spouse outside.

Suddenly, the car rose.

She was weightless.

Ground sped by the windows wrong, ground moving along the side of the car rather than under it.

Then the car folded in half, wedged tight into the underpass.

She looked from what felt a million miles away out the passenger door window. Cracks spider-webbed the glass, expanding as she watched.

Teri blinked.

The wind howled.

Teri blinked.

It was dark.

Teri blinked.

Bright sunlight shone on a lobster-red patch of her shin.

Her neck hurt.

"Mels?"

It came back to her in waves…their vows…the dancing…playing on Hollywood Boulevard….

…and the storm.

"Mels!" Her voice sounded small, devoid of the panic rising in her chest. Teri shifted and white fire shot from her left elbow up to the shoulder. She wormed herself free, gritting teeth against tears, each breath faster than the previous until effort brought success and, after two kicks to the cracked window, Teri found herself sliding out of the car and spilling, not unlike a pile of clothes, onto the slope.

Air hung hot and heavy under the bridge, abandoned by the winds that drove it earlier. The sun was in the wrong place. "Is it tomorrow?" It had to already be nearing a hundred. Teri looked back at the car. From its awkward angle Teri felt vertigo wash over her. An empty stomach churned.

"M-Mel!"

Legs shaking, she backed up a couple of feet and sat down against the concrete base of the underpass. Teri's insides clenched, vomit pressing upward. Her insides knotted, and she clenched her eyes shut against rising bile. A moment passed with no resolution to the feeling.

"Shock," she said. Stating the obvious did little to help. Another minute passed as she waited for the nausea to erupt or abate. The latter won out and Teri swallowed hard, choking down chunky bile.

She opened her eyes again and looked to her left—along the four-foot-high wall. Dates, limericks, declarations of undying love covered the concrete in paint, marker, fingernail polish, and some even etched into the man-made rock itself.

I should put Melanie's name here.

Teri scooted down the slope a little and stood again. This time, her stomach barely complained. She turned and looked at the graffiti. A few feet further down, faded spray paint figures stood, their lines marred by years—in some cases decades—old showcased artwork.

Lines that reminded Teri of lines on sheet music.

She heard herself starting to hum a tune.

Wait.

Teri stopped, shook her head in an effort to try to clear it.

The lines.

Feet moved of their own accord, passing where the lines began and continuing to the side of the underpass.

Fingers. Blood from Mel's fingers. Oh, God. "How much blood?"

Drag marks continued to the corner then vanished, much as Melanie had.

Teri stepped from the shade and looked up the short man-made valley between the Interstate lanes. Its slope appeared empty. She staggered to the middle of the dip and started walking up, moving in the direction the storm had blown Melanie.

Silence, like the air, hung heavy. No rumble from cars whizzing by…no horns beep beep beeping as they blew past her. Not even birds squawked.

The blurry world fell into differing levels of an impressionist painting mere yards away. Teri reached up to push her glasses higher on her nose and found them missing.

"The accident."

She continued walking the center divider between the road's lanes and looked at the twin strips of pavement.

"Mels?" She parroted the call every minute or so. Teri turned around and looked behind her. The bridge was nothing more than a dark blob in an equally blurry world.

"Fuckin' eyes." A laugh escaped her as a bark. "Well," she said to herself, "Mels wanted me to find a new curse." The empty laugh gave way to sobs, and Teri cradled her injured arm and kept her slow pace forward.

Time passed.

The sun rose higher.

Teri wasn't sure how much time had gone by, but at some point she'd fought and finally succeeded in pulling the scrunchie from her hair and letting it fall free.

Not as good as a hat, but at least it's keeping some of the sun off me.

Teri looked down and discovered at some point she'd left the center divider and walked along the road's right shoulder. The backs of her legs burned, as did her left shin. A quick glance down showed her left elbow an angry purple.

"Broken. Got to be."

Another look back yielded nothing other than blue sky and brown earth.

Sand crunched under foot. Asphalt vanished under increasing layers of dust and sand. Ahead, the black lines thinned, became spotty and ultimately vanished from view in the blurry distance.

"Mels?" she parroted for what felt like the thousandth time, though now little more than a whisper. The tears had long dried, but anguish still rang fresh in her raspy voice.

Still no answer.

The sand grew thicker. Heavy grains covered the ground, barren of the lighter dust that the storm ferried away. Something else was in the road.

Shapes.

Blobs.

Shades of brown, black, even reds rippled into view.

"Cars!"

Her shambling footsteps became a half-hearted jog, each step a jarring painful reminder of her broken arm.

"Help!"

Like her cry for Melanie, the call went unanswered.

Teri reached the rear car of the traffic jam—a green Taurus. She smacked the trunk.

"Hello?" she half-yelled. "I need…I need help!"

She banged on the door.

It was empty.

The car's front end was wedged under the rear bumper of a black SUV. It, too, was void of passengers.

"What the hell is this?"

Thoughts of her church upbringing came back. Warnings of the Rapture and what happened to those who didn't follow God's plan danced in her mind. She shook them off with a shudder.

"They were outside when the storm hit…or in another car."

Teri crouched down and looked underneath the vehicles as best she could. Nothing human shaped was wedged between any of the cars' tires.

Only sand.

And cars.

As she stood, hot, sweaty fabric fluttered against her back.

Her shirt was drenched with sweat.

Teri staggered to what had once been a white Subaru and opened the back door. A cooler sat in the middle of the seat. Inside rested half a dozen beers floating in ice-filled water. Her right hand left an orange ring as she ignored the beers and grabbed a handful of ice. Teri swished the first chunk around her mouth and, resisting the urge to swallow, spat it out onto the ground. The action was repeated with the second and third chunks as she worked to free her mouth of caked dirt. Droplets from the fourth slid down her throat like mother's milk—an icy pleasure cooling the inner-most part of her.

A fit of coughing followed. Inky-brown droplets of mud fell from her lips, and she reached in, scooped a handful of water, and brought it to her lips. She swished and spat, then took another handful and swallowed it.

Teri looked around, suddenly feeling guilty.

"Hello? Is anyone there?"

Nothing.

"Mels?"

Not even the wind answered.

"Maybe there was an evacuation."

She looked down and considered the beer a moment before taking it and setting the wet can on the car's roof. Three tries and one broken nail later, she'd managed to open the can. A full can became half in a quick series of swallows.

Braaaaaaap. The belch came with such force that it hurt her throat. Teri tried to wipe the leftover beer from her lips with the back of her good arm but only succeeded in creating a dirty smear.

Tossing the beer aside, Teri dug into the vehicle and looked for anything that might shield her from the unforgiving sun.

Nothing.

She repeated the process on the next vehicle and was rewarded first with an umbrella and second with a backpack. A quick tip dumped the contents onto the car's floorboards and she refilled the shoulder bag with bottles of water also found in the car.

Teri did her best, one handed, to manage both the backpack and the open umbrella. What felt like another hour passed before she tired of looking into the never-ending line of cars in the hopes of finding someone. Her elbow throbbed in time with each step, creating its own painful rhythm.

Teri blinked away sweat and squinted at the road ahead. Reflections twinkled in the afternoon sun. Ant-sized shadows shifted at the horizon. The shadows moved a second time.

"They moved," she gasped. "People."

As before, her steps quickened, each landing more reckless than the last.

Shapes grew and what were once formless blobs solidified into vehicles lining an intersecting road. Further on, beyond her limited vision's capabilities, stood a structure she couldn't quite make out, something resembling a giant mound with so many sunlight reflections that even looking in its general direction hurt.

Teri stared, first at the road before her then off at a forty-five-degree angle to the mound. Heat radiated through the soles of her shoes and rivulets of salty sweat cut trails along the dust on her skin.

"Stay on the road or go cross country?" Words from all the reality survival shows flooded her memory and better judgment won out against desire. "Damned road," she muttered and started out following the barely visible dotted yellow line. A distant thumping resonated throughout the Utah flats, working its way into her eardrums and inadvertently setting her pace.

Voices and the groaning of metal wafted on what little wind the day offered. Teri passed the sign for the upcoming exit.

WHAGEENEE ROAD NEXT LEFT

"Whageenee," she muttered. "Melanie will be there."

As she grew closer, a chorus of voices overlapped, with some crying, others barking expulsions of anger, all of which were still unintelligible as anything other than raised tones.

"Must…" Teri gulped air as a new wave of pain shot through her arm. "Must be…an…emergency tent."

Another scream rang out and her steps faltered.

The off ramp had become a blurry reality, its sandy slide slipping off the highway to Whageenee Road. A crowd stood at the edge of the ramp. Sand blew across the distance between her and them, whipping a dust devil of debris into the air. Six figures broke away from the cluster, surrounded an SUV and began moving it down toward Whageenee's underpass.

"Hello?" Her voice came as little more than a whisper. Teri tried again, putting a lung full of air behind the word this time. "Hello?"

Figures stopped moving and looked toward her. Two, standing a full head taller, broke from the group and approached.

"Thank God! Oh than—"

"*Oph!*"

The first figure focused into stark reality. Leathery flesh clutched exposed bone in a stiff embrace. Nose, eyelids, and lips all drew back in an exaggerated manifestation of dehydration. Empty sockets each held a beetle, both buzzing in agitation. In lieu of a shirt, the cadaver wore an Audi leather seat cover as a tunic, leaving shriveled genitalia exposed with each step.

Teri stumbled back, falling hard on her rump.

It towered over her as did its companion, similarly garbed in its own seat cover, and stood at Teri's feet. The first reached down and grabbed her by her broken arm.

She howled.

The creature eased his grip but didn't let go. It leaned forward and studied her eyes before presenting her to the second.

"*Ehmet tont phu,*" the first said.

"*Pok tont phu,*" came the reply, and it drew a tire iron from its belt.

"*Ehmet tont phu,*" the first insisted.

Teri watched with horror at the exchange going on between the two.

The second replied, "*Dah!*" and stiffly waved at her arm and walked away.

White fire shot through her as the corpse jerked her to her feet.

It pulled her beside him. "*Toh!*"

She stayed at his side, slowing her pace to match his. They passed a cluster of people at the ramp's edge. Teri counted nine, mostly children, surrounded by five of the walking husks.

"Please," she uttered, fearful of some supernatural wrath. "You're hurting me."

The creature jerked her arm hard in reply.

They left the ramp and stepped into the bridge's shade. Children lined the underpass, scrawling on the concrete with everything from crayons to makeup. Sobs sang out in chorus as Teri passed them. One sat up straighter, and she glimpsed eye sockets as empty as the thing leading her. A glint caught her attention, and Teri looked away just as quickly, seeing a beetle's exoskeleton wet with blood as it peeked between the child's newly ruined lids.

They left the shade of the bridge and continued along the shoulder of Whageenee Road, moving ever toward the reflective mound. Vehicles were pushed by groups of four and steered by a fifth, lining both lanes of the road. Bordering them stood more of the husked creatures, each wielding fan belts as makeshift whips.

Teri looked up at the mound and lost her breath.

"Cars."

Cars, trucks, even one house door, were stacked neatly, creating an ever-growing mound. The flow of vehicles never slowed, only kept the same steady pace. Sun reflected off dozens of windshields and car doors.

"I don't…I don't understand."

"*Toh,*" the thing leading her repeated and shoved her toward the line of vehicles. It pointed casually to the cars and made a pushing motion. The beetles moved around in its eye sockets, shifting for a better position.

Teri looked to her left at the caravan of metal. Two cars up, a familiar clutch of hair caught her gaze. Though dirty and clotted, it could only belong to one person.

"Melanie!"

Teri scrambled out of the husk's reach and broke into a full run, clasping the broken arm to her chest, toward Melanie. She passed the first vehicle and was nearly to the second when her head snapped back and feet shot out before her.

The husk jerked Teri back to her feet by the fistful of hair it clutched. "*Pok tont phu*," it said and reached for a wicked-looking length of rusty car metal wedged in its belt. She smacked at its arm with her good hand and pulled free, running the last few steps behind Melanie.

"Stop!" she yelled and pointed at Melanie's back. "I want to be here." She made a pushing motion to the car.

Suddenly her back lit up, hurting as bad as her arm. Teri looked over her shoulder and saw another of the husks pulling back on the fan belt it had just lashed her with.

"*Ehmet tont phu*," it said and pointed to the car.

Teri wedged herself between Melanie and some man that sobbed quietly to himself. Her bare arm brushed against Melanie's.

Too rough.

Melanie's mane of ebony hair covered her face and most of her body to the waist. The narrow bare patch along her upper arm was leathery, pitted, and nearly as dry as the husks.

Voice half-hitched in her throat, Teri whispered, "Mels?"

Melanie's head lifted slightly, but she never stopped pushing.

Teri tried again. "Melanie?"

A quiet rasp came from beneath the hair. "E-Ems?"

"Yeah." Teri shifted so she was still pushing with her shoulder and reached out with her good hand and put it over Melanie's. "I'm here."

Melanie's hand slowly pulled away. "Don't look at me, Em. My eyes—"

"I know, baby. I saw in the storm."

"But I'm not blind." Melanie's voice rose. "I can still see. Oh, God, I can see the most horrible things. The sky...the *things* flying overhead...and all the faces looking up from the sand."

Teri stayed silent but kept staring at Melanie, waiting for her to continue. No more was offered other than a hitch as she worked to get her breath.

"What's happening?"

The man next to them said, "We're pushing."

"No, I mean…all this. What's going on?"

Melanie groaned. "I think we're in Hell. That's what's going on."

The man cut in. "You know what this reminds me of?" He didn't wait for a reply and laughed. "A pyramid. A big fuel-efficient fucking pyramid!"

Teri ignored him and said, "Mels—" then fell silent as Melanie looked up. Ruined sockets that once held chocolate brown eyes now housed two large green beetles. Mandibles quickened in agitation.

"My…."

My what? My God? My goodness?

"Oh, Mels."

Melanie's head looked back down. "You don't know how horrific you, and—hell, everything looks now. It's all so alien and…." Tearless sobs broke free. "I can hardly move. Everything's so stiff. The skin on my neck split right before you found me. I…I didn't even bleed. They're…they're *inside* me."

They pushed in silence for a while longer before Melanie asked, "What do I look like to you?"

"The same. You're the same beautiful woman I fell in love with."

The man next to them stopped pushing and grabbed her by the arm. "Wait—you still have *your* eyes?" He turned her and his beetles gripped the edges of their sockets, mandibles clicking.

A crack of the makeshift whip brought him to his knees. Another strike followed the first. Then a third. He threw up his hands in supplication and pointed back at Teri.

"*Oomph*," the husk said and closed in on him.

"She still has her eyes!" He motioned with two fingers to his own missing eyes then back to Teri.

"*Pah?*" It bent over him, then craned its head to look at Teri and Melanie.

"*Chelah neh pah!*"

Teri quit pushing, grabbed Melanie by the hand, and backed away. "Can you run?"

"What?"

Teri hissed, "Can you *run*?"

"Ems, I can hardly walk. They…they won't let me."

Melanie's arms lowered. Leathery skin stretched, showing minuscule pincers pierced flesh from the inside on either side of split skin, holding it together. A dozen small lumps along the injury told of where each of the younger beetles rested just below the skin within Melanie's body. One small insect, barely the size of Teri's pinky nail, crawled to the injury. It probed the rip a second before retreating from the blistering sun by forcing its way into her body.

Three whip cracks struck Teri in quick succession, bringing her to her knees. The husk in front of her stepped closer while shadows from three others approached from just out of sight. They pinned her, even pulling her broken arm out and pressing it into the dirt. A splintering sensation, like a stick wrapped in steak being twisted, radiated up her arm into the shoulder.

"Gahhh," was all Teri could manage to mutter.

"*Oomph Tallah?*" One of the other three husks leaned in close and forced her left eye open with a bony finger and thumb.

Teri froze when a second lowered a shimmering green scarab beetle down beside her opened lid.

A finger, impossibly large from Teri's perspective, pointed first to the beetle then to her eye, his fingertip actually pressing against her orb.

"The pain's not so bad, Ems," Melanie said from behind the car, head hung in supplication.

The beetle fell from the husk's grasp, landing on Teri's cheek. Talons dug into her sunburned flesh as the insect righted itself before mandibles scissored into the orb and the delved into its new home.

Behind the story...

"Sandcastles" came about from an open call from a friend, Greg Norris, for an anthology called *Canopic Jars—Tales of Mummies and Mummification*. I'd never written a mummy story before, but most horror writers want to salute all of the big movie monsters at least once.

I wrote the first half of this story seven different times. Each incarnation just didn't fit the protagonists. I just couldn't seem to get it right. I tried the couple angry. I tried the couple tired. Hell, I even tried them lovey-dovey. Nothing felt *right*. I ran this through my writing critique group a few times and everyone agreed that *something* was off, but no one could really put their finger on what it was. That's when it was Hollie's turn and she commented, "Steve really gives off feminine energy. Are you sure he's a guy?" Steve was Teri's husband in the original version.

I looked at Hollie....

I looked at my stack of critiqued stories....

I looked back at Hollie....

...and with a simple Find and Replace, I fixed the story.

That's what every writer *wants* to say.

What *actually* happened was a bit of research and two months of rewriting and personality tweaks to get the characters right, not to mention a fair amount of ripping my hair out in frustration. In the end, I was happy with how it turned out, but getting there was a hell of a ride.

SOMEONE TO WATCH OVER ME

"Moonlight and Roses" echoed throughout the makeshift speakeasy, drowning out most of the conversations. Several couples clung to each other and swayed to the slow song. Hanging lanterns cast a sleepy amber glow over the patrons. Elsie Blankard stared into the gloom wreathing the far end of the great room. There, in the darkness, a solitary man drank from a tin cup. Behind him, shadows had their own momentum, shifting with the subtle movements of couples taking advantage of dim illumination.

"Is that him?"

"Easy, Els." Mary shook a bit of spilled bathtub gin from her hand. "This stuff's expensive."

Elsie leaned in close. "I said, 'Is that him?'" She pointed at the dark-haired stranger.

Mary nodded a confirmation. "Yeah, that's Charles Machon. Word has it he just got in a couple a' days ago. Old money. Had some problem during the war." Another song started, this one enticing the masses into drunken renditions of the Charleston and forced Mary to speak up. "Nearly got blipped off during some battle and lost his noodle for a bit."

Elsie tapped her heel to the music but never took her eyes off Charles. Her flapper dress, which cost nearly two weeks' wages, sparkled hypnotically. "He's a real sheikh, you know?"

"Oh, deary." Mary draped an arm across Elsie's shoulders, "Sheikh's so yesterday." We're in the land of talkies now. Haven't you heard?"

She pulled away, skirting the crowd.

"Els! Where ya goin'?"

The blonde threw a wicked glance over one shoulder. "You can't expect me to bump gums with you here all night, now can you?" She slid between the masses, snaking her way into one corner of the designated dance area and narrowly dodging a couple kicking their heels up. A handful of steps later Elsie bumped into the intended quarry.

"I—oh…sorry." She giggled.

He looked down, eyes black in the limited light. "I assume you were looking for me?" His thick, British accent cut against her McKee's Rocks, Pennsylvania twang and left them both straining to understand each other.

Elsie feigned innocence. "No…I don't—"

"Well," he cut in with a sad smile. "I don't think you were planning on going back there alone?" He nodded to the half-dozen or so couples clutching at one another, actions hidden by well-placed coats.

"Oh." She stood a little straighter. "And you think you're the man for the job, do you?"

Charles looked left, then right before settling his gaze upon her once more. "I think I'm the only man in the vicinity at the moment."

"Brazen." She smiled.

"Just observant." He took a long, slow swallow from the cup.

Elsie moved a little closer. "You're the talk-o-the-Rocks here, Chuck."

"Charles," he corrected.

"Charles. Sorry." She shifted from one heel to the other and looked down at his cup. "Offer a girl a drink?"

"Certainly. I believe—"

Elsie snatched the cup from his hand and took a swallow, making sure to lick her lips slowly afterward, stealing a glance to see if he was paying attention.

He was.

"That's not gin," she said. A new song started up and dancers cluttered the floor.

"No. I believe it's made from corn."

"Mash," she said over the increasing din.

"Of course."

"Do you wanna…" Elsie motioned to the dance floor.

"I'm afraid that seems a bit active at the moment. Perhaps you would be content with a walk, miss?"

"You mean leave all this?" She waved an arm at the convention of lawbreakers before answering the second question. "Elsie. Elsie Blankard. Now, lead on." Her hand grasped the crook of Charles' elbow. The flapper gave a devilish look, winking across the barn to Mary. This was met with riotous laughter.

A full moon lit up the night, making the hill country stand out like a minimalist painting. The two walked past the dozen or so wagons and spattering of Fords filling the otherwise empty field.

"Look at that." Elsie pulled free and walked to the side of a newer convertible.

Charles sounded bored. "What about it?"

"It's yellow," she stammered.

"I like yellow."

She stared back at him, slack jawed. "You mean this is yours? Is it new?"

He popped the door open for Elsie. "This one is a twenty-three. Only a couple of years old, but I still like it."

"But it's yellow," she repeated.

"I know."

"But they're *never* yellow."

"This one is. My father knows Henry and managed to talk the moose into making this one a color other than his obsessive black." Charles offered the last swallow from the cup to Elsie, which she took and downed in an unladylike gulp. "Now, about that walk."

"What about a ride instead?"

"You want to go for a ride? With me?" he asked. "A perfect

stranger?"

"You don't seem that strange to me. Maybe a little stiff, but not all that strange."

"Won't your friends be worried about you?"

"Them? Nah. They're already trolling for beaus."

Charles opened the door for her before rounding the Ford, stepping up onto the sideboard and sliding behind the Model T's wheel. "Then a ride you shall have." He retarded the spark and throttled down before turning the ignition switch. A hard stomp on the starter and the car rumbled to life. The sudden noise disturbed the horses. "Direction?"

Elsie thought a moment. "Pull out onto the main road and go left."

"Toward the river?"

"Yeah. There's a place my granddaddy worked one summer called 'The Mound.'" She flicked a lock of bobbed hair behind one ear. "It's an Indian burial mound."

The car turned in a tight circle and started down the muddy field's access. He cut a sideways glance at Elsie. "You want to take me to a cemetery?"

"Not a cemetery. A burial mound. It hasn't been used in ages. Some professor hired Papaw away from the mine to help on a dig." The flapper slid a little closer. "You know, like that tomb they found in Egypt."

"King Tutankhamen?"

She clapped Charles on the arm and he visibly winced. "That's the chap."

"Chap?"

"Sure." A grin crossed her face, makeup exaggerating it in the moonlight. "Isn't that what the British say? 'Pip, pip' and 'cheerio' and 'chap?'" Elsie adjusted her coat as a cut of cool air sliced the side of the car. "Besides, there's a beautiful view of the Ohio River there. We might be able to even see Brunot."

Charles slowed the Ford and navigated a handful of axle-busting rocks at the road's edge before the car turned onto the hard-packed earth. "Who's Brunot?"

Elsie laughed, then choked on a mouthful of dust. "No, no.

Brunot's a little island to the south."

"And what's so interesting about this island?"

She shifted, uncomfortable with the jostling vehicle. "I dunno. I just like it. That's all."

Bugs peppered the windshield as they flew down the country road. Sounds changed when the car left the field behind them and entered a wooden grove. Trees whipped by with a repetitive thump-thump sound while scattered beams of moonlight broke the canopy and danced along the forest floor.

"You're going to want to slow down here," Elsie shouted, now unable to suppress an excited grin. A low branch whooshed by and almost snatched her hat.

Charles acquiesced and slowed the convertible to a more reasonable speed. A rough patch in the road jostled the car so severely Elsie almost lost her grip on the dash. The high bounces rode her dress up. Seconds later she realized this and caught him staring at her legs.

"Eyes on the road, buster," she said with a laugh. "It'd be a heck of a note to be killed because of my gams."

"Killer gams," Charles said with a smirk.

Elsie pointed to the right. "We're nearly there. It's just a cut in the woods. I'm not even sure we can get up there with this bucket."

A darker patch of woods appeared in the general direction she pointed. Charles stepped on the gas, shot off the road and down a slight embankment before spewing rocks as they skidded around a bend.

"Slow!" She grabbed a handful of his upper arm and he screamed, stomping on the brakes until the car skidded to a halt. Charles cradled his bicep, just over her grip. Elsie let go and leaned back. "I didn't mean—"

"It's not you," he managed through gritted teeth. "It's just an old injury acting up."

"Was it—"

"The war? Yes." Charles rubbed his arm through the jacket. "Isn't it always the war for anyone my age?"

Elsie slid closer, looking around. "Turn the car off. We're here." She looked at him, placing her hand on his gently. "You're not all that old. You're what…thirty?"

He managed a grim smile. "Twenty-three…nearly to the day."

"So, you went in when you were…?" Elsie let the question drift off.

Charles sighed and looked up at the hint of moon visible through the lush greenery. "Fourteen. I stole my brother's papers and enlisted. By the time my parents sorted out what happened I was already neck deep at the Battle of the Somme under Sir Douglas Haig."

She returned a hand to his arm and mimicked the soft massage. He winced again and she eased the pressure. "What was it like?"

In lieu of a response, Charles turned and caressed the side of Elsie's face, trailing one finger under her jaw and tipping her head up in preparation for a kiss. Lips met, parted and released tongues to explore new territory.

They shifted, Elsie's hand slid across his body and around his neck, while his own slid from face to arm, to hip and rested on her coat-covered thigh. The time-immortal dominance dance played out in the front seat, Charles urging her to lie back. She pressed her own advantage by shifting and made access to anything other than her lips more difficult.

The kiss broke and left each flushed.

"Would it be more comfortable…?" He nodded to the back seat, but Elsie had already slid across car's width and gotten out on the far side. She turned and rested her forearms on the door.

"So, are you coming or not?"

"I thought we were enjoying the evening here."

"We are, silly." Elsie backed away, illuminated by the car's headlights. "Up on the Mound. I'm serious about wanting to show it to you."

Charles let loose a laugh. "You actually think you're going to entice me into following you into the night?"

Elsie grinned and lifted the hem of her coat and dress, flashing a glimpse of knee.

"You're incorrigible." The driver's side door swung open and he climbed out, alcohol making legs wobblier than when they'd left the speakeasy. "Lead on, milady." He clicked off the lights and followed her through the foliage.

The couple ascended the low hill at a snail's pace. Undergrowth gave way to trees and dried remains of leaves. They peaked the crest and Elsie sat on a rotted pile of lumber looking down into a cone-shaped depression. The remnants of the dig spanned a good thirty feet and better than a third of that in depth. Just beyond the far side's lip lay a ledge. The Ohio river flowed past more than a tree's height below.

"My Papaw worked this with the archaeologist from some college. I grew up with him telling me and my brothers stories about what they found here."

Charles leaned against a tree and hunted for a match. "What, pray tell, did they find here? Gold? Jewels?"

She scrunched her face up as only a young woman still on the shy side of twenty could. "No. They were Indians."

A match bit back the darkness as it jumped to life. "Then what?" He drew deep against the flame, and the cigarette's tip pulsed yellow-red.

Elsie leaned back. "Over thirty Indians. Tools. Seashells. Pottery. They said the Mound is probably full of bodies going back hundreds of years."

"Really?" Disbelief hung heavy in Charles' sarcastic tone.

"Yes, really." She stood, walked over and took his cigarette as her own. The ember glowed hot as she drew deep on the oily smoke. "They think there may be hundreds more deeper than what they dug out."

He reached out, put a hand on Elsie's hip and pulled to close the distance between them. "Fascinating."

"It is," she insisted. "The Hopewell Indians took this area over from the Adena." A schoolmarm quality overtook her, enthusiasm coming across like a lesson. "They don't know what happened to the tribe. From the artifacts they found, the Adena—at least this particular tribe," she corrected herself, "—just died out and then the Hopewell were here."

"Hmm." Charles leaned down and nuzzled her neck. "Sounds like the Hopewell killed them off."

"No." Elsie stepped back, wrapped up in sharing this all-too-well-known local story with someone new. "The Hopewell were peaceful for the most part. The last Adena found were buried like the Hopewell did for their own dead."

"Fascinating," he repeated. Charles closed the distance between them. One hand met another and the cigarette changed partners again.

"Isn't it? Hey, there's Brunot." She pointed through a copse of trees to a split in the river a few hundred yards distant. The land mass lay as a dark patch of blue-green encompassed by a silver chain of water.

He dropped the butt and pulled her tight, lips searching. Elsie resisted for a second then leaned in, pressing herself against him. The couple found their way to the ground but never broke contact. Elsie wrapped her arms around to the small of Charles' back. His palm, hot in contrast to the night air, rested on her leg just below where acceptable modesty placed this season's hemline. She shifted and felt a hand move up a foot before realizing it. Fingertips, softer than those of local beaus, danced at her stocking top, though stayed well below the garter belt's fasteners. Knees relaxed, then parted to allow better access. His nails drug upward and slid from silk to naked thigh. Hesitant caresses teased scant inches away from her sex. With no rejection, the journey continued under the short-bloomers and made quick work of her folds. As digits met their target, Elsie let loose a gasp and drew her own attention to just below Charles' belt buckle. Another hesitation for propriety's sake, then nature took over and she rubbed the front of his trousers, increasing pressure along his rigid length.

Minutes passed as they groped in the moonlight and Charles grew more aggressive with his ministrations. Elsie's pulse pounded in her ears. The flapper's stomach tightened and the forthcoming wash of pleasure made itself known. Then, just short of a quivering release, fingers slid lower, searching for her center. She stopped him short of actual penetration.

"Whoa," she said through the kiss. "I only pet."

A familiar sigh of frustration escaped Elsie's new suitor. She shifted her hand, allowing two fingers to slide past trouser buttons, through underlying fabric, and touched his length in an effort to regain the enthusiasm he'd shown a moment before. He flexed, then pulled away and sat up.

"I...I need a moment."

"I'm sorry."

Charles patted her knee. "It's fine."

Elsie watched him rub at his shoulder. "How bad was it?" The question blurted out and she found herself adding, "When you got hurt?"

He rested elbows on knees and looked into the night. "You know, I knew I would end up out here in the woods tonight."

"With me?" She smiled and propped her head up on one hand.

"With someone."

The smile faded.

"How about a story?"

Before she could answer he continued.

"It was a full moon in 1916. Jerry was coming into the trenches faster than the rain. A bomb went off nearby, but it wasn't the same as the others. Smoke and rain kept us from seeing it. Melburn saw the cloud first—this dingy brown mess that covered everything."

She realized he wasn't really with her anymore. The question put Charles back at that night almost a decade earlier. "I didn't think anyone called the Germans 'Jerry' anymo—"

"We heard the screams from the trenches as soon as it hit them. We thought Jerry was using the cloud for cover, but no one was shooting." His hands shook. Elsie reached out to comfort him, but he pulled away, still favoring the old injury.

"Chuck...Charles," she self-corrected.

"Then it got to us. This oily...it burned and we couldn't get it off. It itched at first, like when you don't get all the soap off from a bath." Charles' eyes were wild in the moonlight.

Fear crept along Elsie's spine, raising hairs. "We don't have to talk about this."

He turned to her then, mask of kindness gone, now replaced with an anger she'd only seen in men her mother dated over the years. "Oh, but we do, Elsie. We do."

She straightened her dress and coat. "I think it's time you took me back."

"I remember running, jumping over my friends, getting away from the gas."

"Mustard gas." She pulled back into the story at the mention of the horrific weapon.

His look became a sneer. "Of course it was mustard gas! Another bomb went off nearby. Everything went black. The next thing I remember I'm wrapped up in bandages and lying in bed looking up at a doctor."

"I want to go back," Elsie said simply.

"I saw Jerries along with a few of my friends standing over by the window, but they didn't fight with each other. They just stood there looking at me." Charles held a hand out as if showing her where to look. He shook his head. "There weren't any Jerries in the hospital and the friends I saw couldn't be there. They were already under mud and forgotten at the Somme."

Elsie rolled onto her side and got up, trying to understand what Charles said. A glance around reminded her just how truly alone they were. The occasional whisper of music echoed down from where everyone else drank, laughed and danced a mile or so away. She held a hand out and forced a smile. "Come on. Let's get us both a drink and get back to the party. You can drive me home later," she lied.

He looked at her outstretched arm then disregarded it. "They said it was because I died that night. My mind must be hurt from the blast. I wasn't breathing when Walden found me. He pounded on my chest and I came to. I was dead. The men, even the doctors, said it was a miracle."

"Well, that's a good thing." She let the hand drop and decided to push the point. "Look, I'm heading back. Are you going to drive me or not?"

"The moon looked like it does here…just not as sharp." Charles stood, moving between Elsie and the makeshift path back to the car. "I found another two that could see. Both died like me." Moonlight caught his eyes and reflected a soft blue. "Died and came back on the full moon."

Panic nibbled at her. "You're just trying to scare me because I said no." She tapped a nervous foot and tried to stare the Brit down. "The sheriff's my cousin. Do you know what he'll do to you if you try anything?"

The threat fell on deaf ears. "They didn't see the same people I do. We talked about it for days, but never around the doctors. We knew they'd take us for loonies and place us in a sanitarium." She stepped to the left and Charles mirrored the action. "It's only the dead that are around when you come back. None of us saw each other's audience, you see." He stepped forward.

"N-no. I don't see."

Spittle fell from his lips. "The people that came back with us. Our audience."

Elsie looked around for a means of escape and backed to the excavation's edge, glancing warily at the thirty-foot drop to the water below. Charles closed the distance in two steps.

"Riley killed the doctor before he hung himself."

"Ch-Charles—"

He took another step. "Pulled the man's insides out like he was looking for something. I knew he was going to do it. He said that's what they wanted—for him to close the door that coming back opened. I think...I think the doctor was just because he harassed the private so incessantly." His hands clenched and opened, clenched and opened. "Johnson..." Charles choked on his words for a second. "Johnson clawed his own eyes out so he wouldn't have to look at them anymore. But you know what?" Arms stretched out for her then jerked back. Elsie retreated, working her way around the narrow lip by the excavation's ledge. "Do...you...know...what?"

Her heel caught on a root and Elsie pinwheeled both arms, righting herself just short of disaster.

"It didn't help. He could still see them...still *hear* them." He stopped the advance. "I shipped home a couple of days later to recover from the burns the gas left on me."

His demeanor changed with a simple exhale of breath. He took off his jacket and held it out to her. "Here. You look cold," he offered with a grim smile.

One shaky hand reached out and Charles snatched her by the wrist, jerking the flapper off balance. Elsie fell to her knees and he shoved her onto her back.

"And do you know what *my* audience says, bitch? *My* audience says little girls shouldn't tease." He climbed on top of her. Hands went to Elsie's throat and thumbs dug deep, cutting off her air. She kicked out, legs splayed on either side of the Brit in a perversion of the very act he'd striven for earlier. "You bitch," he screamed. "*Du dumme schlampe!*"

Her eyes teared and she beat at his arms. Strikes against his right side brought a roar of rage and pain from Charles. He squeezed harder.

"*Schlampe,*" he repeated. He kept the grip around her throat, lifted Elsie a foot off the ground and slammed her head down against the rocks.

Lights danced.

"Bitch!"

More pinpricks of white pain winked before her eyes. Movement came from all around them. Her body scraped against the rocks as Charles dragged her to the ledge.

Figures in the shadows shifted.

Then the lights were gone.

So was the pain.

She was flying.

Her entire body struck something and Elsie went rigid with a sudden bone-numbing cold. Her gasp came as little more than a wheeze and water flooded an open mouth. Feet found shaky purchase in mud and the flapper pulled herself first to the water's surface then to the river's edge. Elsie looked up at the ledge Charles had flung her from.

"*Schlampe,*" echoed a scream from upstream. Branches broke nearby.

Words, guttural and hollow, echoed all around her. Words that made no sense, in some language she didn't understand, but their meaning was clear. "*Get up.*"

Elsie shook her head in an effort to clear foggy thoughts. What wasn't frigid from the river hurt. Her face felt like she ran into a door. So did her chest, but it ached deeper, all the way through to her back—the way her grandfather's had when his heart had nearly given out while working a plow. Though a struggle, she inhaled deep past blue lips. Words came faster, overlapping each other until a cacophony of verbiage rattled her eardrums. She pressed palms against her head trying to block out the voices. Foggy shadows moved all around her, shapes appearing more recognizable with each breath she took.

⤝✕⤞

"Bitch," Charles screamed again. "Shut up! I can't hear her with all of you yelling at me!" He turned in a slow circle as he called, "Where are you?" She saw the Brit kick through a cluster of weeds. Her arm cranked back, aimed, then shot forward.

A speeding blur of gray flew through the air and a fist-sized river rock struck home, impacting wetly against Charles' temple.

Elsie's hands grabbed a broken branch, its raw end jagged and menacing. She staggered over to the moaning form at her feet and stood over him. Moonlight caught her eyes, reflecting a powder blue iris.

"Th-The Hopewell killed off the last of the…" She swallowed hard and forced another painful breath. "…the Adena tribe. They'd gone inbred and the few remaining weren't right in the head…started doing things that weren't…weren't *natural*." Elsie kicked Charles onto his stomach and squatted over him with one knee planted in the small of the man's back. A single jerk to the collar of his shirt ripped the fabric free and exposed a large patch of mottled, leathery scars blanketing the entire right side of his back, shoulder and arm. "You…you were right when you said the Hopewell killed them."

Charles didn't move.

"Are you listening?" Elsie smacked her palm against his ruined shoulder blade.

He spasmed in pain. "*Schlampe*," he managed. "Teasing little bitch."

"They want…." Another breath. This one came with less effort as the knot in her chest relaxed a little. "They want…to know something."

"Who?"

"The Adena…*my audience*." She grabbed a handful of hair and turned his head so she could see his profile. Eye shine met eye shine as one predator recognized another. "They want to know what you taste like."

46

Behind the story...

Ah, "Someone to Watch Over Me," the story that, for me, felt like Alice going down the rabbit hole. This all started with browsing through history magazines and stumbling across an article about Olive Thomas (*Duffy*), a silent film actress, model, Ziegfeld Girl, and hailed as the first "flapper." I read a bit on her and used Olive as inspiration for Elsie, placing my story a decade after Olive's early days in McKees Rocks, Pennsylvania.

Many of the locations are real. After the research and writing the story, I found myself on Google maps and just wandering, virtually, through modern-day locations of places within "Someone to Watch Over Me." I added a few tweaks to better align the actual places with the story I had written and to match what the area was like in 1925.

When it came to my antagonist, Charles, I dipped into my own family history. My grandfather and namesake, Henry Snider, Sr. (*yes, I'm a "third" which translates to "child who struggles to express their own personality and not seen as simply an extension of the previous generation"*), actually experienced the injuries I gave Charles. My grandfather, as the story goes, lied about his age and joined the military for the first World War. He was mustard gassed and lost the skin on top of his head, shoulders, and upper back. Now, fast forward to World War II. He pushed to join up, even with his injuries. They approved him to ride over on the ships with the new recruits and help prepare them for battle, then ride back with the dead to ensure no looting of the fallen soldiers occurred.

I never met the man as he passed away before I was born, but I heard a lot about him. The wars left him with severe PTSD (*"shell shock" back in the day*) and left him divorced from my grandmother, ultimately homeless and trapped in a bottle for the end of his life. It's a dark reality that variations of still occur to this day with our military servicemen. While a depressing history to know about my grandfather, I also know he loved a good story and always had at least one book with him. I believe he'd approve of lifting this horrific experience to tell "Someone to Watch Over Me." My father agreed when he first read this, commenting about how his father once said the edges of the burn, where skin became scar, still hurt when clothing brushed it.

Being honest, this was difficult to write.

WHERE THE PRETTY THINGS ROT

Some of the factual places you can hunt for include McKees Rocks, Brunot island, and the historical dig site (*if you find the football field, you're on the right track*).

TASTE

An October breeze filled the air, and its bite tasted of decay. Mason Wells stared through the '72 Mustang's cracked windshield as the first snow of the season fell. Snowflakes, innocently white against the stark countryside, danced on the wind before they succumbed to the pull of gravity. A hundred and thirty miles east of Denver felt like another world.

His mind drifted back to the orange VW bus that blew by a few minutes before, and way over the speed limit. The type A in Mason screamed to put the pedal to the floor and teach the driver that classic muscle cars trump old hippie buses every time…but the greasy-haired little girl in the back window distracted him. Unblinking pale blue eyes stared out the rear window as the vehicle pulled away and disappeared over a slight rise, appearing as little more than a dot on the next hill as he peaked the first. Then they were gone.

Only a powdery landscape cut with a razor stripe of a county road lay before him. Mason shook his head and focused on the task at hand. "Get Harmony."

This was the third time they fell off the wagon. Parties and the fast lifestyle of the elite stock trading up-and-comers drew them in the first time. A little nose candy fell into a habit that cost them six years-worth of savings, the last of which went to pay for a stint in rehab.

Mason downshifted and slowed around a corner. Barren fields allowed the snow to drift. Armies of flakes accumulated on the road and filled the ditches. A hazy sun hung low in the sky and glowed dull through the storm.

The odometer ticked off another mile and the flea bite of a town—Joes, population 82—faded in the rear-view mirror.

"Not much farther."

Both stayed clean for over a year, until the Christmas party in Cherry Creek. With all the holiday spirit and goodwill, neither thought ill of a little holiday blow. Three months later they were jobless and in the middle of an eviction. A five-year trading suspension landed on Mason's shoulders for being caught in the middle of a line while the floor was still open. Harmony begged a loan from her parents to get out from under their addiction's merciless hunger. Mr. and Mrs. Krenshaw relented, as loving parents of an only child tend to, and paid for a second trip to the "cleaners."

"Damn it…c'mon!" He slammed the shifter back into fourth and felt the Mustang slide. Teeth gritted, his foot eased off the gas and let the car work itself out of the impending fishtail. A couple of seconds passed before tires gripped the asphalt's slick surface. Farms drifted by, their bounty harvested for the season.

Mason's foot danced with the accelerator again and pressed harder where opportunity allowed.

Following the second stint at rehab they got matching rose tattoos after spending the day window shopping used bookstores on Broadway, Mason on the inside of his wrist and Harmony on an ankle. Petals lined in black peeked from the edge of his jacket's sleeve. The artist went too deep with the needle and the artwork's detail ended up hazy, like a testament to the last several years. Harmony's turned out better but still not worth the money they paid.

The Mustang's odometer ticked off mile 141 He slowed and stared hard at the two farms paralleling each other.

"Lady or the tiger…lady or the tiger." Fingers strummed on the steering wheel as he weighed which driveway to turn into.

This last time they both walked the straight and narrow for nearly six months. Mason took a job as a bookkeeper's assistant, unable to return to the stock market until the suspension expired. Harmony pulled in fantastic tips at a local bar, averaging five times his meager salary. The uniform's short skirt didn't hurt matters, either. A flash of upper thigh and a smile easily made the difference between a dollar tip and a ten-dollar tip.

Then the tips stopped coming home.

A week ago, an amber vial rolled out of her jacket. Harmony just stared at him and waited for the argument which lasted all night. Tears and cold-turkey promises flowed like water. Then the accusations fired back and forth. Mason lost control and slapped her. It was the first time he ever hit her…first time he ever hit any woman, for that matter. The tiny container disintegrated under an unopened soda can he smashed down, sending powder peppered with glass shards all over the kitchen table. He left her there trying to pick out enough glass to allow for one last snort.

Mason selected the farm on the right, the one with the double-wide mobile home spearheading a century-old cluster of buildings. Recent tire tracks marred the thin sheet of snow and sporadic tufts of yellowed weeds added a nicotine tint to the otherwise pristine landscape. The driveway went straight as an arrow past the side of the mobile home to the homestead's remnants. Its original house, rotted and beginning to fall in on itself, leaned precariously. Nearby, a barn and paddock fence lay colorless against time's embrace. A splash of color pulled his gaze to the same parked VW bus that passed him earlier.

For the last seven days he'd searched for Harmony and followed a spiral trail, first from regular connections made at the bar to seedier dealers who didn't just trade for money. A pistol-whip delivered from a lowlife named Eddie cost Mason a tooth. Now, two hundred bucks later, he brought his own gun to level the playing field. A distinctive lack of quality reflected the price paid. Rust ate at the .38 Special and after two hours with a brush and solvent, he was confident the hunk of metal wouldn't just blow up in his hand.

The Mustang pulled to a stop behind the bus and Mason got out. The little girl still stared out the back window, greasy blonde hair framing a grime-smeared face. He left the car door open in case things turned sour, which, considering his luck as of late, was a distinct possibility. The child's eyes stayed on his car, without so much as a glance in any other direction.

She's not moving.

No breath fogged the rear window.

Stomach-churning reality set in as what he took as pale blue eyes were actually clouded green ones. Mason staggered back, butt knocking the driver's door closed before he lost his footing and fell, the pistol digging into one hip as he struck the ground.

The child's forehead pressed against the back glass. An unfocused stare looked to Mason's right and panic caused him to pull the gun for the second time in as many days and, still seated on the frozen ground, thrust the revolver in several directions in as many seconds. Convinced he was alone for the moment, save for his audience of one, he got to his feet.

"Son of a bitch!" The words fell lost in the snow and he crept to the back of the bus to look at the young corpse.

The girl appeared to be seven or eight—pretty in a sad sort of way. A bungee cord attached on either side of the glass anchored her in place like a demented ornament. Dusty-purple lips remained parted and revealed a missing front tooth, mirroring his own. Mason stepped forward and saw a massive brown stain across the lower portion of her t-shirt—the kind of brown that only came from dried blood. Sickened by thoughts of what kind of torment the child went through before death, he pushed himself onward.

Mason had drawn his gun for the first time the previous day at an east Colfax fleabag apartment. A twenty got him the same address given to Harmony. The two guys there freely admitted she left just a few hours before. Then they talked about how the cute little brunette was short on money. A laugh and a nod from the smaller of the two directed his attention to the far wall thumb-tacked with dozens of panties. The red spray-painted words "Wall of Shame" added a bit of color near the ceiling. Shock set in when he recognized a sheer pair of pink underwear from the white iron-on letter "M" Harmony put on the butt for Valentine's Day. The pistol ended up in his hand, thrust in the dealers' general direction. Mason left with her panties and the dealers' lock box containing a little over eleven grand. Enough to start a new life somewhere else. Another day of questions and hundreds of dollars in payoffs brought him here.

Nothing moved on the farm, save that of falling snowflakes. He gripped the pistol tighter and crossed the yard. Midway through the brittle grass, he altered direction, wary to stay in the dead child's gaze as he walked to the front of the manufactured home, ducking under each window just like the cops on Harmony's favorite crime shows. He stopped at the front corner of the house and surveyed the scene. White snow covered the front lawn, and a "Welcome Friends" sign hung cock-eyed on the front door.

Each step felt heavier than the one before and left Mason ready to drop by the time he got to the small deck. One clay jug, overflowing with cigarette butts, lay toppled by the door. A handful of the scattered filters were chewed midway along the shaft just like Harmony did when she was nervous. Seconds ticked by as Mason stood on the stoop, half waiting for someone to open the door on their own and see who was there.

He grabbed the knob, turned it and swung the door open.

A wall of marijuana smoke hit him in the face, the smell tickling his senses. The television cast a blue glow inside the living room. Some misadventures of a cartoon deer danced across the screen. Entangled in a mass of sheet lay an unconscious man, beard and long hair giving the impression, if only for a second, of a drugged-out Jesus complete with caked white smear over his upper lip. Harmony's jacket served as a wadded-up pillow for the junkie. Mason kicked the door closed with his heel.

Through a door to the right rhythmic sounds of ecstasy ceased, replaced with a man's scream of rage and pain followed by, "What the hell?" A smack of fist against flesh followed, audible over the music. The bedroom door ripped open and a man, built heavy and wearing only a jutting pair of boxer-briefs stepped from the bedroom. Blood ran down the hulk's chest as he pressed down on a nasty neck wound. He saw Mason and bellowed, "Who the fuck are you?"

The junkie on the couch coughed, getting everyone's attention, then rolled over and returned to snoring.

"You come for him?"

Mason's eyes narrowed as he recognized the hulk as Eddie, the scum who'd knocked out his tooth. His gaze fell from the man's face to the protruding underwear then over to his wife's jacket. "No. For Harmony."

As the name passed his lips Mason raised the gun and fired. Eddie's underwear dimpled between waistband and jutting member. Its depression darkened and blood spewed low in the man's abdomen, the inflicted injury still higher than he'd aimed. The muzzle flash lit the room up for an instant.

A nasally grunt came from Eddie as he fell over, hands clutching at the bubbling wound. The erection deflated in a purge of blood that underwear failed to contain and a small crimson pool spread.

He stared at the gunshot victim for several seconds as shock set in for both of them.

"Oh, God," Mason muttered. "I didn't…I didn't mean to."

More noise came from the bedroom.

"Harmony," Mason whispered, then yelled. "Harmony!" He ran to the doorway and stared into the bedroom.

Murky light wept around the edges of a tacked-up blanket serving as a window curtain. The room lay barren except for the queen mattress and a nude woman sprawled face down on its sheetless surface.

"Ha…Harmony?"

The figure stirred, rolled over and exposed a bloody face and torso. A Chinese dragon tattoo emblazoned across the stranger's left breast, its mouth frozen in the midst of biting down on the areola. She stirred a second time, but beyond that appeared oblivious to the gunshot just fired.

"Gawwwwd," the woman purred, "that was so goooood." Words drew out as she spoke them and hung in the air. The woman's hand slid across her collarbone, a single nail raked over the dragon's nipple, before sliding perversely lower. "Eddie…come back to bed."

"I'm—"

Eyes snapped open and silver orbs focused on Mason. "You're not Eddie." The sex kitten drone vanished. Blood, already drying, stuck the corners of her lips together.

"Harmony," Mason said again. "I'm here for Harmony."

The woman rolled to the right and propped herself up on one shoulder. "That brunette bitch?"

"She has a tattoo like this on her ankle." Mason extended his wrist and exposed his tattoo. A black stem with two thinly lined leaves bloomed into red petals. Any excuse to look away from those eyes was welcome. "Have you seen her?"

Locks of blonde hair, the same greasy shade as the little girl's, met the meager light. *She's the girl's mom*, Mason decided and resisted the urge to tell the dragon-lady how he found her daughter. The dragon swayed, drawing his attention from her face.

"Oh, you like Puff?"

"Huh?"

"Puff. My magic dragon, of course." She pushed herself upright and stood on the bed and faced him. "Would you like a closer look?"

"I…no," he said, suddenly embarrassed. "I don't want a closer look. Harmony," Mason said again, raising the gun in her direction. "I'm looking for Harmony. Is she here?"

Dragon-lady stared with the same flat, unblinking gaze Mason thought her daughter had. "Come here."

He met her gaze.

At the party, he looked across the room and saw a brunette stealing glances in his direction.

His pulse danced as Harmony touched his hand for the first time.

Vertigo played with his equilibrium. In direct contradiction to the woman's demand, he stepped back, ankles inadvertently kicking into Eddie's calves. "Don't." Mason's voice wavered in time with his gun hand.

"Gnuhhhhhhh," Eddie managed to mutter while clutching himself. Aside from the moan, he lay frozen in pain.

Mason chanced a glance down at his first gunshot victim. The man rolled onto his back and convulsed. A small amount of foamy spittle erupted between clenched teeth only to be caught by grizzled hair well on its way to being a beard.

"No running," the woman voice said.

She suddenly stood right in front of Mason, clearing the ten or so feet from the middle of the bed to the doorway in a single blink. Breath, cold and metallic, puffed into his face as she spoke and brought forth an urge to vomit.

Mason staggered back and tripped over the legs he'd already kicked once. He landed hard and wind knocked from him in a single whoof.

The dragon-lady knelt by Eddie and drew in a long breath through her nose. Eyes closed, she looked like a person savoring the smells from a kitchen. One hand, the left, slid seductively down Eddie's chest, snaking its way back and forth as if in the midst of foreplay.

Mason backed up further, distancing himself from the scene as it played out.

"Hel…help," Eddie muttered.

Her pale hand met Eddie's crimson ones, moved up and over them, resting as if a spider ready to leap. She looked from the clenched hands to his face, then without warning shoved her finger between his and buried the digit up to its third knuckle in the wound.

The couple's eyes locked as gender roles reversed in the sudden penetration. His hips bucked in an effort to extricate the invading digit.

"Shhhhhh, baby." She slid her finger in and out, keeping time with Eddie's weak thrashing. Swaying nipples hardened and Mason saw in disjointed fascination that the dragon appeared to bite down on her breast.

"F…f-f-f-f—"

Her hand jerked free, drenched in blood. She licked the digit seductively, never breaking the locked gaze with Eddie. "Fuck? Isn't this what you said you liked, Eddie? Something *different*."

Mason pistoned his legs, gaining momentum moving backward until his head hit the television with a loud thunk.

She looked over at him then, silver eyes reflecting the television's glow. A snarl escaped and the dragon-lady's crouched form went from erotic to predatory. Bared teeth, stained orange from blood and saliva, grinned with a savage fury.

Mason's eyes went to the mobile's front entrance.

Rather than trying for the door, Mason pushed himself up and jumped against the picture window. Thin drapes padded the escape and the window glass resisted, cracked, then gave way. A white-hot knife of pain shot through his side as he tumbled out the window, slid off the stiff branches of a Pfitzer bush and landed in a tangled heap on the snowy ground. Mason reached down and pulled a pie-sized shard of glass from just above his hip bone, the jagged slice ended no more than an inch from where he'd put the bullet in Eddie.

Blood steamed in the cold air.

"Cosmic joke," he muttered, parroting Harmony's constant comments about ironic justice. With one hand gripped against his own bloody wound, Mason pointed the other, the one with the gun, at the gaping window. No figure moved in the black maw of an opening. He blinked against the brighter light and waited.

Nothing.

Silence.

Snow.

Then a click as the front door unlatched and swung into the relative darkness of the mobile home. The dragon-lady stepped out onto the small deck and shielded her eyes against the cloudy day. Natural light did nothing to compliment her. An addict's body, emaciated except for silicone breasts, stood nude on the deck. Xylophone-like ribs protruded and she descended the steps one at a time, toes stepping carefully on the wood planks.

Mason got to his knees, bit his lip against the pain until blood filled his mouth. "Stay...back." The gun stayed pointed at the ground.

Dragon-lady walked onto the lawn and turned to him. Her skin darkened, hue deepening by the second, the shades changing from milky to tanned leather. The hand shielding her eyes browned further and took on a mummyesque appearance like he'd seen once on a special about hikers frozen in the Alps. Multiple splits along the palm and arm opened and showed a raw redness underneath beginning to char with exposure.

"Ow," she said in a small voice and looked at the fresh wounds.

Snow fell onto her shoulders and refused to melt, even where flesh glowed like embers.

That unblinking gaze focused on him.

Mason stared into eyes so reflective he saw himself.

She stepped closer.

Ten feet...Harmony was reflected in those eyes.

Five…Harmony waited for him, arms wide.

Mason's arm rose and he fired a single shot. The dragon lady's head snapped back and her feet kicked out, leaving her sprawled on the white lawn like a sacrificial snow angel. Blood and brain matter sprayed the scene in vivid color.

"I…I warned you," he managed. Bile sat at the back of his throat, threatening to erupt at any second.

"Me-yuhhhh," the woman groaned and worked to sit. A neat hole sat just above her right eye, the surrounding skin ballooned as it kept the shattered skull contained. The right eye itself ruptured from the bullet wound's pressure and the reflective orb wept clear fluid in an oversized crocodilian tear. A matted mass of pink and gray lay entangled with a clump of hair a few yards away.

Mason fired a second time into her face and she fell again. Spasming legs kicked out a rhythm only she danced to. A third and fourth bullet struck her, all but obliterating her features from the nose up. Legs quit moving and Mason stared at the spongy mess that had once been a face—nose hanging on by nothing more than a flap of skin still attached to the cheek, one eye collapsed like a crushed grape while the other bulged in its socket from shattered cheekbone, palate splitting into an artificial harelip.

The dragon relaxed its bite on her nipple.

"Hechsssst," passed misshapen lips.

Then quiet hung as cold and heavy as the afternoon chill.

Staring at his handiwork, he felt the bile churn higher. It spilled from Mason's lips and onto his shirt. He regained shaky footing and looked at the blood-stained snow. The pattern took on the form of a Rorschach test print.

"Thuh-thuh-thuh," sputtered from the dragon lady.

Mason turned away, unable to witness the dying woman's last moment. He walked slowly back toward his car but continued to look over his shoulder every couple of steps.

"Maaaaasonnnn," a whisper on the wind called.

Mason stopped with his hand on the car's door.

"Maaason?" The whisper became a voice. Harmony's voice.

"Harmony?"

"Mason? Oh, God, Mason." Her lyrical voice echoed off the

cluster of structures and he had trouble figuring out what direction her voice came from.

"Where are you?"

"Here," she called out.

He turned, sure it came from the old homestead just ahead of the VW. Hope renewed, he sprinted past the cars.

Smack!

Mason ducked at the sudden sound echoing behind him and half-buckled from pain.

"Christ," he half-shouted.

The VW bus driver's side window spider-webbed as a small palm struck it. The hand disappeared only to be replaced with the ravenous face of the dead child. She pawed at the window like a dog, pink drool falling from colorless lips. And there were those damned silver eyes again.

He was sitting with Harmony in the cafe' where they had their first date.

The little girl shifted, eyes reflecting more.

They were throwing water balloons at her cousins' pool party.

The child's palm smacked the glass again, adding more intricate lines to the webbed glass.

"Blink, damn it." Mason tore his gaze away and felt dizzy. Shaking the disorientation from conscious thought, he stepped past the front of the bus and chanced a backward glance. The child-thing scrambled to the front seat and kicked at the windshield. A collection of boot prints marred his view of the crazed figure who, luckily, didn't seem to understand the concept of a door handle.

"Mason!"

His head snapped to the left and Mason saw a low shadow shift through the house's missing window. Decades of neglect showed in the frame's swelled wood, remnants of white paint flecked the building's empty panes. Inside, a figure swayed rhythmically back and forth, head and shoulder silhouetted before a stark wall.

Smack. Smack-smack-smack. The fourth impact with the windshield produced an audible crack.

Mason moved forward and stepped through the doorway. Warped planks creaked underfoot as he went from the small alcove into the nearest room. Generations' worth of rodent feces—now the consistency of dirt—covered the floor. Holes from some attempt to run proper wiring ran shin-height along the nearest wall while vandalism had torn through horsehair plaster on the other. A ten-foot-long gash exposed ribbed wooden backing, a mortal wound open to elemental infection.

Harmony sat on the floor with her back against the wall, her physical condition paying homage to its abused state. Her pallor matched that of the dragon-lady and her offspring, the one who still pounded away at the windshield. His wife still wore her work clothes, white blouse now stained with filth and the miniskirt exposed bare legs to frigid air. Shoes had been lost somewhere along her journey down this particular rabbit hole, leaving her feet black with mud and grime. A thin, pencil-sized length of silver dangled from one hand, its end sharpened to resemble a giant hypodermic needle. Mason recognized it as the silver coke straw he'd given her before their troubles started. She bobbed her head and shoulders back and forth, almost imperceptibly, attention focused on her right forearm.

The length of sharpened tube lined up with the crook of her elbow and bit into flesh.

"Harmony!"

An audible sizzle ran the length of the tube and blood welled. Her head dipped with slow determination and a snort, the ferocity of which only a powder-lover could properly appreciate, shook her body. A second nostril-clearing sniff followed.

Harmony's head rose with obvious effort. One single trickle of crimson cut a path from her nose, through the clotted vestiges of former indulgences, and pooled at the corner of her mouth. An all-too-familiar shiver ran through her body, bare heels raked along splintered floorboards. The straw pulled free and smoke rose from a perfect round hole, one with four identical mates along her arm.

"Maaaaaaason," she cooed as euphoria took hold. Her eyes opened and orbs the same reflective silver as the straw focused on him. "Oh…Mason."

He stood just inside the room, frozen in place as she stared at him.

He was caressing the back of her hand while she slept.

A crash came from just outside the missing window, but Mason couldn't bring himself to look away from the scene playing out before him.

"I—I tried, Mason." She looked down at the self-inflicted wounds, breaking the trance. "Funny how they kind of look like cigarette burns."

"Honey, we can—"

"They don't hurt, though."

Harmony shifted, exposing both more leg and an amazing amount of mottled bruising along the underside of her thighs. He stared and a memory ripped him back to the age of fifteen—to when he found his grandmother sprawled half out of the tub, two days dead. Meemaw had the same purple-gray bruises, a discoloration of blood settling along her legs.

"Oh, God, it's sooooooo good," she drawled, ecstasy apparent in her voice. Sporadic convulsions rippled through her.

Mason walked over and squatted beside her. Smells of stale sex and burnt ham brought a surge of hate, disgust, depression, anger and love, vying for control in a swirl of emotional cacophony. Flashes of their first date, their first heated encounter on a friend's apartment building's roof, their first declaration of love to one another—these and a hundred other memories reflected in her mirrored eyes.

"Honey," he repeated. "It's going to be okay."

"I don't know where I am." Harmony's eyes closed and his love's confession spilled forth. "They kicked me out, Mason. She's the one who bit *me* and they kicked *me* out!" A second wave of pleasure took hold. "It wasn't so bad up 'til then…nothing we hadn't done before. But it hurt."

Guilt added itself to the whirlwind of emotions. "We can—"

"D-don't. They wouldn't even let me have my shoes." She clutched the gleaming metal in both hands. Underneath, the palms darkened, taking on an ashen look. "I came in here to try to get warm." Her eyes opened, then rolled back up into her head, lids closing once more. "When…when I woke up I was so thirsty. I cramped worse than the first time at rehab. So much worse."

"Come on." Mason reached for her and she knocked his hand away.

"I couldn't walk. I was so cold. Then the cat came in." An almost imperceptible nod to a bloody mess of orange fur in the corner. "And I wasn't cold anymore."

"God." The song playing earlier came to mind.

Confusion crossed Harmony's face. "I…I can't—I can't stop." She held the straw up, words falling in quick succession. "But it's better with this. You can feel it so much faster."

"We'll get you some help." He caressed her cheek. It felt like running his hand along a leather jacket left to the elements overnight.

Another, louder, crash came from the window. Mason looked up.

The little girl was trying to extract herself from the VW bus, attempting to push through the vehicle's windshield in a bloody mixture of gouges and glass. She screamed as hair and a patch of scalp pulled free before jerking herself back inside.

Mason grabbed Harmony by the arm. "We've got to go!" When he pulled, he heard her lower back pull free of the frost.

"No."

He looked down at her as if the word had no meaning and pulled a second time to pull her up.

"There's no time!" Mason felt his bladder tighten, fear pressing the need to relieve himself.

The little girl pushed an arm through the windshield and smacked it down against the front of the bus. Flesh split against glass, bloodless. Just beyond, in the back yard, Mason saw the monstrosity that was the child's mother, complete with deflated mass serving as a head, stagger around the corner.

"Stay," Harmony whispered. She reached up, nearly pulled him off balance in a grip stronger than he remembered, and said, "You swore we'd be together no matter what. I—" she sniffed again. "I can't go with you. I can't walk."

"Oh, Jesus. But…."

Her hand ran down the length of his arm and gently placed the metal tube between shaking fingers. She offered her perforated arm as one would a dinner roast. "Here."

"Harmony—"

"Just this once." She smiled the way she did the first time he said, "I love you." Her eyes pulled the cold from him and he felt the world tilt.

Harmony was squealing as he shoved wedding cake into her mouth.

They walked around the lake holding hands and not saying a word, content to just be together.

"I—"

"Shhhh."

Mason glanced back one last time as the child fell from the front of the bus, then gingerly took the straw and bowed his head to Harmony's outstretched arm.

Flesh sizzled and the world fell away.

Behind the story...

You know those days when you're sure of what the plan is and things go delightfully wrong? "Taste" came about because of a day like that. This tale actually has two instances of Behind the Scenes.

For years my day job has been as a media guy. I'll keep the description brief because it branches out in so many different directions depending on the year. "Media Guy" encompasses work as a trial technician, website designer, photographer, audio mixing tech, cover artist, layout designer...the list goes on. Basically, I'm a nerd with more monitors than I have eyes.

I was shooting a location near Eleven Mile Reservoir, Colorado, of an old stagecoach inn. This was just for fun. For those who don't know, many stagecoach inns are essentially two houses under one roof. The front house— the "owner's" house—was comprised as any house is: basic rooms on the first floor (*living room, kitchen, parlor*) then bedrooms upstairs. The long portion of this particular house had a larger room (*potentially a dining room*), attached barn for horses, and stairs going up to a set of rooms that went over the dining room all the way out to over the attached barn. These were for guests. The second floor of this part of the house did *not* connect to the second floor of the owner's house. A wall separated them. Right by the building was a well, partially filled in with debris.

The first part of the back story occurred during shooting this location for fun. I arrived about noon, so the sun was high in the sky. I brought three camera batteries and was shooting the owner's side of the house, inside and out. Just a note on camera battery life—historically,

I've swapped out the battery on this camera once after shooting all day at an event. Each battery lasts hours without a problem. I shot the dining room of the guest side and went upstairs. I took a few shots of the rooms on the second floor. That's when it got significantly darker and cold. In fairness it was fall in the mountains of Colorado, but there wasn't a cloud in the sky and I discovered while standing at a window that the air outside was significantly warmer than inside compared to just a moment before. I lifted the camera and my battery was dead. I popped in my second…also dead. I ended up yelling down to Hollie to check my third battery that I left in the camera bag in the car. She said it had a full charge and ran it up to me. I checked it when she handed it to me—about 20% power. I popped the battery in and fired off about a half dozen shots before the battery died. Those photos turned out slightly out of focus but showed how dark the second floor was compared to the outside. We walked around a bit before leaving. Once home I charged the batteries again—no problem. No odd drains ever since.

I did have a few people ask if I had my phone with me if it drained as well. No, because I didn't have it on me. When I'm shooting I tend to leave my phone off or in the car. The running joke is that I'm Gen X, the cell phone is for my convenience, not others'. Hollie did have her phone on her but was in the house for only a minute or two and we didn't think to check it out.

I guess we failed the Scooby Gang test on that one.

That brings us to the second segment for "Taste." A friend and fellow author, Morgen, was looking to do a "40 and Fabulous" shoot. We all figured that the stagecoach inn would be a great location and went there in November. There are no real trees in the area, meaning that when there is wind, it's wicked cold in the late fall and winter. The initial shoot was fun and playful. As the day wore on Hollie, Morgen, and I started bouncing around ideas. The poses went from playful to provocative, then from provocative to dark. In three steps, the 40 and Fabulous photo shoot descended into a vampire crack whore photo shoot.

Try saying that three times.

Once home, I went over the images and with a little Photoshop magic, there were fangs, bruises from pooling blood, a silver straw with smoking holes in the crook of an emaciated vampiric arm. A little while later I showed them to Mo and she loved them. I ended up thinking there was a deeper story there and kept explaining Harmony's background to Mo and Hollie. Mo and Hollie both told me to quit telling what the woman's history was and to just write the damned story already.

Needless to say, Morgen's weird, too.

SINGED

Flames licked from broken windows on the first and second floors of the six-story building, leaving char in their wake. Late October snow turned to rain in the heat, coating the Detroit street in a fine mist that acted like glue for airborne ash. Matt Dempsey sat on the ladder truck's bumper and watched his fellow firemen soak the corner store in a nonstop flood of water. The hose snaked back from Martinez and Wolcott, across the empty street and through the front windows of an illegally parked Chevrolet. It was a nasty little pleasure all crews savored when they found a car parked beside a hydrant at a fire. Today Matt took his turn to smash a little glass.

Captain Martinez, relieved from nozzle duty, jogged back to the truck. "You about ready?"

"And able. What's the word?"

The captain wiped one gloved finger across his bottom lip, leaving a charcoal smudge. "Building's mostly empty. There's a couple of families on five and one with a kid on six."

"Almost got it, Cap," Nelson said while working the ladder gears. "The bitch won't move. Gotta be a clamp." He pushed past Matt and climbed up into the rig.

"I thought Devil's Night was supposed to be a thing of the past. With Angel Night we shouldn't be having this much arson. I mean, this is worse than back in the '90s."

Matt put on his gloves. "Ever think of telling Detroit's pyromaniacs that?" He turned and felt Captain Martinez help with the air tank's weight as it slipped on.

"Point taken."

"Think they'll find the missing people?"

"What, the Angels?"

Matt snapped the chest harness closed. "Yeah. I mean, that's a lot of neighborhood watch volunteers to go missing, right?"

Nelson called over the side, "Almost got it."

"Sounds like my cue."

The captain nodded. "I'm betting gang activity."

"But over eighty? I've heard word that the FBI's going to be called—"

"Got it!"

They both moved to allow Nelson some room to hop down.

"Enough chatter."

Matt attached the air hose to his mask, put it on and crowned himself with a helmet.

"Lookin' good!" Martinez gave a thumbs up. "Ass in the bucket."

The fireman went around the side of the truck, climbed up behind the cab and slid into the bucket at the end of the ladder. He reached over and pulled the fire axe from its holster and felt gears jerk to life. Vertigo danced along his innards during the initial rise, as it always seemed to. The bucket lifted and swung out over the chaos. Matt tried the remote controls.

Still dead.

A second story window exploded and peppered him with crystalline shards. Instinct took over and he attempted to duck, rocking the bucket.

"Shit!"

The mask's mic and earpiece squelched to life. "You okay up there?" Captain Martinez's voice sounded more bored than concerned.

"Just enjoying the view."

"What about the controls?"

"Deader than Nelson's love life."

The bucket jerked a second time and the ladder extended from its nested position atop the three other layers. Matt bobbed once, then a second time as the angle of ascent steepened.

His earpiece crackled. "We're putting you in on four. Three's an oven."

"Roger."

More yellow light caught his attention. Two blocks down, another brick apartment building burst into flames. Tanker Seven pulled away with a cluster of firefighters atop it.

"We've lost Seven," barked Martinez over the air. "Too many fires going at once. There's more people at that one so we're keeping five men here and one ambulance."

"Seems a bit light."

"Best I can do—" Background noise howled as a police car's siren started up without warning. "—will assist."

The building was less than ten feet away and he rose to the third floor. "Say again." Heat billowed out from the second floor with enough ferocity Matt felt it warm his boots.

"Nelson. Nelson will assist once the ladder's locked in place."

Seven feet.

"Understood."

Four.

Three.

A third-floor window blew out as he rose past, signaling the building to be a lost cause. The best anyone could hope for was to save a few lives before the structure fell in on itself.

The bucket struck the fourth floor's windowsill and tipped Matt forward. Motion stopped, then reversed itself several inches until the ladder barely met brick.

"Paydirt," Matt said. "Going in."

His axe made short work of the glass and in three swipes the window was open and the base cleared of frame and debris. A heavy metal hook flipped forward over the sill and anchored the ladder in place. Matt stepped into the gloom and flicked on his head lamp.

Shadows mimed furniture under the unforgiving beam and shifted with every move.

"Hello?" He panned left and right, looking for signs of life. "Fire department!"

No one answered.

He went through the five-room apartment, making sure to check under beds and in the wreckage of each closet. Nelson straddled the windowsill when Matt exited the second bedroom.

"Luck?"

"None yet." Matt motioned with the axe to the other firefighter's groin as he climbed in. "Watch your boys. Glass is bad."

"Gotcha."

Matt pulled a glove off and put the back of one hand to the hallway door, then checked the temperature of the doorknob. Both were cool to the touch. He opened the door a crack, ready to slam it. Smoke wafted along the hall's ceiling, forcing them to stoop in order to see better.

"Matt, you do that side and I'll—"

"No. We stay together. Remember your training." He rapped knuckles on the younger firefighter's helmet. "We start across the hall and then work our way up. Close the door behind you so we don't chimney the fire."

The two went from apartment to apartment on the floor, finding nothing except empty rooms until they came to the last door by the stairwell. Nelson banged on the door. Thunks reverberated through the frame.

"Nelson, give the door a kick."

"We have two more floors of this?"

"Yup." Matt moved to the left and tried to glance down the smoke-clogged stairwell. Soot already coated the paint and took the muted blue walls into murky blackness. "Can't see squat down the stairs."

Nelson kicked at the door, rebounded and prepared for a second assault. "Yeah, well at least you don't see flames yet." He struck the door a second time, cracking the wood down the middle. "How's the heat?"

Matt pulled a glove off and stuck it out at head height into the stairwell's airflow. "About Bermuda, going on Mount Saint Helen's."

"Great." His third kick broke the latch and the door swung in. "Deadbolt was thrown. Has to be someone here."

"Hello?"

Nelson parroted, "Hello? Fire department. We need to clear the building."

Matt motioned the junior fighter ahead and tapped at his earpiece as he entered the apartment. "Captain?"

A muddied squawk resounded, followed by, "…ead you well."

"Captain," he repeated and yelled this time, "We're at the end of four." The room was an easy forty years out of date and told the probable age of the tenant.

"Roger."

"Getting hot in here and we're moving too slow. Can you move the bucket to the roof and we'll recover from there?" He stepped past the Formica kitchen table into the living room proper. Decades-old furniture filled the room, fabric worn smooth from repeated use. Even the television, while newer than the rest of its surroundings, still relied on tube technology rather than the plasticized panel units that everyone now owned.

"Not a good…." Crackles overtook the superior's voice.

"No choice," he shouted. "Four's about to light and we won't be able to exfiltrate from here." Matt looked back and saw smoke darken as it billowed in through the open door.

"Affirmative."

"Back here!"

Matt navigated furniture and walked into the bedroom. Bed linens lay in a pile at the foot and Nelson stood by the bathroom door, doubled over without his mask on.

"Nelson!"

He waved the forthcoming order away heaved great gulps of smoky air. One hand motioned toward the open bathroom door. "In…in—"

Remains of the chicken salad dinner spewed, splattering the floor with creamy color contrasting the blue carpet.

Matt reached over, grabbed Nelson's oxygen mask and shoved it into the man's right hand. "Puke, then inhale clear air. I can't afford to be hauling you up and out too." He moved to the door and pulled it all the way open. Mint green tile blanketed the walls and white ceramic ones covered the floor, giving the room more of a subway bathroom feel than that of a washroom inside a private home. He looked across the tiled floor toward the sink.

A drying pool of crimson covered a half dozen tiles from the bathtub's edge, under the sink, and ringed the toilet. Shorelines of scabbed blood gave way to its still-tacky center. Droplets still fell from a nude elderly man's face as he lay slumped with his torso hanging over the side of the tub. Deep cuts and blood hid his features. A box cutter still rested in the suicide victim's grasp.

Now bile danced at the back of Matt's throat, threatening to bubble over. He swallowed hard, knelt by the old man's side and pressed two fingers against the man's carotid artery.

One thump.

Two thumps.

"Nelson! Get in here!"

The old man jerked back at the sudden sound and swung the cutter with wicked intent.

"Nononononooooooo! I'm a good boy," the man said. "A good boy."

"I'm sure you are," Matt said from the doorway. He glanced around the corner to see if Nelson recovered.

Twin, skull-deep crevasses ran from forehead to chin, splitting eyelids in a mock fleshy four-petaled flower. Other cuts zigzagged across the senior's face. One sliced so deep, a full third of his nose hung in place by the thinnest piece of skin. That same cut continued, creating an artificial harelip. A fine mist of blood and spittle sprayed with every word.

"I'm a good boy!" Coughs choked him and the word "boy" came out more as "doy."

"I'm sure you are," Matt repeated and tried to keep his voice calm but still loud enough to be heard over the rising din. He caught a glimpse of Nelson thumbing through a handful of envelopes strewn across the dresser, then thrust one letter into Matt's hand. He looked down at the name. "It'll be okay, Father McKittrick. Just stay calm and we'll get you out of here."

Hearing his name spoken slowed the blade's vicious arc. "How did—"

"Your mail."

The blade lowered further. "And you're...."

"Firemen, Father. There's a fire on the floors below us and we have to get to the roof so my friends can lower us to the ground."

Father McKittrick's blade rose again. "Not upstairs. That's not for us."

"We don't have a choice, Father. All the floors below us are on fire."

"Better to burn." He slid the box cutter along the inside of one thigh, pale skin parting to show red meat beneath. The priest didn't even flinch as his flesh split.

Blood pooled.

"Stop that." A single step was all it took for the priest to jerk the blade from himself and fling it at Matt. The instrument glanced off his mask and clattered to the floor. Now weaponless, Father McKittrick clawed at his face. One pinky finger snagged itself in the segmented eyelid, pulling the wound flap open. Raw flesh and a deflated orb beneath peeked out.

Matt closed the distance between the two and grabbed the old man by the wrists. "Easy, Padre." He held the man of God's clenched hands down towards his lap where nails scratched rhythmically against naked thighs.

Nelson watched the wrestling match from the relative safety of the bedroom. "You got him?"

"Yeah. But I need binders."

He tried to hold both the priest's hands with one of his own, but the man proved to be stronger than his age portrayed. The scuffle resumed and Matt jerked Father McKittrick out of the tub, pinning him to the sticky floor with one knee. Nelson passed the flex-cuffs over—the very ones his captain complained about him carrying— and watched his partner bind the priest's hands behind him.

"We can't—" the priest began.

"Stow it, Padre." What little patience Matt still possessed withered. "We have two more floors to still do. If you keep it up, I hogtie you and you get dragged."

Nelson piped up. "Understand?"

Father McKittrick thrashed again before he settled down and nodded.

Matt ventured an, "Okay?"

"Yeah."

"I'm going to help you up now and you're not going to give us any more problems." Matt gripped the old man by the elbows and pulled him first to his knees, then again to unsteady feet. Blood covered the priest's front, leaving him looking anything but holy. "Can you walk?"

A single nod.

"Nelson, grab that robe off the bed and tie it on him."

The firefighter wiped his mask with the back of one gloved hand. "But we'll have to untie him."

"No." A sigh, audible even through the mask, heaved from Matt. "Just put it on him backwards and tie it. That'll be good enough until we can get back on the ground."

A boom sounded somewhere deep in the building and shook its charring foundations.

"Time to move!"

They guided the priest through the apartment and into the hallway. A single breath of the black smoke was enough to drop the old man to his knees. Fire crackled from the stairwell as Matt handed a mask over to the priest and let him draw deep on the clean air, then helped him up a second time in the last few minutes.

Nelson, who led the way, stopped short of the alcove.

Matt said, "Move it!"

The lead firefighter waved them back as he moved closer to the alcove and stared down toward the floor below.

"Nelson!" Matt kept his grip on Father McKittrick's arm with one hand while still securing the mask with the other. Once up, he knocked on the junior's helmet.

He looked back with a scared expression. "I thought I saw—"

"Later." Matt waved a hand in front of his face. "Too hot. The priest'll cook." He moved the old man to the far side of the well where stairs ascended.

Smoke shot up, using the stairway as a chimney. Each step brought memories of practice fires. Sweat beaded between flesh and mask, loosening the connection. Twelve steps and the trio reached the midway landing. Runnels of sooty sweat streaked the old man's face and left clean marks in their wake. The three pushed up to the fifth floor and moved left into the hallway.

"You live here," Nelson yelled through his mask. "Which apartments are occupied?"

Father McKittrick just shook his head.

"Father!"

"I don't know." Breath fogged the clear plastic mouthpiece. "Some."

Matt helped the priest to the floor and leaned him against the tan wall. "Stay here." He produced a knife, cut the plastic tie and moved the elderly man's hands around in front of him before securing them again. The portable oxygen tank they wedged between forearms was balanced against his chest.

Nelson stayed on his heels as Matt broke in the first door, not bothering to waste time knocking anymore. Furniture guaranteed to be rejected from any yard sale littered the apartment, but its overall layout was identical to the old man's. They rushed in and checked the place room-by-room, ensuring no one was home.

The next place lay empty, as did the following one. With each open door, smoke churned past them, insistent on being first.

The fourth and last dwelling on one side of the hall met with resistance. Nelson's boot bounced off the door as if he'd kicked into a brick wall.

"Son of a bitch!"

"Door blocker."

Nelson rubbed his knee. "No kidding."

Matt banged on the door. "Fire department! We need to evacuate this building now."

Silence.

He swung the axe and let the blade bite deep into the wood about a foot to the left of the doorknob.

"A little low."

He ignored his partner, swinging again. This time Matt arced the descent slightly and completed an "X" in the wood. Two hard strikes with the axe head and the area splintered, leaving a softball-sized hole in the door.

Nelson muttered, "What's with the Devil's Night comeback?" He looked back to check on the old man.

"You know Detroit. Nothing's ever really gone." Matt focused on getting his arm through the hole.

"I remember this stuff from when I was a kid, though. It was usually just warehouse fires and little shit."

"Stuff?"

Nelson laughed. "Shit. Stuff. I'll tell it to the priest when we get out of here."

"Hell, tell him now." Matt reached in through the door and a moment later the tell-tale clatter of a piece of metal hitting the floor rang out. A turn of the knob and the two men entered the living room. Newer paint—blue and brown hues, rich in contrast to the hall's earth tone slop—covered the walls. "Move slow. I can't carry you out, too."

"Yes, Mother."

Books, an expensive entertainment system, props and posters promoting '90s movies littered the area. Bedrooms and bathroom were the same. A king-sized four-poster bed filled one room while a home office setup occupied the other.

But no people.

"This one's clean, Nelson." He motioned to the far side of the hall. "You ready to take on the other side of the hot potato?"

Nelson turned to Matt. "There *has* to be. The door blocker—"

"Chalk it up to gremlins. Now are you ready or not?"

"Do I have a choice?"

Matt looked out the door into the hall, gauging the smoke volume roiling in. "Well, you could play wet nurse to the padre."

"Man, did you see what he did to his eyes?"

"Keep it down."

"But to do that just because of Devil's Night?"

Matt sat and angled himself so the kitchen chair's arm took the brunt of his oxygen tank's weight. "Things have gone crazier than usual since the economy collapsed. My kids are growing vegetables in the vacant lot next to the house. A garden…in downtown Detroit."

"Wasn't Angel Night supposed to put a stop to all the arson?"

He pushed himself back up. "On to the next place. Time's getting short." A nod to a corner of the room was all it took. There, low but spreading, smoke pushed itself up from the floors below.

Nelson's voice dropped. "It's moving fast, too."

"So we move faster."

They made their way into the hall and looked down at the hunched form of Father McKittrick. Bound arthritic hands clutched the mask and small air tank they'd left with him. With the slumped posture and grimy appearance, he looked more the part of a hobo than a man of God.

Nelson yelled, "Hey?"

The father didn't answer.

"Hey, Father? You still doin' okay down there?"

Father McKittrick gave a slight nod and a half-hearted thumbs-up before cradling the air tank once more.

Matt looked at the hall window. Red lights strobed and a white ladder ascended twenty or so feet above their heads to meet with the edge of the building. City noises were muffled by the incessant crackling of encroaching fire. Memories of a fallen comrade tickled at his senses. He banged twice on the door and leaned to one side. No one yelled a response. No trio of bullet holes perforated the door, either.

He felt Nelson's gaze on him.

"Gerard."

The name played as the gospel cautionary tale of not knowing whose door they were actually knocking on. His partner nodded.

Matt banged again then kicked the door. Boot connected to wood and the jamb separated, falling away. An empty living room and open bedroom doors told of the vacancy.

"This is taking too long."

"Easy, Nelson. We'll get it cleared."

Nelson moved ahead to the next and kicked out without bothering to knock. A second well-placed kick opened the door just like its predecessor. "So," he asked while entering the apartment, "What about Angel Night?" Furniture similar in shape to that in the first apartment on this floor cluttered the living room to its limit.

"It ain't working." Matt went in first.

"I know it ain't working. I mean, why 'Angel' Night."

The answer came slow. "Because 'Take Back the Streets Night' was already taken. How the hell would I know?" He gave an easy shove to Nelson. "Check the bathroom and bedroom. I'll hit the other one."

They confirmed the place clear in under a minute. No people hidden or unconscious, and no signs of pets. Then it was back into the hall.

Nelson noticed the priest paying attention to their conversation. "What about you, Father? Any idea why it's called Angel Night?"

"It was a play on All Saints Day. The church made that holiday in response to Samhain. For non-believers, the masses made Angel Night to combat all the Devil's Night arsonists."

"Looks like they failed."

The priest repeated himself. "Angel Night is when citizens patrol and try to stop the fires from being set."

Matt adjusted his gloves while listening to the exchange.

"I grew up here. I know all that."

"Are...?" Father McKittrick looked up, clotted blood held the sliced eyelids in place. A glint of white bone was visible in the slice through the left brow. "Are you sure we can't go down?"

"What's wrong with up?" Nelson shot a wink at Matt. "Closer to Heaven." He reached down and helped the priest up.

"Nelson...easy." An angry look drove home the point that the firefighter crossed a line. Matt led the trio back to the stairwell. "Last door, then we're up to six."

"Can't go up." The priest visibly shook.

They leaned him against the stairwell railing and kicked in the closed door.

Empty.

The pair turned back in time to see the father lean back and allow himself to tip over the railing.

Matt reached out. "No!"

The priest went horizontal on the banister, then further. Pasty-white legs pointed skyward as the fatal descent commenced. Nelson dove toward the wooden rail. Fingertips brushed the ball of McKittrick's left foot as the priest fell. Both firemen looked down as the flapping robe disappeared into the smoke-filled shaft.

Nelson moved to the stairs.

"No. Up."

"But—"

"He's dead! There might be survivors on six." He patted his comrade's shoulder hard and waited until Nelson led the way up to the final floor.

They slowed at the final few steps up to the sixth and final floor. Oily smoke rippled along the ceiling and gave a vertigo impression of black water running along its length. Brown streaks muddied the walls. Pigment changed.

Blood.

Gallons of it.

Matt gripped the axe tighter and put a cautionary hand out.

Nelson leaned in. "I see it too, boss."

"Slow."

"Sure you don't want to have them link up to the window?"

Matt pointed to the end of the hall. Glass and frame were smashed in. He went from the alcove into the hall. The worn wooden floor vanished underneath a coating of visceral fluid. A sidestep allowed Nelson through.

A backward glance showed glowing embers rising with the upward current of air.

"Gotta hurry. With that window open—"

"Chimney effect. Got it."

"—and keep the axe handy."

But Nelson already headed for the doorway across the hall. Two bangs, then a kick to open it. The door opened, slammed against the wall then swung closed again from the concussive force.

People.

Nelson kicked the door again, this time using the axe to keep it open.

Nelson backed up, stomach convulsing with the threat of another expulsion.

Matt pushed past and bit down hard on his lip, forcing himself to look past the threshold.

Beyond lay a nightmarish parody of life.

Couples sat in chairs, throats slit. Others were posed as if in deep conversation, skulls concaved from blunt force trauma. Spotless white Angel Night arm bands adorned every body.

They went into the room, using the axe to nudge the people. Most were still in a state of rigor, while a few others, further along in their state of decay, were past that and lay lumped against furniture or walls. The problem was, they shouldn't be. Rigor shouldn't have resolved this quick. A four-man game of poker, complete with the "Dead Man's Hand," played out in mannequin form at the kitchen table.

"Matt!"

He moved through the masses to the bedroom doorway. A lifeless orgy of the dead were frozen mid-act. A woman, chocolate against white sheets, lay on her back. Her head hung off the bed's side with a flashlight shoved to the hilt into her throat. Batteries still offered enough life to light the bulb with a dull amber glow. Eyes bulged, bloodshot in death. A man stood before her, positioned in such a way as to receive fellatio…if his penis hadn't been removed.

"She choked to death," Matt rasped, staring at the light.

"What?" Morbid fascination overtook him and Nelson moved around the bed. "She was alive when—" he motioned to the woman "—this happened?"

A man whose eyes matched the priest's self-inflicted mutilation lay over her, positioned in a mockery of copulation. Broken table legs propped him up over the woman. Blood encrusted handprints covered the bodies, murderers not bothering to worry about evidence. The exposed angle showed this man's castration as well.

Nelson elbowed Matt. "They're all dead! That crazy priest did this."

"We don't know—"

"We *do* know!" He backed out of the room, pointing at the corpse with identical wounds. "Do you really think that's coincidence?"

Matt followed his partner into the hall.

"We have to check."

"To Hell with—"

Barking cut him off.

Between smoke and noise, neither could tell which apartment

the dog was in.

Lights flickered.

Nelson looked up at the ceiling. "Aw, come on."

Illumination winked out, leaving them with the twin beams of the helmet lights.

Matt keyed his mic. "Captain? We have a situation."

"…Flo…Chr…." The rest fell to squelch.

"Captain?"

The airwaves were left to background noise.

More smoke flowed.

Matt took in a deep breath. "We get the dog, and anyone else, then get the hell up top."

"Man, I really don't want to."

He stood and led Nelson to the next door and banged on the door. It swung open without resistance. Matt's beam went to the broken jamb.

"Fire department!"

A fruit bowl sat on the kitchen counter, complete with severed hands, fingers splayed in floral bloom.

He pulled the door closed.

The dog barked again—a high pitched panicked yapping.

They followed the noise, bypassing two other apartments, and stopped at the end of the hall.

Rather than banging this time, Matt tried the knob.

It turned and the door swung in.

The white blur of a Jack Russell Terrier shot between their feet and skidded to a stop at the stairwell before it barked at them again.

Laughter echoed from the bedroom.

Matt and Nelson looked at each other, debating the other's courage or preparation to flee.

Both moved into the room and found the same insanity of flesh as the others. The missing genitalia from the other apartment lay on plates around the six-person table, waiting for a Dahmer-worthy feast. With axes at the ready, they moved to the door and pushed it open.

Inside, a live-action rendition of the orgy, right down to the castrated men, played out. Bodies groped each other, smearing blood, feces and other bodily fluids with each caress.

More laughter from the man positioned between the corpse's legs. "Take it! Take it! Take it!" He thrust his hips at the corpse, as blood flecked in every direction from his missing genitalia. The man's eyes, as were those of everyone in the room, were gone. Blood and gore covered the four adults on the bed.

Then Matt saw the girl.

Not yet ten, a blonde-haired child sat, pajama-clad knees-to-chest, curled into a chair. Blue eyes peeked at Matt through the ratty mop of curly locks.

He motioned for her to come closer.

One of the men stopped and looked directly in Matt's direction.

He put a hand up for the child to stop moving.

Gore-encrusted sockets appeared to look as the head turned left then right. Seconds passed and the gyrations from the bed once again got his attention.

The girl tiptoed past the blind quartet and took Matt by the hand, allowing him to lead her out. Nelson pulled the bedroom door closed, then did the same with the apartment door once they exited to the hall. The terrier yapped again and started down the stairs before returning up to the hall. His bark took on a hurried repetition.

Matt knelt down to eye level with the child. "What's your name?"

"Beth."

"We're going to get you out of here, Beth. Okay?"

"But my doggy—"

"He's fine." Matt looked her over. No visible injuries. No obvious signs of abuse beyond witnessing the events in that bedroom.

"Roof," Nelson said.

Embers popped up the stairwell and landed on the hallway floor. One connected with the dog's nose and elicited a yelp of pain.

Matt scooped the girl into his arms and followed Nelson to the padlocked door. A swing of the axe gave them access. Fifteen stairs later, they pushed open the roof's fire door. The dog followed a few paces behind and took each stair as an old man would—one step…a pause…then another—always looking ahead. Nelson held the door open an extra minute and coaxed the canine from the stairs. He finally shot past and ran to the edge of the building, looking down over the edge.

"Nelson, it should be over here." Matt pointed to the near ledge then stopped.

Detroit's city skyline glowed from the multitude of fires. Power failures to the south enhanced the burning glow—so many that they appeared as a poor rendition of city lights. Gunshots echoed and peppered the night with explosions of sound.

A nearby condo high-rise's eighth floor was ablaze, trapping people above. Dozens stood on balconies to peer over the edges, pointing at other fires or talking on cell phones. The apartments faded from view as smoke billowed up from the building they stood on.

"Nelson!"

Nelson stood by the door. He stared up at the smoke's low ceiling. The dog continued to bark and nip at the man's heels.

Matt put the little girl down on a vent, then walked over to the door and shook his immobile partner, ending the minor assault with a hard slap across Nelson's face.

"I…huh?"

"Wake up, junior. Time to go."

A small voice asked, "Sir?"

Matt knelt by the girl. "You're going to be okay, honey."

"It's warm," she said.

Nelson dropped his mask, coat and gloves onto the roof. He stood in his suspendered pants and boots, dripping sweat.

"Nelson, get'cher gear back on!"

The little girl slid from the vent, landing bare feet on the tarred roof. She ran past both men and went to the ledge, climbing up on the narrow lip.

Matt's stomach dropped.

"Whoa, there. Let's get back from the edge, okay?"

Greasy blonde hair danced on the wind as she did a tightrope walker imitation with arms outstretched for balance. One dirty foot went in front of the other. Embers crackled and rose past one arm. A few stuck, darkening the dusty pink cotton sleeve.

Matt moved toward her.

"Mister, ever see the old films about the atomic bombs?"

He ignored the question. "Down, *now*, young lady."

Beth did a cartwheel, feet and arms locked straight.

"Damn it!"

"That sounds about right." She giggled.

Nelson wiped more sweat from his forehead and looked at it.

"They called where the bomb went off ground zero." Beth repeated the cartwheel, ending the execution just short of the corner of the building.

"Ma…Matt?"

He looked back at Nelson.

"I…don't…feelsogood." The end of his sentence ran together as if he were in a rush to finish it.

Hair clung against a sweaty brow, but part of his face looked distorted.

Matt grabbed his mask and pulled it free.

The marred look remained. Nelson's forehead smeared, skin sloughing to the side and exposing wet bone beneath. His right eyebrow now clumped closer to the edge of the eye socket and skin bunched up. Dribbles of perspiration beaded on exposed skin, soaked the blue t-shirt's pits and chest.

"Nel—"

"I *really* don't feel well." His hand rose to his face a second time.

"Don't," Matt said low.

The back of Nelson's hand bore flesh in a similar condition to the forehead—skin pushed to the side, exposing wet meat beneath, ligaments contrasting white against red. "What the hell…?" He reached up and wiped again. Skin fell away from face and hand alike. Newly exposed bone and muscle glistened in the firelight.

Barking came from behind one of the two roof-mounted fans.

"Shhhh," Beth said and brought a finger to her lips.

The dog continued, more agitated than before.

"It's hot," came from behind shaggy hair.

Nelson aged in a second as flesh took on a pudding consistency. Features drooped then slid along a frame that no longer supported it.

Matt felt himself back away from the melting man.

"Noooooo," came a voice housed in a body of melting flesh. Lips took on a respectable rendition of a frowning theater mask.

More barks.

The girl put hands to her hips. "I said, shush!"

Barking, louder this time.

"We can't talk like this," Beth said matter-of-factly. "Here, boy. Get the stick. Get the stick!" An empty hand waved back and forth to get the canine's attention. Once she had it, her arm craned back then mock-threw the imaginary item. The dog shot out and ran full force in the non-existent stick's direction, cleared the ledge in a single jump and snapped at the air.

Gravity took over then and the terrier vanished from sight.

Matt took a step in the dog's direction, then realized that took him closer to both Nelson and the little girl. He stopped.

"This is ground zero."

"I don't—"

Nelson sobbed, holding hands that dripped flesh out in front of him. "Make it stop."

The child sat cross-legged on the ledge. "If you touch your friend, he'll get it and you'll be okay again."

"J-just make it stop." Nelson's belly bulged as stomach muscles liquified.

"I promise you," she said with an innocent smile.

"I…I…." Nelson moved toward Matt, effort apparent in each shaky movement. "I'm s-s-s-sorry."

Matt backed up and brought his axe to the ready. "Nelson…."

Both hands came up and reached for him. The distance between them closed to less than ten feet.

"I mean it."

"I can't—"

The axe rose and lowered in an exaggerated swing.

Nelson's right hand dropped.

Both men stopped and looked first at the severed appendage, then at the bloody stump.

In the background, Matt caught sight of Beth. She sat with elbows on knees and fists under her chin, watching with amused interest.

"Ow," Nelson muttered.

Beth's soprano voice piped, "I left some nice cool water down on the third floor. I bet you'd like some."

Nelson started toward the door, then turned and did his best to run at the girl. "You! You did this!"

"You're hot." She didn't move. "You're burning up."

Pieces fell faster. His other hand separated, followed by the entire arm. Matt looked away as Nelson's jaw lost cohesion and fell, taking the lower lip with it. He stopped as his upper body dissolved and collapsed onto the rooftop. The legs still stood, spinal column upright, wet and glistening.

The child giggled and clapped her hands in delight. "And then there were two."

Matt, axe still in hand, moved to the ledge where he believed the ladder to be.

"You wouldn't abandon a little girl up here, would you?"

Matt staggered back. "You're not a little girl."

She hopped up and walked over to him. "Of *course* I am. Look at me. The cherubic face. The blonde hair. If I were any more a little girl, I'd have a dolly in my arms."

Ponies on her pajamas moved on their own, racing across the fabric. More patterns bloomed from her back just as the equines disappeared around her hip. New shapes slithered out in different directions, snaking in every direction.

"Where were we?" Beth's small hand brushed the surging shapes of black and green from her front. They fell from the cotton, animating from two dimensions into three with the flick of the child's wrist. The lumps landed with a small plop and spread, growing at an impossible rate. Tentacles tested the air as teeth gnashed where none were a second before. "Ah, yes…ground zero."

Matt jumped from the roof and landed hard across the top of the ladder's bucket. The pick portion of the axe dug deep into one shoulder and drew blood. He pulled himself across and onto the rungs before daring to look back.

Beth stood at the ledge where he'd jumped from, leaning casually, and looked over at him. "Don't worry." A grin, quickly growing too wide for a human mouth, split her face from ear-to-ear as she pointed down. "I have plans for you."

Below, the street lay coated in blood. Exoskeleton monstrosities dashed along the ground and tore chunks of flesh from those few survivors. A cop fired a shotgun at a vaguely man-shaped thing. Bits of charcoal and flesh struck the ground and sizzled on hot pavement. The creature stayed on its feet and continued the chase. An arm, the only one of four to have been blown off, drug along the ground in pursuit.

The ladder jerked, then extended toward the girl.

Monsters.

No way down.

Torture.

Captain Martinez controlled the ladder. Fishhooks imbedded in his face and arms, actions controlled by two emaciated puppeteers, each sporting four pairs of eyes sitting high atop hairless heads. They jerked lines and purposely tangled them amidst maniacal laughter.

Judgment day.

Matt's bladder loosened, urine spilling hot against skin. He shook all over.

Suffering.

A man bellowed in agony as he was bent over a patrol car and sodomized by a reptilian nightmare that clawed flesh from the man's back.

Madness.

Things, little more than spiders with shoulders, arms and teeth, climbed over each other as they started ascending the ladder. Wide-set insectoid eyes focused on him while outer mandibles chattered in excitement.

Insanity.

"Come back up. Besides," she reached out a hand, offering it to Matt, "the view's better from up here."

Behind the story...

The background on "Singed" isn't all that deep. I was watching a horror movie double feature, *Demon Wind* followed by *The Crow* (the original). During the first movie, there's a scene where an angelic little girl grabs a young woman's arm, speaks in a demonic voice and they both vanish. That launched me down the "what if" string of ideas about having kids be the little monsters we all know they are. By the time I was halfway through *The*

Crow and the movie's comments about Devil's Night, I was elbows-deep in my own fire, writing notes and cutting scenes I deemed too extreme. Considering this story has a fruit bowl full of castrated genitalia and an orgy scene with the damned, let's all be happy some things were cut.

ROOM SERVICE

(Author's note: "Room Service" was originally written for a virus-themed anthology on a luxury liner attempting to avoid a super-plague. Each author was supplied a character and back story to work with.)

John Hoyt rolled off the bed, leaving Thyla—the fellow stow-away he'd discovered—tangled in the sheet and softly snoring. He gathered his things and stepped out into the empty hallway. *She might want to consider getting out of the room before too much longer.*

"Four thirty and all's well," John mumbled. His headache was back in spades. He worked his way down one deck to where rumor said a few empty cabins were—their occupants never having made the launch. "I still can't believe she didn't realize I stowed away like she did."

An attractive stewardess walked past with a covered plate of food. She took him in with one glance, smiled, then flipped her auburn ponytail as she walked past. Smells of eggs and sausage gripped his stomach in a tight knot.

John ran his fingers through his hair, realizing midway through how messy it had to be. Then he looked down at himself and laughed. "Walk of shame."

John tried the keycard he'd lifted on door after door until number 211 released with a click, swinging inward as a gentle wave listed the ship starboard. Dark paneling covered the walls identically to the room Thyla was in with…*what was that guy's name?*

He shook his head. It didn't matter.

There was a suitcase on the bed. Large, leather and the brand screamed a pedigree that was more expensive than every suit he owned combined.

"It's four in the morning," he said to himself.

He looked through the case, then through the maroon one sitting upright on the far side of the bed.

Both empty.

He went to the closet. Designer suits bordered some of the nastiest Hawaiian shirts John had ever seen. Dresses filled the remaining two thirds of the tiny space.

John looked back at the bed.

Still made.

"Four thirty and the bed's still not messed. Something tells me I missed one hell of a launch party."

Temptation overtook better judgment and John started rummaging through drawers before returning to the closet. In the bottom, nearly out of sight, sat the child-sized safe every stateroom had.

"Don't supposed they'd be as stupid as…."

John thumbed the door and it swung open. He knelt down and looked inside. There, on top of a stack of cash was a couple of zippered sandwich bags. One contained smaller bags of pills and the other a respectable stash of white powder.

"Now we're talking." John stumbled onto a cluster of jewelry much the same way when he'd snuck into a motel room being cleaned back in Vegas. A smile rose as he pulled out his prize. The bag turned out to be smaller than he originally thought, and half the pills were in prescription bottles.

A quick dusting and snort brought him a happy little winter storm in the midst of all the tropical air. He sat on the edge of the bed for a few minutes waiting for the effects to kick in. His headache eased in direct contrast to his heart which started hammering as the cocaine kicked in.

A few more minutes and nothing was wrong with the world. "About fuckin' time," he murmured. Josh stood and started collecting baggies.

The door jiggled, turned, then opened. There, in the doorway, was a bear of a man. He looked in his early sixties and between the leathery skin and work-hardened muscles, there was no question how this was about to go down.

"What the—?"

John looked around sheepishly. "Heyyyy," the word came out in a drunken tone, "this isn't *my* room." He smiled, offering the same friendly look that had gotten him through most of his life.

The man's face softened, gaze dropping to the clutch of drugs in John's hand before returning to lock eyes.

"I…uhh—"

The man barreled into the room; arms extended to grab John. He backpedaled the single step before being backed into the outer wall. His fingers fumbled with the slider to the tiny balcony. The glass door opened just as the actual tenant's hands clamped down around his throat. Icy air he couldn't inhale danced at his lips.

John pushed back, lost balance and fell on his rump, his attacker followed him down, tightening his grip and cutting off what little air John gasped in.

Instinct kicked in and John brought up a quick uppercut first to the man's ribs, then two more right between his legs.

Stars blinked behind his eyes as the world started turning black.

I'm dying. I'm dying because of a bag of blow.

The grip loosened.

Beautiful air whipped in. Before he released it, John used the last of his strength and hooked the tenant's knee and lifted with everything he had.

His back cramped under the weight. Then, in a sudden backward jerk that cracked John's head against the rail, the weight was suddenly gone.

John sat there for a second, trying to understand what happened.

The man wasn't in front of him on the balcony…wasn't on the floor by the bed in front of him.

He looked up at the balcony's railing.

There'd been no theatrical scream on the way down…no last-minute grab for the railing. Just here and trying to kill him, then gone.

"Misha," a voice obviously more drunk than John had pretended to be a moment before echoed from inside the cabin. "Where are you?"

John struggled to his feet and did his best to press out of sight.

"Are you…heeeere?" The voice sounded playful. The door to the pillbox-sized bathroom clicked open. "Nooooo?" Mock disappointment carried in the lilt of her voice.

Silence.

Shit. She saw the open slider.

"Out there?" Her voice was closer, more velvety. "Where everyone could see?" A giggle. "You are the wicked one tonight."

John looked to the next balcony which sat a good five feet away, before moving to see what was below them. Multiple rows of identical balconies before a black ocean churned against the hull.

A bottle-blonde wearing an obnoxiously tacky floral cocktail dress stepped onto the balcony carrying two full champagne glasses. She looked at him for a second before her expression shifted to panic and she drew in a breath to scream.

"No," John said and reached out to cover her mouth. The instant his hand covered her mouth she bit down, teeth cutting into flesh.

The glasses fell, breaking upon impact.

John stepped forward and, with the other hand, fired a short jab to her temple. Her head snapped to the side and she stumbled back, falling onto the bed with a plug of flesh still clamped between her teeth.

John looked at his bloody palm. "Bitch!"

Still stunned from the punch, she gave a half-scream as John moved in, jumped on the bed and straddled her before clamping both hands around her throat. Her eyes bulged as he worked to get a better grip through slick blood weeping from his palm.

"Shut up," he growled.

She thrashed harder, trying to buck him off. They bumped the wall at the head of the bed repeatedly.

John pressed down harder on her throat.

Her tongue protruded between perfectly capped teeth.

John felt himself growing hard as he pressed down with his thumbs on the woman's throat.

What the hell's wrong with me?

"Just…fucking…stop," he spat.

He felt something pop in her throat. She twisted hard, rolling him off of her and freeing her neck from his grasp.

John rolled to his side, preparing for the forthcoming scream.

It never came.

She looked at John, still as purple in the face as when his hands were around her throat. Sitting up, her front-to-back motion mimicked convulsions as she worked to get air in. The woman fell off the bed right in front of him. Getting to her hands and knees she looked at him again. Eyes, once brown, now were redder than anyone infected. Spittle fell from her open mouth as her jaw worked as if a fish out of water. The gaze went from pleading to terror, then finally to focusing on a spot on the carpet between them before dropping face-first to the floor, nails digging into the carpet repeatedly before slowing, then finally stopping.

John sucked in breath, staring first at her, then at the jutting tent in his pants. A single bark of a laugh escaped him.

Thrill kill.

He looked back at her. But a hard on while killing some guy's wife? He looked to her left hand. Party girl, he corrected. No ring.

A smell wafted up with a quiet poot sound as the woman's bowels released.

"Really?" John asked. "Really? On top of all the shit I'm dealing with, I'm now dealing with…with…shit?"

He glanced to the balcony. The first signs of dawn sliced in the dark sky, cutting the slightest gray into the horizon. John grabbed her by her arms. The body barely moved. He pulled harder. Still nothing. A third attempt had him holding one wrist and the other gripping a fistful of hair. With each lift of her head, John was able to move her a foot toward the balcony.

"Whoever…" *pull*, "said…" *pull*, "moving…" *pull*, "bodies…." He stopped to get his breath. "Was easy…." He let the rest of the thought drift away.

When John reached down to get a better grip, he patted her head first. "I didn't mean to." His throat felt thick. He wiped a snot trail away, seeing a wet trail tinged with blood on the back of his hand.

John resumed working her to the balcony, then, while avoiding the stain spreading across the woman's backside, lifted her up and tipped her over the rail. She dropped faster than he'd expected. Nearer to the bottom, he saw her head connect with the last balcony before hitting the water.

Even in the dim light, the ebony stain of blood shone against the white of the rail.

"Shit."

He ducked back in, then looked at himself in the bathroom mirror. His eyes returned to a pair of bloodshot orbs.

"I'm…not…sick. I can't be. I beat the odds." His head began to throb again.

John went back into the room and looked for the cocaine bag. It was pressed up against the side of the bed, side split, and leaking better than two-thirds of its contents into the carpet.

"No, no, no, no!" He dropped to his knees and pressed his nose to the floor. Almost nothing invaded his sinuses. John got back up and caught a glimpse of himself in the mirror, looking like any other junkie, right down to the white pasty line smear on his cheek.

John did what he could to salvage the powder and took a collected bit to the bathroom. Two sniffs later he felt a bit better and the headache started to ease. He stripped, squeezed into the tiny shower and rinsed the sweat off. The cold water helped, waking him up.

Once out he cleaned himself up and, after scrounging through the *previous* tenant's toiletries, found what he was looking for.

"The first line of defense for anyone playing with powder." He held the eye drops to his reflection in the mirror and winked. Moments later the red in his eyes was all but gone.

Once he dressed, John checked around for keycards. However, a quick search revealed that they, like their owners, had gone over the balcony.

Dawn was about to break. Filled a small duffel with whatever he thought he could use including over twenty thousand dollars, the drugs, a two Rolexes and some cufflinks. None of the clothes fit.

John opened the door and looked out into the hall. It was as empty as when he'd first entered the room.

He made his way back down to the laundry room and retrieved the rucksack containing everything that mattered and went down to the cabin below. He knocked.

No answer.

He knocked again, adding, "Room Service." A muffled voice echoed from the other side of the door. John offered up his more polite smile for the peephole.

An elderly man opened the door. "You don't look like—"

John punched him in the face as hard as he could, knocking the old man into the room and leaving him on the floor unconscious.

A quick check through the room showed this was a solitary passenger. John grabbed him and pulled passenger to the balcony. The man started to struggle and John flipped him over the side before the guy could call for help. The passenger's expression as gravity pulled him away from the railing was one of confusion—still not fully processing what was happening to him.

John stared first at the empty space the man once occupied, then to the gore-splattered stain on the left corner of the balcony. He grabbed some wet towels and scrubbed the gray matter and blood away, then dropped the once-white linens over the side.

"All clean," he said, looking at the balcony. "Nothing happened." His hands shook and he grasped them together. "Nothing happened here," he repeated.

Another small snort and the shakes were gone, leaving him looking as pleasant as he had when he'd gotten aboard.

Morning was uneventful. He enjoyed the buffet, chatting with a mostly elderly bunch. Not exactly the group of people he wanted to be around, but most of his crowd were still in bed nursing hangovers.

He excused himself after the third round of, "I have a daughter who stayed home I'm sure would love to meet you." He stepped out onto the deck and looked at the people around him. Older males accompanied by women barely out of their teens…power couples that made his wallet burn when they walked by…clustered families forcing laughs out—all of them pretending merriment with the same scared glint in their eyes.

John leaned on the railing and looked over the side to the deck below. Thyla was camped out in a deck chair checking out the crowd, too. He considered going down and seeing if he could cajole her into another round in the sheets. A second look at the sour expression on her face killed that notion.

"Not a happy camper," he said.

"Excuse me," a man in a day-glow t-shirt asked.

"No, I…I was just talking to myself."

The man extended his hand. "Ted Rossen."

John took it.

"Look," Ted leaned in before John could offer his name, "I saw you with that hot little blonde last night. Guess you two had an awesome party."

A familiar throbbing pressed behind John's eyes. *Shit, not now.*

Ted went on. "Anyway, we're past the seven-mile line, so we're in international waters."

John's nose got a tickle signaling that it was about to run. He reached up, scratched his head and drew the back of his arm at an angle to press his nose in the hopes of quelling the itch.

It didn't work.

"I'm saying," Ted went on, "that if you'd like, I have what you need."

John fought against a sneeze. "Meaning?"

"Room 304. I'll be there from five until eight. After that, I'm at the parties for the rest of the night. Bring your wallet." Ted patted him on the shoulder then went farther down past a cluster of deck chairs and struck up a conversation with two bikini-clad women.

John worked his way back to the second cabin. Though smaller than the first, if felt more like the man was one of those big-dollar donors that was just worried about surviving the next month or two. The first cabin felt too warm and inviting.

He slept the better part of the morning and into the afternoon. At some point housekeeping knocked on the door and left when he hollered out to come back later.

John woke to another splitting headache. This time sneezing accompanied it, making each expulsion pure agony. He staggered into the bathroom and flicked the light on.

Dried blood crusted his bottom lids and a similar dark stain clumped at the entrance to his left nostril; his face screamed *virus*.

"No," John said flatly. "I'm fine." He stepped out and picked up the baggie of powder and took a healthy snort directly from the bag. A second look in the mirror reminded him of some old Chevy Chase movie where the star had snorted an immense amount of white powder.

The buzz kicked in a few minutes later.

"Mmmmmmmmmmmmm—IIIIIIIII like it!" He laughed at the poor imitation of an actor from some forgotten movie and set about getting ready to go out before the dinner rush hit.

Another shower and change of clothes later and he felt like a new man. He'd used the eye drops again right after taking the coke. His headache was all but gone. There was a pep in his step and he checked himself out one more time. Sandy blond hair…tan looked perfect, as did his smile.

"What was I thinking? I'm fine." With that self-diagnosis, he stepped out of the room and went to find the gambling tables.

"Seven thousand," John said walking down the hall. "Seven fucking thousand dollars." He shook his head in disbelief. "How the hell did I lose seven *thousand* dollars?" He'd always made jokes about gambling addicts losing everything and how short sighted they were. Today, he hadn't even warmed up at the blackjack table and was down thousands. What caught him off-guard was that he didn't want to leave the table. There was no doubt in his mind that the next deal was going to be a winner. That bitch of a dealer just batted her eyelashes, smiled and kept dealing.

His head was pounding by the time he managed to pull himself away from the table. On a whim, John tried a couple of the red pills to see if they'd have the same effect as the blow. Instead of easing the pain, they made it worse and, in the process, made him feel sluggish.

He leaned into a corner and snorted the last of the coke, licking the inside of the baggie to get every last granule.

The pain eased.

His heart hammered.

John went into the nearest bathroom and checked himself out in the mirror. He needed more eye drops. Beyond that he just looked tired.

"I'm fine," he said. "I'm just fine."

John knocked lightly on the door at five sharp.

"Go away. Come back in five."

He knocked again and held up a wad of hundred dollar bills by his face.

The door opened as one of the power couples exited, doing their best to conceal a bag very similar to the one John had "inherited" early this morning.

John gave a knowing wink to the woman and her man scowled back.

"Come in. Close the door." Ted went over to the bed and motioned him in beside him.

"Before we get down to business, I was hoping you could answer a question for me."

Ted's eyes narrowed. "I'm not in the information business, friend. I just offer a happier time in this stressful world we live in."

John pulled the bag of pills out and dropped it on the bed. "I just want to know what these are."

Ted picked up the bag, looking intently at each colored pill inside. "The white ones that look like aspirin are oxy. The others are…," he turned the bag twice, "some downers…a few uppers. The blue ones to be precise. And the rest of these I have absolutely no idea what they are. Something lab-quality I'd guess. The molding looks clean."

John stared down at both the man and the baggie, making mental notes about every word Ted said.

"Now, to actual business." Ted handed the bag back. "What can I offer you to separate you from the *gorgeous* wad of cash you flashed a few minutes ago?"

John shifted, uncomfortable with how up-front Ted was about the drugs. *Here goes nothing.* "Coke. I'm looking for coke."

"How much are you looking for?"

"A lot."

"A lot I can deliver. How much money do you have?"

"Enough. And…" he grinned, "I might be coerced into sharing a date with my lady-love."

"You mean that blonde?"

"I mean *that* blonde."

"Sold." Ted hopped up with a huge grin.

"Let me write her number down." John pulled a pen out and popped the cap.

John punched out with the pen wedged between two knuckles, and connected three short jabs into Ted's stomach, a fourth landing between ribs and getting stuck.

The drug dealer's mouth opened in an exaggerated O as he fell back onto the bed, holding the three red spots expanding across his midsection.

John rifled through drawers and found a large brick of cash wedged in the nightstand. The bathroom offered two bags similar in size to the one he'd finished off.

Rage boiled. "This is it?"

Ted didn't respond, other than to make a keening sound. His bladder released, soaking through his Bermudas and into the bedspread.

John leaned over the bed and smacked Ted. "I said, 'is this it?'"

"Wuh wuh we don't keep it all…I don't wanna die, man. I'm just the cashier." The keening started again.

"Shit," John said. It was beginning to feel like this was his favorite word. He climbed on the bed and straddled Ted, pulling a second pen out and popped the cap free. He grabbed Ted's jaw with one hand and placed the pen against the man's left eye.

"Nooooooo," Ted managed a pitiful cry.

"Listen," John said, "You're going to tell me where the rest of the stuff is or it's..." he tapped the pen tip against Ted's bottom eyelid, "lights out."

Ted nodded his head slightly and John pulled the pen lower.

Then Ted coughed. Wet bloody spittle sprayed across John's face and shirt.

"Asshole!" He shoved himself up, Ted, realizing too late he'd pushed against the pen stuck in his chest. It dislodged under the pressure and slid deep, causing another wave of coughing.

"You're fine!" John leaned back low over Ted's face and smiled. "You're gonna be fine." He lightly stroked the other man's chest as one would a lover.

Spittle formed in the corners of Ted's mouth and pink bubbles pushed out around the end of the pen.

"Where," John gently turned Ted's face to him, "are the rest of the drugs?"

Ted nodded, trying to get more air into bloody lungs. He shook... slowed, then stayed still on the center of the bed.

He stared at his latest victim with a mild sense of awe. "I—I'm starting to get good at this."

John tore the small cabin apart, finding only a handful of tiny baggies of coke.

His headache was threatening to make a return, so he opened one of the tiny bags and emptied it with two large sniffs.

After cleaning up in the bathroom, John changed into one of Ted's shirts and took everything of value back to the small cabin that he was beginning to think of as his base of operations.

Along the way he swiped a crew member jacket from a linen cart and went to look for the couple he'd seen leave the dealer's room. He passed two rooms with doors ajar, each with occupants lying on the floor not moving. Coughing came from others as he passed by. Halfway down the hall a room sat silent. John stopped and knocked.

Who knows? They might need room service, too.

Behind the story...

Notch Publishing put together an anthology called *Sick Cruising* that was inspired—of course—by COVID. It revolved around a massive cruise ship full of the rich going to sea in an effort to avoid the plague affecting mankind. For those old enough, think *The Love Boat* meets the black plague. The concept our editor put together involved a stack of characters whose storylines would overlap from one story to the next, meaning authors had to coordinate—at least a little bit—to ensure character personalities and descriptions were consistent from one story to the next.

A fun little tidbit about *Sick Cruising* is that the story that follows "Room Service" is "Stowed Away," written by my wife, Hollie Snider. There are a couple of overlaps in both of our stories, and her central character, Thyla, makes an appearance at the beginning of "Room Service."

LUNAR DESCENT

13:01 COORDINATED UNIVERSAL TIME

Garbled transmissions plagued yet another day aboard the Beethoven. Irina Volkov blew a stray brown lock of hair out of the way and thumbed the reception dial for the third time in as many minutes. Back on Earth, the press took great pleasure in equating Saturn's newest listening post's failure to that of its namesake.

Deaf.

"*Chert voz'mi.*"

"Language." Captain Geary's voice echoed from the open hatch.

"Sorry, Captain."

"You know half the globe records every whisper…every *cough* we make." He pulled his not-quite two-meter form through the opening, stopping himself as he floated to the seat neighboring hers. "So, I take it we still can't hear anything?"

"No, sir." She looked up from the display and glanced over at him. The white stubble on his face was well on its way to matching the length of his crew-cut.

"Can we at least *see*?"

Irina dragged her finger across the screen, opening the catalog of options. She selected L419 and accessed the live feed of Enceladus, Saturn's sixth largest moon. Two bookmarked selections later and the pair were staring at over 100 geysers spewing into the night sky from its south pole. Another thumb tap and the view jumped to the deck's main viewer.

"Nice," the captain commented. "So, we have one eye. What about the rest of them?"

"All working within expected parameters." She backed out and brought up the first of seventeen screens each displaying thumbnails of forty different celestial views, totaling all 680 of their onboard external cameras.

He nodded. "Back to the elephant in the room…."

"Elephant?"

He chuckled. "To the *problem* at hand."

Irina rolled her eyes. "Americans and their colorful turns of phrase."

"What? You didn't think that there was an actual elephant—"

"Of course not. However, I *may* have questioned your psychological competence." She exited the screen and flipped to the daily results from their neighboring moon, Dione.

The captain pulled himself into the seat and buckled in, switching on his own set of displays. "So, did Matthias get back to you?"

Irina reached to the mic hanging just in front of her and keyed it. "Lieutenant Lowe?"

Silence for a handful of seconds before a static-filled replay. "I thought I told you to call me Matthias."

"Captain Geary would like an update on your progress." Irina clicked camera T19a and pulled the focus all the way back, angling the lens to the outskirts of their orbiting station. A neon green-suited figure leaned against an antenna array, arm extended as a tiny flash winked from his suit.

The captain took the mic from her hands and said, "Looks to me like you're working on your fan base and not on my array."

Lowe grabbed his belt and whipped himself back around to the open panel.

Irina grinned. "He will blame me for that."

"Well, if you prefer, I can say you fought the valiant fight to keep me from finding out."

She blew air out in a, "Pffft. I think I would rather he be irritated at me."

Captain Geary's screens lit up in a festive series of system errors. More red and orange flashes filled the screen than the preferred green ones.

"Shit," he mumbled.

"Language," she chided.

"Do we know how the Sir John Herschel is doing?"

Irina flipped to her notes screen. "Life base Hershel is in stationary orbit, centrifugal force from rotation equals point eight Gs. One G expected within the week. They took on supplies from the Dyatlov at twenty-two hundred before continuing on to orbit Enceladus."

He looked at her full screen of notes. "All that from last night?"

"Yes, sir." She leaned her neck from shoulder to shoulder. "Couldn't sleep."

"Missing your kid?"

"Anna turns twelve in a few days. I miss her."

He unclipped and pushed up, socked feet clearing the workstation. "I'll make sure you're the first on Satlink…*if* we ever get Satlink up and running."

Irina changed the subject. "I wonder whose idea it was to name our cargo vessel Dyatlov. Such a tragedy from so long ago."

"Superstitious?"

"Ukrainians aren't superstitious. We're cautious of bad decisions. Naming a deep space cargo vessel after doomed Russian hikers is the choice of a fool."

"Superstitious," Captain Geary repeated.

"Bah," she said and focused on clearing her own list of error screens.

"We have no external transmission or reception capabilities?"

"*Nemaye.* Very limited."

"Do we at least know if the Herschel received all of its cryopods?"

A proximity warning blared from every speaker.

Irina tapped the red bar at the top of her screen. The Dyatlov's trajectory had the ship on a collision course with the Beethoven.

"Fu—"

Irina snapped her fingers at her superior officer, then returned to accessing screens.

"Dyatlov. Dyatlov. Dyatlov," she yelled. "Proximity warning."

No response.

The captain slapped the emergency lock-down button, sealing all hatches and warning crew to get into their suits.

Irina's fingers flew from screen to screen, accessing first the maintenance bay, then the army of drones they still had on board from the Beethoven's construction. Blanking their commands, then input the Dyatlov's coordinates and gave the simple command *PUSH*.

"Irina!"

She ignored him, going beyond the simple command given and directing where along the Dyatlov clusters of drones should attach and, pulling a subroutine from construction files, organizing the push to miss the Beethoven with 300 meters to spare.

"Irina! Now!"

"Captain, the immediate danger to Beethoven has been averted. Dyatlov is now in a lower orbit to Saturn."

Captain Geary took a deep breath. "Quick thinking, Volkov."

"Ukrainian efficiency. It's like German efficiency, but it doesn't crumble under pressure."

"What the hell, Beethoven!"

Irina keyed the mic. "Crisis averted, Lowe. Please continue your repairs."

"I damned near shit myself."

They both grinned before Irina responded with, "The captain wishes to speak with you regarding your use of language when you return."

Lowe didn't reply.

Captain Geary asked, "Anything from the Dyatlov? Anything at all?"

"*Nemaye.* She's now in a lower orbit, but it's decaying."

"What about her engines?"

"They weren't engaged. If they were, I wouldn't have been successful pushing it out of the way."

"Was she dead?"

Irina looked over her shoulder at him. "Sir?"

"The Dyatlov. Did it have power of any kind?" She returned to her screen and ran the last few moments of footage again. Pinpricks of light were visible along the hull as it passed.

"Internal power is on."

Screeching feedback suddenly screamed from their speakers. A few seconds passed before a cadence to the tones fell into recognizable words.

"…FAILURE…INFECTIOUS…BEETHOVEN…."

"The captain did his best to slap the wall in frustration without floating across the room. "Can you clean that up at all?" He smacked the panic button two more times, disengaging the alarm.

Irina worked on the reception, lowering the wavelength.

"…ODS…ENGINEER…QUARANTINE…WOKE…."   Then static ate up the airwaves.

Muted cussing came from farther in the ship.

Irina pressed fingers to her temples knowing the shit show that was about to unfold.

⤜✕⤏

13:27 COORDINATED UNIVERSAL TIME

"Captain," Lowe said in the same tone he used every time he tried to get Irina into bed. "The Dyatlov's message talked about quarantine." He pushed down from the ceiling and continued sucking on the pack loosely considered tea.

Wessic wiped his bald head and spoke up. "Lowe has a point. Wouldn't it make more sense to focus on getting the array back online and let Stockholm know what's going on?" He crossed both arms and let his knees keep him essentially seated at the magnetic table.

Before anyone else could speak, Irina replied with, "The Dyatlov is not in a stationary orbit. Currently we can reach her and assess their emergency. If we wait, Saturn's gravity will pull them in. Assistance must be rendered now, before—"

"Captain," Lowe cut in. "They said *infectious*. We could be risking everyone here…hell, maybe everyone over on the Herschel, too."

Irina's voice raised. "We haven't yet received *our* resupply from the Dyatlov."

Wessic barked, "We can resupply from the Herschel."

Captain Geary finally spoke up. "The Dyatlov visited the Herschel before heading over to Enceladus."

Wessic put his hands on the table, better anchoring himself. "What if this started with Enceladus base?"

"I doubt it," the captain said. "I've been thinking about a couple of the words that came through: 'woke' and 'ods.' I think they may have said pods. If something came through the biofilters and got loose when they started waking the passengers…."

"Captain…Travis…" Lowe said.

"*Captain*," he corrected. "You can knock off the pillow-talk tone as well. You're not my type."

This brought chuckles from everyone.

Captain Geary continued. "Lowe: you, Wessic, and Volkov are on your way there now. Get moving."

Irina pushed away from the table, angling for the hatch leading toward the bay.

Lowe pushed. "What, you're not coming with us?"

The captain leveled a stare. "No. This isn't some cheesy vid series. I'm in command."

Wessic said, "I guess it's because we're the best and are already up to speed?"

"No," Geary said. "It's because you're all expendable." He gave Irina a wink, then let himself float back toward the central access tube. "Volkov's in charge. No returns unless this is under control."

～❧～

15:57 COORDINATED UNIVERSAL TIME

Irina checked the reception.

Dead air.

"Lowe," she asked, "ETA to Dyatlov?"

He sighed. "Two minutes sooner than the last time you asked. Three minutes to contact. Another minute or so to dock."

She leaned back and looked past him. Beyond them the Dyatlov loomed, nothing more than a shadow against Saturn's bright body. "Quarantine procedures are in effect. Do not open your suit. Do not connect to their cycled air."

Wessic asked, "How are we proceeding?"

Lowe answered, "We'll look for the crew on our way to the bridge. Then—"

"*Nemaye.*"

"Look, Irina, I get it that you and the captain are chummy, but—"

"We will continue to broadcast our hail to the Dyatlov." If we don't receive a reply by the time we dock, we will keep the outer bay decompressed and contact the crew via the internal communication system."

Lowe sarcastically asked, "Paranoid?"

"Always."

They continued the approach, coming in at a forty-five-degree angle to the ship's starboard side. Lowe popped the jets twice, lifting the four person craft to drift horizontal to the windows.

All three strained to see anything of interest. Room after room stood lit, but devoid of life.

"Loving this," Wessic said.

Irina braced herself as Lowe slowed to a crawl when the small, secondary bay access came into view. She flipped the transmission audio on.

Irina's canned voice said, "DYATLOV. THIS IS BEETHOVEN'S CARRIER ALPACA. DO YOU COPY?"

"Anything?" she asked.

"Nothing," Wessic said. "Hell, at this distance they could just come to the window and shine a flashlight at us."

Lowe lined up the Alpaca and transmitted the open code. Seconds turned into minutes as they assumed drones were securing whatever was in the bay before it decompressed. Finally, the door opened, tipping into the ship and displaying the same gray interior they'd all become accustomed to. The Alpaca puffed jets, floating into the bay as drones took over the landing process, pushing the craft against the floor and engaging magnetic locks.

Irina's fingers flew across her displays as she accessed the Dyatlov's intercom system. "Dyatlov. This is Irina Volkov from the Beethoven."

No response.

"Damn it," she muttered.

She saw Lowe try to turn and look at her, succeeding only in seeing the edge of his helmet's view plate.

He asked, "We go out?"

"We go out," she confirmed. They pulled their oxygen lines and opened their hatch. Irina stepped free and took one of the drones by its grip. "Bay door."

The drone, barely bigger than a suitcase, dutifully pulled her to the bay door. Lowe and Wessic followed.

She manually plugged in to Dyatlov's system, accessing systems through her suit's forearm. "Crew of the Dyatlov. This is Irina Volkov of the Beethoven. I am currently in the—"

Wessic's grip stopped her. She turned and looked at the body, strapped down by drones. Dried blood looked black against the dark jumpsuit as white shards of bone bordered the blooming wound that was once his ribcage and stomach.

Irina waved, getting both men's attention. She motioned Wessic to the right and Lowe to stay at the door. Leaving the drone behind, she pushed off and floated to the fabric web securing a half dozen containers and the man's body.

He was little more than a boy…nineteen, maybe twenty—and still well short of growing a beard. The whites of his eyes bore the bright violet hue telling of a recent cryopod occupant.

"Well?" Wessic asked from the corner where he stopped, his voice little more than a whisper.

Irina turned her torso so he could see her point at her eyes. The brightness told all three he hadn't been awake for more than a day or two.

"Volkov," Lowe's voice boomed over her headset. "Get back here. I've got movement."

She and Wessic floated back, turning up their mag boots when reaching the door. Lowe stayed directly in front of the bulkhead, staring through the eight-inch glass window.

"Well?" she asked.

"I don't know. A shadow on the other side of the airlock. Couldn't see who."

"Or what," Wessic said. "There's drones all over the ship. Might've been one of them."

Lowe reached over, grasped the access grip, then hesitated. Irina pushed over to his side to see him in profile. Sweat ran down the man's face. She reached out and touched his shoulder. The contact seemed to jolt him free of whatever was going on inside his head and pulled the lever, opening the door without so much as a hiss.

They pushed in, secured the door behind them, then the audible noise of air rushing into the room broke the deafening quiet.

Three minutes passed before the pressure light went from red to a soft blue, resulting in the ship-side hatch releasing on its own and sliding up into the ceiling.

A gray wall met their gaze, followed by the most unpopular gray hallways.

Wessic was the first to say the astronaut motto of, "I fucking hate gray."

Lowe floated to the nearest internal intercom and switched the destination to shipwide. "Hello, crew of the Dyatlov. If there's anyone able, please respond."

All three stared at the screen, waiting for a blip to light.

"Awful rude," Wessic said.

Irina pushed away from the wall at an angle letting her float ten meters down the hall before connecting with the opposing wall with an audible click as boots connected with the wall plating.

"We splitting up to cover ground or what?" Lowe asked.

She considered her options. "We stay together and go to the infirmary."

Lowe countered, "We should go to the bridge and announce ourselves."

"*Nemaye.*" She was getting tired of saying no over and over today. "If there's a biological agent the place to start is the infirmary… especially since no one is responding to our calls."

She led the way, all three hop-frogging their way across the floor, walls, and ceiling. Storage compartment after storage compartment met their gaze. No living quarters at this end of the ship, Irina reminded herself. Even the Cryopods were up three levels. She slowed, nearly passing the central access tube leading to the other levels. Wessic pushed past her and launched himself up.

"What the…?" A second of silence, then, "Damn it!"

"Wessic," she called over the headset. "What do you see?"

"Blood."

Lowe repeated, "Blood?"

"Yes, blood. It's peppered all over the tube. I'm stopping just before the next level." He cut his mic.

Irina followed him into the tube, killing the power to her boots and free floating up. A couple of tiny brown flecks bounced off her visor…then more, a lot more. They drifted past like sand falling through an hourglass, bouncing from the helmet and going every direction. She slowed herself and turned in a circle, studying the sides of the tube.

No smears. Not so much as a dusty handprint marring the tube.

"Wessic? Can you see me?"

"Yeah, Volkov. You've still got another couple of meters before you get to me."

She resisted the urge to try to look up. Innumerable headaches from astronauts had forced the reality that EVA suits do not, in fact, offer that option, and instead had reminded each and every one of them of that fact with sore heads from repeated helmet impacts.

Lowe ran into her feet, starting Irina's assent again and speeding more coagulated blood bouncing past her in every direction before she bumped into Wessic's shins.

"We should have brought a sidearm," Lowe said.

Ignoring the statement, Irina nudged Wessic. "Medical is another level up. Please continue your assent."

Wessic grabbed a rung and tugged, propelling himself up. Irina followed, slowing at the level he'd been hovering at. A little more blood floated in the hallway, but no smears or gore.

"Irina, the man in the bay was ripped open. No one on the Dyatlov is responding. We need to get to a weapons locker."

She stopped, floating close to Wessic again, but just short of impacting him. "Lieutenant Lowe, what is the access code for the Dyatlov's weapons locker?"

A grumble was all that he offered in reply.

"In the medical bay," she continued, "we can access their weapons locker by triggering their emergency protocols."

"Clear," Wessic said and tugged himself out of the tube and into the hallway.

"We will also have access to all non-command records." She followed the stocky man and was still bumped into the far wall as Lowe shot into the hall, ricocheting off the ceiling before his boots locked down on the far wall. "*Mudak.*"

Lowe turned. "*I'm* the asshole?"

"That is one translation. The rest get more vulgar…and accurate." She pushed off as on the previous level, leading the way as they hop-frogged their way along the hall. At the first corner they found what was left of another crew member.

This one, a middle-aged black woman, was shredded, deep gouges along her chest and legs, her torso eviscerated and bulging the remains of intestines. Blood left the wound only to coagulate at its tips, leaving a macabre bloom in zero gravity.

Irina had trouble focusing on the wound itself because of all the floating material—*human material,* she reminded herself—floating all around body and slowly drifting down the hall.

Wessic pushed up, flipped, and locked his boots to the ceiling, walking past the scene and repeated the process a couple of meters beyond. He stared at the corpse from the other side while Lowe looked behind them.

Lowe's mic chirped.

"Hmmm?" Irina asked.

"Anything we can tell?"

Wessic knelt and answered, "These gashes don't look right. They're too uniform to be slashes from a knife. And too many to be bites."

Irina looked over at him. "Claws?"

"Wait a minute," Lowe said. "First we have an infectious agent we don't know about. Then murders implying one or more of the crew could be raving madmen. Now you're talking about boogeymen?"

Wessic stood. "You forgetting about the Toldgrom subway release a decade ago? People ran out of there with bone growth protruding out of…fuck, *everywhere* and slaughtering anyone they came across. Took two weeks to get them all."

Irina pushed off and went around the body the same way Wessic had, dropping to the floor just beyond him. "Are you saying this is a similar agent?"

"All I'm saying is that whatever did this looks animal, not mechanical."

Lowe put a hand to his hip. "*Not* mechanical? Really?"

"You know what I mean," Wessic said.

Irina put her own hand up. "Yes, we do. Thank you. Let's continue to the medical bay." She looked at the nearest intercom station and selected ship-wide, as Lowe had earlier. "Crew of the Dyatlov, this is Irina Volkov of the Beethoven. We are making our way to your bridge. Please have someone meet us there or respond now."

Both men looked at her and nodded. Wessic added, "Better a lie than…," and motioned to the corpse.

"Beckett," Lowe said aloud, reading her body's name tag. He flipped up to the ceiling and launched himself past Irina and Wessic, floating down the hall to the next hatch. They followed just as he pressed the access button. The door slid open, showing thirty cryopods, all empty.

"So…" Wessic said, "Somebody didn't get their full shipment of workers." He floated over to the nearest two and switched his camera to take screencaps of their identifying codes.

They looked around the cargo hold, noting that only about half the room was empty.

"Wessic, Lowe, we continue to Medical." Irina looked out into the hall before exiting the room. "No more exploring. Whatever has happened here, our suits won't protect against."

"At least not against its effects," Wessic added.

Fifteen minutes of movement had them find five more bodies, the last two little more than parts blocking the hall and forcing the three to physically move through the gore.

Irina, in the middle, stopped midway through. "Stop."

Lowe asked, "What is it?"

Irina stared at the semi-clotted smear. "The blood. It's still fresh."

Wessic held up his forearm. "Here too." A larger piece of flesh stuck to the wrist of his suit. He flicked it and it drifted away, leaving smeared residue in its wake.

Lowe started them moving again. "Medical is the next doorway."

Irina felt the need to say, "Look first. Then open."

He turned his body mid float to look at her. "Ya think?"

Irina and Wessic worked to catch up, meeting him at the door as he stared through the small rectangular window in the center of the hatch.

Wessic was the first to speak. "How's it look?"

"Clean…messy." He moved away, making room for Irina.

The medical bay was exactly as he described. Five bodies could be seen, all under stasis glass. Clothes floated above them in clear bags, all stained dark with blood and organic matter. Drones had done their due diligence and everything exposed in Medical was pristine. One white drone, bearing the typical red cross on its dome, whizzed past carrying a severed hand in two of its six pinchers.

Irina pressed the access button.

Nothing happened other than the red light over the door began flashing.

"UNAUTHORIZED ACCESS," boomed overhead.

"Damn it, Volkov," Wessic hissed. "The whole damned ship can hear that."

Irina brought up her forearm display, thumbed through subroutines, then accessed the Dyatlov. Seconds ticked by and the door slid up.

"Hacked the system?" Lowe asked.

"*Nemaye*. Registered us as visitors to the ship. We now have medical bay privileges."

They entered, looked around without going too far into the vast room.

Lowe walked across to the nearest bed, boots tinking with each impacted step. The door slid shut behind Irina and Wessic, startling them both.

Wessic went to the nearest terminal while Irina joined Lowe, looking first at the nude patient, then at the bloody bag of clothes near the ceiling.

"Immet, John Jay," Lowe stated after tapping the side of the glass and reading the popup. The patient appeared to be of middle eastern descent, excellent shape, about thirty-five. Curly hair mopped his forehead, disappearing below his shoulders. Not a speck of dirt or blood marred his body. His only visible injuries were two gashes across his abdomen and a wickedly puckered bite where shoulder met the man's neck. Both wounds were open, but blood-free as nanobots worked to repair the damage. Immet's chest barely moved with each breath.

"Well," Lowe said, "he's alive."

Wessic called over, "One of the five are alive. All arrived victims of animal attacks. Two are brain dead, but bodies are salvageable." He muttered something unintelligible before continuing. "The remaining two…well…." He motioned to the far beds. One body was missing so much flesh and muscle it looked skeletal save for the torso. The other had its face bitten off.

Each body was pristinely clean and nude, leaving nothing about the wounds to the imagination.

Irina moved to the two brain dead bodies. One male, the other female. Both Caucasian. Mid-twenties. The male's left side of his face was missing, bone, inner ear, side of tongue and throat were visible. She tapped his case. The floating display popped up. LINCOLN, WILLIAM. CAUSE OF DEATH: BLOOD LOSS. She could see the carotid artery repaired, but not soon enough to save his brain. His chest, like Immet's, rose and fell.

Then his skin fluttered, darkened, then lightened to its pale state again.

Irina backed up a step, bumping the woman's bed. The glass display read CULLING, HANNA. CAUSE OF DEATH: HEART FAILURE. In fact, the gaping hole where her left breast should have been screamed that fact. Brown hair, disheveled and disappearing behind her head in what may have once been a ponytail went from clean near her brow to scabbed starting behind her ear. Glittering specks along her hairline led to where the nanobots were as they worked on the body. Inside Culling's chest cavity, the micro machines weren't anywhere near as far along with their repairs. The heart had closed and artificial blood flowed from the IV, but rib and muscle were still hours from being repaired.

Irina watched the woman…waiting to see if her body did the same as Lincoln's.

Seconds passed.

Then, like before with the woman's crewmate, portions of her skin rippled, darkened, becoming rough. Downy filaments rose from tissue. Her upper lip pulled into a rictus of a smile. Muscles flexed, hand bumping the glass. Beside Irina, Lincoln's body did the same, kicking up at the top of the enclosure."

Lowe's voice came over the headset. "It's happening over here, too."

Irina moved over to where Lowe still stood by Immet. His clean-shaven face was now patchy, easily a day's-worth of growth. Brown skin had turned nearly black with what appeared to be bruising in places. Like with the other two, skin rippled, almost looking like something shifted just under the surface.

Lowe murmured, "Mary and Joseph."

Immet's lids snapped open, golden irises focusing on them. "Hel-help…me."

Irina leaned closer to the glass. "Do you know what's happening to you?"

He struggled, head and neck arching. "Two…two alpha nine seven…six…." the last word fell into a groan of agony. bruising widened, filaments growing the same as Culling.

"Wessic," Lowe said, "enter two, two, alpha, nine, seven, six."

"Nothing."

Irina corrected, "Two, alpha, nine, seven, six." She looked at Lowe. "He repeated the first one."

"Still nothing."

She went to the terminal beside Wessic and entered IMMET, JOHN JAY. Then repeated the access. The screen displayed emergency access to first officer files. Irina clicked on the most recent three files. Each option responded with ACCESS DENIED—CAPTAIN OSGOOD. "The captain's locked the files."

Lowe leaned over Immet. "Your captain's locked your files."

"B-b-b-bastard," Immet managed.

Irina returned to Lowe's side, staring down at Immet. His features relaxed, blotching evening out as filaments withdrew back into his body.

"C-captain delivered to Enceladus." He breathed hard, as if just completing a run. "They called back just as…as we were leaving to deliver their second load." Immet coughed, spittle sliding down his cheek toward his ear. "Crazy talk. Monsters and people dead." He shook his head, as if trying to deny what occurred. "They emergency-podded three."

"Wait," Lowe said. "Emergency pods have sequential destinations to prevent overdemand on resources. Enceladus sends to you…us… and—"

"Herschel station," Immet finished.

"Shit," Lowe said.

"We need to contact Sir John Herschel station now!"

Immet's head shook again, this time deliberate. "Captain locked the radio then set us…on a collision course for you.

Wessic came over. "Every file I could think to access is either locked or offline."

Lowe leaned over more. "Why hit us?"

"The infection. It spreads so fast." He tried to turn on his side, succeeding in only causing fresh blood to weep from his stomach. "Everyone on the ship…one bite and they were gone in seconds."

Irina tapped the glass. "Who released the agent?"

Immet just stared.

Lowe yelled, "Immet?"

"The commander…on the moon…on Enceladus. He said he knew what it was. That they just had to get of the moon and they'd be fine."

Noise from in the hall got their attention. Wessic grabbed a tablet and floated to the hatch, covering the window.

"He left them! He and his command staff." Immet worked to slow his breathing. "He came here. Fucking Jones. The other two…."

Something scratched along the hall, octave changing as whatever it was dragged across the hatch.

Lowe said, "We've got to warn the Beethoven."

"We need to warn the Herschel. There's over five thousand people there. Only forty on our station."

"Now it's a numbers game?"

"It's always a numbers game."

"Guys," Wessic breathed, using the headset, "whatever is outside is still there."

Immet said, "It's better in low orbit. It—it hurts less.

Something struck the hatch.

"Fuck!" Wessic cried out. "I actually felt that."

Irina said, "No use hiding. See what it is."

Wessic lowered the pad and looked through the window. A low chuckle grew into a laugh. Not the jolly laugh the man was known for, but something more akin to madness. "It's…for you."

Lowe cocked his head as much as the helmet allowed before walking over to the door. He stood, motionless, for a solid ten seconds before leaving the hatch and going to the medical bay's weapon's locker. "Code?" he called out.

"A moment," Irina said as she scrolled through files on her suit's forearm. "Eleven, beta, beta, *cem*—"

"*Cem*? What the hell's a—"

"Seven! Nine, two, omega."

The locker popped open revealing a dozen pulse rifles. Lowe grabbed one, pushed another toward Wessic and started bagging batteries.

Irina looked up from Immet. "What did you see?"

In response, Lowe pushed the third rifle toward her. She caught it by the barrel.

"Lowe, what is out there?"

Immet screamed. His skin darkened, going from bruised to black, filaments grew out into hair, spreading across his chest, down his stomach, then to his groin. "No!" he screamed. "Not again!"

Irina watched the hair thin, then fall away from the body. Flesh lightened, appearing blotchy once again.

"The nanos…they…help."

Pounding on the door became more incessant…urgent in its violence.

Irina looked down at Immet. He was whispering something just beyond her hearing.

"EMERGENCY PROTOCOLS GRANTED."

All thirty of the enclosed beds burst into flame. Immet thrashed, flesh burning to char in a handful of seconds, as did the other four bodies. Sickly yellow light filled the room, casting shadows in every direction.

Irina sighed, placed a hand on the glass, then moved to the door.

The side of a lupine face pressed against the other side, eye locking onto Irina's own. It huffed, steam fogging the bottom of the glass.

Lowe went to the station Irina had accessed moments before. "Enceladus's pods are still in route to Beethoven and the Herschel."

Wessic turned his rifle around, pointing it at the floor. "There's only one. We can get back to the bay and take the Alpaca."

Irina shook her head. "It's too slow. We need to warn the stations."

Lowe said, "The Dyatlov's emergency pods."

"No way in hell," Wessic said. "We'd get split up. What if I end up going to Enceladus?"

"Relax, hero." Lowe sighed. "*I'm* going to Enceladus. The first pod will default there because it's closer."

More pounding on the door. The face pulled away, creature floating back to the hall's opposite wall where it, alongside two others, crouched. Irina took the opportunity to take the beasts in. Vaguely man-sized, ribcages vertical to the spine rather than a human's horizontal oval. Wiry hair covering the body in wisps, giving both a rough, yet downy, appearance. It was their heads that transfixed her—instead of the fairy tale werewolves, these had long, downward faces, still shaped like a wolf, but with dimensions similar to those of a horse. Their noses pointed down, simulating a chin where the nostrils flared. This left the main portion of the face with no features, save for eyes.

Then one snarled.

Its head tipped back and the skull opened up, pink tongue lashing between nightmare canines.

"Irina."

It smacked the other, then launched itself at the door with a dull thud. Four more…then a fifth, joined the increasing group.

"Irina!"

She jerked, then looked away from the beasts. "Yes?"

Lowe asked, "The emergency pods. Where do we find them on the Dyatlov?"

Irina looked at the glass again. "One of these times they're going to hit the access button and open the door."

"Irina! Focus."

She looked at Lowe a second time, this time stepping away from the door. "Sorry. Emergency pods should be at every level unless the captain's locked them." A few taps on her arm pad gave the answer. "They're all unlocked."

Wessic moved beside Lowe. "Where are they?"

Irina kept tapping. "Everywhere. Every level. Ten are in here." Another few seconds had the wall on the right opening, a gurney sliding out.

The three moved to the gurney.

"Order?" Lowe asked.

Irina said, "You first, to Enceladus's moon base. Then me to the Beethoven. Wessic to Herschel station."

The medical bay's door slid up amidst howling and snarls. Furry bodies launched into the room, bouncing off beds and gurneys, still not acclimated to zero gravity.

All three astronauts raised pulse rifles and squeezed the triggers. Black slashes appeared on walls and melted glass like butter. Five wolves were similarly sliced, wounds instantly sealed from the laser's heat.

More poured in.

"Go!" Irina shouted.

Lowe got on the gurney, placed the rifle on his chest and disappeared into the wall.

Seconds ticked by. More lupine flesh sizzled. The few in the medical bay were either dead or in no shape to attack. Irina and Wessic focused their fire on the doorway, effectively jamming the access with bodies.

The gurney slid back out.

A legion of howls rang out. Bodies pressed against the dead, pushing the fleshy cork free and letting wolves pour in.

Wessic shoved Irina, taking the gurney out of order, and firing wildly as it retracted, with him, into the wall.

Irina stood alone, staring at dozens of figures staring around the room. She froze. She remembered stories of when wolves were rampant in her country, remembered that wolves hunted by scent. With her suit they couldn't smell her.

What if they still retained some of their humanity?

More moved into the room.

Irina struggled to remember what Immet had whispered at the end.

Sigma, nine, fourteen, gamma…gamma what?

She tapped her arm pad and glanced down. It was still logged into the Dyatlov's systems. "Sigma—"

Every pair of eyes in the room locked in on her. "Sigma, nine, fourteen, gamma…."

They moved as one on her.

"Epsilon four! Medical Bay Three. All!"

A siren blared in the room, startling everyone present, especially Irina."

Flames poured as water from the floor vent, licking at fur, catching and dancing along the lengths of their bodies, then everything, even the air itself was on fire.

Visibility fell to nothing as flames engulfed the room, turning it into a blast furnace. Irina pointed the rifle, firing it twice and thrashing shapes before the hardened plastic failed against the heat.

Something bumped her and she screamed, whipped her arms around blindly only to strike the gurney. She rolled onto it and waited.

Something black, charred, and more pitted by flame than any living thing should be struck the wall right where she'd stood a second before, bouncing away and back into hell.

Light faded and then she was surrounded by black. Several bumps jostled her, then the familiar feel of several Gs as the pod ejected from the Dyatlov into space above Saturn.

It was still black. Only a hint of light beyond her visor made it through. She reached up and wiped at her visor, streaking the greasy ash covering her entire suit. It took a full minute to streak enough of the grime away to see more of the coffin-sized pod.

"Pod?"

"DYATLOV POD TWENTY-SEVEN ACTIVE."

"Destination?"

"HERSCHEL STATION."

"ETA?"

"PLEASE REPHRASE YOUR REQUEST."

"Estimated time of arrival?"

"FOUR HOURS, NINETEEN MINUTES, FORTY-ONE SECONDS."

"Redirect to Beethoven Station."

"INVALID REQUEST."

Irina felt around, found the oxygen hose and plugged it in.

22:57 COORDINATED UNIVERSAL TIME

"OCCUPANT?"

Irina snorted, fighting her way up from sleep.

"OCCUPANT?"

"*Tak*…yes."

"THERE IS AN INCOMING MESSAGE FOR YOU FROM ENCELADUS'S BASE. WOULD YOU LIKE TO HEAR IT?"

"Stupid hands-free…yes."

"Wessic," Lowe's voice sounded pained.

"Fucking Wessic," Irina said.

"I can't get a response from Herschel station. It's too far beyond Saturn's horizon. Beethoven's quiet, too." He laughed. "But then, that's nothing unusual. Irina should be safely on board. She's the lucky one."

"Idiot."

"You've got another twenty minutes before you hit the station. In other news," another half-hearted chuckle, "They took care of everyone, and I do mean *everyone* down here. Bad asses vented the entire station. The only living thing down here is me. Luck to you. Tell Irina she really needs to call me by my first name."

"*Nemaye*," she said to the empty pod. "You must work for that."

She settled back, watching the station grow as she approached.

"OCCUPANT?"

"Now what?"

"INVALID RESPONSE."

"What…do…you…want?"

"THERE IS AN INCOMING MESSAGE FOR YOU FROM

BEETHOVEN STATION. WOULD YOU LIKE TO VIEW IT?"

"Fucking Wessic," she repeated.

"INVALID REQUEST."

"Yes, pod. Display the message."

A grainy image came through, showing Wessic's empty pod, alongside another, equally void of occupant, in Beethoven's main bay.

A second image came in, this one from the station's security camera in the galley. Dark smears streaked the gray walls, crimson showing against plastic housing the room's lighting. One figure clung to a table. It was covered in fur…face and head snow white.

"Captain Geary."

The third frame blinked in front of her face. This one was another security camera capture from Beethoven's command deck. Wessic stood, helmet off, posing. He looked sad. Then Irina noticed the two slashes across his torso.

"Couldn't happen to a nicer guy," she said, giving her best American accent. Lowe was alive and awaiting rescue on Enceladus. The Dyatlov was a lost cause—its orbit was too low, so salvage was impossible. *What's left?*

It blinked, taking time to load.

Werewolves. Really?

Immet's words came back to her.

The nanos…they help.

She closed her eyes, refusing the reality before her.

The pod jolted Irina awake as two drones latched onto it, guiding the craft into the bay and placing it into a tube directed to the station's main medical bay. Another lurch and the pod increased speed.

It's better in low orbit.

She passed hallways, then out into an arboretum, tube hidden underneath the running pond held in place by centrifugal force.

Something jumped in the water. Red tinged the liquid, then it was gone and she was back along the halls again.

The infection. It spreads so fast.

"Pod! Emergency stop!"

"INVALID REQUEST."

The fourth image popped up. It was from one of the long-range cameras on the Beethoven. A crisp image of the base from one of Herschel's domes. The image of a person pressed against the hardened clear material mid-scream and something blurry just off camera. A crimson spray haloed his form.

Another hallway. This one a tribute to the brutality on the Dyatlov, complete with bloody appendages littering the access.

The pod slowed, sliding onto a gurney in isolation. Wolves saw the movement and smacked against the room's glass, breaking it.

Everyone on the ship…one bite and they were gone in seconds.

"Pod, emergency lock."

"INVALID REQUEST." The pod's lid clicked, releasing the latch. She grabbed onto it, trying to lock it back in place.

A fist smacked against the pod's glass.

One bite….

Irina laughed, letting go of the hatch.

Of course, they were gone in seconds.

Saturn has more than 250 moons.

Behind the story...

This confession about the origin of "Lunar Descent" is the silliest one in here and rather short. I had just stumbled across an open call for werewolf stories and thought it'd be fun. My problem: I had absolutely no idea where to start. I know plenty about the lore but just couldn't come up with a story to save my life. Worse yet, the deadline was looming (*cue ominous music*).

When I outline, I tend to have something on my computer or television for white noise. On this particular day it was *The Muppet Show*. In the background I hear, "Piiiiiiigs in Spaaaaaaaaace," to which I mumbled, "Werewolves in spaaaaaaaaace." Thanks to Jim Henson, I now had a location to put my furry friends… er…fiends. Next came the questions of Why and How.

During this time, it seemed every time I visited a science site they were changing the number of moons orbiting Saturn. That just clicked into place without much effort. For this anthology I've kept the number of moons vague because, even now, it's changing.

I so wanted to put a Muppet doll somewhere on the ship, but I was talked out of it.

SONGBIRD

The laughter started again.

Jen Wells groaned.

"Wh-where…?"

She tried to swallow and failed.

Somewhere in the distance a motor hesitated, coughed, then resumed its staccato rhythm.

One cracked eyelid met with the seam of a filthy mattress, her lashes mushed down against it. A tattered hole the size of a softball lay ripped open midway along the bed's length. She focused on the batting that bloomed from the opening for a moment, then on the vertical bars beyond.

Bars?

Jen's hands went to her face, rubbing first one eye, then the other. Remnants from sleep clogged the corners, sandy grains biting as she wiped them free with the back of one hand. She winced as fingertips traveled over a large knot rising from her temple. Her gaze focused on the bars, following their lines up nine or ten feet, then across to where they partially blocked a single dingy light umbrellaed by a metal shop shade.

"Cell? I'm in…a cell?"

Jen pushed herself up to a sitting position and the world swam. Both legs drew up instinctively and her head rested against knees as nausea came and went in angry waves. A deep ache pressed deep from her back, making each breath a struggle. Minutes passed and the tingling in her lips eased enough to chance another look around. The cage appeared to be made from panels, pegged joints were replaced by heavy weld marks. Bolts went through eye holes and into the concrete floor.

"Thirsty."

Jen crawled to the edge of the mattress and looked for a bottle or cup. A plastic bucket was the only offering the search yielded, and, judging from the stains and smell, the last thing she wanted to do was drink what it held.

"Hell-hello?"

"Shhh," whispered a feminine voice off to Jen's left.

The darkness beyond the cell was absolute.

She managed, "Who…who's there?"

"Just go back to sleep." The voice, though distressed, reminded her of her mother's.

"Yes," a second echoed nasally. "Go to sleep."

Jen whispered, "Water?"

The second voice spat, "She wants *water*." A rustling sound had Jen searching the black for even an outline of a figure to focus on. "We don't have any water to give you."

"But," hope rose, "you…" Her voice gave out, becoming little more than a rasp. "You *do* have water, though?"

"*You do have water, though,*" the second woman's voice mimicked, sounding as dry as her own. "You already screwed that one up for yourself, Little Miss Priss."

Jen cocked her head, trying to understand the aggression. "I—"

"Great," the second voice barked, "she's going to start again."

"Be quiet," the first voice cut back in. "You don't remember, do you?"

Jen remembered finishing midterms and going to a party with her friends. She remembered dancing, drinking, even the impromptu fooling around with the DJ's sidekick before drifting away back into the crowd. But after that…nothing. It was all a blank up until she woke up here a few moments ago. She sucked hard on her tongue trying to force a little moisture back into her mouth before answering. "I…no."

Jen grabbed the bars and pulled herself up to a stooped position. Her forehead met metal and the cold steel helped to clear the fog. "Where are we?"

The second woman's voice echoed, "We've already done this with you!"

"Please," Jen managed, "I don't—"

"For Christ's sake, just go back to sleep." Venom came with each word from the second. "That's all you're good for."

The first voice repeated, "You don't remember anything, anything at all?"

"No." Jen sat, looking at the dried blood covering the wound in her palm.

"We've *already* done this!"

Jen asked, "What's your name?"

The second voice parroted, "*What's your name?*"

Ignoring the question, the first asked again, "What can you remember?"

"Hurry up," the second said. "Time's wasting. Tick. Tick. Tick."

There was something vaguely familiar about the first woman's voice.

"The Klepto," Jen managed.

The voices fell silent. She listened to the generator run, cough occasionally—always in time with the single bulb dimming from dirty orange to rust brown—before revving up to a steady rumble.

Denver's newest serial killer had been busy the last two months, always taking a girl then mailing a personal item of the victim's to the authorities. Sometimes it was a simple item, like a driver's license. Once, at least according to Jen's roommate, it was four fingers—not from the same hand, but from different people.

"This," Kylie had said while doing a sawing motion with a steak knife, "let the police know they were dealing with a serial killer." No complete bodies, though. No actual leads to get the powers that be on the right track. No victim to give an accounting of what kind of monster they were dealing with. The nickname was given after the fingers were discovered. She guessed it had to do with the girls disappearing, the severed fingers, and some reporter's twisted sense of humor.

As Jen's mind cleared, she took better stock of herself and the meager surroundings. An over-sized undershirt, covered in stains changing the original white to a muddy yellow, hung on her like a mu-mu—the neck hole being so large that Jen could fit her head and an arm through the opening without really stressing the fabric. It stank. The odor coming off her wasn't just the sweat of an unwashed body, but something more primal.

Stale sex.

Revulsion set in and she felt the fabric; patches of crust left no question as to their source. Jen pulled at the shirt, stopping cold as her bruised genitalia and thighs were exposed. Morbid reality surfaced as a multitude of other injuries covered her legs, groin, and stomach. One, a purplish handprint, covered the majority of her upper right thigh. Jen's own hand mimicked the purple area, taking up no more than a child's portion of the marred flesh.

"Big bastard," the second woman's voice confirmed from the dark.

Jen's voice quavered as she managed, "Did he…?"

"Did he what? Treat you like a dog treats his favorite chew toy?"

She shook.

"Remember yet?"

Reality set in and Jen ground her brow against the bars until the ache throbbed in her ears of all places. "No," she moaned.

"I don't know," the second mocked. "I think you just might—"

"Enough," the first spat.

"Yes," Jen confirmed, "enough." The shirt dropped from her grip, falling back into place and tickling her knees.

"Maybe you should write your name somewhere," the second chimed in. "You know, just in case."

"For the love of God," the first said with a tired sigh, "Could you just shut up for a minute?"

The second pressed, "I did it."

Jen managed a dry, "With what?"

"What?"

"What did—what did you write with?"

"My finger," the second said. Then in a lower voice, "I used my…waste…to put it on my mattress."

"No," Jen mumbled against doing the same.

"I *did*," the second insisted.

"No…not you." Jen's voice was past hurting, taking on a dry ache akin to when she'd had her tonsils out at eleven.

"Great," the second muttered. "Now she's crazy."

Jen turned around, pressing her back against the bars, cringing at the pressure, and looked up at the bulb. Its tin shielding kept the meager glow from going anywhere except directly down on her. Stains covered the ancient concrete, giving patterns to the chipped and cracked expanse. With a hand over her eyes, she could just make out a darker mass in the direction of the voices. That, and a little reflection which could only be the gleam of an eye.

"Yes, you're looking at us now," the first confirmed.

"Do you…do you have any light?"

The second scoffed. "I thought I was kidding when I said she was crazy! Open your eyes. Of course we don't."

"Did," Jen corrected herself. "*Did* you have any light?"

The first answered in a whisper of her own. "Not anymore."

"Oh, yeah," the second continued, "I just wrote my name in the dark."

"Shut up," the first said again.

Jen stood fully and made fists with her hands. "We have to get out of here."

The second grumbled, "She said this before. Look where that got her."

She continued to focus on the shade. "If I can move the light maybe we can get a better lay of the land."

Flaked paint and rusted metal ran in even lines along the cage with maybe six inches of space between them. Jen shifted her stance from one foot to the other, staring at the light beyond, gauging how far beyond the top of the cage she'd have to reach. Less than a yard…maybe two feet.

"Out," Jen said firmly. "There's got to be a way out. We need to see our surroundings." She reached out to grab the bars and, in the midst of pulling herself up, white fire shot around her back, centering on two vertebra just where the ribs start and brought her to her knees.

The second said, "Guess you forgot about that, huh?"

"God," the first breathed, exasperated.

With a self-conscious sigh, Jen pulled the shirt off, spun it like a wet towel, and flipped it up, wincing as the shirt strummed the underside of the cage top's bars before falling down to her. "Not like that," she told herself and turned ninety degrees before flipping the shirt again. This time it went through the bars and landed across two more, allowing the fabric to stay up for a second before falling down once again. "Damn it."

She did her best to find a clean spot before biting down on the shirt, then grabbed the bars. The rib protested and she ground down hard on the fabric, denying the pain a hold. Feet pushed against cold metal and hands slid up, pistoning opposite each other as she inched up to the chest-high crossbar. Her gashed palm started to bleed again, slowing progress. First a knee, then the other. One last pull had both feet on the bar and her head at a precarious angle as it bumped up against the top of her prison.

"Great monkey impersonation. Now what?"

Pulling the cloth from her mouth, Jen made a pfft sound in the general direction of the voices. The action hurt her already dry throat, but any act of defiance was worth it. She moved her grip to the cage's top bars.

"You'll never swing over there again," the second said.

She stopped and rasped, "Again?"

Silence hung for a handful of seconds.

The first spoke up. "You've done this before. I said that, already. You fell. That's how you wrenched your back and hurt your head."

Fingers left the bar and touched the tender spot on the side of her head. "Not this time." The shirt went up through the cage, across two bars, then back down. Jen tied it off, making a loop of the fabric and a makeshift swing for her to slide into. A look down gave new respect to how high ten feet actually was. The mattress, though just a single, looked unusually small from this perspective.

"Maybe it's the lines," she muttered before gripping the top bars and pulling herself into the sling.

Fabric sagged and Jen waited for the knot to slip loose. Seconds turned to a minute, yet the swing still held.

The second chided, "Now you look like a songbird in a cage."

A flash of memory surfaced. Someone doing something repulsive to her while whispering, *"Come on, sing for me, Pretty."*

Bile suddenly rose to the back of Jen's throat and her grip loosened. "No," she croaked. "No. No. No. Nonononononono."

The second said, "I think it's coming back to her."

"Not now," the first said impatiently. "Leave her be. At least she's doing *something*."

Vertigo danced at her senses, offering a ride she'd apparently already taken before. Jen reached out and grabbed the ceiling bars and pulled herself and the sling along, moving from the cell's barred wall out into open air. Two more pulls had her under the light. "Careful," she said to herself and reached out with one hand to the bulb.

"Don't," the second said.

Jen reached out and fingertips came just short of brushing the bulb. Years of grime and insect droppings covered the glass.

"Don't," the first echoed.

"I have to," she said through gritted teeth and swung up hard, both hands extended and smacked the side of the shade. Dust showered down into her face. On the downswing, her fingertips missed the bars and she fell back, screaming in pain as both legs tangled in the shirt, keeping Jen from falling, but leaving her body swinging inverted, back and forth, nearly in time with the light.

White hell shot along one side of her back.

Shadows.

What appeared to be a warehouse, long empty and forgotten.

Shadows.

A form on the floor.

Shadows.

The crystalline reflection of a water bottle.

You do have water, though?

Shadows.

Her eyes focused on the giant form gripping the bottle.

A hulk of a man, seven feet tall, lay on his back a handful of feet from her cage. His telltale brown delivery uniform appeared nearly black in the shadows. A wavy sliver of metal jutted from the Klepto's nearest eye socket, coiling back on itself. She stared hard at the spring wedged into his ruined socket like some sort of spike, then darted back to the mattress and the fist-sized hole in it.

"My palm."

You already screwed that one up for yourself, Little Miss Priss.

Jen jerked her head to where the companions were.

Shadows.

More warehouse.

Shadows.

A pile of clothes.

Shadows.

Tangled within the clothes two forms lay heaped. Gray mottled flesh covered the women's bodies, decay obvious even in the dim light. Clumps of hair, one blonde, the other red, draped over one head, but left the other prone, its eyeless face staring accusingly at Jen, mouth open in a rotted scream. Rats chittered as they worked on the latter's lips as water dripped with an annoying pinging sound.

Hurry up. Time's wasting. Tick. Tick. Tick.

Jen's hand went to her mouth.

"We said, 'Don't.'"

Eyes went wide, recognizing her own voice speaking as Jen felt her lips move beneath trembling fingers.

I used my…waste…to put it on my mattress.

Her eyes darted to the side of the mattress.

What's your name?

There, scrawled on its side as if written by a child, JEN WELLS.

The knot came loose.

The laughter started again.

Behind the story...

I've had a question or two about whether "Songbird"

has inspiration from any case I've worked on for my day job (*trial technician*). The answer is no, not even a little bit. That's a taboo line I've never crossed and never will. However, I did get inspiration from the multitude of serial killer documentaries and biographies I can't seem to get away from.

As someone who spent their teen years in the '80s I enjoyed my share of horror movies…okay, I watched them all! One of my biggest annoyances was the stereotypical girl in the woods with high heels, hiking in a white t-shirt when the weather called for rain. Now, don't get me wrong, I definitely enjoy a wet t-shirt as much as the next person, but it was the characters setting themselves up in such a way that the audience actually cheered when the butchering scenes finally came around that was amazed at.

The core story of "Songbird" came from a dream I wrote in my journal and came back to a few months later. I find it a great example of "out of the frying pan and into the fire." Just when you think it can't get worse it just "does" somehow.

FELLOWSHIP

Melinda stared out the Dodge's window at the blur of trees. The Maine foliage banked the two-lane road, adding to the claustrophobic feeling overpowering her all day. She longed for the next town for, if nothing else, the open feeling that expanse of yards would give. Overhead, thunder rippled.

"It's going to rain," she said flatly and looked over at her husband.

Jason remained his stoic self and tightened his grip on the steering wheel.

"Jason."

"I heard you. It's going to rain." He waved an arm, coming just short of putting a finger in her eye. "Of course it's going to rain. It's Maine. It always rains in Maine."

Melinda returned to her lack of a scenic view. "The…rain in Maine stays mainly on—"

"Us," he cut in.

A laugh escaped her in the form of a decidedly unladylike snort which sent them both into hysterics. Their rental car drifted over the ever-unending solid yellow line and into the oncoming lane.

"Better straighten it out, before we get creamed."

Jason let the car drift all the way across the line. "Creamed?"

"Yes," she said, her giggle fit subsiding. "Creamed. As in greasy yellow corn."

A blind curve banked to the left and the Dodge took it at better than fifty, still on the wrong side of the road. "We've seen one car in the last fifteen minutes, and that was a tractor." They pulled out of the curve and eased back into the proper lane. "Besides, this is unspoiled territory. No other salesmen have been up here. From what I hear, that goes for the competition too."

"Now that I can believe." Melinda shifted her gaze to the long stretch of road before them and to the gray churning mass above. "I mean, there's nothing up here and if we keep going like we have been, we'll end up in Canada."

"What's wrong with Canada?"

"French Canada to be exact."

"Do I get to make a froggy joke?"

"Up here?" She shoved Jason lightly, sending the car back over the line. "You're likely to get your head clubbed. Besides, I bet you can see into Canada if you stood on the rooftops."

Their radar detector blipped and Jason instinctively slowed. A muddy set of ruts came into view on the right side of the road, leading into the veritable wall of trees and dense foliage. As a mid-nineties sedan, complete with light bar came into view, the detector fired, sounding off an electronic woodpecker tone.

"Shit," Jason muttered.

Melinda craned her neck to watch the state trooper pull out onto the road behind them, a spray of mud arcing off the rear wheels. The patrol car flew up and began to pace, keeping back about a hundred feet. She watched the silhouetted figure shift back and forth. A drizzle started, distorting what little could be seen of the officer. The misshapen form shifted again, appearing as more of a bulbous mass than a person.

"Better hide the pot," Melinda quipped.

"Ha…ha…ha."

The spatter of rain ended as they crested the next hill, though low rolling clouds still threatened to release their burden. Lights flared red and blue in the rear-view mirror, adding an artificial splash of color to the muted countryside. Jason looked to the side of the road. A dip led to ten feet of wet grassy mud that served as a soft shoulder. Visibly gritting his teeth, he pulled the Dodge off the pavement. Both passenger side wheels were off the road when a horn blared.

"Back on the road," came from the patrol car's speaker. "Pull the car back on the pavement and stop."

Jason pulled the wheel to the left and felt the right front tire sink and catch. A sickening grinding sound thrummed as the undercarriage rubbed against asphalt. They lurched forward, caught by their seat belts, as the car jerked to a stop.

"Shit," Jason muttered a second time.

Melinda opened the glove box and rifled through the maps and cluster of suckers she'd wedged in there the day before.

A tap at the window grabbed their attention. The officer, a stern-faced woman Jason's father would have called "handsome," motioned for him to roll the window down.

"Put it in park," Officer Hoskel—according to the name tag—said.

"Yes sir…er, ma'am."

Melinda watched the officer smirk.

"License. Registration."

"I'm getting it," Melinda said as pleasantly as she could muster. "Just a sec."

"Are you two enjoying our fine state?"

Jason looked up at the officer, trying not to fixate on the hat's rain guard which looked amazingly like a giant shower cap. "How did you know we were visiting?"

Officer Hoskel leaned over, resting her forearm on the car's roof. "Two things. The rental car sticker on the bumper. We don't see too many rental cars up this way. Where'd you get this one? Bangor?"

Jason stammered, "Uh…yeah."

"Ma'am, don't worry about finding the registration. I'm sure you have all the proper documentation." She shifted her stance, stretching to the point that several audible pops echoed from her back. "The reason I pulled you over was a simple spot check. You were a few miles over the posted limit."

Melinda leaned over so she could still see the officer's face. "No ticket?"

"No ticket…unless you want one."

Jason answered quickly, "No, that's okay."

"Hop in the back of my cruiser and we'll get you up into Fellowship for a tow truck."

The couple grabbed their carry-ons from their trunk, deposited them into the officer's and climbed into the back of the patrol car. Climbing in, Melinda noticed that the hard plastic seat had strange depressions in the backrest.

"It's for suspects cuffed hands and arms—so we can still seatbelt them," Officer Hoskel offered before being asked.

"Looks uncomfortable."

"The seat is, but it's safe and that's what counts these days."

They got into the patrol car and buckled up. As Officer Hoskel pulled away from the Dodge, Melinda asked, "What was the other reason?"

"Hmmm?"

"You said there were two reasons you knew we were visiting the state. What was the other one?" Jason elbowed her and gave his animated "shut up" expression.

"Oh, that was the dead giveaway. You pulled onto the shoulder. Locals just stop. Mainers stop or put on a signal and just drive up to the nearest road or dry patch."

"So, I'm an idiot," Jason said.

"So, you're an idiot," Officer Hoskel confirmed, bringing a Cheshire cat grin from Melinda.

The next ten minutes were met with relative silence. Jason glowered, Melinda returned to her staring out the window and Officer Hoskel relayed what happened to the dispatcher. The patrol car slipped past a massive moose carcass lying in the middle of the road. They rounded another bend and were suddenly in a little hamlet of a town. A dazzlingly white sign—FELLOWSHIP: CLOSER TO GOD THAN THEE—announced the town proper. Their patrol car slowed a hundred yards short of the sign and turned into the only visible gas station.

"Not exactly a friendly welcome sign," Melinda said.

"I'm afraid it's not exactly a friendly town." She pulled into a single-bay gas station and got out. Rain started to fall again.

The door on Jason's side of the patrol car opened to reveal the typical jump-suited mechanic. "Keys," the man said flatly. Jason fished the single electronic key and handed it over. "Two hours. Stay here," and then he was gone, climbing into the tow truck's cab and driving off. A wake of blue smoke hung heavy as testament to the attendant's mechanical skills.

"Kebler," Officer Hoskel yelled, "on the state's tab. Don't burn 'em." She turned and opened first Melinda's door, then Jason's.

Melinda took in the anti-Rockwellian station. Blue paint, now marred by palm sized patches of rust spattered across the "Tommy's Trucks n' Such" sign painted above the picture windows. The street contained no children playing stickball, no bicyclists making their way to or from a favorite watering hole. The closest thing to humanity, aside from their benefactor, was the incessant shrieking of a baby somewhere down the street. The wind blew through the summer leaves and flashed her memory to their two nights in Bar Harbor earlier that week. This sound matched in pitch and volume, though lacked the intensity of the water crashing against the rocks.

Jason's arm slid around her waist. "Quite a view, isn't it?"

"Yeah," she leaned into him. "Almost feels like the end of the earth."

Officer Hoskel called out from the back of the car, "Not the end of the earth, ma'am. That's about five miles up the road. At least that's what the locals say." She stood, hoisting the couple's two bags out and setting them to the side before slamming the trunk. "Might want to just wait it out here. It's Sunday so you're not going to find anything open."

Melinda looked over her shoulder, "Why not? We did everywhere else…even over in Skowhegan."

"This isn't Skowhegan. No tourists and as of a couple of years back, no mill either. You never did say what you were doing up hereabouts."

"Work," Jason said simply and turned to the officer.

"Up here? There's no work up here." Officer Hoskel's friendly demeanor shifted into an official tone.

Melinda turned to join the conversation, smiling. "He's in sales.

Incorporating business websites for towns and villages. New territory here."

Hoskel looked down the street "Be a short list here. Seems hardly worth your gas."

"It's the residuals once the sites are built. That's how I make my income."

"Mmm-hmm," was all the officer offered.

Jason pressed, "Is there a place here where we can get something to eat?"

"About a half mile up on the left is a restaurant. Doubt they're open." She opened her car door and climbed inside. "Best of luck to you."

"Um, miss," Melinda stammered. "Do you think we could get a lift?"

"For a five minute walk?"

"I mean, the mechanic's gone and it's about to rain." Two large drops landed noisily onto the roof of the car, offering nature's version of a rim-shot.

"Nope. Town ordinances keep me from going past that sign we passed…officially. Nothing much up here anyway." She tipped her hat. "They'll probably still complain that I came as far as the gas station. Have to pull that moose off the road. Got you here. Got you help." She grabbed the door. "I'll be back to check on you in an hour or so. Best I can offer. I'd head somewhere else to stay the night, though."

"Why's that?"

"No hotel in Fellowship." The door slammed and Officer Hoskel's car pulled away.

Jason turned to his wife. "So," he said, placing his fists on his hips, "Captain Screwup has done his duty and now the trusty sidekick will be driving them back down the lonely highway sooner than she anticipated. Tune in tomorrow when…."

She jabbed him in the stomach. "Quit it."

Another drop landed in a puddle by the gas pumps.

Melinda grabbed her shoulder bag and passed him the computer backpack she'd gotten him for the trip. The red stripe down the side reflected sharply even in the cloudy afternoon light. She couldn't help but to notice that aside from the neon "OPEN" sign and the pack's stripe, no colors stood out, giving everything before them a muted sense of reality. Red brickwork framing the store had a brown tinge, The red and white striped barber pole mounted above a mailbox down the street had the faded look of an old instamatic photo. Down the road she took in the various driveways and parking spots for the township. No, not a township, a—

"Hamlet," she muttered.

"This, above all," Jason bellowed, "to thine own self be true."

Melinda fought back a smile as she fired another jab to her husband's gut. He doubled over, catching her hand and held it against his stomach.

"O," he continued, "what a rogue and peasant slave am I!"

A devilish grin escaped her and she pressed forward, grabbing the front of Jason's trousers, fingers slipping inside the waistband. His smile matched hers until she jerked the hand up, bringing with it his underwear's waistband. And initial look of shock shifted into an exaggerated expression of discomfort.

"I must be cruel," she said, falling into his Shakespearean platitudes, "only to be kind."

Before he could retaliate as playful couples tend to do, she set out walking past the town limits sign and into what served as the business portion of Fellowship. Jason caught up after repairing his chafing wardrobe malfunction. They passed rotted doors hiding the volunteer fire department's truck. Flaking paint revealed weathered wood bleached light gray with age. Curled shingles gave, to her painter's eye, the impression of birds mid-flight. Another short volley of drops splattered across the road and grass, missing them by scant feet.

"Jesus," Jason barked, "is it going to rain or what?" Just as the genie granted Aladdin's wish, the skies opened up releasing a torrential downpour onto them.

Plodding steps fell into a quarter-step beat as they ran the remainder of the distance to the gravel parking lot of "Jenny's Diner." Melinda grabbed onto the glass door's handle and pulled. The door opened and they pushed into the cinder block restaurant. A dozen pairs of eyes looked at them from around the room. Well, Melinda corrected herself, eleven pairs of eyes and one thirty-ish woman with an eye patch who stood in the corner with a Bible. Overhead, the fluorescents were off and what little light illuminated the eatery came from the storefront's windows.

"Sorry," Jason said to the group which continued to stare, unmoving, at them. "We'll just seat ourselves." He looked at his wife and nodded over to an open corner booth. They dropped their bags and slid onto the vinyl benches. Water sluiced off their clothing and spread a widened pool on the seats. "Mel, what do you want?"

"Huh?" She couldn't stop returning the stares of the restaurant's patrons.

"Lunch. We're here. We might as well eat."

"I…," Melinda shook uncontrollably. "What do they have?"

"I don't know—what do you want?" He leaned back and looked at their audience. "Guess we're celebrities here, huh."

"Guess so," she shifted and stared down at the table.

"Hey," Jason called out to the one-eyed employee, "could we get a little service here?" No one moved.

"Jason!" Melinda hissed his name.

"It's okay," he chided, "*I'll* get the menus." He got up and grabbed two laminated sheets from beside the fifties-era register. "Thank you *so* much for your assistance. I…*see* you're busy."

Melinda felt herself blushing at Jason's digs at the waitress. "Stop it." She took the menu from him and watched as he slid back into his seat, brushing away the pooled rainwater as he did so. A rip in her own seat had sucked much of the puddled water away. Glaring over the menu she willed her husband to return the gaze and, a handful of heartbeats later, he did. An unspoken conversation ensued.

Stop it.

What did I do?

Stop it now.

They're being rude.

Stop being an ass or I'm leaving right now.

Okay. Okay. Jason gave an exaggerated eye roll after acquiescing to her demands.

Melinda raised her hand to the woman who, now a couple of minutes later, still hadn't moved. "Um, miss?" Breathing and blinking aside, the waitress remained immobile.

Jason asked, "Could we get a couple of waters?"

A cook looked out from the kitchen and said, "Water's the last thing we—"

"Jason," Melinda hissed a second time.

Jason avoided returning the look, only a seasoned wife is able to give. Instead, he produced a broad smile and said, "Water sounds great!" He shifted in his seat, opened the multimedia backpack and began rifling through it searching for what Melinda assumed was a little bit of dignity after his childish display. He produced his notebook computer and placed it lovingly on the table before returning to rooting around in the bag's various zippered pockets. She watched his neck flush deep red as his actions yielded nothing of substance before turning her attention to the slowly approaching waitress. The patch over her right eye masked the connecting point of two deep slashes, one horizontal ending at brow and the bridge of her nose while the vertical one began within a forehead crease, parted the plucked and arched trail of hair and continued down to her chin before ending at a point. At her cheekbone the scar split the skin deep, leaving a visible seam where it met healthy flesh.

"No water," the waitress said.

Melinda leaned back and looked at the patrons. No water glasses adorned their tables either...no food for that matter. "I don't... ohhhh, the rain. Did it cut power?" She offered the woman a friendly smile. "I just noticed the lights aren't on."

Jason looked up at her. "How about a Coke?"

"No Coke." She continued looking at Melinda.

Melinda tried, "Do you have a special?"

"No specials. No Cokes. No nothin." The waitress raised her Bible. "Today's Sunday."

"I don't understand. Ummm," Melinda made the "c'mon, please tell me your name" motion with her hands.

"Julia."

"I don't understand, Julia." Melinda tried to sound polite, but even she was getting short tempered with the waitress. "I mean, I understand it's Sunday, but why are you open if you're not going to serve anyone?"

"Missy," an old codger sporting what looked to be an even older pair of coveralls spoke up, "we've been here since sundown yesterday. We'll be here 'til sunup tomorrow."

"Amen," a family of four said, each parent clutching one of two twin boys. The boys looked dirty and tired, dark circles under the eyes visible even in the limited light.

"It's the Lord's day," a woman, primed to have been a circus fat lady in a 1930's circus, chimed in. "You can't partake of anything on the Lord's day." Her words took on a scolding tone, as if a parent speaking to a child. She gripped her own Bible in a sausage-fingered death grip. "You…you should *know* that."

It was then Melinda noticed the smell. While the waitress' clothes were clean and pressed, her exposed skin had a telltale mottling left for the unwashed masses. Scents of sweat and other distinctly feminine odors wafted across the booth. She locked eyes with Jason and knew he'd made the same discovery.

God's personal fat lady glowered at the notebook computer sitting on the table and continued, "On the Lord's day, His children don't work, don't partake of the garden's fruit, and don't partake of man's bounty."

Jason couldn't suppress a chuckle, "what about Soft n' Gentle?" He grinned at the blatant laundry quip.

Shocked and angry expressions marred the shadowed patrons.

The obese woman jabbed a digit at the couple, "Do not mock the Lord!"

The waitress, who now stood glassy eyed, stared out the window. A tear escaped the patch and trailed down her puckered scar. "You should pray," she mouthed more than said, only visible to the couple.

"Tell them," the fat woman bellowed.

Melinda and Jason watched the waitress shake uncontrollably, then raise her right hand to her patch. "If thine eye offends thee…" she pulled the swatch of fabric back, exposing slit lids covering nothing but wet pink tissue. As the waitress blinked the scarred lids puckered, pinching a touch of what looked surprisingly like chewed bubble gum, between eyelashes.

"We're sorry," Jason said with a level of decorum that, to Melinda's knowledge, he'd never before possessed. While still staring with morbid fascination at the remains of the waitress' eye, he pushed himself to the edge of the bench and stood. "We didn't mean any disrespect. We'll just be going."

Their waitress grabbed him by a shoulder. "You can't leave. It's the Lord's day!"

"Lady," Jason's temper began to flare, "we just came from out there." He shook off the waitress' grasp.

"The Lord," the fat woman said, "brought you into our garden. Be not the sinner." A volley of amens echoed throughout the eatery.

"Mel, let's get back to the car." He pointed to his computer. "Put it away, will you."

Melinda lifted her husband's lifeline to civilization and reached over to grab his backpack. Something smashed into her hand and the computer fell to the table, a starburst crack in the top of the plastic housing. A napkin dispenser clattered to a stop beside their property, its contents fanning onto the table. The patrons stood as one and grasped things within reach—another napkin dispenser, two plates, a glass salt shaker and a butter knife. She looked to Jason who stood between her and the group. His shoulders squared like before a wrestling match back in college.

"Mel," he repeated, "let's go."

"Sinners," the father of the two boys said. "You defile the Sabbath." He stood, skeletal frame rising well over six feet. "We know how to deal with sinners."

Jason turned to Melinda, then, without warning, grabbed the computer and hurled it like a discus at the father. The wedge of plastic and electronics struck the fanatic just under the nose, separating him from his front teeth in a spray of blood worthy of any slasher film. Customers, along with Julia the waitress and the fat lady, directed all attention to their fallen comrade. Melinda scooted out of the booth and Jason jerked her by the wrist and pulled her out the door and into the thinning rain. Four men and a rather homely woman strode while watching them intently, all showing the soaked telltale signs of having walked to this destination.

The oldest of the clutch, eighty if he was a day, spoke up. "You all new in town?"

Melinda gritted her teeth against the vice grip Jason had on her forearm. "Just leaving," she managed to call out before being guided onto the road's shoulder.

"You two should stay for evening services."

Jason stopped cold, jerking Melinda's attention toward the street before them rather than the group in the parking lot. Better than forty people stood in the road, or alongside it, framing their path back to Tommy's station. Many of Fellowship's population carried different items clutched in their hands, just as those in the restaurant did, though a few of these were more menacing. She counted five young men casually holding onto hay forks.

Melinda rasped through clenched teeth, "What do we do?"

"We go the other way and if they follow, we duck into the woods on the far side of the road."

She looked to her left at the wall of foliage. No break in the undergrowth offered entrance to the woods, much less a visible means to escape a town full of Jesus freaks. Then a dark patch caught her attention—a depression in the leafy barrier with a muddy patch of standing water carpeting the area.

"Got it," she said, her pulse beating rabbit-fast.

Jason turned to the old man in the parking lot just as the fat woman emerged from the church. "Where's the service being held?"

"Don't you even speak to them, Ezekiel! Their evil ways smote Michael!"

"Smote," Jason said, "doesn't that mean *kill*?" His hands started shaking uncontrollably. "I...didn't kill anyone!"

A thunderclap ripped through the sky overhead followed by a deluge of water. Melinda ran for the tree line. She plowed into the standing water and trudged into the forest's access. The shower's roar deafened her to any sign of Jason's—or anyone else's—pursuit. Sneakers filled with runoff, muddy sludge soaking into her socks with each step. Further she plowed, branches raking across her face and shirt, tearing fabric and drawing blood. Dozens of steps passed, then the undergrowth suddenly thinned, held at bay by the carpet of pine needles blanketing the ground. She stumbled, then a hand grabbed her forearm, jerking her back to her feet. A scream escaped her.

"Shhh," Jason said. "Keep moving! They're right behind us!"

Melinda fell into step behind her husband, content to let him lead after her experience with getting into Fellowship's woods. Ten steps became twenty, twenty became forty. After seventy she lost count in an effort to keep up with Jason. Behind them an occasional call echoed out over the rain's din, sometimes far away—but never far enough. They stopped to catch their breath which came to both in great heaves.

Melinda spoke up, gulping air before each word. "We…should… circle…back."

"We can't," he whined.

She stared at him in disbelief. He actually whined.

"They said I killed him." Jason dropped to his knees before falling onto his side. He grasped a handful of muddy needles in his right hand, letting fingertips burrow into the soft soil.

Melinda looked down at the man she married, unsure how to deal with this broken representation of the dreamer she loved. After a moment of watching him she knelt, "You didn't mean it. We both thought that guy was getting up to hurt us. You did what you had to…to keep us safe. But," she put a hand on his hip, "you need to get up. We need to circle around and get our car."

Jason sat bolt upright. "No."

"Honey—"

"No." He turned to her and grasped her still outstretched hand in his muddy grasp. "That's what they're expecting. We need to continue north." He pushed himself to his feet using her as balance. "We'll come back after dark."

"What we need is to call the police."

"With what?" he spat. "The cell phones haven't worked for the past hour. Do you really think that one of those nut jobs is going to let us use their phone? They want blood, Mel. My blood." He looked into her eyes, "Yours too."

"Jason—"

Another call echoed closer than before.

"C'mon."

Melinda pulled free of his hands and brushed the soil on her jeans. She sighed and waved him on, following close behind.

They continued in what they hoped to be a northerly direction, but with the dense trees and on such a cloudy day, it was hard to tell anything beyond the fact that it was slightly brighter to their left. Evening light on the left meant they were going north, right? She pondered this as the growth thickened once more.

A river? A road maybe?

Suddenly Jason wasn't in front of her and nature's roar grew in intensity. She stumbled, right foot slipping on mud worthy of a pig pen. Arms pinwheeled and she lost her balance, tumbling down the hill in a nursery rhyme parody of Jack and Jill. An icy splash of water broke the fall and her senses went from a vertigo strewn tumble into an uncontrollable spin in the water. Face down, she fought to right herself. Foam splashed up, filling her open mouth and stealing what little air she'd managed to hang onto. Melinda splashed her hands down in an attempt to get her head above water. Her body slowed and pulled against the current. *I'm hung up*, she thought. She splashed a second time, drawing in a lungful of air before sinking once more. Foreign fingers tangled in her hair and, with a root-ripping jerk, she was pulled onto a rock by Jason.

While vomiting and coughing helped clear the water Melinda'd taken in, it didn't help the overwhelming sense she was going to choke to death any second. No clear lungful of air could be gotten at any cost. She lay on her back, legs still in the icy river, and stared at the sky. The rain continued. Jason lay beside her, his own expulsions more evident than hers with white residue both on the rock and down the front of his polo shirt.

"There they are!"

Instinct took over and they pulled themselves the rest of the way out of the water, numb legs slowly responding to commands given them. Jason stopped her and stared back across the river. "They can't get to us." He pointed excitedly. "Look, Mel!"

Melinda stared at the boulder-strewn waterway. A clutch of seven townspeople stood at the far bank's edge, fifteen feet away.

"Murderers!"

"Sinners," cried another!

Jason stood and yelled back at the overall-wearing old man they'd seen in the restaurant, "You started it! You hurled—"

A baseball sized rock thwapped right beside Melinda's leg.

"Stone them!"

"Jesus," Jason said, unintentionally infuriating their religious pursuers.

Melinda stood beside him. "We've gotta go!"

One man carrying a hay fork, younger than the others, took a running jump at the river. His legs pistoned through the air as he crossed the majority of the distance before crashing chest deep into the river. As the man landed he stabbed his fork into the water, using it to gain better purchase. A volley of rocks flew from the far side of the river, showering all around Jason and Melinda.

Jason grabbed a stone of his own and hurled it side-armed at the wading aggressor. It arced high and, to the surprise of everyone, struck the man in the collarbone, knocking him off balance and into a heavier part of the river's current. The river whipped his flailing form as it shot out of sight. He bobbed like a cork then disappeared from sight.

"They're trying to kill Ethan," Julia, the waitress from the restaurant screamed!

Melinda yelled, "You crazy bastards! You're trying to kill *us*. What did you expect?" She backed up further on the bank, careful not to catch her foot in one of the ankle-breaking holes boulders left. Her husband followed, scooping up two more rocks as he went. They watched, warily, as the old man said something to the group and pointed upriver. Their gaze followed his and Melinda felt a sinking feeling in the pit of her stomach with what they saw.

The highway's bridge was less than two hundred yards away.

"Shit," Jason yelled. "Shit. Shit. *Shit!*"

Backs turned, the two scrambled up the rocky bank and plowed their way back into the woods. Smells of mud and decaying plants assailed their nostrils. Waning light gave the surroundings a more ominous look and Melinda couldn't help but to expect a crazed townie to jump out from one of the trees they ran past. While none did, they did have a near miss with a wild pig, its surprised screech matching her own.

Without warning they burst from the woods and back onto the road.

Melinda bent over, hands on her knees, and worked to catch her breath. Blood wept from a half dozen places where branches snagged both shirt and skin during their escape. She rubbed at one on her left shoulder, mindful of the stinging sensation radiating down her arm, and watched Jason as he stared nervously back in the direction they'd come.

"I figure…" he said, his own breaths coming in gasps, "we've got…ten…maybe fifteen…minutes on them." Jason bent at the waist, mimicking Melinda's stance. "They'll have to go back…into the woods to…get to the road. The bank was too steep…on their side."

"That's if they don't…go after Ethan." She felt her teeth chatter and wondered with disjointed curiosity if it was from the onset of hypothermia or simply shock.

"Good point."

No double yellow line marred the asphalt on this side of the bridge. Trees hung over the road, giving only a little more light than when they'd been in within the tree line. Flowers and grass grew in the increasing number of unsealed cracks in the pavement. The rain eased to a fine mist, and while it still pelted their exposed skin with icy aggression, the numbing effect eased.

Jason started across the road to the opposing tree line.

"Wait," Melinda said.

"Hon, we've got to keep moving. They're not that far behind."

"On the road."

"What? No!" He shook his head emphatically.

Melinda stood and crossed the half dozen steps to meet him on the far shoulder. "Just for a couple of minutes. The mud's killing my feet and I can't keep up with you. We'll stay on the shoulder so we can just pop in." Pop in, she thought. Plowing into this excuse for woods was more like trying to navigate a blender.

Jason looked back down the road and then North. "At some point we're going to have to either try to flag someone down or climb a tree and try to call for help."

"The phones!" Melinda grabbed at the holster on her hip and pulled the phone free. Water dripped from the unit's jack and the LCD display offered nothing save a dark gray smear along the right side of the screen.

"Just put it back." He started walking along the shoulder as she wanted. "Maybe they'll work once they dry out."

Re-holstering the device, Melinda followed, picking up her pace until she stepped in time with her husband. "North, huh?"

"We really need to be going South, back to the car." A laugh escaped her.

"What?"

"Think Tommy's pissed?"

"Tommy? The tow truck guy?"

She mimicked his Mainer accent, "Back in two hours. Stay here."

"Best God damned advice I've heard all day."

Up ahead the road petered out, going from painted pavement to dirt. Though still hard packed, the diminishing aspects of modern society fell heavy on the two. They continued along the road, each taking an unspoken turn to glance warily in the direction they'd come. Thirty minutes passed without incident. No visible pursuit ensued. Only the road, red clay beaten to a respectable impersonation of rock, lay before and behind them.

Jason stopped. "What was that?"

"What was what?"

"Shhhh."

Melinda kept walking but craned her head and listened. She could only hear the softer hiss of the mist impacting everything around them.

"There it is again."

"You're imagining things." Then she heard it—an engine, driving slow and getting closer. Fear grabbed hold and she stepped off the road and into the undergrowth, following Jason's retreating form. They watched from the embrace of two pine trees as a patrol car rounded the bend and passed.

"It's Haskel!"

"Hoskel," she corrected and pushed from their hiding place, emphatically waiving her arms. Jason followed suit.

The patrol car skidded to a stop in time with the bubble gum lights flicking on. Strobing red and blue shot fiery color against the woods. Officer Hoskel stepped out, pulled her sidearm and drew a bead on the two of them.

"Freeze!"

Both did, already having their hands up in the air.

Melinda took a step forward. "Oh, thank God you found us."

"I said *freeze!*"

Melinda did as she was told. "The town, they're full of crazies."

"Just keep your hands where I can see them." She took two steps to the side to get a better view of Jason, who unlike his wife, had stayed frozen in place upon being told to. Her gun lowered some, but still pointed in their general direction. "You two look like a couple of drowned rats."

"The town—"

"I heard you, 'full of crazies.'" Officer Hoskel's stance eased. "The way they tell it, you," she motioned to Jason, "bashed some poor guy's face in with a computer."

"They threw a napkin dispenser at me first. Smashed my system's screen."

"So that gave you the right to—"

"They acted like they were going to hurt me," Melinda cut in. "They'd already thrown the dispenser and this huge guy started to get up." Tears, so unlike Melinda to shed, started to fall. "Jason threw it so we could get out of there."

The gun lowered, now pointing at the ground.

Jason lowered his hands some, still keeping them above his head. "We're just glad you found us."

"Okay, okay." She holstered her weapon. "They yelled at me for driving a car on a Sunday in their little town. Either way, you two get in the back of the car and we'll see exactly what hap—"

A rock flew out from across the road and struck officer Hoskel in the temple. Her right eye suddenly bulged from the impact. Her hand grabbed the pistol but seemed unable to draw the weapon from its housing.

Bam!

A shot rang out from the holstered weapon and a spatter of muddy clay erupted in the soil by her feet.

Bam!

Another shot fired down, this time striking the officer in the foot.

Melinda stared at the fresh gunshot wound, expecting to see a fountain of blood fly up. None did.

Officer Hoskel staggered forward, trying to keep on her feet. A mask of confusion marred the woman's face as another rock flew out and struck her in the same spot. The eye burst free from its socket and offered the law woman a decidedly unnatural view down the side of her nose. Knees buckled and the Maine patrolwoman fell, twitching, onto the road.

Jason lowered his hands and ran to his wife's side. "C'mon!"

On queue, townsfolk emerged ahead and behind them, effectively blocking the road in both directions. The number of hay forks and lengths of wood reminded Melinda of a gathering of movie extras from an old Frankenstein film.

"Angry villagers," she whispered.

The people of Fellowship closed in around the two and the car, stepping carefully.

Jason shoved her towards the open driver's door. "In!" Melinda dove into the front seat, jamming her pinky finger as she struck the center console. Jason piled in behind her, forcing her legs out of the way as he fell into the seat and slammed the door behind him.

A knife blade shattered the passenger-side glass and severed the skin between Melinda's middle and ring finger. She jerked her hand away and screamed. A hay fork handled by a middle-aged man with jet black hair thrust into the front driver's side tire. Jason pulled the lever into drive and stomped on the gas, the tire's momentum jerking the fork from the man's grasp and slamming it back to strike a woman forearm with a bone crunching thwack before continuing its journey and slapping against the ground.

The patrol car lurched forward, knocking into the angry mob which parted rather than be mown down. Rocks smashed against the glass, spiderwebbing them. A sickening grinding sound emanated from the car's left front. Men and women followed alongside the vehicle as it picked up speed, slapping whatever they had, bare palms in the few cases where no weaponry was carried.

"Oh God, it hurts," Melinda screamed holding the split hand together.

Jason ignored the cry. "The pitchfork must still be in the tire." A second thwap came from the flattened tire and this time a clunk followed by constant metallic scraping screeched through the vehicle. The steering wheel jerked to the left and Jason fought it back to the right, fishtailing the car as he sped away from the psychotic foot traffic behind them. They rounded a curve and smashed through a logging gate. Steam started to billow from around the buckled hood.

"A gate? A friggin' gate on the highway?"

Melinda snaked around in the seat until she was upright. "This isn't the highway then."

"It's got to be the highway."

They slammed into something. Air bags released, snapping Melinda's head painfully against the seat. Jason beat against the bag, trying to force the safety device aside. A handful of seconds later all of the air bladders deflated and lay flaccid against their housings. The car's hood had buckled further, erasing what little could be seen through the shattered glass.

Opening the driver's door, Jason stepped out of the patrol car and placed both hands on its roof and rested his forehead against the exposed weather stripping. Melinda climbed across the seat and started to push past him.

"What's wrong with your door?"

Melinda looked at him a moment, then at the passenger side door before holding up her bloodied hand.

"Oh crap. Mel, what happened?"

"The mob…back at the car…" she corrected herself, "…back at where the car was."

He helped her out of the vehicle, lifting firmly on her good arm as she extricated herself.

"What in hell?"

Jason looked in the same direction she did. They'd slammed into a parked car…one of many parked cars…a veritable parking lot's worth of parked cars. The hilltop clearing was filled with vehicles of all years and makes, though most didn't appear to be in junkyard condition. Granted, there was a lot of mud and rust on ones further back in the clearing, but most had more of an abandoned appearance, neatly positioned alongside others, all with windows rolled up and doors closed.

Yells came from the direction they'd retreated.

Jason, still holding onto her arm, jerked her along. "Move! Into the lot!"

Vehicles blurred by as they made their way further up the hill, kicking away whip-like weeds and escaped tire rims. Fords, Chevys and GMCs populated the portion of the lot they navigated. Melinda couldn't help but to glance in the windows as they passed. Long forgotten open cans of soda occupied holders, cars with CDs piled on the seat gave way to clusters of tapes occupying the same position in others. As they weaved past pickup truck the voices got louder.

"There they are!"

Melinda looked over her shoulder and ran into Jason, who'd stopped without warning.

"What're you doing?"

"End of the earth."

"What?" She looked around his shoulder.

A fifteen-foot high cinder block wall barred their way, going the width of the open lot in either direction and into the tree line. Directly in front of them were the words, "END OF THE EARTH," spray painted in fluorescent orange. She looked along the wall's length. Where the tree line on their side met the wall, no trees mirrored them on the far side.

Jason stood, staring dumbfounded at the construction.

"Jason!" A thought struck Melinda. "The wall!" She grabbed him with her good hand and pointed as best she could with the other. "We can use the trees and get over the wall!" A single look over her shoulder at the closing group of people was enough for her to take the lead.

The statement seemed to shake Jason free of the surfacing shock and he followed her to the right. They navigated trunks. A family of field mice were displaced by one vehicle shifting hard as Jason slid across the back of one car and the windshields of two others cracked as the two scampered across their hoods.

Behind them, the townsfolk pursued, many choosing more dangerous paths of access to gain ground on the couple. Windshields smashed and boots met with car roofs. A few angry shouts came from those tearing clothes, or in some cases skin, on the rusting hulks. Each shout of pain was followed with a, "Praise Him."

Neither one spoke as they navigated the next thirty cars, before coming to three pickups with campers parked tightly bumper to bumper and a newer RV backed up against the block work, creating a vehicular wall of its own. Jason looked down the four vehicles' length, gauging the distance from the farthest pickup and the ever-closing people of Fellowship.

Too close.

He grabbed the door handle to the RV and lifted.

Nothing happened.

Jason jerked on it a second time yielding the same results. He kicked at the door repeatedly and on the fifth strike the latch gave way, swinging the door and inner screen door open. Shoving Melinda inside, he slammed the door closed and set the lock, adding the ineffective chain lock as well. "Look for something!"

Melinda stumbled into the shifting vehicle's kitchen area and looked for a towel, finding none.

Something slammed into the RV's side.

Jason reached up and smacked the skylight which doubled as the RV's emergency roof access. It popped free and he pulled himself up. Melinda looked up and through the square hole leading out as another series of smacks echoed through the mid-eighties recreational vehicle. She raised her hands, feeling blood trickle down her arm, tickling the inside of her elbow. Hands shot down and grabbed her forearms and she looked up into her husband's face as he hefted her up and through the ceiling. Breasts dragged painfully against the skylight's lip and she was out as far as her waist, though still kicking the air inside with her legs. Then she was free and on the roof with him.

Men and women stood on either side of the vehicle, while still others arrived.

"Come down," the black-haired man who'd stabbed the car's tire said.

Jason turned to her. "Up on the wall, we can drop to the other side." He turned and took a running jump at the wall, catching the top and pulling himself up.

Melinda followed suit, jumping for all she was worth and grabbing onto the lip with both hands.

Jason sat there, straddling the wall and stared into the expanse on the far side. A confused expression marred his face, and he cocked his head like a dog who's heard something unusual.

"J…J…Jason," she managed. Her grip started to slip.

Still he sat there, ignoring her, transfixed with whatever lay beyond the brick monstrosity they were navigating.

"J…Jason!"

Jason suddenly smiled broadly and laughed, putting his clenched fists in front of his eyes. Jerking his arms down for a second, he brought the right fist back up in a wicked arc, striking himself in the face, never looking from what lay beyond the wall. His left followed suit, striking his nose with an audible crack. "Hallelujah!" He started a new volley of blows against himself. "Hallelujah!"

Melinda dug in with her sneakers and pushed up, getting her chin over the lip and using it to help keep what purchase she had. Her gaze shifted from Jason to what the wall hid and her eyes went wide.

Someone grabbed onto Melinda's foot and jerked her free of the wall. She fell, smashing through the bubble-like rear window of a Pacer. Pinpricks of glass sliced along her entire body. Something in her right leg, the leg she'd been grabbed by, gave way and felt somehow loose under the skin. She lay among the mouse-nested mass of what had once been packages of diapers and stared up at her husband, who still straddled the wall and had already beaten his face into a bloody pulp which resembled a post-match boxer.

"The end," she managed. "The…end."

"Hah…yay…yuyah," Jason cried out.

A man's voice outside her limited vision asked, "What about him?"

"Leave him," a woman's voice answered. "He's seen the Lord's plan." Julia stepped into view. "Now, what about you?"

"The…end," Melinda said, trying to convey what she'd seen. "The end." She held out her bloodied hand in a feeble attempt to hold off whatever assault they had planned, a wad of glass falling from the already injured palm.

Two men stepped in, each carrying a length of wood.

Julia's face went gaunt. "Stop!" She shoved past them and grabbed

Melinda's hurt arm. "She's got the mark!" A sigh escaped from her. "Who will take this newest child of the Lord?"

No answer came.

Above them, Jason's self pummeling had slowed, fists swelling in time with his face. "A…yay…yuya," he cried out as best he could past broken teeth.

Melinda turned her own hands to see the mark the waitress had spoken of. The gash opening her hand had been sectioned by another slice, this time by the car's glass. The two together formed a crude representation of a cross.

"I," Julia said with pride, "will house you then."

"The…the end," Melinda stressed, tendrils of madness picking at what was left of her sanity.

The waitress leaned inside the car. "I know, Sister, I know. I climbed a tree as a little girl once and glimpsed…." She brought up a pair of kitchen scissors and drug them down the length of her scar. "I felt better once Momma had done it. More worthy of *His* love."

"I…don't," Melinda screwed her face up and tried again. "The… end."

"It's better this way," Julia continued, "if thine eye offends thee, pluck it out. If thy tongue offends thee…."

Gargled screams echoed through the afternoon.

"A…yay…yu…ya."

Behind the story...

For "Fellowship," this ended as more of a story "after" the story.

I chose Maine as the location for "Fellowship" because—as many of us are—I'm a huge Stephen King fan. I did more research than I really needed to for this and had great fun tormenting my loving couple.

A while after publishing "Fellowship," we went to Maine for the first time for a vacation. Now, a little history here: my son reads King, my wife reads King, and I read King. This was a fun trip taking the Stephen King tour, driving the area where *'Salem's Lot* and *Castle Rock* supposedly existed.

Then our experiences took an odd turn.

We were in Dover-Foxcroft, Maine, and stopped for

lunch at the Nor'easter restaurant (*now closed*). The place was quiet, almost too quiet. Everyone in there really didn't seem to be engaging with anyone else and they all ate with damned near funereal reverence. I kept looking around, a bit baffled by how familiar everything was. This was not a good feeling. Hollie felt it too and kept commenting she was sure we'd been there before even though this was our first trip to Maine. About that time Josh reached over and picked up the stainless-steel napkin dispenser and asked me if I wanted to hurl it at someone.

My jaw dropped and all three of us kept looking around. This place was *exactly* how I described the restaurant in "Fellowship."

Once we finished our lunch we continued east into Milo, then north on 11. About a half hour into driving north, we realized we hadn't seen a car in either direction, causing more uncomfortable laughter. At one point we pulled over to handle the needs of the body and saw a rock with a painted "You can't get there from here" on the front.

More uncomfortable laughter and a photo or two later, we were back on the road.

Sometimes "*odd*" finds you.

1865

Dew evaporated in morning sunshine, leaving the Virginia landscape blanketed in knee-high fog. Captain Gregory Danfield took a sip of the makeshift "coffee" confiscated from a farm five miles back. Powdered okra seed served as a pitiful replacement, but he still managed to choke down the final swallow. In the distance, a few scattered shots rang out and signaled the start of another day full of bloodshed. From his troop's location, more than two miles' worth of fields and homes were visible, cut from forested landscape.

"Sir?"

Captain Danfield turned to his second in command.

"Yes, Sergeant McKay?"

"Orders from Grant." The man's beard, a scraggly excuse for a rat's nest of hair, rested to the left of his collarbone and obviously hadn't been trimmed in more than a season.

"Let's have it."

Sergeant McKay eyed the tin of steaming okra-coffee by the fire. "We're to stop at the next plantation and hold the line. Word is the greybacks are setting fire to the city."

He cocked an eye. "They're burning Richmond?"

"Yup. You can see the smoke just over…there." He pointed to the south. Amidst the morning haze a darker patch rose in the distance taking on the appearance of a half-formed thunderhead. "Banes says this'll be the death rattle for the South. War should be over in under a month."

"Hmmm—homeward bound in April, huh?" The gossip's namesake caught his attention. "Wait. Who's Banes?"

"The private sent down the line to pass word."

Captain Danfield stood and pushed himself up from the squatted position he'd been in for the better part of a half hour. His knees creaked, reminding him of fewer years ahead of him than behind. "I should meet this Private Banes, then, shouldn't I?" He clapped the sergeant on the shoulder and walked back into the tree line. Just within the limited cover of a stand of pines were half a dozen men packing up what limited gear they possessed.

"Private Banes," the sergeant barked.

At the far end of the camp, a short figure stood with his back to everyone, relieving himself. He shook, turned and approached, buttoning his britches as he passed Danfield's men. The teen stood no older than sixteen and smooth-cheeked except for a few stray chin hairs yet to meet a razor. The youth's blues were relatively clean and free of patches.

"I see Grant keeps a clean house."

Private Banes flushed red. "Captain Danfield, sir. I have word from General Grant."

Danfield extended an open hand. "Let's have it."

The teen shifted uncomfortably. "Sir, I wasn't sent with written orders for you—only word of what the general said."

"And how do I know you're not a Confederate sent here to pass along misinformation?" Danfield caught sight of Sergeant McKay struggling to stifle a grin.

"I was told to remind you about…." The private drifted into silence.

The captain sighed, patience growing thin. "Out with it or I'll have McKay shoot you where you stand."

"To remind you about your dad catching you riding a Dutch girl in Maywether."

Sergeant McKay burst into laughter. "Captain Danfield and a whore?"

It was Danfield's turn to blush at the statement.

Private Banes went on. "The sawbones knows you and said you'd know my words as truth."

He took the teen by the shoulder and led him away from the men. "What is this doctor's name?"

"Cauldwell, sir. Benjamin Cauldwell."

A smirk crossed his face at the mention of the name.

"Sir?"

"Yes, private?"

"What's the big deal with your pa catching you bedding a whore?"

He released the teen and crossed his arms. "Because my father is a minister. Doc Cauldwell treated me after I got the lashing of a lifetime. I swear his salve burned worse than the licks I took."

"So…so was it worth it?"

"Worth what?"

"The whore."

"Every lick." Danfield stepped over to his own bedroll and took to the task of packing. "What are your orders from here?"

The private stood straight. "You're the end of the line for delivering new orders, sir. I'm to stay with you until you either have word to send to General Grant or I'm ordered back to his regiment."

"So, I'm stuck with you." Danfield licked his tongue against grime coated teeth. He looked back at the men. "Pack up, we leave shortly."

An hour later Danfield and his eight men skirted the edges of fields with Banes leading the captain's mare. Caution kept them to the last vestiges of high grass after a winter full of snow. Three fields later they met up with Creighton Road and followed the muddy way to the nearest plantation. Two ruts separated woods from cornfield and a lynched body hung from an oak. The man swung slowly against a gentle breeze, wearing only soiled trousers. He'd been white, though a day or more of exposure to the elements and birds looked to have taken its toll, leaving the corpse a mottled blue-gray and eyeless. Lidless sockets stared down at the men. The word "SECESH" was carved across the man's chest, blade marks digging so deep that ribs shone through.

Sergeant McKay took the opportunity to roll a cigarette. "Looks like we're not the first Union troops through here."

Private Banes paled and stared at the corpse swinging fifteen feet from the ground. "But to carve 'Sec…sec….'"

"Sess-esh. Like secessionists. Greybacks." McKay looked over at Danfield. "You sure this sprout is one of ours?"

Banes ignored the age jab. "To carve 'secesh' into his chest?"

"He is a secesh," the burly man said matter-of-factly. "He's down here on Confederate soil and probably did something to piss one of us off."

Meyer signaled an all-clear and the troop started down the road. Someone yelled, "Shit!"

Everyone stopped, drew weapons and pointed in different directions, at the ready. Seconds ticked off with no assault and Captain Danfield looked back to the soldier bringing up the rear, Jonah. The soldier stood below the hanged man, staring up at him with awe.

"Sorry, sir."

"Keep it down. We don't have to let the entire countryside know where we are, now do we?"

"Captain," the soldier said around a mouthful of chew, "He's alive." He pointed with the end of his barrel up at the man. A handful of seconds passed and the secesh's feet twitched, one kicking out in a lazy half-kick in search of purchase. Jonah pulled his knife free and started toward the tree.

"It's just death twitches. We've all seen them before."

"No, sir, it ain't." Jonah stared up and the secesh moved a second time, motions apparently agitated by their conversation.

"Leave him," Danfield said in a low voice. "Move out."

Neither Jonah nor Banes moved to follow.

Danfield looked back at them. "Do I have to remind you about the penalty for refusing an order?"

"But, sir," Jonah pressed, "Leaving him up there just goes against God."

"If we cut him down, we look like seceshes, too." Rather than directing his attention on Jonah, he looked to the teen. "Do you want to be accused of being a Confederate sympathizer?"

The private's eyes widened. "N-no."

Danfield moved his gaze over to Jonah. "Do you want to let any of our troops that might be down this road know you considered helping someone they took a lot of time and effort to string up?"

Anger blazed as Jonah stared back at him. Teeth gritted, he managed, "No…sir."

"Then leave him alone." The captain took on a less oppressive stance. "If there's no troops at the house, I'll put you on first patrol. I can see where a well-placed rock would be a blessing to the man."

Jonah hesitated a handful of seconds before responding with a cursory, "Okay." He continued to stare at the man, mottled and bruised skin appearing as a type of camouflage. Encrusted empty sockets stared down to where he stood. The secesh's jaw sat off center from the noose's pull and what few teeth remained in the man's mouth ground together awkwardly.

The captain spoke softly so only Jonah heard. "Then as I said, let's go."

All nine walked along the ridge between the two ruts hoping to avoid the spring mud. Smoke rose from Richmond and filled the southern half of the sky. Each man watched the black curtain thicken. An occasional boom shook the air as cannons, miles distant, ripped into what flame hadn't yet laid claim to. Nary a sound came from the woods to their left and the men's fingers rested nervously on triggers.

"Banes, come back here a moment," Danfield said as they approached the edge of the woods.

The private slowed until he paced the captain step for step.

"Any news about the cracker line? My men haven't had much more than scraps to eat in over a week—and those we scrounged for."

Private Banes' hand dropped to his pistol as a rabbit tore from the corn field, darting past their line before disappearing into the woods. "I…." He took a moment to compose himself then began again. "Food stuffs are coming down the line soon and we'll all be enjoying biscuits and fat-back for cooking."

Danfield pursed his lips together in a tight frown. He'd heard the same tongue waggling from everyone the troop came across for the last month. "Then I guess it might be a good idea to hope the previous patrol didn't empty out every tin in the house."

McKay, now on point, motioned for everyone into the trees. They did, each cringing at the sounds of winter-dried twigs and leaves as they crunched underfoot. Danfield squat-walked his way to the crouching sergeant. The woods abruptly stopped teen feet ahead, leaving a cornfield identical to the one on the other side of the drive. A hefty glob of spit shot from the man's mouth as they looked at treetops four hundred yards distant framing a plantation house roof.

"That's a long way to hoof it out in the open," Jerod McKay said around a fresh lip full of tobacco. "Even with the stalks still standing it wouldn't be nothin' for a single man with a Springfield to just pick us off."

He nodded past McKay to a small cluster of trees near the halfway point. "What about the apple trees?"

"What about 'em?" The captain and sergeant exchanged a knowing look.

"Banes."

"Sir," came the whispered reply from behind them.

"I want you to take up position in those apple trees. Climb one, check for opposing forces, then signal us if it's safe to advance." Captain Danfield pulled out a large sliver of mirror acquired from a house a few weeks before. "Two flashes close together means it's safe. Three close together means stay put. Got it?"

Nerves visibly bit at the teen's resolve. "But why—?"

"Because you're the smallest of anyone here and will be harder to see…and because I said so." Danfield let his voice take on the same tone used with his children back home. "Now move it, son, before you get a bayonet in the backside to speed you along."

Banes huffed twice then moved from cover and into the corn stalks. He kept low and soon all the men could make out was the top of his hat popping up every so often to gauge where he was compared to where the grove of apple trees stood.

Sergeant McKay scoffed. "Smallest, huh?"

"After having my men die one after another, I think it's only fair to let one of Grant's pets have a chance at playing fox. Don't you?"

Banes' hat popped up again about fifty yards to the right of his goal and vanished just as quickly.

McKay spat another wad of brown juice. "When I was a pup we

called that prairie dogging." He nodded to the field. "Playing hide and fetch out in my pappy's wheat."

Danfield snapped his fingers twice, getting everyone's attention. "He's there."

A handful of minutes passed with no response. The Gideon brothers wagered Banes' lifespan once the largest of the trees started shaking as the private scaled it, creating a huge dark shadow in the middle of the tree's skeletal fingers. Then from the top of the branches a flash of light. Then another. After a pause the paired winks of light repeated…and again a third time.

Sergeant McKay slid past the captain and led the men into the corn. "Think Banes is smart enough to stay up there until we join him?"

"Probably not."

Meyer tied the captain's horse to a tree far enough in the woods to not be easily noticed and brought up the rear of the eight-man line.

The only practical reference point Danfield could use for direction was the smoke from Richmond. Even with the wind keeping the flames pushing south, the air tasted of soot. Pasty stalks, picked clean at the last harvest made a shushing noise as he brushed past. Twenty minutes passed for all the men to cross the same distance as Banes spanned in less than ten. They moved as a long, blue snake, taking more time and moving slower because of the noise they made.

A ruckus sounded ahead of the captain just as he breached the line where corn and fruit tree met. He saw a girl—twelve, maybe thirteen, but not as old as his own Flora—jabbing a pitchfork at a stone-faced Sergeant McKay. One look at the torn and bloodied remnants of her nightgown told what the plantation's previous "guests" expected as hospitality. The girl jabbed the fork with wicked accuracy, snaking a crimson line down his second in command's forearm. Danfield watched her glare go from McKay's face to his arm. She gripped the bottom of her fork's handle and shoved the business end up as hard as possible into the tree. Banes screamed as a tine caught a piece of his left buttock. Then the girl was gone, a wave of shifting corn shadowing her retreat.

William Gideon leveled his rifle, leading aim just ahead of the stalks' movement. The shooter's breathing slowed just as the captain's hand came down blocking both the rifle's hammer falling and sight of his target.

"She's just a child, William." Danfield looked at the Gideon brother. "Go after her and try not to traumatize the child more than she already is."

The bear of a man tore into the corn, angling to head her off before she made it back to the house.

"Banes, get down here."

The teen worked his way down from the tree, cursing under his breath with each movement of his bleeding posterior. He reached the ground and Danfield grabbed the private before he got firm footing the captain shoved him against the tree.

"What happened here?"

An innocent expression washed across the private's face. "I don't know, sir."

"Hog spit."

"Captain," McKay said as he knelt and placed a palm against a patch of disturbed earth, "she's been here for a while."

"Ain't true," the private said, voice raising. "She come up on me in the tree and was tryin' to kill me when ya'll showed up."

The sergeant looked up. "Ground's still warm from where she lay…" he flicked some loose dirt on a darker patch, "and bled."

"I didn't have nothin' to do with that. There weren't time for none of that. You know that!"

Danfield squeezed the private's chest harder against the trunk, causing the teen to wheeze. "Then tell me what you did have time for. The truth," he said through gritted teeth, "now!"

Banes swallowed and worked to get a full breath. "I got here and she was just a layin' like the good Lord left her just for me. She weren't…" he wheezed as Danfield moved his hand from chest to throat, "blinkin' or movin' or nothin'." The private shook his head as his face turned purple. "I just took a little peek and gave her a squeeze before I climbed the tree. She's a southerner, anyway. No harm done."

"She's a child." The captain's fist flew and knuckle crushed cartilage as Banes' nose angled off unnaturally before he dropped to the ground. The private sat there, holding his face.

"Captain," Sergeant McKay said, standing, "we should follow William. No telling who's at the house." He spat the wad of tobacco onto Banes' britches. "What should we do with him?"

"Take his guns and knife."

"Hey," Banes protested as the other Gideon brother kicked him in his injured buttock and unbuckled the private's belt.

"Bind his hands. I don't want him running off."

"Captain," Banes managed as his hands were jerked behind him. "You can't do this. I'm an official messenger sent by General Grant."

"And you delivered that message. I wonder how Ulysses would respond if I told him exactly what you did to that child."

McKay popped the private in the back of the head with one knuckle to drive home the point that Danfield wasn't the only person there wanting some swift justice.

"I didn't mean no harm. I mean, someone already done soiled her."

The captain's hand went to his revolver, only to have McKay stay his hand.

"Captain, I think it might be a good idea if you and the men caught up with William. I'll stay here…with him."

Danfield sighed. "I don't want any 'accidents,'" he said, staring right into his sergeant's eyes. "Best we all go together and decide what's to be done with him once we've settled in."

"I didn't do nothin' wrong!"

McKay turned and brought his knee up into the private's groin. "Another word from you, shit-heels, and I'll skin you slow." He hauled Banes back up and shoved him in the direction William went. "No one said to stop."

The group moved single-file through the corn. A constant whooshing sound echoed out in every direction. Overhead, clouds worked their way down from the north, leaving the group a wide sliver of sunlight in an otherwise murky sky. Trees bordering the house proper grew larger with every step and Banes continued to quietly protest his lack of guilt. Voices, raised in the heat of argument, reached everyone's ears though lacked enough clarity to be understood.

"…ill him…now!"

Captain Danfield recognized a few words and signaled the men to be at the ready and drew his own Navy Colt. A thunk sounded behind him and he turned in time to see Banes drop to the ground in a heap. McKay stood over him, obviously pleased with the pistol-whipping he'd just delivered and gave the captain an innocent shrug.

"Banes' looked like he was going to holler out."

The captain gave him a disapproving glare. His men fanned out and formed a loose firing line before advancing. Danfield gave the signal and they all pressed forward, exiting the cornfield.

William Gideon stood in a defensive pose with one hand on his holstered pistol and the other outstretched to a frail black woman wielding a wicked looking blade. Behind her skirts stood a boy no older than eight and the girl they'd seen at the apple trees.

"Ma'am," Danfield said as gently as possible, "you need to put the knife down. We don't mean you or yours any harm."

"No harm?" Venom seethed in her words. "You rape and burn." She jabbed the knife with each word. "Look what you done to Miss Elizabeth." She motioned to the blonde girl. "And you say you don't mean no harm?"

The boy cried, "Kill him, Milly! Kill that Blue Belly!"

William had enough, drew his pistol and walked within a handful of steps from her before pointing it at the maid's head. "At this distance this thing might blow your head clean off. Might even hit one of the children." He smiled a grin as cold as the winter they'd just endured. "Now we wouldn't want that, would we?"

She looked from his face to the scatter line of Union soldiers. Defeated, the knife fell from her hand and stuck into Virginia clay. She reached back, gripped each child and pulled them to her.

Danfield motioned for the men to fan out. "Name?"

The maid averted her eyes, choosing to look at the ground rather than at him. "Milly, sir."

He looked at the shuttered windows. "How many?"

"Six, sir."

"Slaves?"

"None, sir."

Banes staggered into the yard and asked, "So what are you, darky?" Dried blood covered the lower half of his face. The broad scab cracked as he spoke.

Milly stood a little straighter, set her jaw then looked the captain in the eye. "I'm free, sir. The Morgans set us free near two years ago."

"It's him," the girl whispered through a matted mess of hair and pointed to the private. "It's *him*."

Danfield kept his stern tone. "I see you, the boy and Miss… Elizabeth, is it?" He nodded to the girl and she leaned harder against Milly at the sound of her name. "What I don't see is another three people."

Milly gaze faltered.

"Where are they?"

Tears welled in the woman's eyes. "Two of your kind are in the cellar. Mistress Bethany's taken abed since last night."

Banes walked toward them, the length of rope binding his hands trailed as if a giant tail. "Why'd you put good Union soldiers in the cellar, nigger?"

McKay's rifle butt met the back of the private's knees, dropping him to a prayer position. "Enough of that or I'll plant you here permanently. Got that, sprout?"

"Damned Irish," Banes mumbled.

"The little bastard does ask a good question, though. Why are two soldiers in your cellar, Milly?"

"One's hurt and the other…the other ain't right. He's got the sickness."

"So you put two men, one sick and the other injured, in a cold cellar?"

"No, I didn't have nothin' to do with that. Major Warner did."

The captain looked along the line of shuttered first floor windows again. "And what of Mistress Bethany? I suppose she's pointing a rifle, ready to add another casualty to this war?"

Milly shook her head. "No, sir. She's taken abed. I already done said so."

"Where?"

"Sir, you can't—"

"Milly," he said gently, "I have no intention of harming your mistress or her children," he placed a hand on her shoulder, "or you, if I can avoid it. However, until I can confirm that there's no threat here, I'll have to keep the children with me."

"No!"

Danfield winced at the word. "Now, Milly, that's not a good word to use right now."

"Please, sir, for the love of God, just let them stay with me."

Cannon fire echoed throughout the valley.

"Sit." He motioned to the ground where they stood. All three complied, though the boy made a point to kick dust in Danfield's direction as he sat. "If what you've told me is true then we won't find anyone else. Correct?"

"Yes, sir."

"Then do I have your word that you'll not only stay here, but the children will as well while we search the premises?"

"You do, sir."

"Then I," Danfield squatted down, "offer you my word as a gentleman that unless I'm lied to or my men hurt, no act of aggression will fall on this house."

She nodded and clung to the children.

"Damnation," Jonah yelled from around the side of the house.

"McKay," Danfield said, "watch them," then with a wave in Banes' general direction, "and him." He stood and started towards the commotion. "They won't give you any trouble."

"And if Banes does?"

The captain rounded the corner. "Shoot him."

Both Gideon brothers were at the back of the house alongside Jonah. All three stared out around the far corner of the home.

Jonah looked back and said, "Captain, this may not be the best place to set up camp today."

"How so?"

He pointed around the corner to a dark heap taller than him. As Danfield approached, it looked like a massive pile of clothes just a few yards away from the wall of the Morgan home. Then the smell hit him.

Bodies.

Blue and gray were piled together, easily numbering over a hundred. Predators left raw nubs where bare feet and hands protruded from the heap. On the near side an effort to stack the dead like cord wood succeeded in keeping the pile from getting any closer to the house. Flies, early for this time of year, gave aerial assault in a feeding frenzy.

"Can you believe this, Captain?" William Gideon voice held a tone of amazement Danfield never heard from the man before. "A shot to the head for so many." He walked over to the edge of the pile. "I've never seen so many…but," he poked at a nearby body with the end of his rifle, "this doesn't make sense."

The captain chose to remain upwind of the site. "What?"

"A lot of these bodies have more holes than a rabbit warren." He popped the buttons free on another, exposing a pasty-white chest at least three days dead. "Shot in the chest but there's hardly any blood. Looks like someone might've used them for target practice. Most of these top ones've been tagged in the forehead." William tapped two of the nearest misshapen heads with a boot.

"Get out of there and check the rest of the property. McKay and I'll check the cellar." He used the statement as the perfect opportunity to retreat to where Milly and the Morgan children sat.

"McKay, cut Banes loose."

"Captain?"

"I need him."

The sergeant cut Banes loose then started to take off the teen's belt he carried as a bandolier.

"He won't be needing those."

Banes rubbed his wrists then gave a wink to Elizabeth before McKay shoved him forward. "March."

Danfield said, "Milly, you'll stay right here with the children. Correct?"

"Yes, sir."

He turned his attention to the private. "Banes, you're going into the cellar with us to secure it."

"Then I'll need a gun."

"No, you won't." He shoved the teen ahead of him. "Sergeant, if this soldier doesn't follow orders, you're to shoot him."

"Captain," Banes said. "C'mon now. You can't be serious. All of this because I peeked a girl?"

Danfield added, "in the gut."

McKay motioned for Banes to open the cellar door. "You heard the man; get going."

"But what if I'm shot?"

"What if? Now move it."

Banes opened the cellar and descended half of the dozen or so steps. "Sing out if you're friendly." No answer came and he eased down into the darkness.

McKay nudged the captain's arm. "You think it's a good idea letting junior out of sight?"

The two followed Banes into the cellar and were immediately assaulted with the all too familiar smell of decay. Shadows were heavy, few distinctions made visible by the rectangle of light streaming down the stone steps. A couple of feet ahead the private stood peering into the gloom.

"Christ," McKay managed and wiped his nose.

"There," Banes said low and pointed further under the house. A flickering glow, barely visible to their unadjusted eyes, danced against a rock wall.

The sergeant moved forward and brought his rifle to ready. He advanced past several brick pillars, glancing around each, then moving forward with the rifle. After the final pillar between them and the lamp glow McKay stepped out of sight for a moment then waved an all-clear sign.

Danfield followed, dreading the idea of leaving the comparatively fresh air at the stairs. Bins, usually full of winter necessities ranging from wood to water and jarred goods, sat half full of body parts. Feet, based on what he could see, made up the majority of the human refuse. Banes slowed and the captain ran into him then stumbled against the nearest bin. A rat squeaked a warning at Danfield's intrusion on the rodent's feast.

"Forward," he managed.

Past the last pillar they came upon a makeshift operating room. Several mirrors had been brought down from the house to better reflect the light. An operating area, converted from a canning table, lay stained with blood aged black. Atop it lay a soldier, eyes closed and moaning.

Banes asked, "He gray or blue?"

"Can't tell," McKay said. "He doesn't have a proper uniform."

"Blue," the soldier managed through cracked lips. He coughed and a sticky wetness pooled on his belly. "Bastards left me."

"I don't understand," Danfield said and leaned over the man. The soldier soiled himself at some point and the smell did nothing to alleviate the nausea threatening to overwhelm the captain.

"They thought it was funny." Light from the solitary lamp flickered.

"What was funny?"

"Warner and his men…gut shot me and left me for the rats."

"This Warner, is he a greyback?"

"No," Banes piped up, "he's Union. I was supposed to get word to him, too, but couldn't find the regiment."

The captain looked around. "What about this other soldier Milly says is down here—the sick one?"

"Dead, sir. Warner tossed him back in the cell, yonder."

One rodent chased another across the dirt floor, skittering past Danfield's boot.

"Captain," the soldier said, "I don't want my last breaths down here in the dark. Take me out."

McKay passed Captain Danfield his rifle and helped the soldier sit up. Taking an arm, he shouldered the man. Banes took the other arm, and they dragged him as gently as possible across the cellar and up, into the light. The soldier cried out when they ascended the stairs.

Danfield stayed by the table and gripped the rifle, staring back into a cell made from boards. Beyond it something moved. Something significantly larger than any rat. Another rodent appeared as if from thought and shot forth from the cell, squeaking in terror. A mental tally of Milly's accounting left every person accounted for…providing the maid was being honest. Soldiers as cruel as what Warner's troops appeared to be were men he preferred not to deal with alone in a dank cellar. The captain backed out of the room, keeping the rifle trained on the area where the noises were loudest until sunlight fell on his back.

Back topside, Danfield saw the soldier resting against the side of the house with Milly and Elizabeth attending to him. Only now, in the daylight, was the extent of the soldier's beating revealed. Blood flowed from the soldier's wound, a kind of dark crimson that only comes from deep in a man's body. The side of his head looked the shape of a fall melon, especially with one eye swollen near shut from some kind of a beating. Three fingers on the man's hand bent backwards at an obscene angle, now useless. Banes stood at the top of the cellar steps, absent his watch dog, McKay, and puffed a pipe to life.

"I can't believe you're still drawing air, Mister Joles," Milly said while propping the man up. "Not after the beating they done to you."

The captain walked to the far side and crouched down, choosing a place by the man where he could still see the private. "Tell me, soldier. What did you do to have such a punishment placed on you?"

"I…I had the—" A coughing fit took hold and blood wet the man's lips.

"He said, 'no,'" Milly answered for the soldier. "Fighting was bloody here for what seemed forever. Devil sat the shoulders of both sides when they fought. Mister Morgan says to close up all the shutters and for everyone to stay indoors. I do it. Warner's men took hold of the house after the second day, and I hid the children in our shack. The Morgans did what they was told the first day. It was that night when the blue bellies found the whiskey stashed in the cellar."

Elizabeth kept hold of the soldier's arm, making a point to avoid his broken hand.

Milly went on. "That night they locked Mister Morgan in the attic and took to havin' their ways with Mistress Bethany."

Danfield saw the girl bite her lip. "Milly, maybe this isn't—"

"She was so brave, sir. She endured it and tried to stay quiet, but Mister Morgan knew what they was doin.'" Her voice turned to a wail of despair. "He beat on that door all night. The soldiers outside got riled and by mornin' were ready to serve Warner to the Virginians."

"Thirsty," Joles rasped.

"Elizabeth," Milly said and gently touched the girl on the shoulder, "go get Mister Joles some water…from that pitcher inside the house."

"I'll send Sergeant McKay with her." He stood and realized the missing sergeant still hadn't returned. "Speaking of which, where is he?"

"Last I saw," Banes said around his pipe, "he took to his heels into the corn."

"I'm sorry," Milly said, "I tried to keep the children with me, but young Thomas is headstrong. He took off into the field."

Danfield furrowed his brow and listened to the volley of shots fired out every few seconds. Some were miles away; they didn't concern him—it was the increasing number of reports echoing closer as the day wore on. "Damned fool boy's going to get himself shot. Gideon!" Then to clarify which one of the brothers he wanted, added, "William!" The big man came around the corner holding a dipper of water.

Milly's eyes went wide. "No!" She stood, letting the soldier's head drop to the ground, and slapped the ladle from William's grasp. His hand knotted into a fist and drew back to deliver a blow. She cowered, waiting for him to deliver the blow. "You can't drink from the well!"

"Well why the hell can't I?"

"It's cursed, sir! This whole damned area's cursed."

A laugh escaped Danfield. "Cursed? You mean the water's bad?" A more somber tone followed. "That's what you were going to give this soldier?"

"No. I was going to give him rainwater we collected."

"Captain—"

"William, go tell the men to stay away from the well. If any of them drank from it, have them retch it up and drink something hard. Milly," he said, turning his attention as the Gideon brother trotted back around the side of the house, "is there any more whiskey stashed around here?"

"No, sir. Not a drop. What the men didn't drink for fun the doctor used."

"I need to know what happened…now."

"Milly," Elizabeth said, her voice barely audible over the early spring breeze, "Mister Joles really needs some water."

The freed servant looked back to her ward.

"Miss Elizabeth," Captain Danfield said as friendly as possible, "go get that man some water."

"Captain, I'll go with her," Banes offered.

Danfield's revolver was out of its holster, beaded in on Banes and cocked in less than a heartbeat.

Milly and Elizabeth watched and waited for the deafening boom to add to those peppering the landscape. Banes' hands slowly came up in a position of submission.

"Miss Elizabeth," Milly said, "Go get Mister Joles his drink. You'll be fine. Mister Danfield and I—"

"Captain Danfield," he corrected.

"Captain Danfield," she relented, "and I have us some talking to do."

"Tell her she can clean up," he said under his breath.

"…and Miss Elizabeth…." Milly walked over to her and whispered something in her ear. The girl looked over to him, gave a little nod then disappeared around the front of the house. Milly returned, absentmindedly wringing her hands together.

"You seem a goodly man, sir."

"I have a daughter about her age, Milly. All I want is to go home."

"I understand, sir. I have words for you," she pointed at Banes, "but not for his ears."

Danfield crossed his arms. "Just speak."

"Warner kept Mistress Bethany in a bedroom while all this fighting was going on. Made my Isaac, George…all the men folk here gather bodies and pile them on the side of the house." Another volley of rifle cracks sounded a few hundred yards distant and Milly cringed. "Said no soldier could crawl up on this position and play possum if there weren't no bodies out there in the first place. All the men folk come in covered in blood…other stuff too, smelled like they'd done rolled in stagnant water. Pater come down with it first, sweatin' like he was a shovelin' coal for a week."

Thunder boomed overhead and the band of clear sky between cloud and smoke closed to little more than a sliver.

"Wait. There is a sickness here?"

"We tended him as best we could, but I'm the housemaid. I don't live in the shacks with my Isaac and boys."

"Shit."

"Isaac said he died that night." Her hands clenched and rubbed each other faster. "But then early the next morn Isaac saw him out at the…what do you call a pile of bodies, sir?"

"The pile," he offered. "Go on."

"Isaac saw him out at the pile that evening eating—oh God, save us all, eating the dead." Her lip quivered as a child's would when scolded. "Isaac called out to him and tried to make him stop, but Pater bit at him like a dog. He shoved Pater and he done lost his footing and fell into the well."

Danfield felt his stomach tighten.

"Isaac said not to tell no one because they'd say he'd done it on purpose. So we kept quiet about it. All the men camped here started getting sick, sweatin' and a cryin' out for their mommas. Better 'n fifty died that first night. Others weren't so bad and still went out to fight. A few come back carried by others who didn't drink from that Devil's dipper."

"Walk with me." Danfield looked over her head to where Banes strained to listen. "Banes, get over with the rest of the men. Pronto." The private pulled the pipe from his lips and trotted after William.

"I can't, sir. Someone needs to keep an eye on Mister Joles."

"He'll be fine. Your Miss Elizabeth will be down momentarily."

They walked around the front of the house and stood at the open door. Inside looked like any one of the other houses looted over the last few years: anything of value missing and the majority of whatever was left broken or abused in some fashion. A faint hint of urine wafted in the air, leaving the captain grateful they still stood outside on the porch. Danfield shook his head in disgust and pointed to a small row of shacks on the far side of the home.

"Which one's yours?"

Milly pointed to the nearest, and largest, of the shacks, measuring maybe fifteen feet on a side. "Mister Morgan gave it to Isaac and me because we never gave him no trouble."

"Where is Isaac?"

"Gone. Cursed."

He took off his hat and slapped it against one thigh. "I'm getting sick of hearing about curses, Milly."

Wind carried the screams of men, not too far distant, dying. Both looked to the south where the skies over Richmond went from a muddy brown to dark charcoal. A heavy rumble rolled over the landscape, its sound not distinct enough for either to identify as thunder or yet another explosion from the city.

"That third night—last night—that's when it really started. Just after supper a bunch of blue bellies…sorry, sir—"

"Go on," Danfield said, ignoring the insult.

"Those that died of the sickness got back up as if the Angel of Death wouldn't have them. They were all through the camp." She pointed back to the shacks. "Just at the edge of the corn. I weren't out there but I heard the screamin' then the shooting started. Reminded me of Tuckahoe on a Saturday night with all the whoopin' and hollering. Mistress Bethany ran out to the young'uns. Warner followed her and found 'em."

Glass from a second story window shattered in time with a gunshot fired from somewhere out in the corn.

"That's Mistress Bethany's room, Mister Danfied, sir!"

He grabbed her by the arm. "Finish it."

Milly strained against the captain's grip then let her shoulders sag in defeat. "They shot 'em. Gray and blue. Fired until their hog legs clicked dry and still they pulled triggers! Warner drug Miss Elizabeth back into the house by her hair. Mistress Bethany and young Thomas ran in behind and closed the door."

Danfield looked at the door beside him and noticed a trio of bullet holes in the wood.

"Warner took to acting like a crazed bull. He was sure all this was some Virginian trick to get his men to kill each other. He had Mister Morgan brought down and threatened to…undo Miss Elizabeth's youth if he didn't tell them where the Gray Backs were hiding. Mister Morgan couldn't tell him nothin' because none of us knowed nothin'." Tears cut rivers along the dust covered woman's face. "That demon-made-flesh asked Mister Morgan if he wanted to see that. Mister Morgan said no."

More shots rang out and William appeared out by the shacks.

"Noise over here, Captain."

"Get your brother and check it out. Be careful."

"Tell him to aim for the head," Milly said.

"What?"

"Sir, please, just do it."

"Gideon," Danfield added as the brothers headed in the direction of the shacks, "take your shots at their brain pan."

William barked, "But Gray Backs ain't got no brains," then was gone, followed by his brother.

"They carved 'secesh' into his body trying to get him to talk. He weren't no secesh, sir. He didn't even go to war. With Thomas being so young he couldn't afford go to war." Her eyes darted to different places in the field where corn stalks moved. "That ain't the wind, sir."

Danfield's gaze followed hers. The breeze did blow most of the stalks, but some, some shifted to and fro against their brethren. A tightness clenched his belly.

"They cut out his eyes."

Memory flashed to the man hung at the head of the Morgan's drive.

"They cut out his eyes then played with him, shoving him back and forth while Warner took...." Milly looked into the house, expecting to see the girl. "Took something no man has a right to take from a child. That's when they shot Mister Joles. He'd been raising a lot of hullabaloo about reporting what the men had done to Mistress Bethany. Said no good Christian man would ever think of such a thing. He drew down on Warner when the major threatened Miss Elizabeth and one of the other men gut shot him. They drug him down to the cellar and left him there with the surgeon."

Danfield kept looking to the shacks, waiting for that first shot from one of the Gideons. None came. Only more screams echoing across the field from a multitude of places. Clouds and smoke closed the gap, matching light to the mood.

"After Warner...was done with Miss Elizabeth, he took to beating on Mister Morgan. That's when Miss Elizabeth done run off into the night.

"Smart girl."

"Warner had two of his men drag him out and string him up. He said to be sure that Mister Morgan was still kickin' when they left him."

"Shouldn't Elizabeth be back down by now?"

"Sir, she might be taking more time at the basin." The understanding fell heavy between them.

"Is that the whole story?"

"The men that took Mister Morgan out last night never came back. A few showed up on the door from the camp all chewed on and such. Warner wouldn't let 'em in. Told 'em to stay in the shacks with the slaves 'til morning. He and the five others he had inside took off at first light. Heard them call out at the shacks, but I didn't see a soul step out. They took off on foot towards the James place."

"I heard noises in the basement where we found Joles. Sounded like there were still a couple of folks down there."

"No one you'd want to see."

"So there are people there?" Danfield stood a little taller and shoved Milly.

"Not like you're thinking, sir! They're cursed, like the others out there in the field. Their souls is gone!"

Meyer cried out in pain, then follow it with a, "Son of a bitch!"

Danfield grabbed Milly by the wrist, drug her off the porch and around the side of the house.

Meyer stood with Jonah facing the now-standing Joles. A plug of flesh was missing from Meyer's right arm and he gripped the elbow just above the bloody wound. Jonah skinned his revolver and pointed it at the soldier's legs.

"Hold that shot, Jonah."

"But sir—"

"I said hold."

Jonah turned slow, now facing Danfield and Milly. She pulled hard against the captain's grip, but only succeeded in losing her footing and sliding to the ground.

"You said once they get like this, they've got this sickness…this curse?"

"He ain't Mister Joles anymore!"

"Joles. Sit back down."

The soldier took a shaky step toward Danfield.

"That's an order, soldier. Sit. Now."

Joles took another step.

"Jonah, put a shot in that man's heart."

Danfield's soldier lowered his pistol further. "In the heart, sir? I was just going to wing him."

"You heard me."

Jonah moved to a better position and pulled the trigger without hesitation. The hammer fell and a cloud of smoke followed the ear-popping report. A hole appeared in the soldier's back and a thunk sounded against the side of the house with a black pit showing where lead met wood.

The soldier staggered off balance, teetered, then fell onto his back.

"Should be more blood," Jonah remarked as he stared at the fresh bullet hole.

"I'm bleeding enough for both of us," Meyers said as he tried to stop the flow of blood running down his arm.

Joles kept moving, first as twitches that looked like death spasms, then with more intensity, rolling onto his side and pushing himself up to his feet like a toddler just learning to walk. He turned to Jonah and took a shaky step.

"Again," Danfield said, feeling the first serious signs of fear bead along his forehead. "In the heart."

Another shot fired; its echo rebounded off the side of the house with an ear-ringing boom. A second hole, an inch to the side of the first appeared, and Joles staggered back but didn't fall.

Jonah cocked the pistol a third time. "What the hell is this, Captain?"

"The head," Danfield directed.

A third gunshot went off and the top of the Union soldier's head snapped back. A bloom of crimson spray across the grass and the bottom foot of the house. Joles' legs buckled and he dropped to his knees, eyes bulging from the concussive force. His head bent forward, chin meeting chest then moved no more.

"I'll be damned," Danfield said.

"We'll all be damned," Milly said, still pulling against the captain's grip.

"Pass the word, any shot you take needs to be between the eyes."

Jonah's gun hand shook but stayed trained on the now-immobile body.

"Jonah?"

The man looked up.

"I said pass the word. Get Meyer cleaned up too."

"That son of a bitch bit me!" Meyer gripped the wound itself, palm covering the exposed meat. "What in God's good name is going on here, Captain?"

Danfield ignored the question. "When I say pass the word, I mean pass it now, not later."

Jonah and Meyer vanished out of sight, heading to where their comrades were.

Another scream, high pitched and full of fear and fury came from inside. Milly took the opportunity to wrench herself free and ran for the house. Danfield followed, putting boot to dirt at a frantic pace. He passed the maid, ran through the door and scaled the steps two at a time. He ran head-long into Banes on the expansive second floor landing, each bouncing in a different direction.

Milly ran past the captain and jumped on General Grant's messenger, nails clawing at the soldier's face and digging gouges in his cheeks.

"Get her off me!"

Suddenly the maid's entire body went stiff. She leaned back and rolled off, landing on her back. The hilt of a knife jutted from her chest. Her mouth formed an exaggerated "O" as her hands gripped the hilt and held it steady.

Banes got to his feet. "Can you believe that, Captain?"

Danfield swung hard and connected to the teen's jaw. Teeth clacked together and the soldier dropped faster than Joles had a moment before.

"Miss…" Milly said, spittle already frothing red.

The captain nodded and pushed open the nearest door. Blood replaced paper and paint on the walls. Mangled remains of what had once been Elizabeth Morgan lay draped across the bed and straddled by a woman. The girl's torso sat hollowed out as the woman dipped in a hand to pull out another piece from her daughter. The lady of the house ripped a piece free and set to chewing flesh. Blood coated the Morgan woman from nose to waist and left Danfield with the impression that at some point the mistress of the house had rolled in her daughter's remains. Stench from sex with a metallic hint of blood filled the room, coating his mouth on the first inhale.

Danfield's hand went to his mouth in an effort to keep the morning's coffee down. His stomach refused and fluid spewed between splayed fingers, coating his beard and soaking into the deep blue coat.

"Captain," Sergeant McKay said coming into the house and up the stairs. "You okay? I heard shots." He'd seemed to have aged in the last thirty minutes, looking older than his twenty-nine years. "You won't believe the shit I saw out there. Things my nightmares couldn't fathom."

He started to wave the sergeant away, thought better of it and motioned him up as he wiped his face clean on a sleeve. McKay looked at Milly bleeding on the floor and the disoriented figure of Banes working to get to his feet. Then the soldier's eyes went to the open door.

"Don't," Danfield managed.

"Did he—"

"No…maybe…I don't think so."

Danfield drew his Colt revolver and stood in the doorway with a shocked McKay peering over his shoulder.

"By the Saints' tears," McKay whispered.

The woman straddling Elizabeth, obviously Mistress Bethany, got off the bed and stood on shaky legs. A blood-soaked nightgown clung to her, view giving a perversion of what the woman was in life. Danfield aimed and erased the woman's face with a pull of the trigger. Hair fanned out behind Bethany as the back of her head vomited pink matter. She fell, all but her feet hidden from view by the end of the bed.

Elizabeth's cheek twitched.

"That's what I saw out there," McKay said, pointing into the room. "They're walkin'. They can't be, but they are!"

"I know," Danfield said and adjusted his aim from where he'd shot the mother and beaded in on her child. His hand shook.

The sergeant stepped in front of Danfield, drew his own weapon and fired before the captain registered that he'd been saved that burden. "It's done, sir. The girl…she's at peace."

Danfield turned and went to Milly who looked on in horror.

"Mistress?"

Danfield shook his head.

"Miss…Ellie?"

Again, the captain shook his head, heart sinking at the name of endearment uttered from the Morgans' maid.

"Thomas?" The maid's eyes looked hopeful.

McKay took off his hat and the grim expression hung between them as answer. Milly's eyes glazed and the woman's breaths fell silent. Her chest heaved, strained twice to pull another breath, then went limp as death finally took her.

"Sir," Banes said and held his hands up. "I didn't do none of this."

Danfield pointed his gun and fired, tearing a healthy piece of outer thigh from the private. A fresh wound ran red just below where the girl stabbed Banes at the apple trees. "Run."

Banes clutched his leg and started down the stairs. "You can't do—"

Another shot left the captain's gun, splintering the banister rail.

The private quit speaking and half fell down the stairs before staggering out the door and disappearing to the left.

"What happened to the boy?"

"Same thing as what happened to the girl. I heard the boy scream, but by the time I got to him…." He left the rest to memory.

Both officers walked back into the bedroom, stepped past the crumpled form of Mistress Bethany Morgan and opened the window.

A fantastic view to the south showed the far side of the shacks, the trampled area of field where Morgan's men had camped and the field beyond. The Gideon brothers were nowhere in sight as Banes staggered past the shacks and into the clearing before stopping.

"Captain," McKay said as he motioned to the field beyond.

Dozens shambled toward the house, more than could easily be counted. Those closer showed the damage war took on their broken bodies.

Danfield leveled his pistol and fired off another shot. Dust poofed into the air about ten feet to the right of the private. The teen looked back, fear offering a death mask plastered across the soldier's face. He moved into the corn, blindly limping toward a cluster of corpses.

"Shouldn't the men have come with all this shooting?"

Danfield watched the dry stalks sway as if a great pale ocean. "I don't think they're my men anymore."

McKay pulled his head back in from the window. "Wind's shifted over the city. Fire'll be here by night. Maybe quicker when the fields catch. What should we do?"

Danfield grabbed a lamp, unscrewed the lid and started flinging oil around the room. McKay followed suit.

And Richmond burned.

Behind the story...

"1865" was written well before the resurgence of zombies, so think Romero's original trilogy rather than *The Walking Dead* universe. There are a few tales I could share regarding "1865," but I'm going to keep this one simple.

Every location for "1865" actually existed in my youth. This plantation was owned by my Aunt Connie and Uncle Robert. He was an avid Civil War collector and actually owned the diary of the man who owned the plantation during the War Between the States. It described watching the battles from the second-floor windows. The injured were given aid at the home.

When I was young, I lived there for a time with my parents. I had the pleasure of taking part in some basic excavation where the old slave quarters were (*then a cornfield*) before they burned down and found several bullets around the property which I still have to this day.

The apple trees in the cornfield were also there in the 1970s, as were the woods and entrance to the plantation where, in "1865," they find the twitching man hanged. A small cemetery sat behind the house.

Honestly, I could write about this place for hours, ranging from adventures to ghost stories. It burned down a while back and housing developments have popped up all around it. The remains of the home are still there…still for sale the last time I looked. The location was protected, and with a cemetery there, the last 3-5ish acres are probably a nightmare to navigate building on.

THE VESSEL

Jonah Quint stared along with the rest of the congregation at the kneeling form of Sister Helena as she laid hands on the fourth hopelessly crippled child of the night. Her body rocked in time with the speaker's rhythmic beat, keeping the televised audience enthralled by her healing abilities, and him personally by the mane of blonde hair cascading down her back.

"Camera two, tighten frame on the child."

"Gotcha, Jonah."

One of the fifteen monitors fanned out before the producers zoomed in on the thirty-something and her wheelchair-bound ward. The boy's twisted legs convulsed as Helena gripped his thighs. Tears flowed as the boy's face screwed into a rictus of pain. Without warning the child jerked out of his wheelchair and fell forward, leaning against the healer's shoulders. Helena grasped the boy's arms and stood, further straightening the formerly chair-bound child.

"Arise," Helena shouted.

Applause rang throughout the chapel and the chorus broke into one of the chosen hymns for the evening. Hands rose, clasping each other as one unbroken chain and attendees joined in the song. Three of the four camera crews paced the aisles catching tearful members in moments of prayer and rejoice while the fourth shot up from waist level to get the inspiring "Closer to God" angle.

"Roll credits." Jonah looked over at Karen Finch. "Get me archive footage from tonight's last fifteen minutes."

"Okay. Anything else?"

"Yeah. Fire the hairstylist."

Karen pushed back from the console and smoothed her skirt as she stood. "I thought you liked Helena's hair down."

"I do, and so does every other man out there, but she needs to be seen as the prophet we've built her to be."

"Prophet? You mean healer."

Jonah closed the distance between them, grasped the assistant producer by the arm and led her into back into the sound booth, jerking the door closed behind them. Before she could protest Jonah jabbed a finger right into her chest. "Listen…just close your mouth and listen. Helena's bought out the entire hour and a half following the closing interviews with tonight's saved. She's professed that we're on the verge of the End Times."

"Jonah," Karen took the hand that still jabbed at her and held it in both hands. "Prophets have been saying that for centuries. Many more popular than even the great Sister Helena."

"No."

"No? What do you mean, no? By simple popularity standings, she has less viewers than the—"

"I mean, no." He pulled away from her. "She's healed the sick, and prophesied—correctly I might add—nine events in the last month alone."

Karen opened the door. "Your career's on the line here. Be sure what you're doing is right."

"Of course it's right. We purchased the time just like anyone else."

Karen smirked. "Not right with the network," she pointed up with her pen, "right with *Him*. Are you serving the Lord or are you serving Helena?" Before Jonah could answer, Karen stepped out, closing the door behind her.

Below, Jonah watched the masses extricating themselves from pews and folding chairs, clogging the aisles like rainwater through a downspout. Grandparents, adults, teens and children all wore varying shades of white, reminding him of a white chocolate drink he'd had on the last tour.

"Big J!"

Jonah jumped at the booming sound coming from his earpiece. He keyed it and replied, "What?"

"Helena wants—"

"Sister Helena."

The tech cleared his throat, "Sorry, sir. *Sister* Helena requests your presence on stage."

"Ask her what for."

"Can't, sir. I have to try to get the parishioners back into the seats." An audible click sounded as the crew's newest technician changed channels. "Ladies and gentlemen, please take a moment for the needs of the body, but then return to your seats. Sister Helena has something special for each and every one of you."

A good portion of the crowd immediately returned to their seats while others worked their way to the restrooms. The few that continued toward the exits were met by ushers who whispered something which convinced each person to remain for the upcoming showing. In all, Jonah guessed there to be well over 950 attendees swirling their ways around the chapel's floor.

"Bigger," he mumbled as he exited the sound booth, working his way down the back stairs. "I told her we needed to build it bigger."

Jonah navigated the myriad of parishioners and through the "Staff Only" door which led below the floor and stage. The tunnel stood in direct contrast to the eggshell white walls and crystal chandeliers seen by the public. Here, not even whitewash splashed the concrete walls — only a rough gray cinder block and concrete maze of corridors wound their way under the Sunrise and Be Saved chapel. After two lefts and jogging his way along the hundred-yard shaft leading stage left, he emerged through a tight opening only a child could call an access point. A boom operator, nursing a cup of coffee before the next show, grasped his arm as he extricated himself from the makeshift stairway.

"Helena," he managed to blurt.

The operator finished another swallow of liquid caffeine and motioned with the half empty cup to the layers of white curtains.

"Helena?" Jonah shouted louder than he intended to and won the looks from the stage crew. His cheeks flushed and he walked into the curtains. Slit after slit was found and he stepped deeper into the folds. Thoughts of when he was a boy and would play in his grandmother's laundry as it dried on the line flooded forth, bringing a smile.

"Jonah, here."

Jonah turned slightly to the left and made his way through three more gossamer layers before arriving center stage. With the main curtain down and no less than a dozen layers on either side and behind them, he entered a makeshift room. Two giant spots glowed on the front curtain and filled their space with a softer, but still pronounced, light. That's where he found her. She stood behind her white glass-topped desk as she took off her earpiece, leaving the wire dangling along the cleft of her collarbone.

"We've got twenty minutes before you're back on air. Shouldn't you be in makeup?"

She smiled. "Are you saying you think I need makeup?" With a gentle pull, she drew out the leather chair, also stained white, and leaned forward, resting both arms on the seat's back. Her hair fell down, framing not only her face, but a surprising amount of cleavage from where he stood.

"No…no." He shifted his gaze, albeit reluctantly, away from his benefactor and squinted against the spotlight's illumination. "I mean that you're back on air in just a few and everyone," he returned to looking at her, "and I do mean 'everyone,' needs a little help when on camera."

"Not after tonight." Her smile continued, broadening slightly as she played with the hanging wire.

"There's no time for this. Let's get you ready." Jonah walked over to her and started guiding her to one of the slits in the side curtains. She stopped short of stepping through, putting both hands on his chest.

"Do you remember when we first met?"

"Helena," his voice dropped, "leave that for the P.R. to iron out."

"Do you?"

"Yes, Helena. I remember."

"Me barely out of my teens and doing whatever I could after that horrible marriage." She pushed against him, forcing a foot of distance between the two. "You taking me in, teaching me about everything from psychic cold readings to what most orbs actually are in spirit photography?"

Jonah backed another step, glancing nervously at the front curtain and thinking of the congregation massing just a few yards beyond.

"You remember, right?" Taking another step forward she pushed him back, watching Jonah first stumble, then manage to maintain his footing by balancing against the edge of the desk. "You remember about the half a million in donations that disappeared two years ago?"

"A quarter million," he stammered.

"Oh no. It was a cool half million." She placed a hand on his chest. "I *know* you took it."

Her smile appeared, to Jonah at least, more painted on at this close distance rather than actually there. "I didn't...."

Helena caressed the side of his cheek. "Oh, but you did. I know because I took the other quarter million." She pushed him harder, forcing Jonah off his feet and onto the desk. Following him, she opened the fold in her skirt, straddling him. "It's okay," she soothed, "you swore you were with me in this 'til the end." Her hands fumbled with his trousers, fanning the belt and reaching in to pull him free.

"I..." Jonah looked around in a panic, grabbing at her hands only to get them slapped painfully away. "No! We can't. Not with...."

"Just be quiet and hurry." Helena bent and kissed him, snaking her tongue between his lips as she stroked him to arousal.

Jonah watched, detached as she scooted forward and guided him under the skirt and into her. Instinct took over where decorum left off. He thrusted against her rocking, breathing in time with her and feeling her own passion draw him closer to climax.

"Matheson," she purred.

He faltered at the accountant's name.

Helena ground down hard on him eliciting an uncontrolled thrust from him. "I didn't say stop," she went on, picking up speed. "I know you put the travel notes in his locker." Another push had Jonah returning to sex's fluid motion.

"The police were getting too…ohhh." He lost his concentration.

"…too close. I know. That was number nine."

Jonah grabbed onto her hips, animal tension overtaking him. "I…wha…?"

"Number nine," she grinned and matched his rhythm. "Thou shalt not bear false witness against thy neighbor."

He stopped mid-thrust only to have Helena's motions continue him along.

"Stop."

The grinding continued, pressing his cheeks down painfully on what felt to Jonah like her day planner.

"Oh, no. Not until we're done." She rolled her hips and Jonah clenched his teeth. "You know he was stomped to death while in lockup that first night. That was my doing. I have—Oh God, that feels good." A chuckle escaped the healer. "There's number three."

"Helen," he switched to her actual name, something he hadn't done in years. "Talking about that while we're—"

"Say it," Helena cooed, "say it."

"Having sex."

"*Fucking*."

Jonah ignored the vulgarity of the word, though not the action, he bucked in time with her and felt the clenching of the forthcoming climax.

"Number three," she panted. "You know it…about not taking God's name in vain."

Realization of the statement about orchestrating Greg Matheson's death hit Jonah just as Helena's orgasm ripped through her. Short barks of passion loudly escaped and he tensed, imagining people, of which there were hundreds just a stone's throw away, were stopping their conversations and preparations in recognition of what was heard.

"Five minutes!" echoed throughout the building as one of the producers called out for the final countdown to air.

"Five minutes and you…" she convulsed again, impaling herself against him, "you're making this possible."

Jonah tried rolling onto his side to dislodge her, but she was firmly mounted and drawing him toward his own climax. His hands gripped her waist and held her as he bucked, spilling himself into her.

"Thank you," Helena whispered as she laid down on his chest. "That was the final three."

"Huh?" He pushed her to the side gently, taking the time to make sure that no evidence of their act was visible on the front of her skirt. Jonah stood and quickly tucked himself away and straightened his clothes.

"Four, obviously, seven and ten."

He ignored the statement and went about straightening the desk while tapping his own headset. "Geri, Helena's at her stage desk. Get makeup here right away and touch her up. Micah, switch to camera B and tell the choir that there's a change, we want to start the show with 'Love's a River.'"

"Four's an easy one," Helena said.

He glared at her. "Helena, get your head in the game. We're on camera in just a few minutes. This…" he stumbled for an explanation, "was just too many years of working together and nerves." Jonah attempted a smile while struggling not to catch himself in his zipper. "We'll…we'll get past this."

"Four's 'Keep the Sabbath Holy.'"

"Damn it, Helena!"

One of the six makeup artists stumbled through the same opening Jonah did, catching her heel on the curtain's hem. The artist flushed when she saw Helena's disheveled appearance, obviously certain of what the reason was.

Helena grabbed her blouse and ripped it open, exposing a lacy white bra tinged with red where the underwire portion met her ribcage. She gave a little scream and her stomach distended pushing out, grossly mimicking a hand pressed against a garbage bag. The healer's own hand reached up and caressed the depressions between the raised fingers inside her body. "Number seven I've waited years to know." The statement came out in ragged breaths. Bloody spittle spattered the glass desk, adding a ghastly shade of crimson to the peach lipstick she wore.

Jonah unconsciously grabbed the makeup artist's hand.

"If Tom was dead it wouldn't be worth any…" Helena doubled over, breasts swinging and the bra taking a decidedly redder tinge than a handful of seconds before. "Oh, I didn't expect it to hurt so much." She looked up at her audience of two. "Tom's in California living under a bridge somewhere and stoned out of his ever-loving mind. In six months he would've been dead. I just got…lucky." With the last word, she stared deliberately at Jonah's groin.

"Helena, what in hell—"

"Hell? You have no idea about Hell!" The healer forced herself to stand upright, hand impressions increasing in number and size, stretching themselves between her skin and ribs, pushing upward to cup her left breast in a fashion nature never intended. Skin darkened as it separated from the fascia and lifted. Her eyes rolled back into her head, though through ecstasy or agony was left to each of the onlookers to decide for themselves.

"Aids," she spat between huffing gasps for air. "A stupid needle prick nearly ruined everything." Another handful of gasps followed as one of the hands pressed its way downward, disappearing under the skirt's waistline and doubling her over again a second later. "H-hard to believe it was a different needle prick that 'saved the day.'" She moaned, feet spreading to allow the hand its passage. "Number…seven…adultery." Helena moaned again, letting out a long tone through her nose, blood trickling out and weeping down to the corner of her mouth. "The bastard wouldn't give me a divorce."

Jonah staggered back, clenching the artist's hand harder until the pressure broke the employee's shock and she screamed long and hard at the sight before her, yet somehow stayed rooted to the spot in terrified witness to the horror before her.

"You," Helena looked at her producer, "you were the key." She licked some of the blood from her lips. "You watched me for years. Played with that noodle while watching the security cams in my dressing room. You—" Her words choked off and she convulsed, hips rocking in mimic of what Jonah physically experienced only moments before. A gush of blood dropped from inside her skirt, chunks of what could only be organ material lay against the white satin heels.

Jonah muttered "Dear God!"

"A god…yes. But not…not—"

She looked up, eyes bulging and bloodshot as a subdermal hand forced its way up from under her collarbone across the throat and came to rest along the side of Helena's jaw, cutting off any further words or air. More hands pushed to the surface, stretching the skin everywhere visible, leaving the surface appearing bloated and writhing. One eye fell free of the socket and a single fingertip slid out of the orifice, exploring the lashes in an obscene fashion.

Without warning, all the hands jerked the standing body. Every visible inch contracted. Again this happened, and the internal structure vanished, leaving an upright sack of flesh bearing little resemblance to the faith healer. Her abdomen concaved, drawing in where bones should be, but allowing the outer edges to remain. Skin stretched, then darkened the surfacing bruises. Dermal layers split, the cracks opening further along the breastbone and working downward to where the pubic bone once was. A crevice formed, separating and flapping open as if dried leaves in an autumn breeze.

Light shone into the tunnel that was once Helena, the endless void filled with things crawling toward them, things with segmented eyes and mandibles, yet bearing jutting signs of excited humanity and hands—hands on arms, on legs, one even covering itself in as a makeshift codpiece.

A hand reached out toward the duo and Jonah stumbled back, accidentally pushing the makeup artist forward. The hand gripped her forearm and pulled her inside Helena. Vertigo flooded his perception as he watched the woman fall into a different reality.

Falling deeper.

Deeper still.

Until there was nothing more than a pinprick of shadow awash in waves of gripping appendages.

"Annnnnnd we're on!"

The curtain rose to the makeup artist's screams. White fabric turned red throughout the chapel and a new chorus, one of tortured pain, broke into a song as old as life itself.

Jonah was beyond screaming.

He bore witness, along with ten million viewers, to what the Vessel offered.

Behind the story...

Horror erotica anyone? I wrote "The Vessel" with the understanding that true horror erotica can only exist with equal parts of both.

I remember reading Clive Barker's story "Sex, Death and Starshine," and being both aroused and horrified when the protagonist is being fellated and realizes the woman isn't coming up for air. I found the story disturbing in more ways than one and wanted to see if I could write something along those lines.

The original idea for this came about during one of the never-ending religion sex scandals. All I really had to do was put a Lovecraftian twist on it and let the characters have at it.

TROPHIES

Deputy Derek Mulkens looked out from under his hat at the gloomy March afternoon. Sheets of rain fell, obscuring visibility beyond more than a couple of blocks. The light was gray. The rain was gray. Even the colors seemed somehow muted, adding to the overall washed-out effect.

"Even the Goddamn stoplights," he muttered.

Sheriff Goddard walked past him, her ponytail looking more like a rat's tail in the weather, and opened the patrol car driver's door. "What's that?"

"I was just talking to myself."

"Well, now you can talk my ear off," she said with a smirk and slid behind the wheel. "Get in."

First, being chosen as Sheriff Erin Goddard's number one was rough enough. She was the first female sheriff to ever run the county. Second, and more disturbing—to him at least—was the fact she'd gone to school with his son. Here he was, less than a decade from retirement and some blonde-haired kid who used to cheer for his son on the football field was his commanding officer.

"Fuckin' Murphy's law," he muttered, pulled his hat off, and got into the cruiser. Her perfume, which he was sure she bathed in, filled the car.

"So, tell me about the stoplights."

"I..." Derek sighed, resigned to the fact that she wanted conversation this morning. "I was just saying that everything seems gray today—even the lights don't seem as sharp."

Erin—she'd insisted he call her that when it was just the two of them despite his protests—leaned over the wheel and looked out at the town. "Hmm." She started the car and pulled out onto the street. "Maybe it's just your mood."

"What's so important that we're taking off so close to clock-out time?"

Her smirk returned. "Got a lead on the Boogeyman."

Derek resisted the urge to roll his eyes and failed. "Seriously? There's enough to do here without creating serial killers to chase." He waved a hand. "Granted, it's a small town, but—"

His sentence was cut short as the sheriff jerked the wheel hard onto 2nd Street. The deputy's cell phone dug into his butt cheek, making him shift uncomfortably.

"Ghost gray," she said.

"What?"

"Ghost gray...the day."

"Okay." God, he hated small talk.

"Funny. Did you ever wonder if a ghost dreamt they were alive?"

"Boogeymen and ghosts?" A snide tone followed. "Should I call the news now or later?"

"I get it," she said, all earlier signs of a good mood now gone. "You don't want someone half your age outshining you. But this killer is real."

"Age has nothing to do with it." *Well, not much,* he corrected himself. "You've been on this kick for a while now and there's logical explanations for every clue you have in that little file in your desk drawer." He pulled his phone out from the uniform's back pocket and tossed it on the dashboard.

"Such as?"

She braked for a stoplight.

"Such as the missing teens. It might suck, but we're right in line with the national average for missing or dead teens. Kids run away or get mixed up with a bad element and just fall off the map for years… sometimes forever."

Erin's eyes narrowed as she watched a car shoot by on a hard yellow. "And the children before them?"

"Where are we going, anyway?"

She glanced over at Derek. "To my lead. Now, what about the children?"

"There's no easy answer for that one. Child abductions happen. Murders happen."

"So, which were these?" They weaved through traffic as motorists automatically slowed to a crawl at the sight of their patrol car. "Damn," she said, "I hate it when civies do this."

"They just don't want a ticket."

"Ticket them all," she growled. "Now, you were saying?"

"I was *saying* that bad things happen everywhere. Even if every one of our missing child cases were murders, our numbers are still way below other counties pretty much anywhere." He reached out and nearly took her cup of coffee out of reflex.

She caught the motion.

"It's got cream and a lot of sugar. Help yourself, if you can choke it down."

His hand returned to his lap empty. "Sugar junkie."

"Old fart," she shot back.

Derek grumbled. "So, what's this lead you've got?"

The sheriff took a large swallow of her coffee before answering. "Well, you know how I've been going on the theory that someone is taking people about every four months and has been for a long time?"

"M-yeah?"

"Well, I think I might have a location."

"Sheriff Goddard—"

"Erin."

"Fine. Erin. Our list of missing persons doesn't always match up with four people every four months. Sometimes there's more… sometimes less."

"That's reporting, though."

He shifted.

She said, bullet-fast, "If you match up when the people went *missing* rather than when they were *reported* the dates match up."

"You told me this before."

"And you poo-pooed it."

Did she just say, "poo-pooed?"

He recovered and said, "What I said was—"

"You're smoking again."

"What?"

"You're smoking again," she repeated. "I can smell it on you."

Great. My boss is now my mother. "Can we stick to one discussion at a time?"

"Fine."

Sheriff or not, he couldn't help but to cringe at hearing a woman say that word. It might be sexist. It might be unfair. The reality was whenever he heard a woman say that word it could only mean one thing—he was in trouble. The cherry-tomato-sized birthmark on her jaw visibly darkened as she flushed red.

They drove in silence for a few minutes, leaving the town proper, passed the suburbs, and found themselves in hobby farm country to the south of their town.

"All I'm saying is that the idea of someone snatching people for going on…what, two decades…is a bit far-fetched. If we could close in those dates to the day, hell, even the week, then there might be something to go on."

He grabbed the cooling cup of coffee and took a swallow, wincing at the sweetness.

"So, you're saying there's something to go on?"

Derek sighed again, noticing it was becoming a common practice during business hours. "That's not what I said. I said *if* the disappearance dates were more uniform. These aren't even happening every four months, but you keep quoting like they do. They average four a year. That's different."

She passed a truck and horse trailer, leaving them behind in a spray of water.

"You're blind," she said flatly.

"And you're grasping at straws."

She took the coffee from his hand and downed the last swallow. Derek could just imagine the sugar sludge that lay as sediment at the bottom of the cup and it sent a shiver through him.

"Let's just see if this one pans out. 'Kay?"

"You're the boss."

"That I am."

Erin's smile returned as the car slowed, turning into a long driveway bordered on both sides by empty fields.

He looked out the window. "So, why do you call him the Boogeyman? If anyone picks up on that the news is going to have a ball with it."

"I only use it around you."

"And Thompson. And Adams. And—"

"Okay, okay." She slowed to a crawl and navigated around a couple of puddles that had the suspicious appearance of being significantly deeper than most would assume. "So maybe I use it around the office, but nowhere else."

She can't be this dense.

"Sher—Erin, what I'm saying is that the office is rarely empty. One of these days you're going to slip up when there's someone present to repeat it."

A bunch of rabbits stopped playing in the field and watched them warily.

"Fine, oh great and powerful guardian of the sheriff, I'll watch my mouth. Any other observations I need to take notice of?"

Seriously?

Derek looked out the window. "You're the one who wanted conversation this morning."

"We're here."

The house came into view. A place that, although not occupied, seemed in relatively good condition. All the windows were intact, as were the doors, and even the white paint wasn't in too rough shape. The style was from the early 1900's, its simple two-story design now considered classic by most. One corner of the porch sagged a little, but even that was something so minor it barely registered to the naked eye.

Erin stopped the car hard, jerking Derek against his seat belt.

"Looks abandoned."

"No," she corrected. "Looks *empty*."

Derek continued to take in the farm from inside the car. "Maybe the owner leases the land out."

"That'd explain the fields." He watched her shake for a second, literally shaking off the bitter attitude of the last few minutes. "Let's check this out. I wanted you here with me as a pair of seasoned eyes."

"I think that's pretty much the nicest thing you've said to me all week."

"It's only Monday."

"Still…."

They got out of the car, both staring hard at the place. New grass peeked up through the brown remnants of last year's growth. The lawn, even the flowers, had been cleaned up last fall. No litter, aside from what had obviously blown in, piled up anywhere. This farm even lacked the telltale signs of teenagers using it as a party place.

"It's clean," he observed.

"Homey," Erin commented.

The front door was locked, so they walked around back, doing what they could to see in the windows. White sheets and glass reflected a gray day and little else. No signs of movement—no real signs of anything. A three-season porch sat off the back of the house and Derek pulled on the screen door as he passed.

It opened.

"Hey, Sheriff." He waved the door back and forth, it squeaking in protest.

Erin smiled and shot past him and up the three steps onto the porch. He followed, happy to be out of the drizzle that never seemed to end anymore. Old battleship-gray paint covered the floorboards.

"Before we go any farther, shouldn't we knock…or maybe just call in to see who owns the property?"

"I already called in for that."

She banged on the back door.

No sounds other than the incessant pinging off the porch's metal roof.

Derek reached past her and tried the doorknob.

It turned and the door swung open to reveal a hallway ending at the house's front door. A staircase could be made out at the side of the front foyer. Other than a discarded soda can, the hall was void of any pictures or furniture.

"Looks empty," he said.

Sheriff Goddard stepped past him and into the hallway.

He followed, looking immediately to the right. A small kitchen, complete with 80's era Formica counter tops met his gaze. Flicking the light switch confirmed that the power was off.

Erin stepped out of the hallway to the left. He followed but put a hand on her arm to stop her.

"Sheriff's department," he called out at the top of his lungs. "Hello?"

They both held their breath, listening for any sounds whatsoever.

Silence reigned.

"Guess nobody's home," she said and continued through the empty dining room and into the equally-empty living room. The rooms showed their signs of age. Walls bore the outlines of pictures, and, in the dining room, the large boxy mark of where a china hutch had once stood. Carpet covered the living room floor, and little puffs of dust poofed up with each step.

"Room needs a vacuum," Derek mumbled.

They turned right and stepped into the small foyer, really little more than an entrance, stairs and a couple of doors.

"Erin." He pointed down to the floor. The hall had been swept recently. His hand went from the floor to the stairs. Dried mud, and footprints from numerous different shoes covered the steps going up. Upon closer inspection every one of the impressions was of a smaller foot.

"Looks like teens," she said.

"Girls too," as he noted an impression of wedged feminine sole on the third step.

"You sound surprised. Girls can be vandals, can't they?"

Derek pulled his light and shined it up the stairs. "Not much sign of vandalism here…unless you count tracking mud in."

"A *lot* of mud."

The light beam slid back down the stairs.

He clicked off the light. "Nothing a plastic knife and a vacuum couldn't fix in fifteen minutes."

Erin called out this time. "Sheriff's department." She looked over at him. "Better to be safe than sorry." Her nose wrinkled up at the smell. It was something akin to moldy leaves that finally had a chance to dry.

Still no response from anyone.

The house stood in silence.

Taking the lead, Derek drew his weapon and climbed the stairs. *Might be stupid, but better to have the pistol out and not need it rather than to need it and—*

The upper floor lit up as if it were noon.

Boom.

The house rattled under the thunder.

"Shit," he spat.

"All we need now is someone to jump out."

"Isn't that what we're here for? Your *Boogeyman*?"

She gritted her teeth. "Better than a ghost."

"Ghosts now? Really?"

Another two steps had him on the landing which, like the stairs, were covered with a heavy layer of filth. Gloom painted the day's dimming light in broad strokes, never fully illuminating any portion of the hallway. He switched the light back on and shone the beam first one direction then the other. Dirty tracks led both directions, but the lion's share of dried mud caked the floor going left.

He trailed the beam along the messy floor. "Follow the yellow brick road?"

Erin, still on the stairs, stayed silent.

"Sheriff?"

"Go right first. There's only two doors that way."

Derek glanced over his shoulder. "How'd you know that?"

"It's not a big farmhouse. There's only space for a couple of rooms that way."

"Well, there's three."

"Linen closet?"

The door at the end of the hallway was only about two-thirds of the size of the other two. "Probably."

He nodded and stepped to the right, allowing Erin enough room to join him on the second-floor landing. A single step brought them both to the three doors and Derek opened the smaller door without hesitation. White-washed shelves, heavy with dust and neglect, filled the closet space. At the top corner a web with multiple white spots throughout it, showed how well the spider was eating.

"Livin' it up," Derek said.

"Huh?"

"The spider."

A panicked tone filled her voice. "What spider? Where?" Her flashlight's beam darted around frantically.

"Easy there."

She growled, "Where…is…it?"

Opening the door wider, he shone his own beam on the web.

Her hand appeared right by his face, something dark in its grip.

Her gun?

Before he could move whatever was in her hand hissed and a stream of liquid shot out. Droplets spattered from around the nozzle, covering the side of his face.

Then it burned his eyes.

She was whispering, "No, no, no, no, no, no, nononononononononononono!"

Derek gasped, leaning away from the sheriff who still held her arm rigid and continued to spray the web until was nothing more than a puddle of goo. His vision blurred, tears running down his cheeks in a way that hadn't happened since he was a child. He let his breath out and fell heavily against the door to the closet's right. The smell from the pepper spray filled the enclosed area as he slapped at the doorknob until it turned and he fell into a room, kicking the door closed behind him.

He rasped, "What the hell!"

Nothing mattered but getting his eyes to clear. None had gotten into them, but enough hit his cheek to start his nose and eyes running like a faucet. The single breath he'd taken in the hall left his throat raw.

The hissing noise subsided and the door opened a crack before being blocked by his legs.

"Derek?"

"What?" he screamed.

"Are you okay?"

"What the hell do you think?" He patted himself down, trying to remember where he kept a few sealed handy wipes in case of the all-too-often domestic violence calls. Blood was nothing to play around with. Then again, he reminded himself, neither was pepper spray. Condom-like foil wrappers met his fingertips in the last pocket checked.

"I…I'm sorry." She sounded small, like a small child in trouble. "I just can't…spiders are…you've got to understand—"

All sense of professionalism left him. "Shit, Erin, you just shot pepper spray in my face! Over a fuckin' spi—"

"*By* your face."

"In, by, I don't give a shit. You just can't do that!" He groped one back pocket for his handkerchief, desperate to wipe tears, snot, and as much of the syrupy splatter from his face as possible.

He heard her kneel beside him.

She repeated, "You've got to understand—"

"What?" He pulled the swatch of cloth free from his pocket and began wiping down, away from his eyes. "That you've lost your mind?"

"No. You've got to understand," she repeated. "Spiders. I just can't…."

Derek tried to shake it off, grateful she'd only splattered one side of his face with the spray. "Look," he said, still wiping at his cheek, "I get it that you don't like—"

"*Loathe*." The word was almost a moan coming from her mouth.

"Fine. 'Loathe.' You *loathe* spiders. But, damn it, you can't just go off half-cocked like that."

Again, the young voice came from his superior. "I'm sorry, Derek. I just—when it comes to *them* I just…." She trailed off again at that point.

He sat up and did his best to look her in the eye. "You owe me a steak dinner."

"And this never happened?" She sounded hopeful.

"Oh, no," he tried a smile, but the skin around his eyelids shifted and started a whole new river of tears. "I'll cash *this* chip in when I'm good and ready."

She gave a half-hearted laugh. "Fair enough, big guy." Erin grabbed him by the arm. "Let's get you up."

Derek stood, feeling wobbly as if he'd just thrown up. The sheriff stayed by his side, steadying him.

The room, at least what he could make out through watery eyes, was a pale green bedroom, devoid of furniture. No footprints were on the floor.

"Looks clear."

Erin moved toward the bedroom's closet door.

"Wait," he said, and she looked back quizzically. "Let me. I don't think closets are really your thing."

"Can you do it?"

He snarled, "Just get out of the way," and lumbered across the room, ripping the door open without any concern for what might be in there.

A handful of wire hangers hung on a well-worn wooden rod. On the back wall of the closet, down low, a child had taken crayons and drawn a crude representation of the house and a family of six. Five stick figures, two larger and three smaller, were out in front of the farm while the sixth, a girl by the crude swipes on the sides of its face and drawn in a sickly green, looked out from one of the windows with a frown on her face. Squares and triangle bodies defined the parents' gender as well as the children. Two boys and a girl. Beside it, another representation of the farm showed it during winter, blue snow piled around against the house and car. Yet in this one both girls were in front of the house. The green girl smiled while the other four had pronounced frowns on their faces. One of the boys was missing from the artwork.

Erin's hand on his shoulder drew his attention from the young artist's murals.

"Let's go," she said. "We've still got the rest of this floor to check."

He turned back to the images. "There's more images here. Maybe it'll help your—"

She stepped away. "Guess I'll check the rest alone."

"Damn it, Sheriff. You haul me out here and now don't even want to check things out."

"I *do*. I just want to clear the house first. Or is that too much to ask while you're kneeling there with your back to the door?"

She was right.

He knew it.

Derek stood and walked past her to the door. Stepping into the hall he faced the opposite door and reached for the knob, but stopped short of touching it.

"Who owns this property?"

"What?"

He turned. "It just dawned on me that legally we're trespassing. There's no immediate danger. I don't even know what this lead you were talking about is."

She let loose an exasperated sigh, sounding oddly like one of his, and used her flashlight to push the hall's closet door closed while eying the top of the door warily. "It belongs to a family named Gelly. They're out-of-staters. I got permission to check the place out this morning."

"But what's the—"

"Let's clear the house and I'll fill you in on everything. I promise."

This wasn't how Jenkins, the previous sheriff, did things. He was by the book. Erin, Derek noted, seemed to do everything by the seat of her pants. Though mostly successful, it left the potential for disaster always waiting around the next corner.

Or on the other side of a door.

Steeling himself, Derek grasped the knob, turned it, and pushed the door open. An unsatisfying creak echoed through an identically empty room. Only dust lay on the painted pine floorboards. He stepped in and walked over to the closet door. From the corner of his eye, he saw Erin tense, free hand on the butt of her pistol. As with the bedroom door, he pulled the closet door open revealing a small pile of clothes in the rear left corner.

"Should I read it its rights?" Derek asked over his shoulder.

"Is there anything in it?"

Using his flashlight, just as Erin had with the closet door, he separated the child-sized t-shirt, jeans and underwear.

"And?"

"And," he said, "it looks like they were worn...at least by the underwear." The flashlight's beam centered on a crusty skid mark.

"Eww," Erin said.

"So far we've found a dirty clothes pile and some drawings."

"And a spider," she added.

"Which you shot without reading any Miranda rights."

"Cute." She turned. "Let's finish the upstairs."

"What about the basement?"

"There's no basement," Erin said walking back into the hall.

"How do—"

"I asked the Gellys. Now come on."

Derek followed her to the door mirroring the stairs. She opened it into a bathroom without hesitation. The toilet had been taped down and a piece of paper declaring it had been winterized was stuck to the lid.

He moved to the end of the hall to the two remaining doors, making a prune-face at the spoiled smell. The room on the right appeared to be larger when taking the stairway into account. A trail of dried muddy footprints went into both rooms. The door to the larger room was already ajar and he pushed it open, revealing a furnished master bedroom complete with a queen bed still with clothes draped across its comforter.

"Hello?" Derek called. "Sheriff's department."

Quiet.

Nothing moved.

Hairs on the back of his neck stood up.

He stepped in, raising his weapon.

A dresser stood on the far wall, its mirror showing him in a dusty representation. The closer wall, to his right, held a chest of drawers and a large tube-type television.

"That takes me back," he whispered.

"Me too."

To the left of the door was a double-sized fan-door to the closet. Both stood open, revealing clothes that were more at home in the eighties and nineties than now. Harsher colors, vibrant even with over a decade's worth of dust, filled the wife's side of the closet, while what Derek assumed to be the husband's side offered a darker selection.

Another cluster of webs clogged one corner of the room, white specs visible from over ten feet away.

"No," Erin said, voice quivering again.

"Erin—"

"No!"

He turned in time to see her back hit the wall by the door. She was grabbing at her pepper spray again, trying to free it from the leather holster. A slap at the canister knocked it from the sheriff's hands.

"Calm down."

She was babbling now. "No spiders. No-no-no spiders. I can feel them. I can feel them crawling…." Erin slid down the wall.

Derek reached out, placing a hand on her shoulder.

"Let's get you out of here."

What the hell happened to the "Take care of it all" woman who won the election by a landslide? If she goes to water over a silly spiderweb, how's she going to deal with real problems?

He knelt beside her and said, "Come on."

"No!" She spat the word, and her terrified gaze went from the far wall to Derek. Erin grasped his arm in a tight grip. "We *need* to finish checking the house."

"Okay, okay," he said, trying to sooth her. "Let me check the last room. Once I've cleared it, we can go downstairs, and you can fill me in. Sound good?"

Erin offered a shaky nod of agreement.

He stood and stepped into the hall, taking note of her scratching at her arms and neck.

She's gone batty.

One step into the hall and he traded one kind of tension for another. There was a smell, something like roadkill that'd been left drying on the side of the road for weeks, coming from the door.

"Erin," Derek said. "You might wanna get out here."

"Nononononono," quietly echoed from the master bedroom where she still sat.

"Shit," he said to himself. A quick turn of the knob let the door swing in, exposing a bedroom engulfed in shadow. The air reeked of something spoiled, making it hard for him to draw a full breath.

An eighties-era pull down blackout blind kept most of the outside light from hitting the room. Derek swung his light around the room in a cursory check. One bed, a single, was pressed against the far wall and had clothes piled on it. A princess nightstand, dresser, and desk filled the majority of the room, leaving only enough room for a couple of small bookcases.

Dried muddy footprints covered the floor from wall to wall.

Steeling himself, he stepped in, first taking note of the dresser. Faded pictures adorned the mirror of a blonde girl either alone, or together with others—but always smiling for the camera.

"Why the hell," Derek mumbled to himself, "would they leave all of this here?" Then he reminded himself that out-of-staters bought the house.

But the pictures….

He returned the light to the mirror again. In one of the photos the local school was visible.

"Erin! Suck it up and get your ass in here!" His beam shone more around the room. Simple Plan and Radio Day posters bordered the window. He stared at them, trying to remember what kind of music they played. *Probably awful, whatever it was.*

A second light's beam joined his.

"Y-yeah," Erin managed.

He half-glanced over his shoulder. "Something's not right here." His beam whipped around the room. "Why the hell is there all this stuff…this *dated* stuff in here if those people you talked to bought the place?"

"I don't—"

"I think you might actually be on to something. Maybe not a serial killer, but still…something."

"Hey," Erin's voice perked up. "Simple Plan. I remember them."

Derek's light went to the bed and stopped.

From under the bed's covers and clothes a mummified hand gripped the sheet, ragged fingertips puncturing the aged fabric in two places.

"Oh, no," Derek said as he stepped closer. A mane of blonde hair framed a girl's face. "Boss," he said, forcing himself back into deputy mode, "we've got a body."

"Mmmmm," was Erin's reply and he saw her putting her light on the dresser, pointed towards him, and putting a hand across her stomach.

Not sheriff material, he reminded himself and turned his own beam across the remainder of the room and back in her general direction.

Heads?

He jerked the flashlight back to the closet. Rather than full of clothes or empty, this teen's closet was full of severed heads in varying states of decay. The ones on the bottom were more bone than anything else, telling of years-old murders. As the rows climbed the victims became fresher. Men, women, and even a dog's head lined the closet, stacked in such a way that it reminded Derek of the old castle walls he'd seen on his honeymoon to Ireland. Faces, some newer ones bearing horrified expressions, stared out at him, offering no clue to the basic question of, "Who did this?"

For a second Derek thought his vision swam, seeing swirling movement everywhere in the closet. Adjusting the angle of the light's beam told a more gruesome story.

Bugs.

Hundreds of them, maybe thousands, moved sluggishly in the cool weather. Maggots dropped down from new trophies to old, one thrashing after being caught by an attentive millipede, its pincers locking around the fleshy grub.

Derek looked away as he drew his pistol. "Sheriff, we need to call this in."

She didn't answer. Erin still stood, partially bent over and facing the open bedroom door, muttering incoherently to herself.

"Erin!"

"Nonononono sp-spiders. No more…in the dark. They—they—they—"

"Damn it," he screamed. "Call this in!"

He stepped over to the window and raised the blind, putting a large pale beam of light onto the far wall's bookcase. The rest of the room brightened, making the horrors the closet contained all too real. The deputy focused on the bookcase. A few award ribbons lay under a layer of dust, a few Sweet Valley High books lay out of order. Various knickknacks, mostly equestrian themed, filled the remainder of the shelves.

Then something caught his eye.

Derek took a step closer, dried mud crushing under his footsteps. On top of the shelf, a framed photo of a pretty cheerleader striking a one-legged pose, the other bent, and her pom poms shoved skyward. He recognized the mascot logo from the local high school. A big smile lit her face as blonde hair draped hung over one shoulder in a long braid.

Trying to bring the sheriff back around, he said, "Erin, definitely looks like you found your serial killer." Derek put his flashlight away and reached up to click his radio, then stopped short of depressing the mic button.

The girl in the photo, there was something wrong, something just at the edge of comprehension. Derek looked reluctantly back to the mummified body in the bed, then went over to her, kneeling by the exposed hand. After being in the afternoon's direct light, this part of the room felt in shadow and he retrieved his flashlight again, clicking it back on.

Fingertips were mostly gone aside from bone, making it easier for them to pierce the aged, fitted sheet. A tattoo, or something written in Sharpie—he couldn't tell which, marred the teen's forearm. He leaned forward and looked directly down on the arm, hoping to get a better angle on what the ink showed.

The mummy's face moved.

"Son-of-a—"

Derek fell back on his butt hard.

No, it couldn't have moved. He got up and, unwilling to lean over as he'd been a moment before, stood over the girl.

Incessant scratching noises emanated from the closet, bugs agitated at the room's intrusion. Although the room was cool, the smell was nearly overpowering.

Could use some of Erin's perfume right about now.

His light went up the mummy's form, illuminating a faded Bear Whiz Beer sleep shirt. The beam settled on the girl's slack-jawed face. Empty sockets looked to the ceiling, forever staring at a coffee-colored water stain. There was something on the side of the face.

"Nonononononononono," Erin repeated the mantra beside him and smacked palms against her face.

Something moved in the right eye socket.

A spider crested the orbital socket and perched on the teen's cheekbone. It scampered down the side of the girl's face and across the thumb-sized discoloration on her jaw. Then another emerged from the girl's face…and another. Derek stepped back, light shaking and moving back to the first spider on the—

"Birthmark," Derek said, comprehension finally setting in as he turned. "It looks just like your—"

Erin was gone.

He turned back to the bed.

The girl was gone.

Derek turned once more, and a figure lunged at him. Fabric tore across the front of his uniform and he felt his mic cord catch on whatever struck him, jerking it, and the radio, away as he fell. His head cracked against the nightstand. Instinct took over and he rolled, firing off a shot, not so much for self-defense, but to hopefully startle his attacker long enough for him to get back to his feet.

He rolled up by the door, knees screaming at the sudden activity, and held both his light and gun, at the ready.

By the closet hunched the figure in uniform—in Erin's uniform. Blonde tufts of hair puffed out in every direction. The Erin-thing moved with blinding speed and closed the distance between them in a second.

Did you ever wonder if a ghost dreamt they were alive?

Derek jumped back and slammed the door, pulling against the knob to ensure it stayed closed. His grip was loose between the knob, the pistol, and the flashlight. The light slipped free and clattered to the floor.

"What the—" he panted. "What the," he stated again, trying to bring what just happened into some kind of rational reality.

Something struck the door and he jumped, losing his grip on the knob.

It turned the instant he let go.

Fear grabbed hold and he fired off five shots through the door, then turned and ran past the stairs before he'd realized it and ended up back in the first bedroom, racing to the window. He thumbed the latch and tried to raise it. Nothing happened. Then the handful of nails going from window into frame met his eyes.

He shouted, "No!" and fired through the window until the slide locked back, signaling the gun was empty. Shattered glass lay strewn under the sill and he used the pistol to knock it away.

A scattering sound of something large raced down the hall and Derek chanced a look over his shoulder.

The Erin-thing raced into the room on all fours. Shoes, now too big—like the rest of her uniform—clapped loosely with every quadruped step. Derek threw the empty gun at her, dove to the right, landing in the closet and slammed the door behind him. He gripped the knob with both hands—a true death-grip if there ever was one.

The knob rattled, then came free in his hands. Two weak beams of light shone, one from where the knob was once seated in the door, and the other from a half-inch gap at the bottom of the door.

Erin rattled the barrier, unable to get the closet open without the piece of the knob Derek gripped.

He held the knob between his fingers like a punch knife and laughed.

"C-can't get in!" Breaths came in gasps. "You can't get in!" He reached back for his phone.

The pocket was empty.

"Shit!"

The door rattled again and the light coming from where the knob had been disappeared. Derek knelt, being sure to stay back a bit, and looked through the small hole.

Erin—the mummy Erin—looked back at him through empty sockets. Spiders crawled out…even more literally pouring from her mouth. The thing shook her head, sending arachnids flying left, then right, and silently mimicked a laugh.

Derek's back pressed against the back of the closet.

It got darker and he looked down.

Smaller shadows danced their way under the door, dimming the light as their masters pressed under the door.

Then they extinguished it altogether.

Behind the story...

I wrote "Trophies" when I was trying to get a nightmare out of my head. In my dream I was Deputy Mulkens and all of the events happened to me. On the one hand, this was fun to write...on the other, I have arachnophobia and anything to do with spiders is just a "no" for me. While I was working on this, Hollie sent me to the couch more than once because of how bad the nightmares were.

The way "Trophies" turned out is pretty much how I dreamed it, minus the pepper spray.

A MURDER OF CROWS

August winds pushed through the procession of oak trees lining Highway 217. The season's heat wave struck the nation from coast-to-coast and the Midwest felt most of it. Even leaves took on a brown tinge while suffering the summer's drought. In southeastern Kansas, a murder of crows watched the intruder as she shifted a rucksack from one shoulder to the other.

Karen Elgefson stared at the avian audience. They were the first sign of life she'd seen in the two hours since her last ride, "Davis the hormonal," had parted ways with her.

"Let me tell you about Davis," she said, grateful for anything to interact with along this dusty stretch of backwoods country highway. "He picked me up in Vegas the day before yesterday thinking I'd trade mattress duty for a ride." A flick of her wrist released the last cheese twist from its bag and she watched it tumble to the roadside. One of the crows dropped from its perch with two brethren in close pursuit. He retrieved the prize and scarfed it down before one of his kinsmen could steal it.

"Damn." She looked at the agitated exchange. Feathers came free from the trio as they flapped and pecked at each other. "Guess this drought makes everything hard to come by, huh?" The three birds stopped posturing and watched her pass by. Nothing moved. Even the bugs seemed scarce.

Karen felt a twinge of foolishness for speaking to the ebony onlookers. Absentmindedly, both hands reached up to cover her sunburned shoulders but jerked away on contact. Pain bit across her back and reminded her that the "Miss Kitty, Take 2" tank top didn't cover much.

"Christ…sun must be getting to me." A clear blue sky ensured that, before the day was over, temperatures would exceed a hundred degrees. Rivulets of sweat ran down her brow, stinging both eyes. Karen wiped her forehead with the back of one hand and it came away streaked with mud. "That's just great."

"C-caw."

A crow, significantly larger than the rest, drifted to her side of the road and perched itself on a low-lying branch about twenty feet ahead. He eyed her for a second, then began to preen the feathers under one wing.

"Oh, you want to hear more?"

The crow didn't respond, but a second glided into her field of vision and joined the first.

Karen looked around, half-expecting someone to pop out and catch a crazy redhead talking to birds. Only woods and pastureland across the empty highway met her gaze. A rumble reverberated behind her, rolling through the countryside. An over-the-shoulder glance offered forth a mountainous thunderhead bearing down on her.

"Guess the dry spell's finally over, huh?"

The two birds chattered as if in agreement.

"Anyway," Karen continued, resigning herself to the fact that a downpour was unavoidable, "Davis treats me okay for the first night, not really wanting anything more than a poke and a tickle."

Three more birds settled in as she passed under the branch. The largest shifted its position and continued watching her.

"So I give him what he wants…no big deal, you know? I'm thinking, 'smooth sailing from here all the way into Maryland.' That is until after he's done with me." She stared at the large crow for a handful of seconds. "You're the biggest daddy of them all, birdy. I think that's what I'll call you…Big Daddy."

The five crows, led by Big Daddy—as Karen dubbed him—whizzed past her head, feather tips less than a foot from her face as they glided ahead to the next branch. Two more followed the asphalt and joined the small cluster but chose to reside further up in the tree.

"He no more than snaps the rubber off before sobbing about how lonely he is. I mean, get a fuckin' dog!"

Big Daddy chuffed.

"I'm there holding this…two-hundred pound man-baby while he spills his guts about how he lost his wife and kids because he was on the road all the time. Oh, did I mention there were more girlie pics stuck to the walls of his cab than in any porno shop I've ever heard of?" She flipped her ponytail. "I felt like I was balled on stage."

A horn tapped twice as an old pickup skidded to a stop and surged a wall of dust into her. Classic Hank Williams rockabilly poured from the Redneck Cadillac which, judging by the smell, burned more oil than an Iraqi oil field.

"Hey there, purdy lady, need a lift?"

Karen leaned over, rested both arms against the door frame and examined her potential benefactor.

The cowboy looked to be straight from a piece of Norman Rockwell artwork. Stereotypical faded jeans and a sweat-stained green button-down shirt clothed a forgettable lanky frame. He couldn't have been over twenty-five, but years of work under that brutal yellow globe tanned his skin to a leathery quality far beyond his true age. A fishing pole rested in the gun rack.

Karen turned on the charm. "How far ya' headin'?"

"Only about five miles up, but every mile counts on a day like this, huh?" His gaze shifted from her face to the valley of exposed skin only partially concealed in the position she now stood. Karen righted herself and half squatted to continue the conversation.

Big Daddy dropped onto the truck's back gate and started shifting weight from one foot to the other and back again.

"Whoo-weee, will you look at the size of that sucker?" The cowboy stared into the rearview mirror. "Love to see 'em dance on a day like today."

"Dance?"

"Hot metal. Birds don't have the sense God gave a goose!" He guffawed at his own weak attempt at humor.

Big Daddy chattered and side-stepped towards her along the edge of the pickup.

Another look at the frothing storm cemented the offer.

"Thanks." She swung her sack into the bed, barely missing the crow in the process. The cowboy popped the door open after a couple of attempts and Karen slid in. She slammed the door shut with the same effort he'd used to force it open.

"That-a-girl." He pushed the shifter up until the grinding noise gave way to a sudden lurch forward. Old Hank's music faded in and out on the AM radio, reception victim to every tree along the highway. "So, tell me, what brings you to these parts?"

"Just working my way over to the coast."

"Workin'. Har, har, har."

Karen flinched at both the implied impropriety, no matter how correct it may have been, and the cowboy's laughter, its bark more annoying than the driver's assault on the truck's gears. She stared out the window and counted the seconds to the next mile marker. Each one meant she was just that much closer to escaping this excursion into redneck hell.

"So," he pressed, "what kinda *workin'* are ya' doin'?" His hand maneuvered on the shifter so that his pinky brushed her knee.

"You know, thumbing across the country." She ignored the subtle advance. "So tell me, what's your name anyway?"

"Well, hell."

She cocked an eyebrow. "That's a funny name."

"Naw, not that." He nodded to the mirror. "That sumbitch is still hangin' on back there."

Karen craned her neck and gazed at the immense bird still gripped onto the truck's rear, wings splayed in a woeful mimic of flight. Big Daddy's eyes were clinched shut against the barrage of dust that cascaded back from the front tires. In pursuit, eleven dark specs flew, nearly invisible, against the marbled charcoal sky.

"Huh. Guess Big Daddy really likes me."

The cowboy's hand pulled free of the shifter and landed firmly on her knee. "Yes, siree, Big Daddy sure does like you."

"Not you." Karen shifted in the seat to see the crow better, noticing a dusty palm print now graced her jeans from the cowboy. "Him," she pointed at the bird.

"Never seen one that big, huh?" His hand moved to the bench.

"No."

"Smart fellers, them crows. Look't that murder of them."

"Huh?" Karen's mouth went dry at the word.

"The murder of crows." He guffawed and nodded to the rear-view mirror. "That's what you call a flock of crows…a *murder*."

Her mouth tasted gritty from dust. A stray hair drifted across one eye. Pulling it back, Karen realized her hair felt disgusting and must look even worse.

"So, I've heard."

"Yup. Saw a special on television once about them, too. S'posed to be the geniuses of the bird world. Can solve problems too…use tools even."

"Really?" Sarcasm bled through the word. She tried to change the subject. "How can you see anything through this windshield? There's got more dust on it than the road."

"I know, I know." He emphasized his previous statement with hand gestures before the appendage returned to the bench an inch closer than a moment before. "It sounds crazy. I don't mean nothin' like havin' one use power tools or anything like that, but this show had them using sticks they'd find to dig grubs out o' the dirt."

"No shit," Karen shifted her gaze from Big Daddy to the cowboy.

"Even had them teachin' other crows to do the same."

A volley of ruts jarred her spine. Karen couldn't help but notice his attention had shifted from the road to the jostling motion of her chest.

"To top it all off," his attention returned to the road an instant before they went into a ditch, "there was one who even played checkers. Seemed to be pretty darned good at it too."

The truck backfired and Karen looked back just in time to see Big Daddy lift off from the tailgate and drift back to his companions. A hand returned to its unwelcome resting place on her knee, bringing all focus back to her assumptive benefactor.

"So," Karen said, flashing a mischievous grin at him, "you never did tell me your name."

"Brent. Brent Walker." In an effort to prove his namesake, fingers walked midway up her thigh.

"Well, Brent," her voice dropped an octave and took on a sultrier tone, "what would your wife think about you groping another woman?"

The hand retreated. "What?"

"You heard me."

"I'm not married." For emphasis he held up his left hand and waggled his fingers before returning them to the wheel.

"Boy, they do raise them dumb around here, huh?"

"Look, missy, I don't know what you're gettin' at by this shit, but—"

She cut him off. "Just because you pulled your ring off before you picked me up doesn't mean you're not married." Karen reached over and tapped the clean, pale band of skin on his ring finger. "Ever heard of marriage called a 'brand of love?'"

"Bitch," he muttered and slowed the truck to a crawl. "Get out."

"Stop first."

"I said out!" Spittle, brown with the residue of chewing tobacco, splattered the dashboard.

"B-G-T-nine-seven-six," she said, citing his plate number.

"Out!" He slowed more.

"Stop the truck or the first call I make will be to the police to tell them you jumped me." Her hand gripped the door latch, just in case she actually had to jump with the pickup still moving. Karen pressed, "Imagine what your wife would think."

The ancient truck crept to a halt. Brent stared through the windshield, apparently determined not to acknowledge her existence from this point forth.

"You know," she continued, content with winning the battle of wills, "not every woman on the side of the road wants to be saddled by you." With that final jab, she forced the door open with a shove, extracting herself from the rusted heap. Tires spun and Karen had just enough time to pull the rucksack free from his truck bed before a wake of dirt engulfed her in a final statement of Brent's anger.

A chorus of caws echoed from the trees just ahead. Black dots marred dusty green. The growing audience awaited her arrival. Ten yards further, she paralleled them.

"I guess you tried to warn me, didn't you? Sheesh, what a jackass."

Over a dozen pairs of eyes stared down. Three more crows arrived, joining the growing murder.

"Well, where was I?"

Big Daddy cocked his head and stretched both wings.

"Oh yeah…Davis." Wind picked up and pulled her ponytail into a swarming rat's nest. Karen pulled the tie loose and adjusted it, instantly disgusted by the gritty texture her hair had taken on. With her only bag slung on one red shoulder, the story continued, "Well, Davis blubbered about the need of a good woman to warm his heart." Hiking boots thunked on the dry earth and each of her steps wafted small plumes of dust. "He's spent the better part of the evenings at the bars—last night it was the Pussy Willow—going on about how he was gonna bang me through the cab when we left. Bang me…he hardly lit his firecracker before it went off." She smiled at the insult, its bite lost on the avian audience.

The birds shot by again, cawing as they passed. A small breeze whipped from flapping wings and blanketed her face.

Thunder boomed, startling her. Crows scattered in every direction. What bore down on them was what she'd heard Kansans call a "Twister-Momma." The thunderhead led a group of equally dark clouds, each with its own promise of wet fury.

Karen looked around. The storm couldn't be more than fifteen minutes away and the closest proof of civilization was the road she walked on and a pen for cattle across the way. Not even a driveway marked the quarter mile of visible highway.

"Not good."

Her pace quickened. Karen half-trotted to the bend in the road, finding wooded land on the far side as well. Ahead, a metal chute for drainage cut under a driveway. In contrast to the relief felt, clouds blocked the summer sun's afternoon rays. She looked back to see how long until the rain started. A pillowy charcoal sky blocked the western view, sheets of gray rain cascaded down not more than five miles away, sharp winds evident by the sweeping liquid canvas shifting with each gust. An icy breeze bit into her back.

The murder went past, speed magnified by the storm's tailwind. Four dime-sized white bombs fell to the road as they passed.

She called out, "Guess you don't like what's coming either, huh?"

Karen's hair jerked painfully to the right. Black wings beat from behind her head, nearly meeting in front of her face. Several red strands, pulled out by the roots, were clutched in one clawed foot as the large crow lifted itself up and out of arm's reach.

"Ow!"

Big Daddy glided ahead, the crimson prize clutched against his underbelly. He settled himself on a nearby fence post along the left side of the two-lane highway.

"Bastard!" She instinctively rubbed her scalp and half expected to see specs of blood on her fingertips.

None.

"Caw," came the simple retort to her insult.

More crows flew in and landed on the length of barbed wire on either side of the post. Ten…twenty…Karen counted better than forty before another rumble from the advancing storm broke.

Her pack suddenly felt heavier.

"Caw."

The sudden sound from a crow riding piggyback on her rucksack almost loosened her bladder. Black canvas ripped along with the jacket tied to it as the crow dug in rather than leave its newfound perch. Jacket batting flew free and drifted over twenty feet before being snatched mid-air by another black avian.

Dozens more flew in to join Big Daddy and filled the top two fence wires, not to mention numerous trees on either side of the road. Karen couldn't help but shiver at the Hitchcockian hell she now found herself in.

"Stupid little shits."

"Caw."

Thunder rumbled and silenced both sides of the exchange.

Whap.

A white chunk of hail the size of a dime struck the road's center line.

Whap. Whap. Whap.

Two more icy missiles struck in front of her with and a third knocked one of the crows just down from Big Daddy off its perch, the bird's death throes little more than a mating dance in reverse. One wing beat spasmodically against the earth while the other remained bent back at an obscene angle.

An unvoiced cue sent the entire mass of crows into the air…all except Big Daddy. Karen watched the birds fly up, circle in a lazy arc before zooming down and past her in a frenzy of beating wings before they banked to the left and followed the driveway.

Big Daddy continued to stare as he plucked the strands of Karen's hair from his claw and left them to wave at her from the confines of his beak.

Whap.

White-hot pain permeated her skull as a chunk of hail struck her squarely on top of the head. She staggered, then took off at a trot toward the driveway

Whap.

Though the hail hadn't come down in a barrage yet, there was no doubt the main event was only seconds away.

Big Daddy took off as she passed. Rather than following his companions, he flew directly into the woods.

"Dumb bird." The thought of the crow striking a tree in a cartoonish impact brought a second of joy before reality set in. She looked up. A natural green umbrella offered a good deal more protection than the road. "Dumb bird…dumb me is more like it." Karen cut off the road to follow Big Daddy.

She threw the rucksack across the tightly strung fence and followed it. A heavy gust of wind whipped in and launched her over the top strand. A single barb stabbed through the denim, slicing along her left ankle before she jerked the foot free.

Karen fell and grabbed the injured leg. A small red stain emerged through the jean material. Torn fabric offered a view of the blood-soaked sock underneath. She gripped the ankle with both hands, applying pressure to stave off the crimson flow and, hopefully, dull the pain.

Thunk.

Another hailstone struck the dirt to her left, embedding itself in the soil. This one, she noticed, easily exceeded the size of a quarter in diameter. A distant thrum made its way to her ears, growing louder with each second.

"Here it comes," she said through gritted teeth.

"Caw." The call sounded from deeper in the woods.

She forced herself to stand. A wet stickiness welled in her sneaker, but the foot worked.

Thwap.

Another hailstone struck Karen in the knob of her shoulder and she felt the arm jerk out against the strike before going numb.

"Caw. C-caw."

Thunk.

Bag retrieved with her good arm, she pushed into the woods. The front line of foliage broke into a knee-high carpet of plants and saplings. Leaves fell, casualties of the icy assault battering the stand of trees. Karen watched palm-sized leaves drift down. An occasional splat from an arctic baseball broke through the ranks of branches.

Karen leaned against the trunk of a rather large oak and checked her arm. Slight discolorations of what would prove to be a nasty bruise already began to surface. She flexed her hand. Digits responded without incident, as did the elbow, but when she tried to rotate the shoulder an explosion of pain ripped across the socket, down the arm, ending in the fingertips.

A hollow reverberation from some man-made structure echoed in the distance. She ran from trunk to trunk, making her way across a chessboard of woods and hail in pursuit of adequate shelter.

Thwap.

A hailstone as large as her fist burst through the canopy of trees, shearing bark from the trunk Karen now sought refuge beside. The ice struck with enough force to reverberate through the immense tree.

Thunk.

More leaves drifted down like summer snowflakes.

"Caw," came from somewhere overhead.

An answering call came from the same direction.

As if a single entity, all the trees groaned against the wind. Debris peppered her skin and a twig caught in her small hoop earring. Wincing, she pulled the wooden shard free and resumed course to what she hoped would be adequate shelter.

The first thunderhead's mass overwhelmed her and light dimmed to that of dusk. Shadows encroached from everywhere, escaping en masse from the banishment daylight wrought. Water fell, the canopy no longer able to hold out against nature's will.

Two droplets struck Karen's hair, the third smacked her sunburned flesh. Goosebumps surfaced. More water fell from above in an icy shower.

She pressed on.

Hail-filled rain gave way to the roar of a torrential downpour. Thirty yards more of dodge and hobble brought Karen to the edge of a clearing. Through the sheets of rain she made out a late model black SUV and the skeletal remains of a lime-green tent, its skin covered with holes and mud. Both stood out against the white hail-covered ground. Some large black mass loomed just out of her range of vision, its size apparent, but all semblance of details blurred by the downpour.

"Gotta be a building."

Torn tent fragments flapped against the downpour. She squinted, looking for signs of life inside the vehicle. The most recent wave of rain eased, allowing her a clearer view of the campsite and the barn beyond.

The SUV's windshield sported two fist-sized holes and the passenger-side window was little more than a mass of translucent spider webs. One corner of the hood angled up, an obvious casualty to the frozen barrage of white missiles laying shattered across the vehicle. No movement came from inside the cab.

"Hello?" Karen realized there was no way anyone inside the truck would hear her since she barely heard herself.

She scanned the sky. More sheets of rain fell, escorted by an occasional icy cannonball dropping to earth with devastating force. The barn loomed not more than fifty yards away, red stains blanketed the ground around the structure. Light continued to fade as darker clouds encroached.

The barn.

Thunk. A crater the diameter of a softball pitted the ground to her left.

"No time like the present." Her boot felt sodden with fluid, more so than its mate. Time was of the essence and she tested her leg. Pain throbbed through the calf, but all five toes moved without resistance, as did the ankle. Karen ran from the tree's cover.

Rain instantly soaked her and weighed the rucksack down. She dragged it along, pushing through the pain, focused on the relative safety of the barn.

"C'mon," Karen grunted. Gusts of wind struck from both the front and side, each taking turns in an effort to knock her over.

Flattened grass emptied into a muddy area offering yet another obstacle for her to navigate. No more than ten feet from the door she slipped, landing hard on her butt. A black slick of mud added its own unique touch to soaked fabric.

Crawling the last few feet to the door proved easier than expected on the slippery mud. The red stains seen from the tree line turned out to be flecked paint worn from the walls by sun and weather. She pulled the door open only to have it rip free and smack solidly against the side of the barn. Ignoring it, Karen dragged her possessions inside. The smell of wet hay greeted her as she took in the barn's features.

The structure could easily have been used at one time to host barn dances. Stacks of unbound hay moldered, filling the better part her sanctuary. Shadows danced around spears of light leaking through a dozen holes in the roof, the unintended skylights varying in size from slits to one massive collapse twenty yards distant. A few horse stalls lined the far end of the forgotten building.

"Hello? Is anyone here?" Her voice didn't echo in the empty building.

"C-caw."

Karen looked up to see Big Daddy perched above on a massive beam.

"Well now, I see I still have my traveling companion."

Big Daddy cocked his head and flapped his wings in an effort to dry his feathers out.

"Well, if anyone's here, my name's Karen." Silence met her introduction. "I just came in here to get out of the storm, like you." She hobbled over to the nearest of five stalls and peeked in. A crow settled into its nest, one of about twenty occupying the littered floor. Another three occupied the hay trough. "I don't want any trouble." Something darted by behind her and she turned.

Nothing.

"I saw your truck out there. It's messed up pretty bad. Storm do that?" From the corner of her eye, Karen saw another shadow shift. Hands drew into fists, nails bit into palms as she prepared to meet—

"Caw." The call came out of the shadows. Wings flapped and destroyed the impression of hulking shoulders atop a piled tarp. More birds called out, overlapping one another until the cacophony matched the volume from the storm's assault.

"Caw yourself." A middle finger shot out for punctuation. She retrieved the sack and spilled half its contents onto the dirt floor. "Well if anyone's here," Karen continued, steeling herself for a response at any second, "stay where you are. I have a gun." For emphasis she waved a nickel pistol-shaped lighter around.

"Caw," called a tenant from the loft above.

"Crows." She slipped her hiking boots off, surprised to see the crimson stain covered her entire sock, toe prints offering the only lighter shade of red against the rest. It took more effort than anticipated to peel the muddy jeans off and she dropped them beside the rucksack. The tank top followed a moment later and Karen sat on the ground to examine her ankle.

The gash wasn't long, but pitted midway through, ensuring a nasty scar. Remnants of a bottle of whiskey served as anesthetic; the burning sensation quickly gave way to a distant ache. A quick swig of the "medicine" put things right and a trickle poured across the injury. She probed the quarter-inch wide gash with a finger, transfixed by the blood which slowly filled the wound.

Boom!

The concussion from something connecting against the barn's roof reverberated through her. The crows fell silent. Karen held her breath, eyed the ceiling suspiciously and waited for the first signs of implosion.

"Let's see," her voice sounded small, as if from a child, "I'm half-naked in the middle of nowhere. Where's my machete-wielding knight in his hockey mask?" Fresh bird poop struck the dirt nearby in response.

Karen looked to where the bird's defecation struck the ground. The feces blended in perfectly with the surrounding dirt.

"C-caw," Big Daddy called down to her.

She continued to stare at the barn's floor. Pale dirt, upon this closer scrutiny, proved to be an immense layer of bird feces, covering the barn's floor from wall to wall. The hay piled along the walls and in bins were filled with scores of makeshift nests, all filled with crows tending to their young, mating or going about the mundane preening birds attend to.

Her hand pressed into fresh fecal matter. "Gross."

"H…hello?"

Karen spun on her butt and looked to the far end of the barn, in the direction of a far stall. Instinct took over and she grabbed an over-sized blue tee shirt which doubled as a nightgown and pulled it over her head.

"Who the hell is that?" She suddenly had to pee.

"Help," the sexless voice rasped. "For the love of God, get me out of here."

She gripped the lighter, pointed it in front of her and walked to the back of the barn.

"God," the voice continued, now taking on a more masculine quality. "Please don't let this be another dream."

Hay shifted. Hot pink fabric pressed against the spaced slat walls of the stall.

Karen took a step back and jerked her out-thrust hand in the direction of the voice. "Who are you?"

"Shhh!" The shadow shifted again. "They'll hear you."

"Who?"

"The birds." His rasping voice fell into a fit of coughs. "What day is it?"

"Friday," Karen took a tentative step forward. "Are you hurt?"

Her companion managed a gravely laugh. "You could say that."

Karen took another step and the two were separated by nothing more than the gate. She looked down at an injured man, long brown hair hung loose across his face.

"Tom…. Name's Tom."

"Karen."

"Friday, huh? Been here three…no, four days now waiting for my wife to come back. Guess she's not." He let his head fall back until it struck the wooden wall. "No big loss." Tom's hand disappeared underneath his jacket. "She didn't really like me much, anyway."

Pain stabbed! She looked down to see a black hatchling as it pecked at her injured ankle, renewing the flow of blood. Karen kicked absentmindedly at the chick and returned her attention to Tom.

"Take me with you?" He licked his lips.

"Where am I going? The storm—"

"To hell with the storm!" His hand shot out and grabbed her shirt, ripping it as he pulled himself upright. Darker shadows fell from his lap and an insane flutist's menagerie of peeps filled the ten-foot square pen. "We've gotta get out of here…now!"

"Caw." Big Daddy's call was answered throughout the barn.

Tom's grip on the shirt tightened, knotting the strap of Karen's bra in the twisted grip. His left arm didn't appear to work as he rotated his shoulders to swing it up and knock the pen's gate open. Peeps went to screeches as he stomped on what she could now see were chicks, dozens of them. Bird calls overlapped each other in the barn's great room, agitation evident.

"Move," he urged and pushed her into the adjacent stall. With no gate to slow Karen's sudden advance, she stumbled and fell into the empty stall. Tom followed suit and landed between her legs, pinning her to the ground. "Help…feeding me…" he said then whispered, "starving."

Karen froze, eyes shut tight and waited for a repeat performance of that horrible night half a decade before.

Seconds passed.

Incessant bird chirps and squawks reached their ears from the stall they'd just left as new mothers mourned their crushed young.

"Shhh," he repeated, his mouth rested against her ear, tickling the hairs. "They can't see well in the dark." She heard his tongue snake out of his mouth and slide along his lips again. What the hell was it with him being hungry?

Her grip on the useless lighter tightened, the other hand pushing up in a feeble attempt to keep any sort of distance between them.

No bulge pressed into her thigh.

Nothing ground against her pubic bone.

No demand for satisfaction.

Only breathing.

The rancid smell of human excrement and dried urine threatened to suffocate her.

His breath came in gasps and pushed her further toward the conviction a rape was about to commence.

"W-we need to open the door in this stall. Do you see it?"

Karen, eyes still clamped shut, shook her head.

Tom's lips touched her earlobe again. "It should be right there." His breath smelled sweet, the way cooking roadkill on hot asphalt did.

Bile rose in the back of her throat, threatening to spew the bologna sandwich she'd eaten for lunch.

A surge of adrenaline coursed through Karen and she thrashed underneath him. Kicking harder than the dancers she'd mimicked in youth, her uninjured ankle came up, its foot planting itself against his hip, and flipping him off of her and back in the direction they'd come. Tom rolled on the floor, wheezing with effort.

Not waiting for round two, she stood and frantically searched the outer wall for a door.

A splinter shoved itself into her palm as she found an old wooden slider latch.

"Take me with you," Tom urged. He pulled himself up the stall slats as a boxer would in the ring. He turned to face her. "You can't just leave me here! You…can't!"

Karen jerked the latch and put her sore shoulder against the door.

"Caw." Flapping from a multitude of wings roared throughout the barn, growing louder.

"For Christ's sake!" He stumbled forward as crows came to rest on the pen's rail.

The door whooshed open, caught by the wind. She backed out into the gale. Gray light filled the doorway as Tom emerged.

"Water." His head tilted back and rain cascaded across his face, drenched his hair and pulled the strands away, giving Karen her first good look at the man while he drank.

His left arm was a mangled mass of meat. Discolored skin marred the bicep before disappearing under the tattered remnants of the once-bright jacket. The pinky and ring fingers were gone. Stylish tan pants, once a status symbol, now hung on as little more than a clutch of fabric any hobo would reject, black stains covering the groin and inner legs. Nearly a week's worth of growth covered Tom's face, masking what may have been once a handsome face. And the dark circles around his eyes….

The sandwich would not be denied. Lunch surged forth, spewing onto the dirt between them. Karen spat and looked up. "Your eyes."

Discoloration, mirroring Tom's arm, covered his cheekbones. Shredded flesh marked the edges of eye sockets, now empty save for crusted blood. An eyeless gaze focused on her.

"You can't leave me," he said. Tom's voice took on a more masculine sound since granted the benefit of moisture.

Terror coursed through her. Karen turned and raced around the corner of the barn, heading back to the front entrance. Every horror movie she'd grown up watching told her to run and not look back. Instinct took over, legs pumped fervently, demanding not to be caught by the monstrosity which pursued.

"Come back!" Tom screamed.

Karen slid as she rounded the corner, mud further caking bare legs.

Tap. Tap. Tap.

She looked up and stared at the barn's window. Half a dozen crows returned the gaze with piqued interest.

Regaining her feet, she ran back in her original direction, past the shredded tent and skidded to a halt beside the SUV.

The truck!

She pulled on the passenger door without success. Anger replaced panic and Karen smacked the webbed window with her hand. The flat palm met minimal resistance and cupped a potato-sized wedge of glass as it passed through to the interior. More smacks widened the hole until only shards remained.

"Karen!" Howling wind carried her name.

She jumped into the truck and cracked her head on the steering wheel.

"Starving." Karen drew herself into the driver's seat. "The crazy bastard was going to eat me."

Hands met with an empty ignition slot.

"No!" She popped open the compartment between the front seats and groped for a spare. Empty candy wrappers flew onto the floorboard from the frantic search.

"Karen!" The voice was closer now and she saw him stagger around the corner of the barn, his pursuit blind, yet unrelenting. Tom's one good hand waved in her direction emphatically, something marred the natural shape of his hand.

"Keys." Had she whispered it? Screamed it?

A black carpet of crows dove out from the confines of the barn, wings flapped against the crushing force of the storm, their altitude never exceeding five feet.

"Feeding me," she repeated Tom's words and recognition finally set in, "not 'feeding me.'" Karen's mind flashed to the multiple injuries she'd seen…the wet chicks on Tom's lap…the missing eyes… the deep pock marks. She crawled back to the empty window and watched dozens of crows circle the injured man.

"Caw." A single cry rang out from inside the barn. The circling ring of birds tightened on their prey.

"Tom," she screamed. "Throw them here!"

"No!" He stumbled in the direction of her voice, oblivious to the fatal threat which surrounded him.

Karen shouted over the din, "The crows are all around you!"

His advance slowed.

"Throw the keys here and I'll come get you!" She ducked as one stray crow whizzed past her face.

"You won't leave me?" His voice sounded terrified.

"No! I didn't get it before!"

"Caw." Big Daddy shrieked as he emerged from the barn, beat his wings against the increased rain and took to the sky.

The avian death squad converged on the blind man, blanketing him in beaked attacks. Tom's screams took on a feminine quality as the birds gripped his hair and pecked at the already empty sockets.

She watched the keys fly skyward, lofted over two crows who dodged the metallic projectile and landed on the hood of the SUV. A crow landed on the hood, followed by another.

"Oh, God," Tom screamed. "Please, God, make them stop!"

Karen stuck her hand out through the nearest of the windshield holes only to have the thumb pecked near a knuckle. Necessity overshadowed pain and she continued to grope for the keys, pressing herself against the glass at such an angle that sight of the keys was no longer possible. Stabs continued, covering the exposed wrist and hand with triangular holes. Fingertips met metal, grasped a toothy length of key and retreated with her prize.

A shadow grew in the corner of her vision. Karen turned to see and was struck square in the face by one of the flying marauders. Blood gushed from a freshly misshapen nose. Her eyes filled with tears and all vision blurred. The bird dropped to her lap, dead.

Karen slammed the key into the ignition and turned the key.

It didn't give.

She groped for a release button.

None.

A half-remembered trick surfaced and she pulled the wheel while turning the key. The ignition released, starting up without effort. The truck dropped into reverse and she stomped on the gas. Karen jerked the wheel and sent the truck into a half circle, spraying the barn, Tom and his adornment of killer birds with a layer of mud. A crow smacked into the windshield, burying its broken body halfway through the already-shattered glass.

Karen glimpsed Big Daddy as he flew in the open window, latching onto her face with talons that dug deep into the flesh of both her cheeks. Wings flapped a maniacal rhythm, beating against the sides of her head.

Her hands released the steering wheel and the truck spun as she tried to dislodge the massive bird. Gripping Big Daddy by the neck, she ripped him free and chucked the flailing crow into the back. Mud flew up in plumes and her bare foot continued to mash the gas pedal to the floorboard. One hand found the wheel again while the other held the ruins of her face. Karen focused just in time to see a man-shaped form covered in flapping ebony wings struck by the truck's grill before passing under.

She hit the barn at fifty, the initial contact careening the SUV onto its side. Rotted walls buckled like balsa wood.

～✖～

Blackness.

Tugging.

Her face hurt. Throbbing like when Jimmy Falcone had taken it personal when she'd said no to him.

Karen tried to blink, to open her eyes. The left one refused, the effort causing white-hot waves of pain. Her right lid responded reluctantly, bringing the world into blurry view.

Gravity pulled her to the left. The ground wasn't where it was supposed to be. She saw a blurry feathered form of the giant crow holding something in its claw…something that stared back at her… something a familiar green. He punctured the iris of her severed eye with his beak and devoured the oval delicacy in a jerking gulp.

Karen watched with detached horror as Big Daddy returned for a second helping.

Behind the story...

In many ways "A Murder of Crows" opened the floodgates for my novel, *Drive-In Feature*. This was written a few years before being published in 2012 and, oddly enough, is an unofficial peek into what happened to our avian characters from *Drive-In Feature*.

I've always been fascinated with crows and ravens. Writing "A Murder of Crows" just felt like a dark salute to their intelligence and having their own ambitions and goals, many of which don't align with what people expect.

The story itself came into print after a particularly hot drought. I was watching crows run other birds off from a muddy puddle by a car wash. The water was oily on top, but the birds were so thirsty they just didn't seem to care. From there I started wondering about food for them: rodents, small predators, and so on. The next thing I knew, I had a scantily-clad woman in a barn with nefarious avian hosts. '80s theme anyone?

At the end of this collection is the beginning of *Drive-In Feature*. I hope you enjoy the novel prequel to "A Murder of Crows."

THE LOST

Jennifer Rialto stared through tear-filled eyes at the Lieutenant occupying her husband's chair. The man's thinning hair did little to mask the roadmap of pink interlaced scars which covered the right side of his head. She found it difficult to look away from the pink tissue contrasting sharply against the detective's natural chocolate hue. Though a large-framed man, he appeared, to her at least, to be more of a scarecrow dressed in oversized clothes rather than a representative of the law.

"Miss Rialto—"

"Missus Rialto," she corrected. "I'm a widow, not divorced." She looked over her shoulder and out the window. Outside, children played, oblivious to the pain she felt…oblivious that one of their own had vanished…oblivious to the dangers.

Lieutenant Tulls flipped back a few pages in his notebook before scribbling a correction. Frustration appeared on his face as the eraser tore a corner of the page.

"Missus Rialto, what time was your son supposed to be home?"

"We went over this already." Her voice raised an octave. "We need to find Jimmy!" She stood, walked over to the kitchen table and lit a cigarette. The smoke helped to cover the overwhelming scent of aftershave which now permeated the room.

Lieutenant Tulls' voice took on a practiced soothing tone, one only learned through years of practice. "Missus Rialto, this *will* help Jimmy. We need to be sure of our information before continuing."

Jennifer stared at the image of Christ welcoming a new soul into the gates of Heaven. Today, unlike others, it held little comfort for her. She closed her eyes and inhaled, pulling deeply on the filter of the cigarette, feeling her lungs fill with warming smoke, burning as she stretched them past their normal capacity before exhaling in a long, paced motion.

"Detective?" An officer came into the room. He made a point to look only at Tulls. "Mackintah is at the baseball field."

Tulls stood, bones popping in loud protest as his full height of six foot two was reached. "If you'll excuse me for a moment."

"No."

Tulls looked at the distraught woman. "No?"

"If he knows something about Jimmy then I have a right to hear."

"Missus Rialto—"

"Are you trying to keep something from me?" Her eyes narrowed, intensifying the obvious distrust she felt toward everyone at the moment.

Tulls sighed and took the handset from the officer's vest.

"Mackintah? What's the status?"

"The diamond is…. Sir, I think you should come down here." Static barked as Mackintah released the mike.

"Just give me the twenty."

"He's found my Jimmy," Jennifer's hand started shaking uncontrollably. Ashes fell. A single glowing ember remained lit after falling to the carpet below. "Sweet Mary, mother of Jesus, my boy's dead. He's found my boy."

Mackintah's voice rang tinnily as he spoke again. "The school, sir. It doesn't look right."

"Mackintah. Missus Rialto is here with us listening." He hoped the rookie would understand the statement as a need for caution. "Have you found anything?"

"Not having to do with the boy, sir." The mike stayed open for a handful of seconds conveying only dead air. "Lieutenant…I really think you should come down here."

"Vandalism?"

"No sir. The school looks wrong somehow. The additions that were built are gone."

Tulls rubbed his eyes and pinched the bridge of his nose until the incessant throbbing eased. "What do you mean?"

"The school's *wrong*. Some of the stores I passed, too."

"Mackintah, get back here now." Tulls shoved the mike back into the officer's hands before shooing him away.

"What does he mean the school's wrong?" Panic crept into Jennifer's voice. "Has something happened to the school? Is that why Jimmy's not home?" She crossed the room and grabbed Tulls by the coat. "Did someone blow up the school? Oh my God! Someone blew up the school, didn't they?"

Detective Tulls pulled free of her grip. "That's not what Officer Mackintah said."

She was screaming now, droplets of spittle spraying across his face. "He said part of the school was gone." Jennifer fell to the floor sobbing. "Someone killed my Jimmy. Someone killed my baby."

"Ma'am…the officer didn't say a word about seeing your son." Tulls squatted down beside her. "We *will* find him."

She stared at his face, studying him for any sign of dishonesty. Finding none, she nodded. The jerky motion sent her disarrayed hair forward, masking Jennifer's mascara-stained cheeks. "I—I lost Jimmy's father. I couldn't bear to lose him as well."

Tulls helped her to the couch just as a patrol car skidded to a halt in front of the house.

"Lasser, get out there and see what's going on."

The second officer, who had been standing immobile by the open front door, stepped out into the waning daylight.

The children that were playing now surrounded the patrol car, eyeing it with auspicious wonder.

Mackintah ran into the house and nearly tripped over a throw rug. "Detective!" The rookie yelled. "Sergeant, we've got to get out of here! To get backup! There's a situation."

"What?" Tulls' Bronx temper flared. "Quit with the bellyaching and tell me what this situation is!"

"The city…it's not right. The whole damned city is just wrong."

The phone rang. Its '70s era goldenrod color doing little to aid the color coordination of the room.

Tulls picked up the receiver before Jennifer could get off the couch. His hand went up in a "stop" motion, signaling Jennifer to stay seated.

"Hello?"

A small voice sounded on the line. "Who is this?"

"This is Lieutenant Thomas Tulls. Is this Jimmy Rialto?"

No answer.

"Your mom is worried about you, Jimmy."

"Can I talk to her?"

"Sir," Mackintah piped up, "you need to know. To understand." His eyes seemed wild, nearly a mockery of the tripped-out junkies they hauled into Mathes General on a regular basis.

Tulls continued on the phone, but motioned first to Lasser, then to Mackintah. "We need to know where you are Jimmy. Are you okay?"

Lasser guided his fellow officer out of the room, putting a finger to his lips as a signal to be quiet.

"I'm fine. I just…. Can I talk to my mom?"

"First, can you tell me where you are, Jimmy?"

"I'm scared."

"Are you alone?"

"Yes…" Tulls heard the crinkling of paper. "No. I mean there's stores and I hear people, but—"

"You need to work with me, Jimmy." Tulls could actually feel his blood pressure drop knowing the boy was all right. "Do you know what street you're on?"

"I thought I did."

"Can you see the names of any stores?"

"I passed a Dairy Freeze-It before I found the phone."

Tulls' mind raced. There were no Dairy Freeze-Its anymore. The last one he could think of closed nearly twenty-five years ago.

"Jimmy, do you see anything that might help us figure out where you are?"

Another pause.

"I can see the—"

Click.

"Damn!" Tulls slammed the phone down, an act lost with today's digital technology.

"What?" Jennifer stood.

Tulls looked at her. "He's fine, Missus Rialto. He's lost, but fine."

"Oh, thank God."

"Excuse me for a moment."

She asked, "Where is he?"

Rather than answer, he pushed past and walked outside to where Lasser and Mackintah stood among the few vestiges of grass comprising the front lawn. Mackintah paced back and forth nervously, his gaze drawn to the East and the diminishing light.

"Okay, we have a child to find. Lasser, get on the horn and find out if there's a Dairy Freeze-It somewhere around here. Mackintah, *what* is your dysfunction?"

Lasser looked at his fellow officer before walking to the car.

Mackintah continued to pace, only now at a quickened tempo. "The school…it wasn't all there. Windows…the windows were broken out. It looked firebombed."

The detective winced. "Are you saying someone firebombed the school?"

"No, I'm saying the school wasn't right."

"Damn it, man. Quit talking in circles and answer a simple question."

"The school wasn't *our* school."

Tulls put his hand out. "Officer, your gun."

Mackintah looked at the exposed palm, pale against Tulls' ebony flesh. He pulled the automatic and handed it, butt first, to the Lieutenant, who pocketed it.

"Get in my car and wait for me."

Mackintah did as asked, closing the door with enough force to rock the Chevrolet.

Tulls went back inside. Jennifer Rialto was not in the living room. Sounds emanated from the kitchen, sounds of coffee being made.

He pulled his cell and dialed the station. The phone rang sixteen times before he hung up and redialed in frustration.

No answer.

Tulls dialed three alternates.

Still no answer.

He dialed 911.

The automated machine stated that his call would be answered in approximately thirty to thirty-five minutes.

Jennifer came back carrying a cup of steaming coffee. "Did you send someone to pick up Jimmy?"

"Just a minute." Tulls dialed the direct number for lockup.

No answer.

"There's a problem with the phones." He turned to her. "Your son was disconnected from us."

"You don't know where Jimmy is?" A panicked tone resurfaced.

"He was able to give us the name of a nearby restaurant. We'll be able to find him from that." He motioned to the phone, "I was just trying to call in and relay the information when I discovered that there's a problem with the line."

"What kind of problem?" She grabbed the receiver from him and dialed a number. A soft ringing echoed up from the handset. Someone picked up on the other end.

"Marge? It's Jen. I just needed to see if my phone was working." She hung up without saying goodbye and cut eyes at the detective.

An expression of concern washed across Tulls' face. He took the phone from her and dialed the station again.

Ten rings.

Twenty.

Thirty.

"What part of town does Marge live in?"

"Two blocks over." Jennifer grabbed her coat.

"Missus Rialto. Where do you think you're going?" He sounded exasperated. Tired.

"To look for my son." She wrapped a yellow and black checkered scarf around her neck, tucking it inside the front of her coat. "I call the police," she said, talking more to herself than to Tulls, "and they're either babbling about hallucinations or occupied with phoning in a pizza."

240

"Missus R—"

"Stop saying that! To top it all off, my son is—"

Tulls yelled, "Missus Rialto!"

She stopped, stunned by the outburst.

"Listen closely to me," he addressed her in an official tone, "I can't explain what Mackintah's problem is. Right now, I really don't care. I have only two concerns," he put up a finger in front of her, "the first being locating your son," Tulls put up a second digit, "and bringing him safely home." He lowered his hand and took hers. "Do you understand that?"

Tears flowed free as Jennifer nodded.

"It's just that he's all I have."

"We'll find him." He put an arm around her and guided her to the door.

Air bit at their faces, a winter beast not to be denied. It howled past, bringing acrid taste of the city into the Rialto home. Tulls pulled the door closed behind them with some effort.

Mackintah looked out of the passenger side of Tulls' car expectantly.

"Missus Rialto, wait here." He crossed the handful of steps between the front door and his car, making sure to avoid stepping on the patches of black ice which were quickly becoming invisible in the late afternoon light.

Mackintah opened the door. Ice chunks fell from the bottom of the car and shattered upon impact with the concrete gutter.

"Detective Tulls, I need—"

"Stow it," he growled. "Listen to me. This woman is distraught. She's already lost her husband and now her son is missing. Our job," he pointed a thick forefinger at the younger man, "is to bring her boy home. Is that understood?"

"Sir, I *need* to tell you about what I saw."

He appeared calmer than when first bursting into the Rialto home a few minutes before. Dried spittle at the corners of his mouth did little to alleviate the impression that the man had chosen to stop at the local crack house before completing the task assigned by Tulls. The body language Mackintah showed expressed more terror than signs of drug use.

"What's more," Tulls ignored the direction his subordinate was trying to take with the conversation, "is that I'm left having to figure out what your problem is. *If*, and I stress that word, if there had been some sort of disaster, don't you think we would have been notified by now?"

"I know what I saw," Mackintah's voice rose slightly. "If you'd just give me thirty seconds to explain, I'd tell you."

The detective sighed, his chest forcing the blazer open enough to catch the wind and flap against his arm, cold air snaking inside the sleeve. He looked up at the clouds in the early evening light. City lights reflected against them, giving a false impression of the hour.

"You've got thirty seconds. Go."

"I showed up at the school. There's supposed to be outbuildings there and the north wing that was built in '99. But they weren't there...as if they never existed."

"Are you sure you were at the right school?"

"Positive." Mackintah leaned partially over the car door which separated them. "I went to that school, William Scotts. It's been there for nearly a hundred years."

"Explain what you mean by 'gone.'"

"I mean as in, 'never there.' There's undisturbed snow on the ground where the outbuildings were," he repeated. "It's as if they were never there."

A few curiosity seekers had begun to gather on either side of the street, interested in what may have occurred to require the presence of the police. Mumbles about the sanity of 'one of Chicago's finest' drifted across the frozen street. This single comment spurred others.

Tulls reached with, "It's possible that they may have been moved, right?"

Mackintah shook his head. "No!" He grabbed the top of the door in a white-knuckled grip. "I mean, it's possible that someone moved the cubicles, but what about the wing? It was three stories high and it's fucking gone!"

"Drop your voice," Tulls cautioned. "If there is a situation here, the last thing we need is to cause a panic."

Tulls looked over his shoulder to where Mrs. Rialto stood. She sucked deeply on a cigarette, its glow standing out against the woman's olive complexion. Her expression, Tulls had seen on hundreds of faces over the years, beaten down, hoping to beat the odds in the card game called life, but always somehow losing.

Mackintah complied, lowering his voice to little more than a whisper.

"The north wing was gone. Some of the windows in the basement and first floor were broken. It looked like fire damage."

"And you didn't call this in to dispatch?"

"I tried. Don't you think I tried?" More spittle formed on the officer's lips, some spraying off to be caught by the November air. "I couldn't get an answer from dispatch. On my way back here, I switched over to Highlands channels, they couldn't get a hold of anyone east of 32nd. I figured maybe a blackout or power surge but—"

"But dispatch has battery backup," Tulls finished for him. Mackintah nodded and ran his fingers through what remained of his close-cropped hair. A few snowflakes were displaced by the action.

"You see. There's something seriously wrong here. And on the way back, too."

"Getting tired of the word 'wrong.' I agree something's amiss here, but I don't know about expressing yourself in the way you did here." He gaze bored into the younger man. "I need to be sure you're okay. I can't have an officer out here flipping his lid." His tone softened. "Do we understand each other?"

Mackintah nodded. "I swear it's what I saw."

"Are you solid?"

"I'm shaky."

"Shaky is good enough." Tulls retrieved the pistol from his jacket pocket and returned it. "I'm going to have Lasser take Missus Rialto in his car. You come with me."

Mackintah sat back in the car and closed the door. Immediately he checked the condition of his sidearm before returning it to his holster.

Tulls returned to where Jennifer was working on her third cigarette. He waved Lasser over.

"Missus Rialto, this is officer Lasser."

She nodded. "I gathered that."

"He'll take you to the school."

"Where will you be?"

"I'll be in the car ahead of you." He looked to Lasser, "Have your partner stay here in the event that Jimmy comes home."

Sergeant Lasser nodded and trotted off to pass on the information. Jennifer followed behind, flicking ashes into the fresh snow along the way.

Tulls returned to his car. Whoops from cocky teens erupted from various places accompanied by the barrage of, "Five-O is on the job," and "haulin' away anothah' one."

"I love my job," he muttered, sliding behind the wheel.

"Detective?"

"Yeah, Mackintah?" Tulls started the car and pulled out of the driveway.

"I've been thinking about the school."

"Uh huh." He turned left, heading east.

"I remember hearing about a fire there. Back in the '90s."

"That was quite a ways back. Before your time."

"Still, William Scotts was firebombed back then. I remember hearing about fifteen people who died."

"Sixteen, "Tulls corrected, "Thirteen children, three teachers." He pumped the brake, nervous about the sedan's response on such icy roads. In the rear-view mirror Tulls could see Lasser's patrol car fishtail slightly. "Kind of a morbid interest."

"They taught it in my civics class back in school."

"Ahh."

"The people I saw on the way back…I forgot to tell you."

"And what's that?" Tulls' mind had focused more on the task of not having an accident than on the conversation at hand.

"There weren't any."

"The weather's shitty. What do you expect?"

"I mean anywhere east of 32nd. It was dead."

Tulls growled as the car slid to the left and nearly clipped a parked van before he regained control.

"Did you hear me?"

"What?"

"I said that part of town seemed dead."

"How so?" He eased the wheel to the right, going with the

direction he desired rather than jerking the wheel into the slide. "Because there weren't any people on the street?"

"No, because I couldn't see any signs of life *at all*." He pointed out the window. "Look at the sky. Tell me that's natural."

The clouds directly ahead of them appeared somehow darker than those blanketing the rest of the city. They didn't swirl or bloom, just hung stationary. In the distance the snow-filled mass regained its amber hue.

Tulls responded, "It's just a more condensed patch of weather. You've probably seen it a hundred times before and never registered it."

A Super-Jo lunch truck slid past them at the intersection, making a slow slide down the middle of the street. The driver's face wore a mask of concentration, oblivious to everything except the goal of keeping his vehicle from hitting anything. It skidded to a stop inches before coming into contact with an expensive looking Cadillac.

The light changed and the scene which had just played out fell behind, giving way to another block of ice-blanketed streets and shivering pedestrians.

"Detective, I know what you're trying to get at, but…" he hesitated long enough for Tulls to glance his direction, "but some of the other buildings were wrong too."

"How so?"

"I passed a Dixieland Liqueurs on the way here."

"There's no Dixieland Liqueurs anywhere in our jurisdiction."

Mackintah laughed in a high, cackling way. "Don't you think I know that?"

"There's no way you may have been—"

"There *was* a Dixieland Liqueurs about thirty-five years ago. My Uncle Murdock was shot while working there. Perp killed him for about fifty dollars."

Tulls flipped on the heater, convinced the engine had run enough to offer heat. The fan rattled in obvious need of lubrication. The sickly-sweet smell from a failing heater core wafted through the vents.

"What are you trying to get at?"

Tulls sighed. "The store closed right after my uncle died. They leveled it and put in the Taco Heaven."

He checked the rearview mirror to make sure that Lasser was still behind him. He pressed on the gas and passed 30th Street with the light.

"The place has great enchiladas."

Mackintah turned in his seat. "That's not the point. The point is that the Taco Heaven was gone and the Dixieland was back in its place."

Tulls remained quiet, focusing on both the road and the conversation playing out between the two of them. Ahead, the patch of dark cloud remained stationary, giving off no visible reflection of city lights.

Tulls asked, "Are you sure?"

"I know I may sound it, but I'm not crazy."

They drifted past 31st Street.

Tulls slowed the car to little more than a creeping pace.

"What else did you see?"

"The road had been driven on, but the sidewalks were snowbound." Mackintah turned and looked his window. "It looked like everyone had just up and gone." He paused before adding, "No foot traffic. No shoveled walks. Nothing."

Ahead a gathering of people stood in the street, their backs to the approaching car.

Tulls tapped the horn and received an upturned finger as a reply from one of the spectators.

"Pop the cherry," Tulls said.

Mackintah retrieved the dash light from the sedan's floorboard and plugged it into the cigarette lighter. The light reflected pink on the snow and a rich maroon against the backs of the forty-odd people comprising the crowd.

"Detective Tulls," the radio squawked.

Tulls motioned for Mackintah to take the call.

"Go."

"The boy just called again. Said he was going back to the school. Something about not being able to leave."

Tulls took the mic.

"Did he say anything else? Anything that may give us a better idea of where to look for him?"

"No sir. Just that he was scared. Didn't say why."

"Clear." Tulls replaced the handset and tapped on the horn, advancing the car in the process.

The onlookers reluctantly parted. Midway through he stopped and rolled down the window.

"What's going on?"

"Across the street," a blonde woman, better suited to the role of Fat Lady in a sideshow, answered. Her rose-colored muumuu flapped and exposed more of her leg than Tulls thought any man should have to see.

"What about it?"

"It's…" she worked for the right word to use, "*wrong*."

Tulls rolled the window up in reply to her statement.

The car inched through the remainder of people. Tulls stopped the car, threw it in park, then got out.

Across the street lay the beginning of something *wrong*.

On the north side of the street a Pleasure World porn shop sat where he was sure the corner Gas Rabbit should be. Its sign, lit with a multitude of colored bulbs—mostly blown, rather than the common LEDs or neon that comprised the majority of establishment advertising today—flashed a discordant morse code to the libido of any within sight.

"See," the woman said while waddling her way across the ice to where Tulls stood, "I said it was wrong, didn't I?"

He was really beginning to hate that word. "I…just go home."

"I ain't done nothin'!" The woman's blonde hair fell free of the kerchief covering her head. "You can't make us," she stressed the point by waving an arm to the crowd which now showed equal interest in the exchange as in the event taking place across the street. "We ain't done nothin'. None of us!"

"You're standing in the middle of an icy street blocking traffic."

"What traffic?"

Tulls waited for her to register the fact that he, and the patrol car behind him, were the very traffic he referred to. Half a moment ticked by before she stared from him to the car and walked off in a huff. Other members of the crowd mimicked the action, leaving the street for a safer vantage point on the sidewalk.

"Is there anyone else who feels I'm harassing them?" He already knew the answer to be "no," but the calculated statement had the desired effect. The remaining few people on the street cleared.

He stared at the porn shop suspiciously, taking in every aspect of it. Iron bars covered narrow windows. An advertisement for Shakey's condoms glared out from the side of the store. The cardboard sign declaring them open hung stationary from wire hanger, its once bright red lettering faded to dingy orange.

"Detective?"

Tulls got back in the car and slammed the door. He checked his cell phone.

No signal.

He sighed, looked at Mackintah and said, "We're going," and he stepped on the gas.

The sedan slid into the intersection with minimal effort. The dip on the far side of the intersection caught the right front tire, jerking the wheel out of Tulls' grip.

For an instant the world spun by in a slow carousel view, first showing the block they'd just come from, then the street they'd crossed, finally passing by Pleasure World before coming to a stop facing east.

"Well," Mackintah said, "at least we won't have to turn the car around."

Tulls scoffed, put the car in park and got back out.

"What are you doing?"

He didn't answer. The shop stood before him, appearing as solid as the ice under his feet.

"Sir?"

"I need to check this out."

"Sir, there's plenty more farther on."

Behind him, Lasser's car shot across the intersection fast. It hit the dip straight on and shot into the back of Tulls' car, crunching the two of them in a metallic embrace. Taillights shattered on impact, crimson shards flying in every direction. The two cars pushed past Tulls, missing him by inches.

Tulls took two steps toward the porn shop before slipping and landing hard on his right side. A rib which never healed right bit white-hot at his back while slush soaked through thin trouser material.

"Damn it!"

Lasser's vehicle continued to accelerate, tires spinning with the sound of a thousand angry bees against the slick road, as a black rain of polluted water shot up from the rear of the patrol car. He couldn't see Mackintah, but the locked rear tires of his car told of the man pressing against the brake pedal with his hands. The conjoined vehicles stopped twenty feet past the collision point.

Tulls stood and calmed himself before making his way to the vehicles, determined to keep control of the situation.

Lasser pushed his door open and pulled himself to his feet.

Tulls looked at the heavy dark bruise already visible. "You okay?"

"I'm fine. The damned gas pedal stuck."

Mackintah had already evacuated their car and knelt to examine the two vehicles' damage. Oil dripped in a steady stream from the patrol car, melting the ice and pooling underneath the engine.

"This one's toast," the officer said simply. "The other looks okay… well, except for the rear end."

"Aesthetics aside, it'll do."

Tulls made his way around to the passenger side and opened Jennifer's door. The window had spiderwebbed, a baseball sized hole rimmed with crimson marked where her head had impacted with the glass. She sat staring straight forward, unmoving. Blood matted her hair against the side of her face, effectively masking the severity of the wound.

"Missus Rialto?"

"I…uh…." She slowly turned her head to him.

He placed a hand on her shoulder and kept her still.

"Take it easy. Help is on the way." Tulls looked up at Lasser. "Get on the horn and call for an ambulance."

"My son…we need to find my son." Her gaze seemed to look right through him, focusing on something beyond his view. Jennifer fumbled with the clasp on the seatbelt.

"Easy, ma'am," he pulled the wet locks away from her brow, exposing a two-inch gash which wept freely. Swelling forced the wound open, exposing the wet tissue beneath. Tulls pulled a handkerchief from his pocket and applied pressure to Jennifer's head.

She winced and slowly shook her head from side to side in a muddled attempt to dislodge the fabric.

"Damn it," she managed. "Get off me!"

"Missus Rialto, you've got a nasty cut."

Lasser's voice echoed back from his vehicle, "Radio's out."

Tulls leaned across Jennifer and flipped the radio to auxiliary. No static, calls from other units, or multi-toned squalls were emitted— only dead air. He switched across the dozen direct channels, looking for any feedback. None came up as a winner.

"Damn." He looked down at her.

"Find Jimmy," she said flatly. Breath made from thousands of cigarettes engulfed Tulls' face.

"Right now, we need to worry about getting you some help."

She pushed him away from the car and forced herself to stand. Icy air clotted the bloody wound in an instant and left only a blackened mask covering part of her face.

"What I need," she said with increasing anger, "is for you to get off your collective asses and go get my son. Then I'll go to the hospital or wherever the hell else you want me to go."

Echoes of the Jackson Five emanated from the shop and caused everyone to turn.

The store shimmered, appearance fluctuating as if from a mirage. Walls blurred, momentarily giving way to pumps and the Gas Rabbit's flourescent yellow logo visible through the transparent brickwork. Tulls blinked in an attempt to clear the unnatural double vision. A ripple ran through the porn shop's wall before solidifying once more.

"What in hell," Lasser muttered.

"Missus Rialto, get in my car now." Tulls continued to stare at the front of the shop, not believing the sight before him. "You too, Mackintah."

Lasser and Tulls walked to the sidewalk with the latter tapping the edge of the sidewalk.

"Checking for ice?"

"Checking for a mirage. The entrance to the gas station should be right about here. So, there shouldn't be a curb. Right?" Tulls tapped on the now solid curb. "Odd."

"Odd?" Lasser looked up and down the block nervously. "Odd is finding a finger in your bowl of cereal. This is fucking insane!"

"Lasser...Frank, I need you with me on this. Mackintah's already two peaches short of a fruit basket and the Rialto woman's hurt."

"What are you thinking?"

"Well," he took his foot off the curb, choosing to remain in the street, "Mackintah said there was more farther in."

"Don't tell me you want to continue?"

"Hey Detective," a call from the increasing crowd behind them sounded out, "is that what you call a meeting of the minds?"

Lasser turned and opened his mouth to reply.

Tulls placed a hand on his arm.

"Easy. Remember, it's all part of the job." He motioned the officer towards his vehicle. "We're out of contact with headquarters and about thirty of the patrol cars. What I'm suggesting is that we continue with our case...find the boy and get our asses back to the station."

Other comments, mostly obscenities, echoed across the intersection questioning everything from professional competence to their ancestry. A bottle flew across the expanse, smashing upon contact with the street and showering the two public servants with crystalline shards.

The composition of the crowd shifted.

Shouts accusing the officers of being responsible for the sudden reappearance of Pleasure World were followed by more sounds of glass breaking and dumpsters being rummaged through.

"Detective, this situation is getting pretty grim."

"Uncle Tom!" Another glass missile flew out of the crowd, went wide and shattered against the newly-formed porn shop wall.

"C'mon. Let's see if we can get your car moving."

Lasser slid behind the seat and turned the key. The car turned over and emitted a heavy knocking sound before sputtering to a stop. Green and brown life blood spilled onto the street in a pulsing release.

Tulls laughed.

Lasser looked over his shoulder and watched the increasingly agitated mob.

"What's the joke?"

"Uncle Tom."

"Huh?"

"Nothing."

The vulgarities increased in volume.

"What?" Lasser pulled the shotgun from the lock between the seats.

"Anything in the trunk?"

Lasser got out and moved toward the lead vehicle. "Just a med kit."

"Leave it." Tulls stopped. "Do you smell gas?"

Lasser pulled his light and walked in a squat, shining the beam underneath Tulls' car. "Got a leak…a bad one."

"Doesn't matter," he gave a wayward glance behind him. "We've got a situation brewing here. Get in."

Tulls slid in back, behind the driver's seat, while Lasser took the wheel. Keys were passed and the car started.

Lasser dropped the car into drive. "What about the 'Uncle Tom?'" The officer sounded excited, pumped up on adrenaline.

"Huh?" Mackintah said.

Tulls answered, "Just race and loyalties."

"Thought we were past that." Lasser stepped on the gas and the car moved forward slightly before the tires spun.

"More things change, the more they stay the same." Tulls turned and looked out the rear window. Lasser's patrol car shifted in time with his vehicle. "We're hung up."

A flaming bottle exploded against the patrol car, blazing brightly and splattering the trunk of the detective's vehicle with liquid fire.

"Go. Go. Go…go-go-go-go-go," Jennifer chanted in repetitive steam-engine puffs of smoke.

"Getting bad," Tulls said.

Mackintah had completely turned around in his seat and was looking out the back of the car. "Bad, hell!"

The crowd, sensing the shift in power, converged on the joined vehicles, scampering over the tops and smacking hands and bottles against the windows. Bell bottoms, beadwork, and fringe vests, accented large afros, beards, and shoulder-length hair.

Tulls and Mackintah pulled their weapons.

The cars rocked in unison under mob-enraged power.

A palm smacked by Tulls' window only to be followed by a man's face. His tie-dyed bandana flashed the only color save the whites of the man's gritted teeth.

"Honky!"

Another yelled, "Fuckin' pigs!"

"Get us out of here!" Tulls heard the words, knew they came from his mouth, but the intensity sounded alien in comparison to his otherwise solemn manner.

A revolver's barrel smacked menacingly against Mackintah's window.

Tulls pointed his gun and pulled the trigger in reflex.

The sudden explosion of noise didn't match the quarter-sized hole which appeared in the door glass. Spiderwebbed cracks opaqued any view of the bullet's target.

Something smacked Tulls on top of the head. His vision swam.

As if in a dream, he watched the roof of the car bend in…watched Mackintah fire three times into the roof…watched as the screaming mass fell behind the vehicle…watched as the buildings slowly passed by.

"Tulls!"

"I…" he shook off the converging waves of nausea, "I'm still here."

"Low on gas."

Tulls leaned forward; the needle sat firmly on the "E."

"Leak must be bad. I filled up before heading over to—"

"We've got to find Jimmy!" Jennifer Rialto's gaze burned into Tulls. "Don't you see? He's out there with those…maniacs!"

"That's where we're going right now," Tulls assured.

The car lurched.

"How long since we pulled away? I'm a little fuzzy."

"About four blocks back. Two minutes, give or take."

Another lurch and the car stopped.

"Okay," Tulls looked at everyone in turn, "Lasser, keep the shotgun and take point. Mackintah, you stay with Missus Rialto and I'll bring up the rear.

The four of them got out and looked at their surroundings.

Tulls recognized the closed Chuck's mini-mart, light from the "We Sell Beer" sign shown through barred windows. Cho stood beside a porcelain-skinned woman and looked out and studied them with mild curiosity before disappearing into the storeroom. The woman followed after a handful of seconds, turning off the beer sign as she went.

"Think his phone works?" Mackintah spoke slowly, as if each word was forced from his mouth.

"Wouldn't matter," Tulls replied. "Ol' Cho doesn't open the gate for anyone after closing."

"Did you see…?" Lasser started.

"What?" Tulls pulled hard on the trunk, trying to force the buckled metal to release.

"That woman."

"Yeah. What about her?" The trunk refused Tulls' ministrations and he smacked the hood with frustration.

"She looked like Yoshey."

"Who?"

"Who cares," Jennifer broke in. "Where did Jimmy say he was and I'll get him myself."

"Missus Rialto…."

"No! You have dragged your feet since I first called." She lit another cigarette. "You have to wait a certain length of time. You have to call in. You have to get into a pissing contest with a bunch of nutjobs. You need to do everything but find…my…son!"

"Quiet."

"Excuse me?"

"Shut up," Tulls stressed through gritted teeth.

Snow started to fall as the four of them stood quietly in the middle of the street.

Silence.

Mackintah pointed in the direction they'd come. Just over a block in either direction their view was blurred by snow, eventually being erased into grey oblivion shortly thereafter.

"Mobs don't usually give up that easily," Tulls said.

"Right."

"If nothing else a whoop or two should make it this far."

"Or the sound of them snapping on my car." Lasser turned to him, "You are gonna sign off on that, aren't you?"

"I didn't see a thing."

The two chuckled at the weak joke, laughing more against the lapse in sanity than at the subject matter.

"Missus Rialto, if the information your son gave is correct, he should be a few blocks up on the left."

"And you couldn't say that back at the house?"

Tulls started everyone moving, choosing silence as the best retort to Jennifer's question. They walked down the middle of the street. Snow pulled all smells of pollution from the air, leaving an unnatural freshness. Light from streetlights dimmed, their glow more of a dingy orange than that of the bright bulbs Mayor Fulgribs was so proud of.

At the end of the block Lasser motioned Tulls up beside him and said, "About Cho…."

"Yeah?" Tulls glanced his way then ahead once more.

"That looked like his wife."

"Cho isn't married."

"He's a widower. His wife was a mean bitch."

Tulls gave a disapproving look.

"Fine, she was…*unkind*. Selling drugs, guns, prostituting, whatever she could to make an extra buck without Cho knowing about it."

"And just how do you know about it?"

"My big brother was…a regular customer."

Mackintah looked in every direction, eyes darting from potential threat to potential threat.

The four crossed the street.

"Hey," Jennifer said, her voice little more than a whisper, "where is everyone?"

"Keep moving." Tulls kept his weapon at the ready with his finger on the trigger guard.

"I mean it." She slipped on the ice and fell on her back, effectively smacking her head for the second time in less than fifteen minutes. Her cigarette went out, melting a nickel-sized hole in the piling snow. Jennifer rolled onto her side, still clenching the wet butt. "Where is everyone?"

"We don't know."

"This is what I was trying to tell you back at her place. This area is wrong. We need to go back."

Tulls said, "Back through that mob?"

Mackintah nearly screeched, "I don't care! We could cut a block over and—"

"Enough, Mackintah."

"Don't tell me, 'enough!'" He pointed to a pawn shop on their left. "That should be Razorback Liquors. I buy a six-pack there every Friday on my way home. I mean," he pointed with his pistol, "look at the place. Take a good look."

"Just keep moving."

"Bullshit."

"Stow it and keep moving. We need to get the Rialto boy and find some backup."

Tulls looked at the pawn shop as they passed. Layers of dust covered the multitude of display items in the window.

…at the dozen guitars masked in shadow…

…each with a neatly severed arm wired to it.

A knowing look passed between the officers.

Mackintah clicked his light on, briefly illuminating the alley to their right.

A handful of cans lined one wall while an oversized cardboard box leaned against the building directly opposite.

"There."

The box shifted.

Lasser stepped forward, pointing the shotgun ahead of him. Mackintah stepped farther to the left, keeping the box in his light. Snow came down steadily without wind to veer its course.

"This is the police," Lasser said, bellowing an authoritative voice. "Step out of the box."

A dog crept out. The animal's pedigree little more than a joke between God and Darwin. Mixtures of black, grey, and red mottled hair covered the pitiful beast. It looked at them with a confused cock of its head before tucking tail and disappearing further into the alley.

Lasser kept his pistol pointed in the direction of the fleeing dog.

"Keep moving," Tulls ordered.

The four of them continued down the center of the street. Vague illumination from streetlights gave a hauntingly surreal appearance to an otherwise bland landscape. Two lights ahead, the blurry glow of sequential bulbs winked out.

"Answer me something, Mackintah," Tulls said, surprising all as his voice broke the silence. "Was there ever a Dairy Freeze-It around here?"

"Yeah. Used to be the after-school hangout for kids."

"Where?"

"It was…oh hell." Mackintah stopped walking and brushed the snow from his shoulders. "It used to be just around the corner."

"Left or right?"

"Right."

"Missus Rialto, I think that's where we're going to find your son." Tulls motioned for Mackintah to catch up. "Here's the game plan, we get the boy, get to a land line, call for backup and hold up somewhere until they show."

"Sir," said Lasser, "what makes you think that the Rialto boy's going to be at a parking lot?"

Tulls looked over at him before returning his gaze to the darkened storefronts.

"That's what's there now, you know that."

"Indulge me."

Jennifer Rialto set the pace for the officers to the end of the block and kept the four at a dangerously fast paced stride on the snow-packed ice.

They passed the corner shop and Lasser shone his light through the front window.

Inside lay a soda shop straight out of the fifties. Advertisements for cola and stick figures promoting chewing gum plastered the upper portion of the walls. Stained tile, remnants of its original blue coloring visible between thousands of cracks, blanketed the flooring. White wire-backed chairs were scattered across the room, many piled in a skeletal mass against the kitchen door. In the center of the shop sat a woman, her back to the group. She slumped in her seat, hands hanging limp. Shoulder length red hair contrasted sharply against the bright yellow ribbon holding the auburn locks in a ponytail.

Tulls rapped his knuckles against the frozen glass.

The woman didn't respond.

Mackintah whispered, "Detective, I don't remember this being here."

Tulls looked at Lasser who shook his head slowly in confirmation of the other officer's statement.

The detective went to the door and tried the knob.

Locked.

Tulls rapped on the glass again.

The woman didn't move.

Lasser asked, "Constitutes special circumstances?"

"Special circumstances?" Mackintah's voice shook as he spoke. "Shit! This whole afternoon qualifies."

Tulls kicked the glass door's wooden frame just below the brass knob.

Etched glass spiderwebbed as the door swung open halfway. The reverberating screech from unoiled hinges grated on all their ears. A snowy breeze blew into the shop and shifted the heavy layer of dust covering the floor up into the air, causing swirls of minuscule particles to wisp across the flashlight's beam.

Lasser took the point position, moving ahead of the rest. He kept the flashlight and his pistol trained on the counter and the swinging teal door leading back to the storeroom. Mackintah mimicked the actions and checked under the row of tables lining the far wall while Jennifer stood in the doorway.

Tulls moved to the sitting woman.

Her mummified face stared up at the ceiling, mouth open in a silent cry. A gash across her throat left little question as to the cause of death, its depth nearly severing the woman's head from her shoulders. A spoon had been placed in the wound as if she had continued to eat using the new orifice. Tulls came to the morbid realization that the victim's desiccated condition resembled that of a hornet's nest.

"Detective," Lasser said quietly and shone his beam on the bowl which sat in front of the corpse. Fresh ice cream filled the dish waiting for a bite that would never come. A blackish liquid covered the frozen delight. In the dim light, neither officer could tell whether the topping was chocolate or something more grim.

"What's wrong with her?" Jennifer asked and drew deeply on her cigarette.

"She's dead, Missus Rialto."

Jennifer placed a hand on the door to steady herself. "We need to find my son, now!"

"Shhhh!" Tulls' shooshing echoed through the room.

A clang came from the back room.

Mackintah moved behind the counter and listened at the door before pushing it open and taking a classic shooter's stance with pistol in one hand and flashlight in the other.

His gun wavered.

Lowered.

Tulls moved to the doorway and stole a glimpse into the back room.

Reflective metal countertops bounced the single beam of light all around the narrow room. Industrial sized cans of flavored syrup and other toppings filled metal shelves lining the far wall. In the sink rested a torso, sans appendages and head. Small patches of hair flecked the otherwise smooth chest.

Mackintah's flashlight wavered and light reflected wetly across the wounds.

"Cover me," Tulls said.

"Sir, we need to—" but was cut off by a look.

"The wounds look fresh with no clotted blood."

He approached the dismembered remains cautiously, half expecting them to suddenly become animate. Tulls grabbed a butter knife and lightly touched the neck at the torso's separation point. Exposed meat gave under pressure, leaving a crimson smear across the reflective blade.

Quietly, he returned the knife to the pile and backed out of the room with Mackintah following closely behind.

The Detective whispered to Lasser and Jennifer, "Out. Now."

Following Tulls' lead, the three exited the store and stood on the sidewalk.

"This is insanity!" Jennifer's hands shook violently as she yelled. "Which way did my son say he was?" She turned in a small circle.

All three officers turned and looked at their ward.

Since leaving the vehicle, Jennifer had gone from a callous woman to having the mannerisms of a child no older than that of her son. She turned with her arms outstretched in a macabre visage of the Sound of Music's Julie Andrews. "This is some…some kind of nightmare."

Tulls motioned to the right. "By my guess, he was half a block down."

Jennifer moved ahead of the three men, kicking against the shin-deep snow which continued to accumulate. Just beyond the alley a single phone booth stood illuminated by one of the scattered streetlights, a bright splash of blue pressed against the bottom of the glass cubicle. She quickened her pace.

The three officers sped up to keep time with the distraught mother.

She slipped and fell against the side of the booth, the impact reopening the gash on her head and allowing a new trickle of blood to work its way down the side of her face.

"Jimmy?" Jennifer pushed herself onto her hands and knees. "Jimmy!"

Tulls passed her and opened the phone booth to reveal a green and black "Surfin' Dudes" backpack propped underneath the corner-mounted phone. The antiquated rotary phone looked new enough to have been just installed. It offered direct dial for a nickel.

Tulls picked up the phone and dropped a nickel in. A dial tone crackled and he dialed "0." The rotary dial followed the pull of his finger hesitantly before rotating back to its original placement.

"Operator."

"Operator, this is Detective Tulls. Patch me through to the Thirteenth Precinct."

"Just a moment."

A moment passed by. Two. The distortion on the phone line worsened, background noise dropping pitch and stretching background conversations to resemble a 45 record playing at 33 speed.

"Sir?"

"Yes, operator?"

"I'm not sure I heard you correctly. What precinct did you want?"

"The Thirteenth."

Another pause.

"Sir, I have no listing for a Thirteenth Precinct."

"What?"

Jennifer called out into the night, "Jimmy? Where are you? Jimmy?"

"I have the South Station on line. Please hold."

Tulls leaned back and called out, "Lasser?"

Lasser stepped from behind the booth where he had been dodging as much of the winter breeze as possible. "M-yeah?"

"They're connecting us to South."

"South?"

Tulls nodded.

"Sir, South station is a homeless shelter. We outgrew it in… what…'82?"

"I know."

"Sterling here," crackled from the receiver.

"This is Detective Tulls."

"Tulls? I don't know any Tulls. Anyhow, what can I do for you?"

"We…we're in a bit of a bind down here."

"Join the club. What precinct are you with?"

"The Thirteenth."

"What city?"

"This one! What city do you think?"

"Look buddy, there's no Thirteenth Precinct. Who's your captain?"

"Johnson. Jerome Johnson."

"Johnson?" A throaty laugh came from officer Sterling. "Figures ol' J.J. would put someone up to pullin' my leg."

"You know him?"

"Sure, came on the force last year…best rookie we've got."

"Rookie?"

"Look buddy, you got a grin out of me. Enough of the chuckles and clear the line for people who are really in need." A click sounded the end of the conversation.

Tulls hung the phone up slowly.

"Jimmy?"

Jennifer's voice echoed down the empty street.

"Shhhh."

Rattling noises came from the alley.

Mackintah leveled his sidearm and prepared for whatever was making its way to the alley's mouth.

A small shadow pulled away from the darker blackness. "M… momma?"

Jennifer pushed past Mackintah and scooped the small form up into her arms. The child stood stiff in his mother's embrace, his coal-black eyes staring straight ahead.

Lasser scooped up the boy's backpack.

"Baby, are you all right?"

"I…."

"Missus Rialto," Tulls said, "we need to get going."

The woman nodded through her tears.

Lasser whispered, "Which way?"

"Fastest way is back the way we came."

"But there's one mother of a welcoming party waiting for us back there."

The detective wiped the increasing layer of snow off of his head. "We don't know how much farther this…anomaly goes."

"Well, we *are* armed, sir."

"Against the unknown or against the *Hair* mob back there?"

Lasser shrugged. "After what we've seen so far, I'd have to say I'd rather go back and regroup."

"Can't say as I blame you. But we do have a multiple homicide on our hands."

"Girl's been dead for years."

"But the torso in back was fresh." He peered into the gloom of the alley. "Besides, there's no statute of limitations on homicide."

"Sir, with all due respect, this falls under some pretty extreme circumstances. We're on foot, on the run from a hippie mob, and hurt." He motioned his head over towards Jennifer who, given the blood caked on her face and matted in her hair, gave the strong impression of a slasher-film victim. "One way or another we need to get them out of the elements and call for backup."

"Point taken. So the only question is forward or back?"

"Back. Don't like what I've seen so far, but I'll be damned if I expose a child to…." He let the sentence hang.

Mackintah glanced warily over his shoulder and moved closer to the small group. "Something's moving over there." He pointed with his pistol across the street at the apartment building.

"'Bout time," Lasser said. Then, changing the subject asked, "Go over one block then down or backtrack?"

"Backtrack. My guess is the mob's already broken up and the suspect for the other…issue is long gone. Let's stick to the safest route."

Jennifer scoffed. "Safest." She lifted Jimmy into her arms and carried him as they walked single file in the direction they'd just come.

Tulls slowed the group as the nearest apartment building offered a sign of life.

Among the boarded-up windows, a faint light emanated, flickering a dingy yellow glow that only a candle could give.

"That's where I was," Jimmy said quietly.

"You were in there?" Jennifer put him down and looked at the building.

The three-story apartment building was comprised of decaying brick, the granite cornerstone proclaiming it was built in 1928. Boards covered the first two stories' windows, leaving those of the third broken by the elements and vandals. Snow accumulated on the remnants of empty panes, piling up in a depressing visage of a winter wonderland.

"It…it's where I saw the paper."

"What?" Tulls knelt at Jennifer's side. "What paper?"

Jimmy wouldn't look at him, keeping gaze only with his mother. "It showed me things."

Tulls gently took Jimmy by the chin and turned his head. "Jimmy, I need you to tell me if there's something in this building that answers what's happening here."

The crotch of Jimmy Rialto's jeans moistened, urine flowing down the boy's right leg and into his boot. Steam rose skyward.

Mackintah resumed his nervous hyperactivity. "Detective, we can come back. We need to go."

"The snow!" Jennifer shouted, "Look at the God damned snow!"

Ten feet behind them and approaching fast, snow was kicked up by an invisible force. As frozen crystals arced, they turned crimson, falling heavily with a peppery spray on surrounding drifts.

Tulls grabbed the boy by the arm and shoved him towards the steps to the building. "Inside, now!"

Mackintah pointed his pistol where the footprints approached and fired a shot as he backed up the stairs. The bullet skidded off the pavement and struck a trash can across the street, the "pang" sound reverberating in everyone's ears.

Tulls and Lasser pulled two boards free from the doorframe. Lasser mimicked Tulls' earlier move and kicked the door open, climbed through, and helped first Jimmy, then Jennifer to enter.

"Mackintah," Tulls called from the stoop, "move your ass!"

Mackintah ran up the steps, slipped on the last one and fell to his hands and knees. He continued momentum on all fours and scampered through the opening.

The footprints stopped at the bottom of the stairs, giving Detective Tulls a clear view of the impression made in the snow.

Shoes.

He'd been expecting to see some wide-angled footprint from some unknown mythical beast. Yet here, at the bottom of the stairs was the impression made by two men's dress shoes. Blood appeared at the bottom of the impressions, seeping out and distorting Tulls' discovery. Another imprint appeared on the first step.

The detective turned and dove through the doorway.

Lasser slammed the door, scraping the wood against his superior's leg and tearing a foot long rip in both the detective's pants and leg. A foot-long gouge released red

Tulls rolled away before more damage could be done.

"Shit," Lasser said and knelt beside him.

"I'll be fine; help me up."

"We gotta get that leg taken care of," Mackintah said.

Thump.

All eyes went to the door.

The impact hadn't been otherworldly, only loud.

Light came from the apartment to their left, its missing door allowing all to see into the living room.

Gaslights flickered on the walls, dancing shadows throughout the room. Gold wallpaper blanketed the room, adding to the already yellow hue. Trim, normally painted in such buildings, had been polished to a dark shine with lemon oil. Knickknacks lined an ornate cherry wood sideboard complete with doily. A fainting couch was the centerpiece of the room. Newspaper lay strewn across the antique furnishing, looking as though ants were in the process of crossing it.

Tulls limped through the doorway to get a better look.

Headlines danced across the front page, showing, for an instant, one tragedy after another. Shootings, mob wars, rapes and natural disasters winked across the page faster than Tulls could process what he was seeing.

Thump.

Whatever was at the door rattled the knob with fervor.

Tulls reached down and grabbed the paper with his left hand, unwilling to relinquish the pistol in his right even for an instant. The paper felt new under his fingertips, opposing its brittle appearance.

"Sir," Lasser stressed, "bigger problems."

Tulls looked at the boy. "Where were you in here?"

"The back apartment."

"Everyone head to the rear of the building. Lasser, you in front."

Jimmy pulled against his mother.

"No!"

Jennifer started, "Jimmy—"

Mackintah scooped the boy up and slung him over his shoulder before following Lasser. Jennifer followed behind her panicked son. Light escaped from under the last apartment's door.

The rattling of the front door continued, more urgent than before.

"Don't go in there," Jimmy cried. "Don't!"

Lasser, feeling the rush of adrenaline, turned the knob and pushed.

The door swung in on well-oiled hinges, exposing a nightmarish visage.

Dried blood caked the walls and floor, a drenched mattress the only semblance of furnishings to be seen. Sprawled on the center of the mattress a small form lay unmoving, arms and legs bent and unnatural angles.

"Damn, kid." Mackintah put the boy down. "You peed all over me." He raised his wet hand to see the ruby red fluid coating it.

"I told you," Jimmy said, voice rasping. "I told you not to open the door. I just wanted to leave." The boy backed through the doorway to the room, his chest now seeping blood and soaking the front of his coat.

Tulls looked past the boy and to the body in the room. A Surfin' Dudes backpack was propped against one bare, pre-adolescent leg.

"Why couldn't you just take me home?"

"Jimmy…" Jennifer began and reached for him.

Lasser grabbed her hand.

The doppelganger cried out a pitiful wail. "It showed me things, Momma." He moved farther into the room, stopping beside the dead boy.

Jennifer put a hand to her mouth.

The skin above the child-thing's left eyebrow split cleanly, separating across the bridge of the nose and ending midway along his jaw. "It showed me things…bad things."

"Oh…my…baby."

"Do you want to see?" Puss welled up in the wound, spilling over and running down his cheek.

"Everyone out," Tulls said quietly.

Jimmy-Thing smiled, exposing two broken teeth. "Does that mean you'll still take me home?"

"You," Tulls pointed at the changeling, "wait here."

Jennifer turned on Tulls, shoving him violently. "We…are not… leaving Jimmy here!" She fell back along the wall and slid to the floor. "He's just hurt, that's all…just hurt."

"Momma," Jimmy-Thing said, "hold me."

Mackintah and Lasser backed away from the two, unsure of how to respond.

Jimmy-Thing's body took on more injuries. With each passing second he looked less like the child from the picture supplied earlier in the day and more like some matted pulp wheeled into morgues every day. He crawled up into Jennifer's lap, nuzzling her neck.

Tulls fought back rising bile and swallowed hard.

"What was outside?"

"Just a shadow. What else?" Jimmy-Thing laughed and a bloody bubble formed on his cheek. "There are lots of shadows here. Other things too."

"Here? Where is here?"

Jennifer stroked the changeling's head, humming a lullaby quietly.

"Missus Rialto?"

No response.

Lasser stood his ground as Mackintah backed to the rear entrance of the building.

"We gotta go! Damn it, we gotta go!" Mackintah bolted out the back door and into the night. The door slammed shut behind him.

Lasser said nothing but kept his pistol trained on the macabre pairing before him.

"Jennifer," Tulls said softly, "your son's in there."

She kept humming and looked up at him, followed with her eyes the direction he pointed.

The backpack fell over.

The officer's ward jumped, the noise shocking her out of the insane euphoria she'd slid into.

"J—Jimmy?"

Her gaze went from the battered mass in the apartment to the equally beaten form held in her arms. She tried to push the child-thing away unsuccessfully.

Then it burned her. Her skin grew dark, then softened, melding into the Jimmy-Thing like warm pudding.

"Get it off, get it off getitoff!"

Tulls dropped the paper he held and reached for her. Two of his fingers promptly crumbled and broke off, falling to the floor before shattering to dust.

He raised his hand, staring dumbfounded at where the missing appendages were only a moment before.

"The paper," Lasser cried and smacked the side of Tulls' coat. The jacket pocket which once held it fell apart, allowing the pages to flutter to the ground. The already worn carpet unraveled around it, the floor underneath taking on an aged, fragile look.

Jennifer stood. The Jimmy-Thing's body had fused with her own, flesh melding as butter. It churned against her, working to get more of its body up against its adoptive mother.

"Hel…help me." She raised one arm, the other lay fused into the jacket of the beast.

Bam!

A hole appeared in her right cheek as grey matter sprayed the wall.

She fell over, the Jimmy-Thing still moving.

Tulls looked at Lasser…at the smoking gun he held.

"She said…she said she wanted help."

"You did good," Tulls whispered.

The two went out the back door and into the night.

"Now what?"

Tulls continued to stare at his hand. "It doesn't hurt. That's the funny part."

"Detective," Lasser said.

Hearing his title brought him around.

"We'll go back the way we came."

They walked down the middle of the streets, pistols at the ready.

The neighborhood was coming back to life.

Lights flickered. Voices spoke in a foreign language safely behind drape-drawn apartments. Bodiless shadows moved across alleyway walls…and then the first person staggered out.

A junkie scrambled out from behind a stack of trash cans, needle marks apparent to even the most untrained eye.

"Did you fuckin' see that?"

Tulls leveled his weapon at the new arrival as Lasser pointed his in the direction the man had come.

"See what?"

"The angel, man…the angel." He pointed up. "See…there she is. The angel. Hi—hi angel," his high-pitched voice crooned.

A sheet, blown free by the storm, was thrown violently about before wafting in the direction they'd come.

"Wait…wait for me!"

Lasser stepped in his way.

"But it's my…angel."

Tulls said, "Let him go. Just don't touch him." He held up his grey, withered hand as a reminder.

Lasser said, "The malt shop…look."

The ice cream parlor was lit and open for business. Inside a red-headed teen sat enjoying a sundae while the soda-jerk flirted shamelessly with her.

"You don't think…."

Tull's voice was lost to a bout of huffing as the two ran across the street and into the lit establishment.

"We need some help," Lasser managed.

"Well, dang buddy, I'd say you do."

"Can you call the police?"

"Well now," the soda-jerk's face blistered, "I thought you two *were* the police." He came around from behind the counter holding a meat cleaver.

"God in Heaven—"

"Now, now, now," the burnt visage crooned, "there's no need for taking *His* name in vain, now is there? Right, Karen?"

The teen turned and smiled, showing pearly-white teeth.

Tulls and Lasser leveled their weapons as the soda-jerk raised the cleaver. Burnt pieces flaked off as he continued to move forward.

Karen continued to eat, oblivious to the actions of those around her.

Both officers fired off shots simultaneously.

The figure fell forward, its cleaver striking Karen square in the throat, slicing deep.

She fell back, arms to her sides and legs kicking out uncontrollably.

Tulls turned away from the death spasms they had caused. His gun fell to the floor and fired again, striking Lasser in the ankle. Tulls watched the officer fall with disjointed interest. The pistol he dropped was gripped by a severed hand…his severed hand. He held up his right arm and stared at the dusty stump.

"I don't understand." His voice sounded weak, belonging somehow to another person.

Lasser was on the ground holding his leg, silently mouthing a righteous "O."

A shot fired from outside, striking the officer in the thigh.

This time Lasser howled. "Fuck! Oh fuck! Help! Oh…Oh fuck!"

Tulls tried to move. A popping sound came from both his legs. He fell onto his back. Dust, broken free from his body, skittered across the tiled floor.

He watched as Mackintah stepped, wild-eyed, into the shop.

"I'll help you," he cackled and blew the top of Lasser's skull off. He turned to Tulls.

"I…but…."

Mackintah knelt down and wiped a few flecks of flesh from Tulls' face before placing the muzzle against the detective's temple.

"I'll help you too."

Behind the story...

"The Lost" is what happens when you try to write while you have an especially nasty case of the flu. It was a weird time. I had weird dreams and I had no idea how this was going to end until I clicked SAVE for the last time.

I do remember it started with dreaming about being lost in an abandoned city and seeing severed arms in a music store window. PSA—that is what you dream about if you mix chicken soup, beer, and several slices of pizza in a single evening of being ill.

"The Lost" came about not too long after having a time-travel discussion with my father-in-law, Tom. The conversation left me with more questions than answers and that's kind of how I approached the story, not giving an answer, but playing within the physical laws I set within the story.

SKETCHES

Lani Milton sat in her wheelchair and stared through greasy brown hair at the scrap of paper, torn roughly into a square and brittle with age. Her latest sketch on it was a pile of money occupying nearly all the left side's six-inch length.

"Why?"

The sound of her voice echoed in the cabin's great room.

Deafening silence was the only answer.

But silence was better than all the other placating answers she'd been given during the last eight months of hell.

Why had their car gone off the road?

Why had that branch—that one fucking branch—been bent so low?

Why hadn't she worn her seatbelt?

She pushed back from the desk, sick of looking out the cabin's window at the wishing well. Its paint still looked unusually bright.

"A pile of money? Really?"

Lani drew the money on the old scrap two days ago. Then yesterday a call came from the life insurance company notifying her their investigation was finally complete, and a check would be cut and mailed out sometime in the next two weeks.

She wheeled around the couch, taking notice of the missing chair Trent used to sit in—a chair her father removed while she was in the hospital learning how to use the working half of her body.

Compared to how they'd originally decorated their home, it now felt spartan. Nearly half the furniture they'd found between antique stores and rummage sales now sat out in the barn. Knickknack furniture was gone, replaced with ample floor space for the wheelchair.

"Probably destroyed by mice now, anyway."

She'd gone through the seven stages of grief several times since the accident. Nothing helped and she'd settled on bitterness to fuel the waking hours.

Trent had mouthed words to her.

Lani shook her head, memory refusing to be denied.

His lips….

"No," she said simply, using a tactic—one of many—the therapist gave her to work through flashbacks. "Vocalize control," he'd said. "Deny the memory any power."

Deny what? The fact that he had a branch stuck in him like some kind of marshmallow?

Polished log walls met her gaze, their normal rich honey color appearing more a dismal syrupy hue in the stark light.

"More like shit," she muttered and wheeled to the kitchen counter.

Her great aunt Esther's letter sat folded, still together and just out of easy reach, resting right where Lani threw it after skimming the pages. The contents were the same drivel all their friends and family sent through cards or letters.

Why didn't they just send emails? They're easier to get rid of.

She reached for the papers, fingers coming just short of connecting with the letter.

"Damn it."

Reaching down, her right hand connected with the gator. The hideously goofy grabbing tool she'd been given at the hospital stared up at her from the makeshift PVC holster her dad added to the chair after the third time she'd left the tool in another room.

She slapped the gator down on the letter and dragged it closer.

Lani froze.

Esther was senile, but why share dementia-induced fantasies about an old slip of paper?

Silent words being mouthed popped into her head again.

Trent's eye bulging.

The blood.

So much blood.

A metallic taste flooded Lani's mouth and she released her lower lip from between clenched teeth.

The mangled piece of flesh bore fresh gouges her tongue explored, letting her focus for a moment on physical pain rather than the hell her mind refused to leave.

She pulled the letter free and clenched it in one shaking fist.

Little Lani, the letter opened. She'd been the only one Lani ever allowed to use a pet name. The spiderweb-thin scrawl lined the first page—the only page that contained anything. Most of the words were nothing but gibberish that couldn't be deciphered. All the other pages were just filler, nothing more than protection for the little slip of parchment gifted to her.

And answer to all her woes, Esther promised.

"Woes?" Lani rolled her eyes at the archaic word and felt a wave of wine-infused vertigo wash over her.

"Whoa." A chuckle escaped her at unintentionally throwing out a homonym.

Drunk, she decided. *I'm a drunk cripple.*

"How fucking pathetic."

Placing the letter in her lap, she wheeled back to the desk and placed it by the scrap of paper then stared at the well.

The latch clicked and the door swung open, giving Trent enough room to carry her, hefted over one shoulder like one would a bag of dog food.

"Put me down," she giggled, smacking his low back.

"Across the threshold, mah dear," Trent said, butchering a southern accent.

"This isn't what I meant."

He kicked the door shut and carried her into the bedroom before dropping her in a decidedly unromantic way onto the bed.

"Lani..." Trent breathed into her ear, but his voice sounded far away.

The lovemaking had been sweet, almost as if they were teens groping for the first time. Her shirt went "somewhere" and she'd kicked her jeans mostly free...one pant leg refused to slide free past her ankle. Trent nuzzled her neck, tracing the edge of her bra, fingers tracing lower, past her sternum to—

"Hey, Pumpkin."

Lani's eyes snapped open, dread immediately setting in.

I don't want to be here. I was just—

Her mother's voice interrupted the thought. "Did you sleep in your chair all night?"

An audible sigh escaped. "Hi, Mom." A second sigh came and went before she added, "Hi, Dad." She sat up straighter, knotted hair blocking most of her view. Two shadows walked around the room, growing smaller with every move.

Familiar footsteps approached and she wheeled around, pushing across the room, putting distance between them. Lani finger-brushed the rat's nest on her head back and forced a small smile.

"What brings you two up here?"

With a grunt, her dad set a box filled with groceries on the counter right beside the two bottles of red she'd emptied the night before. He picked one up and looked from her mom back to her, silence saying so much more than any amount of yelling would. Burst vessels marred his nose and cheeks, showing that over the years he'd put more than a bottle or two away himself.

Must run in the family.

Her mom, whose appearance screamed the very definition of "annoying woman," walked to the kitchen area and looked at the two bottles, then at the other four lying dead in the trash can.

Dead like Trent.

"Lani, we talked about this. Your medication—"

"Mom, I'm a twenty-five-year-old cripple who killed her husband. I think that's worth a drink or two, don't you?"

Her mom's lips pursed, accentuating frown lines which only deepened with time. She moved to sit down, then thought better of it after eyeing the layer of dust covering the couch.

"Honey," her dad cut in. "It was an accident." He moved closer and she backed up. "The report said he went quick."

Lani barked a sad laugh. "He didn't die quick, Dad. That branch stuck in his chest, and it took a while for him to drown."

"Lani," her mom snapped.

"Hours, Mom. He didn't bleed out like you two keep telling me. I was awake. He'd cough and make a face telling me I killed him!" Tears welled. She screamed out her frustration, memory locked back in the car, steering wheel crushing her abdomen, "Do you know what he said?"

Her dad moved closer and sat on the couch. "Honey, he couldn't have said—"

"He said, 'It's going to be okay.' Do I look okay?" She'd spent two full months learning to read lips from watching the TV on mute, just to figure out those five little words. "Do I fucking look *okay* to you?"

Silence reigned as loud as when she'd been home alone moments ago.

That was last night.

A minute passed with no one making eye contact before her mom started back up. "So, who'd you convince to bring you alcohol?"

"Liquor stores deliver now, Mom." Lani held up an empty glass in a mock salute. "Thank you, Covid."

"Lani," her dad started. Then, thinking better of continuing, got up, took the glass from his daughter, and added it to the others in the sink.

"George, let's focus on why we're here."

"Hon," he started, eyes staying fixed on the sink. "We want to talk to you about—"

"Moving back in with you."

"Yes." His tone sounded defeated, conveying he already knew the answer she'd give.

Lani gave an eye roll worthy of any teenager, earning a glare from her mother.

"Listen—"

"Hey, you two," Lani cut in, "it's been great seeing you, but I'm feeling a little tired. I think I'm going to turn in." She turned the wheelchair and shot into the bedroom, slamming the door behind her and locking it. She flipped the chair's stops and waited. A muffled argument ensued just quiet enough for her to not understand. One minute became three…then five.

Pressure changed as the front door opened and closed again. Moments later her dad's old Ford, a '78 piece of garbage he obsessed over, started up.

Lani pulled herself onto the bed, reaching down and grabbing each pant leg to lift lifeless appendages onto the mattress.

What if Mom stayed?

It wouldn't be the first time and, unless she found a way to get them to just leave her alone, wouldn't be the last.

Her hand slid under the far pillow—*Trent's pillow*, she reminded herself—and pulled free the cheap bottle of whiskey she'd left for a rainy day.

Morning sunshine lit the yard outside like the set of a romance movie.

She wiped a tear away. "Looks pretty rainy to me," and took a long swig, wincing as amber fire slid past her lips, burning the mangled flesh she'd chewed raw.

Lani huffed, pushing the wheelbarrow through the yard before losing her footing and tipping it, then herself, onto the grass. She stretched, feeling fresh-mown grass tickle her ankles and sunlight beating down on her face.

"Hey," Trent called from the pickup, "no breaks until we get the rest of this dirt unloaded."

Refusing to look in the direction a day's worth of work waited, she stared at the cabin. Newly hung curtains adorned the bedroom, its sheers just barely allowing her to make out the outline of the bed.

Something moved.
She squinted, making out what appeared to be a shape on the bed.
On their bed.
It looked like—

Lani's eyes snapped open, staring at the same sheers she'd seen just a second before from the yard.

She blinked.

From last summer. Not a second ago.

The yard looked neglected, somehow beaten in the early March daylight.

Just like me.

No leaves crowned the trees. No squirrels or butterflies played in the yard. Only remnants from last summer's unharvested garden filled the fenced off area she'd been so proud of.

She pulled herself into the chair, grabbed a handful of clothes to change into and a fresh colostomy bag.

Lani forced herself through the morning routine, noting she was getting weaker when moving from the wheelchair to the plastic shower chair. The act of brushing her hair proved more problematic than expected, knots snapping strands with each pull.

She brushed harder.

Trent always loved her hair.

"I'll cut you tomorrow." Wheeling out of the master bathroom, Lani wasn't sure if she meant her hair or her wrists.

If Mom and Dad were here yesterday, then that had to be Saturday. A glance at the wall clock showed it was closer to lunch than breakfast.

Just the thought started her stomach growling to the point it hurt.

Good.

Rolling back to the desk, Lani looked out at the yard to that damned wishing well.

Esther's letter still lay partially crumpled on the by the paper where she'd tossed it when her parents showed up yesterday.

Saturday.

"Shit," she muttered, noting that today was also her parents' day off and odds were good they'd be making another appearance.

Lani looked over at the groceries neatly lined up on the kitchen counter, sans box.

Her toe itched.

The scrap of art paper was right where she left it, rubber eraser weighing it down. It had been pristine, though yellowed with age, when originally pulled from her great aunt's letter. Now the paper was thin from being drawn on and erased several times. Faded ghosts from drunken scribbles covered different areas on the page.

Picking up a pencil, she looked over the doodles. A pile of money…her walking on a beach…a bird…bottles of wine…and that God damned well.

The itch in her toe started burning.

An audible growl escaped, and she reached for the alligator grabber.

The holster was empty.

Of course it is.

Lani pushed herself over to the kitchen counter and looked for the grabber. *Someone* placed it behind the groceries and up against the counter's backsplash. She knew with every fiber of her being that someone was her mother.

Ever since the car wreck her mom had done everything in her power to convince Lani she needed help and couldn't get along alone. The term the therapist used for what both her parents were doing didn't come to mind.

An unpleasant realization surfaced past the hangover fog. *I'm out of wine.* The open bottle of whiskey wasn't any better; its remnants soaked the sheets.

"Guess I'll be making another call today, won't I, Mom?"

The empty cabin gave the only answer that mattered.

Silence.

Lani popped the wheelchair locks and hauled herself up to a standing position, arms rigid and palms-down on the kitchen counter. Leaning to the left, she reached out with her other hand and snatched the grabber before easing herself back into the chair.

"Easy peasy," she said, and instantly winced at using her mother's favorite saying.

The gator slid back into the sheath and then the search for her missing cell phone began. The thing disappeared nearly a week ago amid constant accusations of her ignoring family calls. Granted, if she did know where the phone was, Lani still wouldn't have answered it, but today was an emergency and she'd turned the stupid thing off.

She was out of wine.

Ten minutes became twenty, then thirty. Nearly an hour passed before she found it wedged between seat cushions on the couch. Once, that would have been the first place she would have looked. Now, why would she? It's not like she sat there anymore.

Along with the phone was the receipt for the last delivery. Bloodshot eyes scanned the thermal paper looking for the store's phone number before stopping on the fifth line.

Two bottles of wine?

Lani looked back to the kitchen counter to the four empty bottles her mother retrieved from the trash can, then to the two empties still sitting on the coffee table.

Six bottles…not two.

She looked at the receipt again, searching for a place where maybe they'd rung up the additional bottles separately. Nothing. Even the final total came out reflecting they'd only supplied two bottles.

The employee delivering this would have caught it. They have to verify—

Lani cut herself off mid-thought, looking up from the slip she held and over to the desk.

How many?

Wheels banged into the end table as she shot back to the desk, armrests banging into its front.

Four bottles of wine. I'm just nuts.

A rare smile started to cross her face when she looked back down at the receipt.

Plus the two I ordered….

Lani stared at Esther's letter and found herself getting winded from doing laps round the cabin's great room in a pitiful imitation of someone pacing. Worse yet, she did this while sporting a mind-numbing hangover.

The words she could make out were *Little Lani,* a jumble of other scribbles, then the word *Love*. At the bottom Esther's name was printed as if by a child. Lani looked at the four legible words. Turning the page slightly, added other words *One side, care*—or *careful,* she couldn't be sure—then a pile of what could only be described as a toddler's attempt at cursive.

The past month was little more than a drunken, self-medicated blur. Pain killers, wine, Mom, Dad, the delivery guy, an occasional meal here and there, and….

"And what? I get an empty letter from a senile old bi—"

She cut herself off before finishing the word. Esther had never been anything but loving. Lani leaned her head back and took a deep breath, feeling the familiar twinge in her mid-back where the rest of her became nothing more than dead weight.

As had been happening more and more lately, she found herself looking out at the yard again…at the well.

A sad chuckle escaped. "I'm a sad piece of work. Nothing more than a cripple hung up on a stupid wishing well."

Her toe was driving her nuts. She pulled the grabber free and scratched at the entire end of her foot.

Nothing.

Then…just at the very tip of her big toe, a sense of gratification as the plastic teeth raked back and forth.

The itch returned and she reached down with the grabber again, only to have her toe twitch in time with the sensation. She opened the alligator's jaws and clamped it down on the toe with no sensation. Then, cocking the head so the teeth would meet the end of her toe between nail and flesh, she repeated the action.

This time a faint pressure registered, like lightly touching an arm through fabric. Her head cocked the way a dog's would when hearing something unusual.

The piece of paper had four bottles of wine. She'd somehow gotten four additional bottles. The paper also had the wishing well and….

Lani stared at the well again as her subconscious bobbed just below revelation, screaming something.

The wheelbarrow.

She looked out the window at the well. It sat right where she tipped the load of soil when they were working on the garden.

"It…wasn't…there."

Every line matched up with what she'd drawn out.

Her sketch of herself standing…and now she's getting sensation in her toe.

How long ago did she doodle that? A week? More?

Lani picked up the page and stared at it. The letter arrived well over a month ago. She'd started doodling on it—

When?

Hell, she didn't even remember doing the drawing of herself walking.

Wine. She got it.

Money. The call came confirming it.

The well.

She stared at the stone lip crowned with a shingled wooden peak, then down to its drawn counterpart.

"It just doesn't make any sense." Lani held the page up in front of her, comparing art to reality. As the page came up, Trent's face blurred into existence on the page and she dropped it with a yelp, fingers jerking back as if just touching a hot stove.

The page fluttered down, coming to rest between the desk and the wall.

"Trent?"

The page didn't move.

Lani used the grabber to retrieve the yellowed sheet. Slowly, she lifted the page. Wine. Herself. Money. Well.

No Trent.

Raising it higher, to the same point in front of the window it had been, revealed the blurry outline of Trent's face. While not a great representation, it was definitely him. She turned the page over and stared at the drunken sketch she'd done at some point on the back.

"This is bullshit," Lani said to herself. "Trent's in an urn on the mantle and there's no coming back from that."

Still…wine…money…standing…well.

Rage rose. "Then where are you, huh? Answer me!"

She wadded up the paper and was about to throw it when the thin pencil strokes outlining his chin and ear appeared.

A dry sob escaped as she smoothed the page and held it up to the light, looking at the back side where Trent's sketch was. Wrinkles now distorted his features, giving the image more of a third dimension. Lani held the page up in front of her by its sides, feeling stupid, but needing to kiss him, even a crude representation of him, just one more time.

Drawing the paper close, features shifted. She moved it back. Light from the window hit it again and the features changed again, growing angular, impressionistic, until he was nearly lost to the image bleeding through from the other side.

"The well."

Lani wedged her phone and scrap of art paper into her shirt pocket and wheeled to the front door, fighting to get it open, then wheeling out and down the ramp her dad built during the winter.

"This is crazy," she said, insane hope filling her. Wheels came off the ramp and the chair slowed after it crossed the sidewalk and rolled into the yard itself. Brown grass, rigid from winter pushed back against her efforts. Her chair stopped less than fifteen feet from the stone ring making up the base of the wishing well.

"Crazy," Lani repeated and pushed herself from the chair, landing in a heap in front of it. She focused on the gray stones as fingers dug into cold earth to pull her a few inches closer. Sock-clad feet dragged behind, the tip of one toe teasing the renewed itch that threatened to drive her nuts.

Ten feet.

The pinky nail on her left hand tore, exposing the quick to gritty soil and Lani sucked in a breath. Momentum never stalled.

Five feet.

I can do this.

Her skin pulled on the right side. A wet spot appeared on the side of her sweats. The colostomy back tore loose. Lani turned back to the well.

He can't be there.

"Crazy," became a mantra.

He has to be there.

Lani's right palm smacked against the side of the well, its stone surface feeling colder than the earth she pulled herself across.

"Tre... Trent?"

An early spring wind blew across the yard, feeling significantly less than warm.

She looked up. The lip of the well seemed so far up.

Four feet. That's not so far.

Filthy fingers dug into any gap the stone spacing offered for purchase. She pulled and rose a little, bringing herself up against the stone. The twinge in her back protested at being stressed.

The odd angle left Lani's face pressed against the stone with no real way to back away. With no other ideas, she finger-walked her hands up farther until they crested the side of the well.

One great pull brought her chin over the lip. Lani stopped, sucking wind. Heartbeats hammered in her ears. She pulled again, flattening out one forearm, then the other. With a final push, she was upright on her hands looking down into inky blackness. Gray rock lined the well, descending into that dark. Cold radiated up out of the hole.

"Trent?"

He can't be there.

Pebbles worked free and fell. She waited for the plops.

A second passed before two distinct wet impacts echoed up.

Lani squinted, trying to see anything.

I know I drew the well before it was here. Uneven rock bit into her palms. *Now it's here. This was the first thing I drew.*

"Trent?" she screamed.

Her voice didn't even echo.

She leaned over, freeing her hands and pulled her phone from its pocket. The scrap of art paper fluttered beyond reach and fluttered down, appearing as little more than a beige speck in a ring of ebony.

"No!"

Then it was gone.

Lani slid forward an inch and grabbed the edge of the well in a white-knuckled grip. Turning the flashlight feature on, she reached as far as possible and shone the light down.

More rock and shadow.

Her body shifted, tipping her farther forward. Self-preservation kicked in and she pinwheeled the extended arm while scrambling for a better grip with the other.

Then the phone slipped, tumbling past fingertips and bouncing off the far wall before strobing down.

No splash.

The light didn't wink out.

There had to be water. She'd heard it.

The light coned out at an angle from the same side of the well she hung over, illuminating something brown and white just breaking the surface of the water.

The paper?

She looked closer. No, not the paper. Water ripples reflected in the light, better framing the object. This had substance.

It was a nose and cheek.

No.

Once recognition set it, dim shapes formed a chin, part of an ear and eye, comprising a distorted—but still familiar—profile.

Trent.

Lani's mouth gaped in a silent scream as her eyes adjusted to the gloom. The cheek, once rosy, now bobbed at the waterline bloated and as gray as the stone surrounding it.

"*Twice,*" fell from her lips.

One arm still reached up; fingers stuck into some pocket hidden in shadow.

"*Twice,*" she repeated, louder this time.

She brought him back.

I killed him twice.

She screamed the word again. "Twice!"

The word ripped from her again and again, until its meaning was the only reality left.

Behind the story...

To understand my reason for writing "Sketches," you need to know a little about my history. I shattered my knee at 15 and have had problems with it ever since resulting in multiple surgeries. For years I wore what I lovingly call a leg cage (*an ankle-to-hip knee brace that had drop locks on it for walking but can be released to sit without the leg sticking out straight*). So, much of my time was spent in the brace, using a cane, or on crutches.

In physical therapy I befriended a wheelchair-bound person and realized while I might be in constant pain and have difficulty getting around, at least I could stand.

Decades—yes, folks, decades—later I felt like I was in a good place to write a story about dealing with disabilities, albeit in a horror fashion. I channeled my personal frustrations, and the frustrations I witnessed in PT so many years before to write "Sketches."

Between using "Sketches" as a little bit of therapy, having a deep, personal, understanding of the statement, "Be careful what you wish for," and a love for *Monkey's Paw* type stories, I was happy with how this turned out.

SKEWED PERCEPTIONS

Lisa Bennett looked through the passenger window as the world around changed from the manicured frontage of some unnamed building to the stark gray concrete of the parking garage. "It's 2028 and it still looks like the mid-'90s. We've done *so* well for ourselves."

"Hmmmm," Izzy managed, entranced, as usual, with her phone.

An hour's ride out of the city, hosted by the government—under threat of stopping her and Izzy's Sensory Screen Technology launch later in the month—a Capitol Hill senator had some vague concerns that could only be remedied through a private physical meeting.

Lisa brushed a brown lock of hair from her face and looked over at Izzy.

"Dress professional," she'd said. Lisa did her best, wearing the same gray skirt suit worn a year before for a televised interview. She'd never gotten used to the heels and absentmindedly slid her left foot out and rubbed the arch.

Of course, Izzy didn't seem to have a problem. At six feet without the four inches her shoes added, she was intimidating… with them she was a force of nature. The wild mane of blonde hair that was subdued with a handful of hairpins completed the scientist's professional look.

The car slowed, and took a right past a pylon, stopping beside a pair of metal security doors.

Izzy looked over at her and took on a stoic expression. "Must be showtime." She looked down at Lisa rubbing her foot. "C'mon. Get your game face on."

The door was opened by what Lisa could only assume was a member of the Secret Service. She struggled to suppress a grin when the man turned his head and she saw the telltale ear bud, complete with curly pigtail, going from his lobe into the folds of his coat.

Lisa pushed the shoe back on, got out, and followed Izzy out the door. She took a deep breath and cocked her head.

Izzy caught the motion. "What?"

"I—"

"Ladies," the security officer motioned to the doors, "this way, please."

"The air's too clean," Lisa whispered. Izzy rolled her eyes before pushing past the escort and opening the door for herself and Lisa.

The three entered an alcove, then the elevator, and ultimately ended up on the seventh floor. Rather than emerging into a business office, they arrived at a hallway as stark and white as the garage's alcove.

Their escort ushered them out, saying, "To your left, please."

Izzy started down the hall and Lisa followed suit, struggling to keep up with her benefactor and friend. White walls were broken up by floor-to-ceiling windows into different labs. Lisa recognized some by the equipment each possessed. Sleep studies. Tactile testing. AI emotive responses, immersion suits.

Immersion suits?

All things *they* were developing.

A man with saucy red hair stepped out from a machine, looked at them in shock, and disappeared through a security door on the opposite wall.

"Son of a bitch."

Izzy slowed, then stopped, turning on a heel. "What Lisa?"

"I just saw—"

"Ladies," the escort said, interrupting, "Colonel Jessup is waiting for you."

Izzy cut eyes at him, then down to Lisa. "Will it keep?"

"I don't think—"

"Miss Holwitz," a voice boomed from the next door up, "I'm pleased you accepted our invitation."

Izzy turned once more and went into the open doorway, followed closely by Lisa. The room held a strong contrast to the hallways they'd seen on the way in. Rich walnut paneling covered the walls, and carpeting muffled their steps. A desk worthy of someone making the mid-six figures a year rested midway along the room, and behind the huge piece of furniture sat Colonel Jessup.

Lisa took in the colonel. Built like a fire plug...white pinpricks of hair on a head that was close to being bald. The career soldier's nose listed to one side, leaving her to swallow a joke about the man probably always having his nose out of joint about one thing or another.

Izzy strode up to the desk, ignored the officer's outstretched hand and sat, crossing her legs in the opposite direction—body language effectively dismissing him. Lisa stood behind her and slightly to the left.

"Miss Bennett," Colonel Jessup said, motioning to the other empty seat.

"She prefers to stand," Izzy quipped. "Mister Jessup—"

"Colonel," he corrected, eyes narrowing.

That took her less than a minute to piss him off.

"Of course," Izzy said, a friendly lilt appearing in her voice. "We're not here for pleasantries, so let's dispose of them. You've threatened to lock up my research and halt the launch date for my immersion systems."

"I'm sure—"

Izzy held up a hand. "Please let me finish. Then you'll know where we stand."

He sat back and opened his hands in a giving gesture. "By all means, please continue."

"Sensory Screen Technology is the newest public gaming platform and stands to make easily fifty million in the first year alone. By threatening that, you're risking lawsuits...not to mention the publicity."

Lisa watched his smile never falter.

Colonel Jessup asked, "Done?"

"For the moment."

The colonel took a deep breath. "Everything you've said up to this point is correct. Bottom line, the United States Government considers your technology dangerous."

"So, we're shut down no matter what?"

Jessup nodded. "Pretty much."

Izzy's legs crossed in the opposite direction but Jessup's gaze remained squarely on her face, not faltering one bit.

Interesting.

"Then why are Lisa and I here?"

"We'd like to offer you a job."

Lisa couldn't resist scoffing.

"Sooooo, I work for you or I don't work for anybody? Is that your pitch?"

"That's my pitch." Jessup watched them as a predator would.

"If I say no, Ol' Uncle Sam will buy my patents out from under me when I'm forced to sell because of investor lawsuits?"

"Yes," he said simply.

"Then why not do that in the first place, and forego the cloak and dagger?"

"We want *you.*"

"*I'm* not for sale." Izzy shifted, positioning herself in the seat as if it were a throne. "What if I have a better idea?"

Lisa watched the colonel's smug expression as he leaned forward and placed clasped hands on his desk. "Do tell."

Izzy raised her hand and fanned manicured fingernails for a wave, then brought them together and snapped her fingers.

Lisa cleared her throat, closed her eyes and began. "When we exited the car, your garage smelled especially clean. Considering vehicle exhaust build-up, odds are you're using a negative air-pressure filtration system to keep contaminants from escaping the building. That means infectious materials. Your security cameras watched us exit the car. The units are Machloung twenty-three thirties—coming with a default red LED that's lit when active. The one at the garage's door, the one on the elevator—that one a Machloung twenty-three seventy-nine, and the two in the hallway all are active, minus the LED power light. Each camera, even when inside the tinted housing, can be seen…and its lens moving as they focused on us at each stage of our journey up here. This means you were interested in how we approached the office as much as what we've said in it. Body language.

"The fact that you sent us up here past several secure labs shows you're confident that we'll…." She faltered there, realizing she'd included herself with Izzy.

Izzy spoke up, "Go on, Lisa. He's confident we'll what?"

"Colonel Jessup's convinced we'll accept his offer. In addition, he's contracted your former employee, Jerry Stallinger, incorporating many of our earlier design and programming aspects. This also means the colonel is aware of the primary project that the gaming gear is designed to finance."

Izzy turned around in her seat and stared at Lisa slack-jawed.

"When did—"

Lisa cut her off. "Right when we were walking down the hall. I tried to tell you."

"Well," Colonel Jessup said, "the cat's out of the proverbial bag."

Lisa watched Izzy shift in her seat, regaining composure. She, however, adjusted her stance, feet cramping in the binding footwear. *Flats. I should have worn flats.*

Lisa cleared her throat, then said, "How much of our research did Jerry share with you?"

He blinked.

Lisa continued. "All?"

Jessup nodded.

Izzy said, "So, you're unable to successfully incorporate the Sensory Screen Technology suit to the synth skin receptors?"

He nodded again.

Lisa couldn't resist and cut in. "That's because when we realized someone was copying files early on, we took steps to protect ourselves."

"It's *gaming* gear," Izzy said.

"Not your original plan," Jessup countered. "What was it…'Total immersion into an artificial device' or something like that?" He picked up a pen and tapped it on the desk. "You wanted to offer mobility and freedom to those who didn't have it for medical reasons?"

Lisa added, "Paraplegics…the elderly…even—"

"Exploration," Izzy finished.

Jessup started up again. "We wouldn't have even known about the potential for this work if you hadn't pitched it to every space foundation on the planet."

Izzy sounded small, almost childlike. "But we couldn't get past the time delay."

The colonel was obviously pleased and parroted, "But you couldn't get past the time delay. Nothing worse than a three-to-twenty-minute delay in every action…every sensation." He leaned back in his seat. "I mean, what's the point?"

"The…point…" Izzy's words came almost as if she were spitting each one, "Is to help people."

Jessup motioned for Izzy to be quiet. "Look, we're having some programming issues and we need your help."

Lisa asked, "Then why not just ask us?"

"You might have said no."

Izzy sat a little straighter. "So, better to strong-arm me than simply ask for my help."

"Exactly."

Jessup interjected, "You've celebrated three times over the last two weeks. It's obvious that you've solved whatever problems you had with the suits."

"You," Izzy's words were low, like a bestial growl right before attacking, "*bugged* us?"

Lisa stammered, "I-I need to have a moment with Miss Holwitz."

"No," Jessup said. "Anything you need to tell her during the course of this meeting can be said in front of me."

Lisa knelt down, getting onto her knees beside Izzy's chair. She looked up into her friend's face, seeing both frustration and confusion.

"You know how you keep calling me your Samwise?"

Izzy nodded mutely.

"I saw someone was accessing files when no one else was even on site. I figured that person put a back door into our system."

"Wait…you knew?"

"I didn't want to worry you. We're so close to completion. I took that bonus you gave me and set up a VQR floating server that backed us up safely, then shifted variables, components, and even left out current coding before saving to the infected server."

"What?" Jessup didn't sound amused.

"So…so we're good?"

Lisa smiled. "We're fine."

"Where exactly *is* this server, Miss Bennett?"

"Nope," Lisa said.

"Maybe you and Miss Holwitz should stay for a bit as our guests."

Lisa sighed. "Look, Colonel Sanders," Izzy snorted again when Lisa made the chicken reference, "I've known our system was compromised since two days after Jerry infected the system. Just to make sure we weren't *guests* for too long, I took my own precautions."

"Oh, should I expect commandos bursting through the door?"

"No, but with how fast you locked us down after completing our work, I figured something was about to happen. So did Izzy."

Colonel Jessup said, "Izzy—"

"Miss Holwitz to you," Izzy said.

Lisa spoke before Jessup could start in again. "Izzy, remember when the notice we were being picked up came? I kinda did something." She took a breath. "You said you'd rather give everything away than have the fu—the government lock it up."

"Yeah," Izzy said slowly.

"I have everything set up to launch worldwide unless we cancel it."

"So, it's ours or it's everyone's?"

"It's yours, Izzy. I'm just a number cruncher."

Izzy took her hand. "It's *ours*."

Lisa looked at the colonel. "Even with your best, you couldn't track down where everything is stored, how many self-replicating copies are going out, or what type of personal introduction these files have." She stood again, taking her original position behind Izzy.

"Meaning?"

"Meaning," Izzy spoke up, finding herself once more, "that she probably listed trace information for the call we received, copies of every piece of legal paperwork which, if I remember correctly, bear your name—along with a certain senator's, and whatever else she could think of."

Lisa shifted uncomfortably. "That about covers it." *God, I hate being the center of attention.*

The three of them stared at each other, then to the pen Colonel Jessup fiddled with. Silence electrified the air, making the tension almost palpable.

Jessup spread his hands across the desk, smoothing imaginary paperwork. "Miss Bennett, please take a seat."

"I prefer—"

"I don't give a damn what you prefer." He stopped himself, ears taking on the same beet color his cheeks already bore. "Please."

Izzy gave a small cough and nodded to the now-empty chair. Lisa dropped into it in the most unladylike fashion she could muster.

"Truth time," Jessup said. "Not going to waste any more effort with confidentiality agreements or threats."

"Good," Lisa said.

"You wanted to use the synth skin to clothe a cybernetic organism, allowing the 'driver' to feel what it feels while on another world."

"Yes."

"The time for the signal to get from other world or asteroids made this task too limiting?"

"Again yes. Get to it."

"We have a location to send the AI where transmissions and reception occur real time."

"Somewhere here on Earth." Izzy rolled her eyes. "That's nothing new."

"No," Jessup said, "not terrestrial."

Lisa and Izzy exchanged glances.

Lisa spoke first. "Say that again."

Jessup pushed back from his desk. "We've *mirrored* a neighboring dimension. We can even physically pass through, but there's too many variables regarding contamination going either direction. We need a way to move forward without losing any more people."

Izzy stood. "Wait, wait, wait. You're saying you've punched through to another dimension and want to use my gear to explore?"

"I'm saying we've *mirrored* another dimension and have been able to observe off and on since the 1980s. There was no punching involved. Last time was in 2020. We reconnected three weeks ago."

Lisa shot her question out, "How long did you know this was coming?"

"We're able to estimate the mirroring to within a few minutes. We need your suit technology. That's when we made Mr. Stallinger an offer he couldn't refuse."

Izzy smirked. "How very Godfather of you."

He nodded.

"*If*," Izzy said, "we decided to act as consultants, what happens to our work?"

"It gets buried."

"No deal."

Lisa let her breath out.

"Miss Holwitz—"

"Did you forget? Lisa made sure it goes public without us stopping it."

"The technology *can't* go public as is. It's too dangerous."

Lisa asked, "To who?"

"To everyone. We're not the only ones who are actively pursuing this." He stood. "In case you haven't noticed, the world's resources are running desperately low. We need clean water, air, minerals, food, lumber. If we can't have that, then we need a good—"

"Plague," Lisa offered.

Jessup looked at her for a moment. "I was going to say 'plan,' but 'plague' works equally as well."

"I'm not burying my life's work," Izzy repeated.

Jessup got up and walked over to the door. "Miss Holwitz, Miss Bennett, come with me."

Lisa looked over to Izzy, who shrugged and got up. Both followed the colonel out the door and farther down the hall.

"Everything here is considered Triple Black, is that understood?"

Izzy cocked her head. "Meaning?"

"Meaning jail time would be the least of your worries."

Neither woman answered.

"Before we go any farther, I need to be sure you understand that.

No discussions over beers, no using it for leverage, nothing." He looked each of them in the eye in turn. "Do we continue or go back to playing poker in the office?"

Izzy nodded. Lisa watched her, then mimicked the action.

Jessup slapped a meaty palm against a hand scanner, then punched in a code.

"Kind of archaic," Izzy observed.

The door clicked and swung slightly open for him. "This plant is secure."

They stepped through and into yet another hallway that was equally as white and stark. No chairs, or even maps to guide a person were anywhere. On some of the doors were alpha-numeric designations, but none were in order or gave a hint as to what was behind them.

They stopped at ADJ-319. Another palm scan, then Jessup ushered them inside.

A lab, uncannily similar to their own, lay before them.

"Déjà fucking vu." Lisa moved into the workspace and checked all of the equipment. Systems…even computer makes and models were identical to their own.

"You would work here as needed. Nothing goes home."

Lisa said, "You're offering us a lab we already have. Besides, Izzy already said 'no.'"

"Show us," Izzy mumbled, still standing in the doorway.

The colonel crossed the room and went through a small door on the far side. He held the door open, waiting for them to follow. They passed him and went into a windowed reception area looking out onto a control center akin to the old NASA war room. Scientists and technicians went about their duties, oblivious to them. But on the screens….

Izzy's hand went to her mouth. "Dear God."

Displayed on one the massive screens on the far wall was a nightmare landscape. Trees—if they could be called that—waved without any wind. Their root systems free of soil and moving, while slow, of their own accord. Each followed the one before it in some form of forest migration.

Another depicted a pixilated view from a hilltop. Charcoal gray valleys and black lines of distant rivers filled the screen. Miles away inky black was sliced apart by the lighter gray of the horizon. The camera rotated to the left, following the horizon and stopping on a mountain higher than anything Lisa could fathom before it began turning to the right once more.

A third screen showed fluid bubbling from a cluster of thermal vents. Every fourth or fifth pop released a cluster of flying insects, each radiating a hypnotic blue color. They swarmed around the steaming vent for a few seconds, then took off in every direction—one angling right over the camera.

Other screens were on, but nothing more than varying shades of black filled the display.

One tech spotted them and mouthed something that Lisa couldn't make out. Apparently, Jessup couldn't either as he opened the glass door into the command center.

He towered over the smaller man. "What?"

"Boots is coming back around. We saw it on the last pass."

"Boots?" Izzy asked.

Jessup moved farther into the room and took a seat in an empty chair. Lisa and Izzy did the same.

As the left-most screen rotated, they took in the dim slope of a horizon, similar to the other monitor, and the gray swirling outlines from trees.

The tech leaned on the back of Izzy's chair and Lisa saw her expression sour.

"Any second now," The tech switched his view from the screen to the top of Izzy's head and, more likely, her legs.

Then it was there. Another tree, moving just as the others were. Only this one had something attached to one of its roots.

A boot?

It was a combat boot. Beyond it, even in the weak light, Lisa made out a leg clad in military fatigues, then a second that appeared to be tucked up and under a genderless torso. The body itself she couldn't make too much of. Roots of varying sizes snaked in and out of the soldier's body, threading it to the trunk. The head rested chin against chest, leaving the helmet to mask his identity.

Izzy pushed up out of her chair, the top of her skull impacting the tech's chin. She was oblivious to the bump and stood, snaking her way through the aisles of computer stations until she was right under the screen showing the tree they'd dubbed Boots. The tech realized he'd been caught ogling Izzy and gave Lisa a guilty nod and small, polite, smile, then stepped aside so Lisa could join her friend and the colonel.

"Who was he?" Izzy asked.

"Someone from our second team," Jessup said, walking up beside her. "We're not sure who exactly."

"We lost the whole team," the female tech added. "We're hoping to be able to read the nametag or see the face this time."

Another tech, this one a woman with hair cut nearly as short as Jessup's, spoke up. "Sunrise in a few minutes. That's when the show really starts."

Jessup handed a folder to Izzy which Lisa hadn't noticed before.

"I'm prepared," Jessup was studying the screen as hard as Izzy, "to offer you this."

Izzy opened the folder, looked at a diagram for what appeared to be biotech in the shape of a tick. The screen forgotten, Lisa watched as Izzy flipped pages back and forth skimming, then reading closely, then skimming again, finally settling back on the front page.

"That's it?" she asked. Looking at Lisa she said, "It's a neural interface."

Jessup lifted his chin slightly. "Self-implanting. Full sensory immersion capability."

"Whoa." Lisa reached for the folder.

Izzy handed it over, but looked at Colonel Jessup and said, "No."

Lisa flipped through the file, much as Izzy did. Detailed schematics. Sensory immersion level initial tests pegging the upper ninetieth percentile each and every time. Rejection ratings showing under a hundredth of a percent. "Wait…this is *exactly* what we need for the core project. We wouldn't need the gaming suits."

"Not good enough." Izzy took the folder back and offered it back to Jessup.

The colonel's face flushed. "Why isn't this good enough?"

Lisa interrupted. "It's *exactly* what we need. Think of the elderly… the coding and writing power. Hell, game immersion would be like nothing you ever imagined."

Izzy looked down at her. "Our investors, Lisa. We don't have the finances or the time to start over that way."

Colonel Jessup looked from the screen to both of them. "I have an emergency situation right now. I've expressed your nation's need. What's it going to take?"

"A blank check," Izzy said.

"No."

Lisa put her hand on Izzy's shoulder. "Let's be realistic." She calculated. "Worst case, it'd take us another four years to have a public-ready device going this route. It'd take a decade going with the suits we're about to launch."

"But, just the first year—"

"Like you said, 'The investors.' Izzy, you keep looking at gross, not net. After paying them, staff, the materials, taxes…."

Izzy rolled her eyes at that one. It was an annoying habit that Lisa wished Izzy had grown out of.

"It would take that long."

Jessup frown eased. "I'd listen to her."

"Don't be so quick," Lisa shot back. "She's right. The deal's *not* good enough. I'm just saying it needs to be realistic."

"What did you have in mind?" Izzy asked.

She looked at Jessup. "Four years projected sales of the suit we're about to launch."

The colonel leaned against the wall. "Okay."

Izzy mouthed, "Twenty billion?"

"Not done," Lisa said. "All our investors get repaid…*and* they get their projected returns for the next four years as well."

Jessup hadn't so much as twitched.

"Payable in Bitmash. Today."

Lisa was thinking she'd gone too far. The man wasn't scoffing or countering her offer.

"For that," he said, "we pull your patents to the suit, its tech becomes ours. You both support all tech and coding for the suits for ten years—renewable at *our* discretion. You get the nano and all rights to it. You keep your coding with all licensing rights to the US government—"

Izzy managed, "Non-exclusive."

He grunted the affirmative. "Non-exclusive," he confirmed. Then, to Lisa, asked, "Anything else?"

Wanting the last word, she included, "Friday dinner and drinks for anyone we employ…on the government's tab."

This actually brought a chuckle from the colonel. "Ten-thousand-dollar tab per month, on a Federal-issued card…for the next five years."

Lisa stuck her hand out, then froze. She'd taken over for Izzy *again*. She looked up at her friend who still had a deer in the headlights look. "If…" she said sheepishly, "that's agreeable to my boss."

That seemed to bring Izzy out of her fog once again. She blinked, appeared to process the exchange and nodded. "My *partner* strikes a hard bargain. That's our price. However, I have a few conditions."

"Well?"

"I'm assuming Jerry Stallinger is going to be a colleague in this venture?"

"He is."

"He's a subordinate or we don't sign." Her features hardened. "He slowed our progress several times because of his misogyny and short-sightedness. I can override him at any point for any reason. *You*," she pointed at Jessup, "get veto power only after hearing any issues that might arise because of him."

"And you think there'll be problems?"

Without missing a beat Izzy asked, "How many harassment claims do you have already? Three? Six?"

"Point taken. Your solution? Without firing him," he added.

"Start him fresh, knowing I'll publicly berate the little weasel, and, if necessary, work him on shifts he hates."

"So, we're in agreement?"

"He *never* enters our lab…under any circumstances or he's gone from the entire project."

Izzy looked at Lisa, who couldn't resist saying, "And two coffees?"

"Mr. Stallinger's a peon, and two coffees to close the deal," Jessup confirmed.

Izzy grinned wickedly. "Brought by Jerry."

Jessup's eyebrow went up. "You," he motioned to both women,

"are going to be interesting to work with."

Lisa returned his gaze. "Did you just P.C. call us bitches?"

He pushed off the wall and headed for the door. "Ladies."

Less than four hours later the specifics of the agreement were ironed out, contracts signed, payment made, and Lisa was downloading the complete files from a remote server.

Lisa stared at the monitor, verifying key information dropped correctly. "Izzy, I didn't mean to take over back there."

"I froze. I'm a badass at most things, but when I'm blindsided I just…lock up."

She turned in the swivel chair to face Izzy. "So, you're not mad?"

"I'm not mad. You made us billionaires, zeroed out our debt, and got Uncle Sam to pay for meals once a week." She spun the smaller brunette around. "Why would I be mad?"

Lisa said, "This is your baby. I didn't mean to step on—"

"This is *our* baby. You're my partner, now. Fifty-fifty."

"No. I—"

Izzy spun her back to face the monitor. "Fine. Fifty-one, forty-nine. That makes me the boss. Get back to work." With that, she popped Lisa on the head.

"I wonder how high Colonel Jessup would've gone." She looked over at Izzy, who was busy calibrating a clutch of sensors. "I mean, he didn't even bat an eye."

Their lab door opened, and a mousy, even by Lisa's standards, tech stuck her head in.

"Miss Holwitz, Miss Bennett?

Both looked over and said, "Yeah?"

"There's an issue."

They followed the tech through the windowless labyrinth and to a smaller, mobile recon room.

"We had another exposure."

Lisa said, "That's not our department."

The tech said, "But it was through the suit." She nodded at the screen showing two personnel in clean suits peeling back a gaming outfit. Blue lights blinked across the neoprene surface, except for around a dozen on the left shoulder-blade.

"He was on the other side?" Izzy asked. "In a suit?"

"No, ma'am. The bio gel we use for the receptors is from the mirrored side."

The suit peeled back, exposing missing skin. Tendons and muscle could be seen underneath, but instead of healthy flesh, a gray tinge muddied the pink. Exposure went deep as the camera changed angles, showing a good inch into the soldier's body. An X covered the audio icon, but judging from the expression on his face, Lisa didn't need it.

He was in agony.

The medics pulled the man free and what material remained on the inside of the suit seemed to wave under its own power. Grayish pink tendrils hovered a good two inches above the garment's lining. Seconds later a bag was forced over the growth and tossed into a clear plastic exam box.

Izzy stared at the screen. "Whose idea was it to use bio material from the other dimension?"

"Ma'am, I just work—"

"Whose?" she screamed.

"Mr. Stallinger's, ma'am."

Lisa said, "That little prick. Always cutting corners where he can."

The tech said, "I don't understand. This was the only way."

"No," Izzy said, "He could have spent a few days replicating a VR representation of the alien DNA."

"You can do that and have it work?"

Izzy ignored the question. "How many others?"

"Sixty-three. I mean the whole ninth floor is contamin—"

"That's enough, Patricia." Colonel Jessup stood in the doorway. "I'll take it from here."

Izzy looked over at him. "Sixty-three people?"

Jessup nodded to the monitor. "Sixty-four."

"All because that little fucker couldn't follow protocol?"

He stepped out of the room and started walking toward the elevators. "Coming?"

Izzy stormed in pursuit, leaving Lisa scrambling to keep up.

"Screw it," Lisa finally said, pulling the heels off, scooping them up, and rushing after Izzy barefoot.

They stepped into the elevator and Jessup pushed eight. "His mistake is one of the reasons we called you in for this project."

The elevator groaned as they ascended.

Lisa listened to the noise and brushed the ever-falling lock of brown hair from her face. "Should've taken the stairs."

"Stairs are currently off-limits." He looked at the elevator button. "Decontamination."

The doors opened onto a portable clean room. Tented material was propped against every wall and several soldiers moved around on the far side in clean-suits spraying something on the nearly transparent material, the floors, walls, and ceiling. They focused their streams on discolored patches resembling mold.

They pushed through plastic flaps, entering what had once been a junction of hallways, but now looked more like a surgical staging area.

Jessup led them from one enclosure to the next, always unzipping and re-zipping each access point.

"Can never be too careful," was all he offered on the topic.

At the far end they came to a plasticized airlock.

"You pushing us out?" Lisa asked.

"Quite the contrary. I need you to see what it is we're dealing with." He closed the airlock zipper then went to the other side of the tent and opened them to the hallway.

Izzy shifted. "Shouldn't we be wearing something?"

"This side's fine. C'mon."

They entered the first door on the right. At least a dozen men and women lay on gurneys in various stages of infection. Autopsies had already been performed on several of the bodies.

An orderly opened a door into the adjoining room and held it for them. Inside, the soldier they'd seen on the monitors writhed in agony.

Izzy covered her mouth. "I thought you said this side was fine?"

"It is," Jessup repeated.

"We shouldn't…we shouldn't be here," Lisa managed.

Jessup pulled a probe from the table and poked at where the

wound once was. Now the area was covered by a second skin. The gray mass was interwoven with what appeared to be burnt flesh.

"It seems to bond to only one person and doesn't mature for several hours."

"Colonel," the soldier managed through gritted teeth. "Please… it…it…it hurts."

Jessup ignored the man. "See here," he indicated to Lisa and Izzy. "The flesh has merged with the biomass, creating…." He stepped back, dropped the probe and lifted a sheet from the printer, and finished, "quad-strand DNA."

"Please," the soldier repeated.

"Shh," Jessup scolded. "In a minute."

Lisa fumed, "What the absolute fu—"

His hand came up in an "in a minute" motion.

Izzy said, "We're just supposed to be here working on gaming suits. Remember?"

"Here's the low-down," Jessup said. "We need the suits to interact with the skinned robotics on the far side. Mr. Stallinger took several…" he looked for the right word, "*liberties* with your coding to keep us ahead of our deadline. Because of that we've had complications."

Lisa stepped in front of Izzy, blocking her from the colonel. "Ever try telling the whole truth in one shot?"

"*Because of that,*" he repeated, "you've inadvertently inherited a problem." He looked down on the brunette, then up to the blonde. "You're not geneticists, but your suits are the problem."

"Our suits," Izzy jabbed a finger at him, "are fine. That little—"

The man on the gurney screamed.

Izzy stopped.

Colonel Jessup motioned to one of the medics then led Izzy and Lisa out of the room, through the morgue, and back into the hallway.

"That," Jessup said casually, "was unpleasant."

"Unpleasant?" Lisa repeated, shocked.

All the lights in the hallway blinked out, leaving them only the fire security lights mounted on the walls every fifty feet.

"What's—" Izzy began.

A bleating alarm sounded.

Jessup screamed, "Not again!" He tore farther down the hall, away from the clean rooms, and around a corner into another hallway. Lisa and Izzy followed, unsure of what else to do.

Three doors opened and closed as they ran to keep time with Jessup. They caught up as he was working his way into another zippered airlock.

"Good," he said. "Get in here and bring up your software."

"But we haven't set the systems on a server yet," Izzy said.

"Everything's linked. That's how it's done here."

Izzy moved into the main part of the clean room and booted up the nearest machine. Lisa did the same on the system next to her, tossing her heels beside the keyboard.

Lisa asked, "What exactly did that asshole do?"

"Nooooo," Izzy said, looking at her screen. "No. He didn't do… why did…oh, that moron!"

"What?" Jessup asked.

Izzy sat back. "Rather than allowing the two second lag for the dimensional shift, that asshat used biomass from the other side to coat the receptors here, and used our biomass to do the same on the robot's second skin." She pulled a pen from her pocket and threw it across the sagging tent.

Jessup bent over and looked at her screen, trying to understand. "Meaning?"

"Meaning he's infected everyone who's put on one of the suits and, dependent on communicability levels, may have just infected us all!"

Jessup picked up a phone. "Lock it down. Lock the whole building down! Now! Code Black!" The phone slammed back into its cradle. "Can you see what the infection rates and incubation is?"

Izzy said, "I don't have access to it."

Lisa was already typing at her terminal. "Just a sec…."

"Lisa," she started.

"He said everything's connected." Her fingers flew over the keyboard. Files popped up only to disappear once more as she sifted through what appeared to be hundreds of simulations, looking for the proper demographics. One of her shoes tipped on the desk and bumped her hand as she typed. She batted it away and kept going.

"And," Jessup said after five minutes.

"Annnnnnd…found it." She brought up a chart listing age, blood type, growth pattern based on fifty specimens.

"Specimens?" Izzy read aloud.

"Soldiers," Lisa said.

"Enough about that. Burn me at the stake later. What's the communicability rating?"

Lisa put the query in.

The computer's answer blinked on the screen: 87%.

"Jesus," Izzy said.

Lisa offered, "But that number's only through direct contact."

Jessup stood back up, putting hands to hips. He paced, working through something silently. Lisa kept trying to read his lips, though couldn't successfully string two words together…and probably hadn't even guessed one successfully.

Banging echoed from down the hall where they'd come. A scream of rage followed…or was it pain? More shouts followed, this time from multiple voices.

"Clean room! Clean room!" Voices overshadowed each other again before falling to one male voice booming over the others. "Jesus Christ, clean room!"

One of the infected soldiers from the lab skidded into view, bare chest covered with pulsating alien flesh. He stumbled a couple of steps their way. Woody tendrils pushed out of the skin only to snake back and pierce his unaffected stomach, one of which forced its way through the dimple of the man's belly button. He doubled over, mouth open in a silent scream. Infected skin started to pulse faster, swelling much the way the bubbles had on the thermal vent they'd seen on screen hours before.

"God," Izzy said.

Lights flashed down the hallway in a lazy strobe, out of sync with the alarm's pitch change.

A shot boomed, opening a crimson hole in the soldier's chest as it exited, and punching a comet-shaped hole into the drywall just at the edge of the clean room tenting material.

Izzy said, "That…was…."

"Close," Lisa finished.

He dropped to his knees. What looked initially like smoke rose from the opened wound. It circled in on itself, forming framework for other strands to build upon. It worked with nearly fluid complexity until a crude formation began to rise.

Izzy squinted. "Is that a sapling?"

In answer, three blade-shaped orange leaves unfurled.

"We're going up to nine," Jessup ordered, controlled fear apparent in his voice.

Lisa grabbed her shoes in one hand and started frantically working on a zipper in the far wall with the other.

Izzy got up. "I thought your tech said the ninth floor was contaminated."

Men in fire gear rounded the corner and pulled the trigger on a sprayer. Fire leapt from the metal nozzle, engulfing the soldier.

"Yes," Jessup said. "No…damn it, it's hard to explain." He shoved Lisa out of the way and jerked the zipper all the way up.

Flames licked at the plastic shielding, instantly warping it.

They pushed through the flap and Jessup pulled the zipper closed just as the tarp on the far side melted through, dripping molten plastic onto the tiled floor.

The colonel took off at a trot, leading them through a series of hallways, jogging first right, then left.

"How do you," Lisa sucked in a breath, "manage to keep all these halls straight?"

He ignored her, skidding to a stop at an unmarked nondescript door. "Here." Jessup fished out a ring of keys and selected one with black tape on the head. "Master," he said, unlocking the door.

Inside was a storeroom filled with metal shelves of cleaning supplies, boxes of paper, and other office materials.

"Why the hell," Izzy said, "are we stopping here?"

"Back corner," Jessup said and pushed past.

In the corner, essentially out of sight, was a floor to ceiling metal door. The colonel pulled it open revealing a ladder access no bigger than a coat closet.

Lisa leaned her head in and looked down. The shaft seemed to go on forever, alternating black shaft and weak lighting every floor exaggerating their height. She turned her head to look the other direction. Twenty feet or so above her was another hatch identical to the one they stood at.

Jessup pulled her back, stepped into the well and started climbing. Izzy followed, with Lisa bringing up the rear, nearly losing her grip on her shoes with each rung grabbed.

Hot, stale air blasted its way up the shaft, heating Lisa's legs and making her want to gag at the same time.

A handful of curses later, Jessup got the ninth-floor hatch open and pulled himself into the light. Izzy vanished as well, leaving Lisa alone on the ladder. She pitched her shoes through the opening, then climbed through.

Lisa blinked, a heavy case of déjà vu setting in. They, once again, stood in a storeroom with all the same materials as the one they'd just left.

Jessup already had the door open and was exiting into the hall.

Lisa called out, "Hey, wait up."

"Keep up, then," he muttered.

Izzy handed Lisa her heels. "Put them on."

"No friggin' way. I'll never keep up then."

Another two hallways brought them to a massive metal door emblazoned with lethal force warnings.

Nearly a dozen white-coated staff ran down the hall in their direction. In the middle of the fray Lisa made out the scraggly red hair belonging to Jerry Stallinger. The group, as one, skidded to a stop at the sight of Colonel Jessup.

The lead woman, gray hair done up much the same way as Izzy's, barked out, "Colonel! Eight has a contamination breach. It—"

"I know, Doctor Mallen. We just came from down there." He started toward a pair of large double doors. "I need you and your team to help in…."

A look passed between the group.

She'd backed away, moving in the direction the trio had just come from. Others followed, nearly pressing themselves against the far wall to get by.

"Doctor Mallen!" Jessup repeated. "I said I need you and your team's assistance."

"No," she said, continuing to back away, leading the group toward the storeroom.

Izzy stepped forward, grabbing Jerry by the arm. The group parted and continued around them. He shrieked at the touch.

The rest left him to her, moving quickly down the hall.

Jessup called out, "If you take the access ladder, skip eight and seven. Grab the stairs down on five."

No one responded.

"This is *your* fault!" Izzy screamed at him. "You're going to help make it—"

His fist connected squarely against her nose.

Jerry looked at his fist and the blood spattering the knuckles.

"Her blood!" He screamed. "Her blood! I've got her blood on me!" He ran after Dr. Mallen.

The group poured into the supply closet faster. The door slammed before Jerry could get in. Noises echoed from inside as shelving was moved. He banged on the door, sobbing. "Please! Please," he begged. "Please!"

Izzy pinched her nose. "Asshole," she muttered, staunching the flow of blood.

Lisa put a hand on Colonel Jessup's arm. "If it's contaminated, would we really—"

"This is command central. The contamination's below us. We need to shut this down before it goes critical."

He jerked his arm free and palm-scanned the door. A blinking red light followed, and Jessup put his face up to it, receiving a retinal scan as well.

The door popped free of its housing and Jessup slid inside.

Lisa took a deep breath and followed him. The bleating of the alarm echoed louder in the confined space. Izzy went to the nearest wall and stood. Lisa stepped beside her and took the room in.

It was essentially empty. Two computer terminals rested atop a folding desk facing a blank wall some twenty-five yards distant.

"There's nothing…" Izzy said.

"Here," Lisa finished.

Jessup barked, "Boot up those systems. We only have another minute or two before the rift opens."

Both women did as directed and booted the systems. The far wall seemed to darken, even with the fluorescent ceiling lights shining at full strength.

The door opened again, and Jerry slipped through.

"They locked me out," he said, wiping his fingers on his jeans.

"Shut up," Lisa said, frantically trying to understand the boot up sequence.

"Thirty seconds," Jessup said.

"Why us?" Izzy asked as she typed. "You should've brought someone more experienced."

All Jessup offered was, "No time."

Lisa suddenly felt nauseous and her perception tilted. The whole world was at a forty-five-degree angle, yet she was still upright.

Then everything snapped to normal.

Except for the wall.

It was gone.

In its place was a mixture of colors seemingly brought to life by some non-existent black light. Trees, much like the ones she'd seen on the screen in the command center clutched the soil, each other, even, in one case, some animal as big as a Shetland pony, but with… ten legs, all ending in knobby hooks. The beast screeched silently, thrashing against the branches that pulled it closer to the trees upturned roots until penetration slowed the thing's struggles.

The beast's face, reflective over-sized blue orbed eyes set wide on an otherwise almost feline face, looked directly at them.

Lisa looked over to see Izzy openly weeping, something she'd never see her do.

"They're coming," Jessup said, pointing past the tree.

Four black garbed soldiers raced toward the opening. Rather than regular military gear, everything they wore appeared to have had plastic melted onto it, creating a seal.

Each ducked under the tree, which was oblivious to them now that it was already working on a meal, and dove for the opening. As each hit the opening they vanished. The last, a true bear of a man even with all the gear, was covered with what looked, to Lisa at least, like golf ball-sized ladybugs…though these were green, not red and polka-dotted. A receiver of some kind fell from the man's hand as he dove through.

"The call box!" Jessup yelled. "We need it to close the mirror!"

"Tell him to go back!" Izzy yelled.

"I can't," Jessup said. "The entrance is here. The clean room for returns is two rooms over."

Lisa took a second to look over to where Jessup stood. He held a dead-man's switch down, powering the gateway. By the size of the activation arm it was a two…maybe three-person job.

"We can't shut the return window without…without." The rest was lost as he struggled to keep the gateway open on this side.

Jerry went to the window and called back, "One of you reach through and I'll pull you back. It'll take two."

Lisa stood and bolted to the wall, reaching out for Jerry's hand, but watching him jerk his hand back at the last second.

Then she was falling through open air. Everything swirled around before gravity pulled her to the ground. Heat enveloped her as if she'd just opened the oven door at home. Bare toes dug deep into muddy earth. Breath escaped her. On her next inhale, sickly-sweet air from decomposing matter filled her nostrils. She gagged, then knelt, grabbed the device, and turned.

The window behind her was a dual image and hurt her eyes. In one visage, the group of soldiers were in what, for all intents and purposes, was a locker room. They were still fully geared up, but showering, scrubbing at each other—especially the one covered in beetles. In the other visage was the room she'd just left. Izzy was standing behind the desk and miming a scream. Colonel Jessup had managed to pull his service pistol out and point it at Jerry, while still holding the dead man's switch down. Jerry had his hands up.

A wink of light brightened the room and a small spray of blood erupted from Jerry's shoulder. The impact knocked him toward the Mirror. He stumbled, then fell back and through.

He seemed to wink out of existence for a second before reappearing on Lisa's side, squealing like a stuck pig.

"He…" Jerry cried. "He *shot* me!"

Lisa ducked, backing away and lost her footing. An embankment sped her tumble down a steep slope.

"Lisa!" Jerry called.

"Damn it," she muttered.

"Lisa?" he repeated, louder this time.

Other noises filled the pre-dawn. Ones on padded feet. Ones that took each step deliberately.

Predatory noises.

The world was like nothing she'd ever imagined. Forests as far as the eye could see, though most moved as if with their own purpose. The air hummed with insects. An azure sky with clouds so black they appeared more as openings to nothingness, canopied the land. Water, the only thing in this world that looked the same, flowed in a small stream not a minute's walk from where she stood. The air was worse down here and she puffed it out only to be forced to inhale once again.

Something small and weasel-like skittered across her leg and continued along the forest floor.

She kicked out, muffling a screech.

Jerry called again. "I need the receiver to go through the mirror." Though he was trying to keep it under control, the panic in his voice started to surface. "Please, Lisa!"

"Fucker," she whispered and pushed herself upright and looked at the receiver. Military grade, it contained a simple button on one side and grooved impressions for gripping fingers on the other. "Let me guess," she whispered, "press and go."

She caught a glimpse of something large, swallowed by shadows.

"Hello?" Jerry yelled. "We can…we can go *together*. I didn't mean for you to fall through."

Sure, you didn't.

Lisa saw his silhouette thirty feet or so above her, not daring to step away from the mirror's light.

She pushed up, stepping away from a tree slowly moving in her direction. Lisa moved as she'd done when hiding from her brothers playing hide and seek, watching with a wary eye and only moving when Larry turned his head, his own motion masking hers.

Twenty feet. It's only twenty feet.

Her toes dug deep into the dirt.

Lisa grasped a root only to have it contract and nearly pin her fingers to the earth.

"Lisa!"

Jerry was turning in circles now, still standing between her and the mirror.

"Damn it," came out as nothing more than a breath.

Leaves fluttered, the action angry, as if from a rattlesnake.

Lisa moved to the right.

Something got caught in her hair. She batted at it and combed her fingers ensuring it wasn't still there.

Whatever was stalking Jerry moved to the left.

Thank you, Lady Luck.

Jerry took a deep breath, "Liiiiiiiii—"

Webbing that Lisa barely saw whipped onto him. It shot out of the darkness and around him, jerking back, vanishing just as quickly. Where its strands met skin, Jerry's flesh changed color. Skin swelled, split, and wept an orange ooze.

Jerry looked in her direction.

Their eyes met.

"L-L-Lisa?"

The web shot out from the darkness a second time, creating a new crimson pattern on his flesh before whipping back again.

A voice, guttural, parroted Jerry from behind her. "Luhhhh… Luhhhh…Liiiiiiisaaaaaah."

Lisa tore from her hiding place and ran for the mirror.

From the corner of her eye, she saw Jerry shamble toward her. More ooze bubbled on him. A third snap of the web and Jerry vanished along with the strands, leaving only his screams to fill the void.

Something broke through the bushes to her left. Izzy rose and pointed in that direction, a terrified look on her face.

Lisa pressed the button and dove through the doorway, landing on hard tiles.

An electric pop sounded right by her ear, and she looked back to see a claw, easily ten inches long, lying on the floor right beside her.

She backpedaled away from it. Yellow ichor dripped from where the talon was severed.

"Who the hell are you?" came a voice behind her.

The four men, soaked, but apparently clean, stepped from the half-wall.

Lisa held up the receiver. "Uh…you dropped this."

Each looked at her for a second, making her more than a little self-conscious. As one, the quartet backed up toward the door, which stayed closed.

Through the glass, Lisa saw Izzy and Jessup.

"It's okay," she yelled. "I got it. I'll just shower too, and—"

Izzy was crying.

Lisa stared at her, then bent down to scratch an itch on her calf. Fingertips met with a bubbled blister. She looked down, seeing others surfacing on her right leg. Beyond them, goo from some insect she must have stepped on splattered her foot, guts creaming up from between her toes.

A touch of red mixing in the mess.

The men started banging on the door as the white lights turned red and an artificial feminine voice echoed throughout the room.

"Foreign biological agent detected. Clean shower removal or decontamination commencement in sixty seconds."

"What?" Lisa screamed. The men were looking back at her and banging on the door harder. She looked down. The blisters on her leg had…*something* in them. Something that *squirmed*. The largest blister ruptured, releasing a handful of centipedes barely the size of a pencil lead. Blooming fibers rose from the wound, reaching out into the air. The wound wept a viscous brown pus.

The men were yelling now.

"Forty-five seconds until decontamination."

Lisa ran for the shower and pulled it on.

It wasn't water.

Chemicals seared her skin, flaying the surface layers off in an instant.

She screamed incoherently, but stayed in the stream, gripping the shower wall.

"Thirty seconds until decontamination."

Lisa ripped at her clothing, pulling it off with shaking hands.

Izzy banged on the far side of the door and just behind her Jessup stood stoically.

She howled, scrubbing harder.

Lisa grabbed a wire brush and started scrubbing at the blisters on her skin. Each blister ruptured easily, freeing centipedes and allowing the wire bristles to dig deep into muscle and tendons.

"Ten seconds until decontamination."

Please. Please. Please.

"Five."

She stopped scrubbing when she saw new blisters forming on her arms, more white larvae squiggled just under the surface.

"Four."

Something tickled her sinuses.

"Three."

What flowed down the drain went from white, to pink, to red.

"Two."

Lisa looked up. "I-I-Izzyyyyy...."

The room was swallowed in flame, yellow light licking every inch of the room.

Outside, Izzy Holwitz banged against the door.

Banged until her hands were bloody.

Banged until Jessup left.

Banged because there was nothing else to do.

Behind the story...

Now we're at the final installment of BEHIND THE STORY.

"Skewed Perceptions" was published in *Darkness Wired* by Notch Publishing, the same publishing house who put out *Sick Cruising*. The open call guidelines were easier than the previous call, leaving the rules that submissions had to: 1) be horror science fiction, and 2) use a character supplied by the editor. I was given "Izzy," a mad-scientist type of person. Not a lot to go on, but I wrote the first draft of the story and sent it in.

The response after reading the first page was, "Izzy was supposed to be a man." So, I'm initially thinking, 9,000 words wasted and maybe I can find a new home for "Skewed Perceptions." During the video call, the editor went on to say they'd really prefer Izzy to be a man. This was one of the few times I fought back on a story, arguing that I'd only known two Izzy's in my life and both were women nicknamed for Isabelle/Isabella. My editor said they'd see how it worked and logged off to read the story. The next day she said, "Izzy works great!" There were no issues with the rest of the story other than Izzy's gender.

I had fun watching Izzy Holwitz flex her personality in this story.

Who knows? Maybe she'll be back.

DRIVE-IN FEATURE

A sneak peek at Henry Snider's new novel

CHAPTER 1

Renna hunched over the desk and surveyed the stacks of research material Jeff had acquired over the last eighteen months. Black and white photographs, maps, and enough paper to have stripped a forest clean cascaded off the desk's top and onto an ever-growing pile that littered the floor. She sat with one leg under her and brushed a brown lock of hair away, tucking it behind an ear. An exaggerated cough caught her attention.

Jeff stood in the doorway, still in his pajama bottoms, casually stirring a cup of coffee. Hair stood out in every direction and gave him the appearance of a mad scientist in training.

"And just what do you think you're doing in here?"

"Oh, you know, snooping."

"Looking for love letters from my other gals?"

She grinned. "I know where you keep those. There's only one and she's ninety-three."

"Youth has nothing on experience." Using his coffee cup to point, he motioned from Renna to the living room. "You…out."

"Aw, not even one peek?" She lifted her oversized t-shirt's hem, showing an additional two inches of leg. "I'll make it worth your while."

He flicked the light off in response and shooed her out of the den. Renna flopped on the living room couch and stretched out, blocking Jeff from sitting next to her as punishment. They stared at each other in the day's early light, her peppy and awake while he still struggled to get both eyelids blinking at the same time.

"You'll get to hear, read and see all about this over the next two weeks. I promise."

"And I can't read right now because…?"

"Because I need your responses at the location to help me flavor the book."

"But a coffee table book—"

"And website for videos."

"And website full of depressing photos and stories?" She furrowed her brow, unsure of the success potential for such a project. Moving her legs, she finally let Jeff sit. "If you're sure this kind of book will sell, I guess I'm in." Renna leaned over and grabbed his neck, "But this better be worth me cashing in my two weeks of vacation." She pulled him forward and offered a quick kiss to drive the point home. "Can I at least know the topic?"

"Bad places."

"Bad places? That's kind of vague, isn't it? Besides, I already know that. I mean, do I need to bring my pepper spray or something more substantial?"

"That's all you get." Jeff pushed himself upright and headed back to the bathroom. "Clock's ticking. Best get your butt dressed. We leave in thirty minutes."

"Ugh!"

Renna waited until she heard the shower running before returning to his office. Binders contained a laundry list of paperwork ranging from handwritten letters and aerial photographs to official documents and bagged swatches of clothing. Unsure where to begin, she flipped open a random manilla folder and was greeted by the color photograph of a brutalized woman. Her green leather skirt, obviously from the mid '80s, was hiked up, showing hose and underwear torn free. Dead eyes looked off to the right and Renna found herself staring hard at the corner of the photograph in an effort to see whatever it was the victim saw. Unable to look away, she focused on a little flag with the number three on it stuck in the gravel beside a scuffed purse. A pair of men's legs were in frame near the woman's head.

All the warmth left her. "What the hell kind of book are you working on?"

&

The drive took longer than expected, especially since the morning's commute fell on a Friday.

"I can't believe you got all of that research into two plastic tubs," Renna said.

Jeff smirked at her. "Tell me, Sherlock, how much did you see?"

"I didn't—"

"You've hardly said a word since we left the house."

"That's not true." Renna shifted to unstick bare legs from the car's leather seat. Guilt bit deep as the lie left her lips. "I only opened one folder."

Jeff frowned.

"It was the one with the dead woman in it."

"Which one?"

"Which one? You mean there's more than one dead girl?"

He sighed. "Just tell me what you saw." Jeff stomped on the gas and the rental car barreled past yet another semi hauling poultry. Even with air conditioner set to recirculate, an overpowering smell of wet chickens found its way in.

"It was a raped woman in a green skirt."

"Kay…gotcha."

Watching the tension in his neck visibly lessen, Renna regretted both agreeing to go on this venture and for playing the part of Pandora. The hum of the highway increased as Jeff sped up.

She turned to stare at the traffic as they passed. "So how bad is this going to be?"

"On a scale of one to ten with ten being The Texas Chain Saw Massacre?"

"Shit."

"Only about a four." Jeff snaked in and out of traffic and Renna found herself wishing she'd offered to drive.

They rode in silence for a while. Renna watched Jeff's mouth moving silently as he worked through some problem she assumed had to do with this damned book. Sometimes she matched things she imagined he said with the movement of his lips, once succeeding in Jeff unknowingly lip syncing the words to the Beatles' Come Together.

The South Kansas town of Kyst came and went, and the Denny's sign faded away in the side mirror. "How much farther?"

"We're here."

Hyper 44 offered weary truckers choices from gas to showers, not to mention everything in between. Semis lined the far side of the truck stop, appearing as if it were a trailer park mobilized to move on a moment's notice. The center's main building sat as a testament to big-rig cheesiness with oversized fiberglass logs stacking their way to the roof. Red neon bit the shade and proclaimed "MOVIES INSIDE." Renna was pretty sure Disney wasn't on the list.

Renna asked, "Why are we stopping here?"

Jeff mumbled.

"What?"

He sighed. "We've gotta meet up with Travis."

"No." Renna said. "No way in hell am I spending two weeks with him."

"Ren, come on. It's not going to be that bad."

"Easy for you to say."

"Trust me."

She crossed her arms. "This isn't over."

They whipped in, coming to a stop next to Travis's day-glow yellow crew-cab pickup. The monstrosity was mobile redneck heaven, sporting oversized tires, a high-water lift kit and the stereotypical 102-inch CB whip antenna waving off the rear bumper.

"Think he's inside?"

Jeff opened his door. "Of course he's inside. This kind of place is like Mecca to him." He grabbed a lone folder off the back seat and got out.

Renna followed him in, blinking away the bright daylight

until the door closed behind them. Travis was at the far end of the restaurant, standing on the booth's seat and waving his ever-present straw cowboy hat like an idiot. Crew cut red hair, dangerously close to bleaching orange, framed an otherwise handsome face. Then, just like the first time she'd met Travis, he opened his mouth and ruined the cute cowboy effect.

"Y'all are late!" The overdone Texas drawl echoed throughout the dining room, causing everyone to look over.

Renna walked to the booth and slid in beside Jeff.

Jeff asked, "So are you two ready?"

"Nope," Travis said. As if on cue, a bleached blonde dropped down in the seat next to him. "I want you two to meet Stacy. She's coming with us." A white halter top and tattered blue jean shorts made her perfect arm candy for the cowboy.

Jeff's lips all but disappeared. "Excuse me?"

Travis smiled. "Don't worry. I already told her all about the trip."

Jeff leveled a stare. "And just what do you think you know?"

"Oh," Stacy piped up and fired words as if from an automatic weapon, "he told me it was some kind of haunted trip and that you were a photographer and a writer and that we'd get to be in the book you're writing and—"

"Whoa, whoa, whoa," Jeff said, trying to calm the girl down. "Take a breath."

"Sorry." She smiled shyly. "I talk a lot when I'm nervous." Stacy's hands went below the table like a child scolded for grabbing a cookie out of turn.

Jeff grumbled, "Travis, can I have a word with you?"

"Wait," Stacy interrupted, "I won't be any trouble. I promise. I've seen all the ghost hunting shows and it looks like so much fun."

"Jeffy, you've got your own plaything. Why can't I have mine?"

Renna kicked Travis under the table at the same time Stacy smacked him on the shoulder.

Jeff gave in, sighing. "Fine. I think I have the release forms in the trunk."

"See." Travis smirked, stretching back and snaking an arm around Stacy. "What'd I tell you? No problem."

All four ordered large breakfasts, per Jeff's suggestion, noting they had some serious road time ahead and the meal may double as lunch. Pancakes, eggs and sausage, which Renna remarked smelled like warm dog droppings, were devoured with quick efficiency.

Wiping a dribble of syrup from his chin, Jeff looked up from the empty plate. "Are you ready for a generalized rundown of what you're in for?" He produced a folded piece of paper smeared with handwritten names and dates.

Renna reached for her coffee. "Judging by what I saw this morning, I'm leaning closer to 'not.'"

"Tough. Here we go…." He took a deep breath. "In 1867 Antoine Lefebvre, fresh from getting rich selling guns to both sides during the Civil War, worked his way Southwest heading toward Mexico. He crossed Missouri and into the southern part of Kansas. That's where he stumbled into Parish Hill."

Travis said, "He sounds French," around a mouthful of biscuit.

"He was. Antoine hits the local saloon and finds out any further south will get him onto Indian lands. Deciding he doesn't want to take a chance on losing his hair—even on a reservation—and buys a patch of land about half a day's ride further west."

"Scalped Frenchmen?" Stacy giggled. "Sounds like a gastropub meal."

"Actually," Renna offered while pushing the remnants of her meal away, "the French started the practice of scalping. They did it to prove they killed the native they said they had…and for trophies. A few tribes realized the trophy angle worked both ways and took the actions as their own."

"Thank you, Miss History, but let me tell the story, okay?" Jeff looked at each of his three companions in turn before continuing. "Antoine buys his little patch of land from the center of a wilderness, a two-thousand-acre wood and names it Le Perchoir au Coucher de Soleil."

"Gesundheit," Travis barked.

Jeff ignored him. "In English it means Sunset Roost."

Renna cut in, "I thought your notes said it translates to 'The Perch in the Sunset.'"

Jeff didn't even glance in her direction. "He hired men to hack out about a hundred acres in the middle and built a pretty decent home overlooking a patch of farmland. That's where his problem started."

"Indians," Stacy offered.

"No. That's just it. The Sioux avoided that area even before the whites arrived. He found out even with the land cleared, most of the soil was too acidic from pine needles to grow anything, but he still tried. Antoine contracted with local cattlemen for manure and hired a dozen newly freed slaves to till fertilizer into the soil. For three years he kept this goal of farming in mind and only succeeded in growing a pitiful crop. The few things Antoine managed to produce all tasted bitter, even the corn.

"After spending thousands of dollars buying land and building this salute to the American dream, he married a local girl. Enter Hanna Wilson." Jeff mimed walking legs with his fingers across the table. "With her being fifteen, she was just the right age for Antoine." He pulled a copy of a tintype and laid it on the table.

There sat a solemn Hanna, hair light enough to be corn silk and wearing a white dress covered with lace. Behind the teen stood a stern-faced Antoine, one heavy hand on her shoulder. Renna stared at the photograph, thinking in today's world Hanna might have been a cheerleader or played volleyball with her friends. Back then, she'd undertaken the role of wife.

"I thought that was only legal in Oklahoma," Travis said.

"God, Travis," Stacy said, "you are so bad."

Renna mumbled, "You have no idea."

The girl looked over. "What's that?"

"Nothing," Renna said. "Go on with the story, Jeff."

"With a thirty-year gap in their ages, neither of them had much to say to each other. She's there mainly to do her wifely duty and bear him children."

Their waitress started collecting plates. "Oh, dear," she cut in, "that really is a tragedy. My own Phil married me when I was seventeen and the bum wasn't good for nothin.'"

Jeff just stared, refusing to comment while she grabbed saucers and silverware. She left in a huff at being excluded from the conversation. A hushed snicker escaped Stacy.

"Thank you," Travis called out behind her, twisting the knife.

Hands became more animated as Jeff fell back into the story.

"Now it's something like 1885 and they've been together for about sixteen years, give or take. Hanna's done her duty and given him three daughters and a son—Sarah, Felicia, Winifred and Michael. The girls, fifteen, fourteen and twelve, all go to school in Parish Hill…and yes, we're talking about an oversized one-room schoolhouse straight out of Little House. At fifteen, Sarah has a beau who's been courting her, much to the disapproval of Daddy.

"The boy's a local, one Thomas Fornier. He's handsome, strong and the son of one of the cattlemen Antoine does business with."

"Sounds decent enough," Renna said.

"It would have been, too, except one of the farmhands stumbled across them doing what comes natural, especially in the springtime, and this was late May…maybe early June. The guy ran off to tell Daddy what was going on in the barn."

Travis chuckled. "So, it was shotgun wedding time?" His hand slid under the table and Stacy's eyes grew wide before offering him a second, half-hearted smack.

"Not quite. Antoine demanded satisfaction and challenged the boy to a duel. This being the United States and not wine-choked France, Thomas declined, sending instead the ranch's foreman to deliver the message…and a letter to be given to Sarah."

"And this is where we're going?" Renna leveled a serious look at her boyfriend. "A dilapidated house out in the middle of nowhere."

"Yes and no."

She rolled her eyes. "Those would be the choices."

"Just let me finish this part of the story, okay?"

Renna said, "This part? You mean there's more?"

"You saw the photo. Did that look like a tintype picture?"

Travis asked, "What photo?"

Jeff shifted uncomfortably. "We'll get to it. Now Antoine doesn't take the news that the boy's refusing to meet his challenge very well."

Stacy thumped her elbows on the table. "What was it? Pistols at dawn?"

"No. Antoine considered himself a civilized man. He challenged the boy to a sword duel."

Travis, now getting into the story, asked, "Seriously? Swords? Like Vikings and all?"

Renna finished her last swallow of orange juice. "Fencing sounds cool until you imagine someone putting a thirty-inch razor through your body. Then it somehow loses its romanticism."

Jeff nodded. "Antoine finds Sarah reading the letter and confiscates it, banishing her, along with the rest of the children, to their rooms…except of course for Michael, who's still confined to a crib. Night falls and Sarah, being the lovestruck teen that she is, disappears out the window, never to be seen again."

Stacy fiddled with the check. "What about Thomas?"

"Same story. He vanished as well. Which brings us to Antoine's drinking like a fish. Weeks go by with no word from either of the young lovebirds. Thomas' family refuses to do any more business with Antoine until the kids are found. Some of the townies accuse him of killing the boy and even go so far as to send deputies out to the homestead. Between the drunken curses and threats of reprisal against the entire town, Antoine refuses to even discuss the matter… in English or his native French.

"A couple months go by with no word from the Lefebvre household…or anyone from Le Perchoir au Coucher de Soleil at all. No workers come for supplies. The children are out of school for the summer, but no one sees them at church for half a dozen Sundays. Pastor Ghausted takes the time to stop in for a visit and what does he find?"

Jeff stared at the three seated with him and waited.

Understanding setting in, Stacy guessed, "A mass suicide?"

Travis joined in, "The entire place burned down?"

Jeff looked at Renna, waiting for her guess.

"Fine, I'll play along. Nothing."

"Wrong on all accounts, but Ren wins the prize for being the closest." Jeff gave her a syrupy kiss, lips sticking slightly as he pulled back.

Travis winked. "Glad I didn't win."

"Pastor Ghausted rode up the path and saw two fresh graves in the front yard, ringed with stones and each bearing a whitewashed cross. He walks around them twice before hearing a tapping from one of the upstairs windows. Hanna's knocking on the glass and looking like a victim from a horror movie. She puts one finger to her lips in a 'shhhh' motion and waves frantically.

"The pastor enters the house, walking as quietly as one can on dry wooden floors. He sees Antoine passed out on the couch, a couple of bottles standing guard to his snoring ass." Jeff, in full character, mimed the story's actions. "He goes up the stairs to a locked door. He turns the key and pushes it open and there's Hanna, sitting on the bed, a chain running from the headboard to her bruised bare ankle."

Travis raised his hand to eye level and finger-waved at the elderly couple listening in from the neighboring booth. "Now wait a minute. How do you know all of this?"

"Research and court records."

"This much detail from way back then?" Renna blurted.

"That's right." Jeff jumped back into the story before Renna could interrupt further. "The pastor knows he can't get her free without waking Antoine, and Hanna's taken to sobbing loudly. She keeps trying to push Michael into his arms. That's when Ghausted hears a creaking from the stairs. Without thinking twice, the man of God shoves the baby back into Hanna's arms, opens the second story window and jumps out, landing—you guessed it—on one of the two graves, breaking his arm. He promises to get help and takes to his horse."

Travis grinned. "Takes to his horse, huh? Quite the turn of phrase you have there, ol' buddy. At this pace I'll make a cowboy out of you yet."

Jeff countered, "Better chance of making me into a pair of cowboy boots."

Renna stretched and felt her back pop against the thinly padded plastic bench. "Are we hitting the road, or what?"

"In a minute. So, Ghausted rides all the way back to town, gets the sheriff and a little posse together. He insists on coming back with them, broken arm and all. It's late in the day when they get there. Most of the house is in shadow. They see Antoine perched on the front steps with a bottle of whiskey planted between his feet and hat tipped low, passed out and sprawled only the way a drunk can. A rider stops by the graves and manages to call out before vomiting his lunch. One of the crosses was broken under the weight of baby Michael, his little body sliced and folded backwards over one of the rocks…glass covered him from the bedroom window."

Loud coughing came from the elderly couple in the next booth over, followed by a decidedly dirty look from the man.

"Just ignore them," Stacy said, entranced by the tale. "Finish it."

"They slap irons on Antoine and go upstairs to rescue Hanna. Only they don't find her. They see where the chain's chewed the floor and scratched the iron headboard, but no Mrs. Lefebvre. Of all people, it's Pastor Ghausted who takes to kicking Antoine awake and demanding to know what happened.

"Antoine claims she left a couple of months ago. That's when the pastor starts in again, reminding him between doing his rendition of a soccer player to ol' Lefebvre's body that he'd been there earlier in the day and seen Hanna for himself. In a stupor, Antoine changes his story, saying that the girls died of the fever a month before and Hanna'd taken the baby and walked out on him that afternoon.

"When confronted about baby Michael, still prone in the front yard, he simply said, 'I never killed no baby.'"

Renna asked, "And this is where we're going to?"

"Oh, honey, I've only hit the tip of the iceberg with this. But you're right about us going there."

Sarcasm dripped as she said, "You take me to the best places."

"I'll make it up to you, hon. I always do."

The elderly man rose, grumbling about a lack of manners in today's youth. Stacy blew him a kiss as he helped his wife out of the booth and led her down the aisle.

Renna hung her head. "I'm so glad I have my back to them."

Jeff lifted his empty coffee cup, getting the waitress' attention after a handful of silent seconds. She nodded and resumed wiping down an empty table in the center of the room.

"Let me finish."

"How much longer?"

"Maybe twenty minutes?"

Renna said, "You're done. You've sold us on participating in this book, but if we don't leave we're never going to get there."

A frown crossed his face, quickly mimicked by Travis.

"You can finish once we get there. Fair?"

"I do have to go by the Parish Hill police station today."

"Willingly going into a police station?" Travis's voice rose, looking for an audience. "What the hell's wrong with you?"

"Have to check in before we go to the drive-in."

"Wait a minute," Renna said. "I'm confused. We're going to a drive-in?"

Jeff scooched her out of the booth. "I'll tell you about it when we get there, like you said."

She slid out and stepped aside for Jeff.

Stacy held onto the check, refusing to give it up. "You guys are being nice enough to let me come along. The least I can do is buy breakfast."

"No, the least you could do is…" Travis said, bending his head and whispered something only she could hear.

Her eyes went wide for the second time that morning. "Renna, what do you think about us girls bunking together?"

Travis slapped her on the butt. "Now it's a party!"

"Stacy," Renna said, "I'm afraid you're on your own."

"I guess we'll have to figure something out." She directed an obvious wink at Travis and led them all to the register.

CHAPTER 2

Renna stretched, doing her best to get comfortable in the afternoon sunlight and blinked away a half-forgotten dream about being lost in a house. The Kansas sun beat down on her legs, contrasting a sensation of heat against heavily air-conditioned skin.

"Good afternoon," Jeff said as the car slowed. "We're in Parish Hill."

Stone buildings offered momentary shade as the car pulled up to a stoplight. An all too familiar engine revved just off their rear bumper.

"One of these days he's going to hit you."

"You should've seen how close he was coming down the highway."

The light changed and they turned left onto Main Street. Brick buildings lined both sides of the block, housing typical small-town businesses. Dan's Grocery offered sales through dusty windows. A drug store, along with the next four buildings, stood empty.

"This place is a ghost town," Renna said.

"All the better for us."

"That's not what I meant."

"When we get to the police station I'll run in and then we'll hit the motel."

She looked over at Jeff. "They're not sharing a room with us."

"It'll save money."

Renna felt her temper flare. "Cowboy Travis and his runaway pecker have plans and you know it. I'm not going to try to sleep with that going on right next to me."

"What if we want to—"

"We won't want to if we're sharing a room." Renna jabbed her finger into his ribs emphasizing each word. "That's just creepy."

"Ow!"

"Got that?" Her fingers held ready for another thrust.

"Yes ma'am."

"Good." A stop sign, faded to the point of being dusty pink and white rested at a forty-five-degree angle. Below it sat a blue police sign with an arrow pointing to the right. "Turn here."

"Why?" Jeff asked.

She pointed to the sign and stared at an empty video store as they rounded the corner. Bright afternoon light lit up the front area. Empty shelves sat testament to satellite television, and ultimately streaming's success. Burgundy bat-wing doors led to an infamous back room that all independent video stores seemed to have. The store drifted from view and the next block offered the police station, volunteer fire department, and library all in one stone monstrosity of a location.

Renna adjusted, facing forward, not really irritated anymore but still a ways away from letting the idea of bunking together go. She put her feet on the floor and sat prim, knowing it drove Jeff nuts.

"How about that," he said, touching her on the shoulder. "There's parking right in front."

She shot a frigid stare at Jeff.

"You know we're getting our own room. I wouldn't do that to you."

"Mmmm hmmm."

"I was just kidding. I swear."

Jeff parked the sedan and opened the door. A blast of hot air whooshed into the car and hit Renna as if she'd opened an oven. Sweat immediately started beading on her upper lip as she got out.

The blast of air continued around her, peppering dust on everything in the car.

"Lovely," she said before looking around. "Hey, where is Travis anyway?"

They both looked around before seeing the pickup in the shade of the last building they'd passed, a pair of crossed bare feet sticking out the passenger window and propped on the side mirror. The twangy tones of a country song filled the gaps between blasts of summer wind.

Jeff held the outer door for Renna, and they went from a hot street to a scorching office. Oscillating fans sat on every desk, totaling four, and all pointed toward the ceiling in an effort to avoid fluttering a tree's worth of papers.

"We just hit Mayberry." Renna saw the joke was lost on Jeff. "I may wait back in the car."

"Hold on a—"

"Can I help you?" An officer looking as if he only needed a curly tail to overemphasize the word pig stared over the dark oak counter at them.

"Yeah," Jeff said. "I'm looking for Sheriff Longberry."

"Why?"

"Excuse me?"

"Why?" the officer asked. "Why do you want to see him." One of the fans started clanging.

"We're supposed to check in."

"Ex con?"

"What? No." Frustration marred Jeff's features. "I'm here on a book project and I'm supposed to check in with him when I get to town."

The officer was obviously enjoying this. "What kind of book?"

"Um, officer…" Jeff read the sweaty uniform's name tag, "Fredricks, I'm not trying to be rude, but we're on a bit of a schedule here and want to get back on the road."

Fredricks stared at them. "What…kind…of…book?"

"A tourist book," Jeff said.

The officer waited a handful of seconds before he nodded noncommittally and yelled, "Yo! Longberry! People to see you."

A handful of seconds later the sheriff's hulking figure emerged from the windowed back office. Rich cinnamon features and drawn back snow-white hair sat atop a body built for lumberjacking. Obviously past the age most people would retire, the sheriff looked strong enough to snap a man in half. He eyed the two for a moment then made his way to the counter.

Jeff started, "Sheriff Longberry—"

"You're Jeff Miller and that must mean you are," he turned the hard gaze on Renna, "Renna Tublonc."

"Yes, sir," Renna said.

"And I'm guessing that Travis Wills is the driver of the pickup outside?"

Jeff nodded, uncomfortable with the interrogation.

"Not sure of the woman riding with him, though. I got your email and verified you have permission to be out there. But," Longberry leaned on the counter and pointed one sausage finger at Jeff, "I don't like this. We're a small town of nice people." He tapped his fingers on the countertop. "Nice people with a nice reputation."

"Sir, I—"

"I wasn't finished." The sheriff's face hardened. "Best case scenario, you're going to have every wanna-be ghost hunter out here snooping in people's backyards where they have no business being. Worst case, your little trip here ends with getting you hurt, lost, or worse."

"Worse?" Renna repeated.

"Bad things happen everywhere, miss. Even in the heartland, bad things happen." He drew an orange paper folded like a brochure from behind the counter and started filling it out. "Keep this in your glove box. It'll let anyone asking know you have permission to be where you're going." Longberry refolded the paper and held it out for Jeff, jerking it back at the last second. "I can't stop you from talking to people here in my town, but if I hear you've harassed so much as one person, and I mean one single complaint, you're out of here. Do we understand each other?"

"Yes...sir," Jeff stammered.

Longberry nodded and placed the paper in Jeff's hand. "Motel's five blocks down Pearl Street then one block over."

"Thanks," Jeff said.

Renna looked from the Sheriff to Jeff. Bad places. Bad things.

"I noticed you only requested two rooms, Miller. I'm assuming you and Wills will be sharing a room and Miss Tublonc will share one with…?"

"The other woman," Jeff said, dodging the query.

The sheriff smiled, obviously appreciating Jeff's response. "There are still laws about unmarried people sharing the same motel room."

Jeff shifted. "I don't think there are any laws like that anymore."

Longberry said, "Town ordinance. Keeps the kids under control."

"We live together," She blurted. "So legally that makes us common-law. Right?"

The sheriff nodded. "And Mister Wills and his…guest?"

"I'm not sure. I think they're cousins," Jeff offered.

Renna bit back a grin. "Officer Longberry," she asked, forcing a pleasant tone into her voice.

"Sheriff Longberry," he corrected.

"Sorry. Sheriff Longberry, is there a place around here where we can eat?"

"Micah's Pizza's right next to the motel. It's your best bet for dinner."

"Thanks."

Stepping outside, Renna realized the air actually felt cool in comparison. A breeze hit the accumulating perspiration, letting her know just how sweaty she had become. "Motel," she said, "shower, then whatever you've got planned."

"Oh, whatever I've got planned, huh?"

"Just get in."

&

The Sunset Motel appeared to have been built sometime in the 1960's. Interlaced diamond patterns made the background for the sign, below which was a mostly empty kidney-shaped swimming pool. Dried mud caked around a pitiful puddle in the deep end, its diameter no bigger than a kiddie pool. Cracked remnants of a sidewalk ran the length of the V-shaped building, plastic chairs framing oversized windows in front of half of the rooms.

Getting the rooms wasn't much of a problem. The morbidly obese woman behind the counter looked to be at least in her sixties and was more interested in the talk show she was watching than checking Renna in.

"You need ice, gotta go to the second floor. First one's busted," she said, then turned and walked back to her chair.

"Uh, thank you."

Renna chose to walk to the rooms, numbers one and two respectively. No other cars sat in the parking lot. No curtains were drawn back for people to see what little view there was of the empty field across the street. She went to the end, opened number one and pushed the door wide.

Beautiful, refrigerated air struck Renna. She entered and closed the door. While the furniture hadn't been changed since sometime during the Carter administration, the mattresses looked decent on both beds. She flopped back, landing on the one nearest the window and bounced once before coming to rest.

"Ahh." She spread both arms and let the air hit everywhere the cool bedspread didn't.

A resounding thunk followed by a string of curses echoed from the other side of the door.

"Yeah?"

"Let me in, Ren."

Renna rose and opened the door. Jeff stood there with two duffels strapped bandolier style over his chest and carrying both locking plastic tubs. "Did you ever hear of a second trip? I mean, we are on the first floor."

"Just move," Jeff said through gritted teeth and pushed his way past her, setting the burden down under the window. "Air conditioning's been on? Nice!" Bags and tubs hit the floor and he vanished into the bathroom, sounds of streaming water cramping Renna's own bladder.

"Hurry up. I wanna take a shower."

A not nearly muffled enough response echoed out. "No time. You can have one when we get back."

"Jeff, I'm not letting anyone else see me until I at least feel human."

"See," came from the still open door, "I told you she was an alien." Travis stepped in, leading Stacy by the hand.

Renna held out her hand with number two's key. "Don't get comfy. Jeff's taking us somewhere this afternoon."

Stacy leaned against the door. "Damn. I wanted to grab a shower before we went anywhere."

Jeff reemerged and Travis pushed past Renna for a turn at the facilities.

"God, you're such an asshole. Why don't you just go in your own room?"

The bathroom door stood ajar, his own expulsion sounding throughout the motel room. "Like yours more," Travis hollered.

"And without manners," she added. Turning her attention back to Jeff she asked, "So, where are you forcing us to go?"

"Well, I figured you'd like to see where we'll be doing some of the work."

Stacy chimed in. "We're going to the farm?"

"Not quite. We are, however, going to the woods for part two of the story."

"What about the end of part one?" Stacy flopped on the bed just as Renna had.

"Not a whole lot left to tell. They arrested Antoine and took dogs to Le Perchoir au Coucher de Soleil, but of all things the damned pooches start whining and pissing themselves before getting a mile into the woods. Once there, they had to be dragged out of the wagon and what did they do once they're on terra firma? They just tuck their tails and hide under the wagon. The sheriff tried to pull one out and nearly got a finger bitten off."

Travis stepped out. "What about the farm dogs?"

"There weren't any. Antoine couldn't get any to live there. He'd bring them in and they'd disappear within a week or just die.

Renna leaned against the low dresser, grateful for the cold wood and tried to ignore the need to pee. "Did animals kill the dogs?"

"Nothing like that. They just died. Even the ones they tied to the house."

"Hold that thought." Renna made for the rest room, taking a moment to turn on the water in the sink for a little privacy.

"Hurry up," Travis called. "Hey, that's a hell of a flow there, Ren," he chided. "Got Niagara Falls for kidneys?"

She flipped off the closed door, thrusting the upturned digit in a silent retort, then finished her business, and returned to the bedroom. "So let's get on with the story already."

Jeff didn't need a second prompt. "They wrapped the sheriff's fingers and start looking for Hanna or any of the farm hands. They spend two whole days there looking for any signs of foul play and couldn't find anything except the scuff marks on the bedroom floor and headboard."

"And the dead baby," Renna said.

"And the dead baby," Jeff confirmed. "They even check a ways into the woods in every direction, following established trails and any fresh ones they find."

Stacy asked, "So…what? They're all expert trackers?"

Renna sighed and gave Travis a look that said, did you get this one out of kindergarten? "No, Stacy. Back then most men hunted. Tracking, to them, was just like us going to the grocery store. It just came naturally."

"No one finds any definitive signs of foul play other than what the pastor saw and baby Michael's death. They charge him with the baby's murder. Months go by before Lefebvre gets his day in court. While the minister's testimony carries a lot of weight, Antoine still has money enough to hire the best attorney in the territory. With no actual proof that Hanna didn't just run off, or that she hadn't killed the baby herself, the judge couldn't get him for murder and the girls were buried for months by this point, so they had little for the prosecution to go on. Antoine persisted he couldn't have killed his son and stuck to the story that Hanna must have done it."

Stacy stood and headed toward the bathroom. "He got off, didn't he?"

"Nearly." Jeff walked to the nearest tub, popped it open and thumbed through the paperwork while Travis' newest gal pal took her turn in the restroom. He stood, grasping an aged newspaper page in time with her emergence. "Here." The plastic sleeve containing the page passed from person to person.

The headline read, "Lefebvre Guilty of Manslaughter." Renna

focused on the etching first, which showed a moustachioed man standing and pointing at the judge. She scanned the message, finding the judge's declaration that the boy's death was Lefebvre's fault since he was the only one present at the time the authorities got there. It went on to say that no woman would leave her dead infant in such a state.

Travis snatched the paper from Renna. "Did they hang him?"

"No," Renna said. "It says he got four years—one year for every six months Michael lived."

"And," Jeff said, gently taking the page from Travis, "that is pretty much the end of that part of the story. Antoine served his time, got out in 1899, and moved back into the house. By this point to say he was a bit off would be an understatement. The Frenchman boarded all the windows and doors shut and just lived out of the front parlor and kitchen. Willshire was a little burg that sprang out from nothing on the other side of the wood. A priest looked in on Lefebvre—who was a devout Protestant, I might add—from time to time to see how the old man was doing."

Stacy asked, "If they were Protestant, why'd he have a priest coming by?"

Jeff tapped the bottom tub with his foot. "I can only go by what's in here. It looks like he converted while in prison. What I can tell you is that on Wednesday, December twenty-seventh, the same year, Antoine went to Willshire and participated in the act of confession."

"Let me guess," Renna stretched and weighed her desire to take her flip flops off against how dirty the tactfully camouflaged carpet probably was, "the priest left the order never to return."

Jeff made a face.

"No? Well, that seems to fall in place with your story so far. Hey, when are we going to get around to the photo I saw?"

"In a couple of days probably."

"Probably? Why not now?"

"The point of this is not only to tell the story, Ren, but to gauge your," he motioned to Travis and Stacy, "and their, reactions to what's happened here."

"And it's not bullshit?"

"No, it's not bullshit. All of these things happened right here.

Antoine sat right in that jail we walked into. He probably even ate meals in one of the buildings along that block and so on. But," he said, popping the top off the second tub and searching through its considerable contents, "we need to get out there before it gets too late. I want to fire off a few initial shots."

"So finish and we can go."

"Antoine gave confession and the priest suddenly started making regular trips out to Le Perchoir au Coucher de Soleil. It becomes a weekly thing. Late summer of 1902, the sheriff makes a call of his own on Antoine, who's now seventy-eight. He finds the ol' guy dead and leaning against one of the boarded up doors leading off the front hallway. Been that way for quite a while from what I gather."

"But the priest—" Stacy started.

"Had been there time and again since Antoine's death."

Renna cocked an eyebrow. "And he hadn't offered last rites or buried him?"

"Obviously didn't bury him. I really don't know about the last rites. Church tends to be tight lipped on the subject of Le Perchoir au Coucher de Soleil." Jeff stood after extracting a thick manilla file. "The official story is that the priest was formally reprimanded and moved to some parish on the East coast. Nothing really came from the official investigation. That's the end of that part of the story."

Travis yawned. "That part? How much more is there?"

"Oh, there's a part two…even a part three." He nodded to Renna. "That's where the photo you saw comes in."

"Great," she said sarcastically.

"Everyone ready?

The four left the comfort of the darkened motel room for the sweltering heat of southern Kansas.

CHAPTER 3

The drive out of Parish Hill left Renna feeling like a child going to the principal's office, full of apprehension and more than a little nervous. Watching Jeff get on the wrong road when there were only two major ones going west helped lighten her mood some. It was petty, she knew, but entertaining just the same. He smacked the steering wheel twice and grumbled to himself.

"What was that?" she asked.

"Nothing."

Renna saw him scowling behind the sunglasses. "You know, we don't have to do this today. We just got here and there's still two whole weeks for you to do your research and take photos."

"Another hour," he said, oblivious to her. "We lost another hour driving the wrong God damned road."

In truth, they barely lost forty minutes—twenty each direction. He'd been the first to notice it, eyes going from his phone's map app to a folded one appearing older than both their ages put together. Jeff's finger nearly took her eye out as he pointed to a black forest north of them. They backtracked and, after the spine jarring potholes of Watkins Road, Jeff found the narrow-paved stretch of blacktop he wanted.

Travis was no help, either. Each time Jeff slowed to look at the print map, a habit that caused the car to swerve and Renna's guts to twist, Travis's pickup rode their bumper, threatening to tap the rental.

"We'll get there. Okay? Look," she did a little pointing of her own, "the sun's still high in the sky. There's plenty of time to get there. Besides, from what you said, we're nearly there now. Antoine didn't live all that far off the road, did he?"

"No. But we have to find the old highway."

Renna sat up. "How hard is it to find a highway?" She chose to leave the obvious chance to jab his directional skills alone. Still, the opportunity hung in the car like a joke awaiting a punch line.

"They shut it down in 2001."

"A whole highway?"

"No. Just this stretch of it. Most of the traffic takes Highway Two toward Miller Falls anyway. So, they shut this one down citing budget cuts for road repair."

"But people live on it, right?"

Silence.

"We're driving on a highway that no one lives on, heading into spooky woods to see if we can do our own rendition of Blair Witch or something?"

The car accelerated. "We're not on the highway yet." He nodded to one of the cows stretching their heads through the fence, reaching for morsels beyond the barbed wire.

Travis's truck whipped past them, and Stacy leaned out the open window, flashing them first a smile and then she jerked her tank top higher, exposing ample breasts before she slipped back inside.

"Well," Jeff said, stunned.

Renna patted his leg. "You've seen breasts before. Blink."

They watched as the pickup pulled away, skidded around a curve, then took off at a seventy-five-degree angle from them. Jeff slowed to a stop. Pastureland ate everything around and just ahead stood a makeshift gate from barbed wire and a couple of dried out pieces of lumber. Visible potholes and pie tin sized piles of manure peppered the pitiful remains of the highway, which shot straight as an arrow for a quarter mile before disappearing over a low ridge.

"This is it." Jeff inched to the curve and stopped. He looked over expectantly.

"Fine." She slid her flip flops on and got out of the car. Renna navigated the low ditch and, after having a weed painfully stab between her toes, made it to the gate. It took a few tries to get the barbed wire noose off the two posts, but she finally succeeded and pulled the triple strands to the far side, making an entrance big enough for the car to go through. While waiting for Jeff to drive the sedan to what he would no doubt call the greener side of the fence, Renna looked down the open road for Travis and Stacy. Unsure if the taillights were lit or just reflecting the intense summer sun, she shaded her eyes just in time to hear the telltale sounds of hot tires sliding across asphalt. The truck skidded out, tires sliding again, though this time in acceleration, and revved toward them.

"Hon, would you…?"

Renna motioned him on, knowing that he wanted her to wait for Travis and Stacy. The pickup bounced through the ditch and slowed as it passed.

Stacy rolled down the window and leaned out. "Sorry. Travis dared me."

"Hey, sweet thing," he called to Renna. "I'll flash you next time."

"You can do that and drive, huh?" Renna waved him on.

Reattaching the fence proved to be more difficult than releasing it, with the rusted wire not wanting to hook the post. After a few more tries she managed to get the noose over the top inch of the two pieces of wood. Renna studied it for a second before deciding that was good enough until they came back in a couple of hours.

"Travis says he's going to flash me later," she said, flopping back into her seat. The door slammed shut as Jeff eased on the gas.

"I'll talk to him. Okay?"

"Don't."

"Why," he teased, "do you want to see him naked?"

Jeff squeezed the car between chuck holes competing to swallow one of their tires whole. "No, but he'll be that much worse if he knows he's getting to me. And you said that we're here for a full two weeks." The woods came into view, closer than either of them expected, slashing a tall charcoal slice in an otherwise dusty yellow landscape.

"Maybe less."

"I know you. I'll be lucky to get home in time for a shower before work."

"Ren—"

"Don't 'Ren' me. I came, didn't I? But if you start getting condescending, you'll be driving me home right now." Her brewing anger finally frothed. "I had plans for these two weeks, Jeff. I wanted us to go to Maui…just us." Her eyes glassed over and she blinked them clear, unwilling for him to think she was just being emotional. "I have to work a full year to get two weeks off. Instead of us basking in the sun and snorkeling, I'm stuck here in the middle of nowhere, sweating myself into a puddle, and why? Because you couldn't go on this little adventure without me."

The car got very quiet.

Renna looked out the window, watching as they slowed before entering the woods. Pines rimmed the forest edge, needles creating a red blanket covering for the road. Branches hung low, free from road crew trimming and assault from vehicles passing underneath.

"Travis is going to love this," she said, glad to have gotten what was pissing her off out in the open. Renna changed the subject. "He'll get that pretty paint job scratched."

"Better him than us."

The car eased into the shadows and Jeff removed his glasses. They could see the road amidst the natural debris and recovery. Renna noted to herself that no more animal feces littered the road and she looked out the side window. None rested under the trees either.

"Odd."

"What?" Jeff's voice perked up that conversation had shifted.

"No manure."

"Didn't we get enough of that back there?"

"Seriously. I thought cattle looked for shady places to wait out the worst of the day's heat."

Jeff pushed the car to thirty, dangerously fast for the conditions. Travis still rode their bumper, revving his engine every so often, goading Jeff to accelerate just a little faster.

"Maybe there was another fence."

"Not on the road."

He tapped his brakes twice before slowing for a downed tree. "I dunno. Maybe it's part of the story."

"Speaking of the story," she shifted in her seat and looked over. "How much of this is fairy tale and how much is history?"

A grin spread across Jeff's face. "Mah dear," he said, doing a horrible rendition of a southern gentleman. "You have not yet begun to see the horrors this here land offers."

"So it's all fairy tale."

"Just the opposite. It's all true. Everything, right down to the minister kicking the crap out of Antoine—literally I might add—are all documented facts."

"…and the dead girl photo?"

"Soon."

"Now," Renna pressed, letting irritation settle back into her voice.

"That was in the eighties, when the drive-in became a more… mature venue."

"Drive-in? What drive-in? I thought we were going to Le Perchoir au Coucher de Soleil."

"We are." He sighed. "See, this is why I didn't want to tell you anything about the picture yet."

"What do you mean about this drive-in being a mature venue?"

"That didn't happen for twenty years after the drive-in opened."

"I don't get it."

"Exactly." He put a hand on hers. "Will you just trust me on this?"

The car pressed over a thick downed branch and it scraped the undercarriage with a wincing screech before the rear tire pushed them over to the other side.

"Not if you don't pay attention to the road."

His hand returned to the wheel. "But will you let me finish telling the story the way I want to?"

Renna's gaze darted from one side of the car to the other, taking in the expanse of woods. Thick pine trunks jutted out from dead foliage and undergrowth, the latter of which took on a decidedly skeletal appearance in the shade. The occasional beam of light broke through nearby, showing her cloud after cloud of mosquitoes and other flying insects.

"It's not much farther."

"Jeff," she said, not looking at him, "I really do have better things to do on a Friday night, on my vacation, I might add, than watch you and Tinkerbell back there do one of your cutesy little photo montages." The F-250 pickup's engine roared as if to drive the point home. Her attention stayed on the side mirror as the caboose of the two-vehicle convoy intentionally fishtailed a plume of dust into the woods.

Renna got back on-topic. "I mean…a drive-in? I thought we were checking out an old house."

"Not just a drive-in. An abandoned one."

"Abandoned, hell. This whole fucking road's been abandoned."

Jeff flushed red. "Ren, could you not? Just this once."

Renna put her feet on the dash, wrapped arms around the underside of her thighs and leaned forward to rest the side of her head against both knees. "How long?"

"A few hours at most."

"Half an hour."

"Three."

She offered up a smirk. "Maybe I take the car and leave you there to ride back with Captain Libido." Trees closed in further, branches blocking the afternoon's orange glow. A barrage of mosquitoes, taking advantage of the shade, peppered themselves out of existence against the windshield. In a flash Renna's smile vanished and she rolled the window up. "An hour, then I'm leaving with or without you."

"You're the best."

"You're an ass."

More places in the road buckled, thrust upward by tree roots. Plants pushed through cracks, creating a low garden of greenery for the car to force its way through. The combination of pavement-to-greenery gave the overall illusion that they were driving along a length of giant scales. The thwapping sound started to give Renna a headache.

"Shit!" Jeff stomped on the brakes, but not soon enough to keep the front tires from going over the lip of a ravine, dropping the front end, and stopping them cold.

Renna braced for the inevitable impact of Travis's truck hitting them. Instead, the horn blared and the yellow crew cab pickup skidded to a halt beside them, only with all four tires still safely on the pavement. His window rolled down and he motioned for her to do the same.

They both heard Travis's muffled, "What the hell?"

"Be nice," Jeff whispered as Renna rolled down the window.

"They must've heard you were coming," she called.

The pickup's window rolled back up without reply.

"I said, 'Nice,'" Jeff said.

"What?"

"I don't want any fighting today. I just want to check this place out and get back to the motel."

Renna dropped her legs. "Checking a place out usually means you shoot five hundred photos, force me into several, then skip dinner while you study what you've shot." She cut eyes at him. "That is not what I call a vacation."

"I'll be quick." He opened the door. "C'mon, we can ride the rest of the way with Travis and Stacy. Then we'll get the car loose and be home before dark."

"Home's over two hundred miles away." She jerked the door open and slammed it behind her.

Travis's window slid down a second time. "Mmmmmyes?" He looked over at them between the top of his sunglasses and brim of the ever-present straw hat.

Jeff opened the door and got out. "This is deliberate."

Renna's attention left Travis. "What?"

"There are old chew marks in the pavement. A front loader dug this out." Evenly spaced teeth marks serrated the highway's edge, leaving the ten-foot gap for a now dry creek to cut through.

"Don't sweat it," Travis called over. "I've got a rope and we'll pull you out later. I know you're jonesing to get to the place, so hop aboard and we'll get this thang done."

"We're close," Jeff said.

"Damned close by the look of it." Travis nodded toward the road.

Jutting out through the trees less than a hundred yards ahead was a sign for the Sky Maiden Drive-In. Once blazing red paint adorned the hooked red arrow underlining cursive white lettering. Years of neglect now left both dull and muddied with rust.

"Travis knew we were coming to a drive-in?" Renna meant it to sound as sharp as it did, leaving the accusation hanging in the air.

"He had to. Him knowing about the drive-in was the only way I could get Travis to come. You know what a movie buff he is."

Travis chuckled. "C'mon, you two. Have the lover's spat on your own time. We're burning daylight."

Jeff looked at Renna. "Walk or ride?"

She opened the rear driver's side door, got in and slid over behind Stacy. "What do you think?"

With the door barely latched behind Jeff, Travis jerked the wheel and stomped on the gas, shooting them to the right and into the woods. The pickup bounced with spine-jarring efficiency as he tore through the creek before the front two tires shot skyward as the truck struck the gap's far side, staying airborne even when rear tires propelled them up and back onto soft earth. A shower of pine needles sprayed through the trees behind them as Travis returned to navigating the dirt-caked remains of pavement.

Before Renna or Jeff could get a grip on their seat belts the truck shot down the road.

"So," Stacy said, "you're a photographer."

Brown fir branches reached out like skeletal fingers, narrowing the two-lane road to an access little larger than that of a one-car garage.

"Getting tight here," Travis said, finally easing off the gas.

"A student," Jeff corrected. "I don't have the arrogance to call myself one yet."

Renna snorted.

"So, what do you take pictures of?"

Jeff leaned forward to better see the drive-in's growing sign. "Stop here."

Tires slid on the bed of leaves and pine needles, coming to rest fifty yards short of the sign and the drive-in's entrance beyond. "Thought we were going in."

"We are, but on foot. I don't want to disturb the area more than necessary."

Travis rolled his eyes and mouthed the word, "artists," at Stacy.

Renna was already out the door with Jeff's camera bag, unzipping the quick-access flap to pull the SLR out. Jeff put a ball cap on his head with a mounted camera to the bill as he followed. Catching up, he took the unit by its bulky lens and managing a whispered, "Thank you," heard only by her.

She nodded, then elbowed him lightly. "Steak and a serious back rub tonight."

"Steak," the blonde cut in, "I just love steak!"

Renna shouldered Jeff's media bag. "How'd you meet Slim over there?"

"I met Travis last night. He said all of you were going on some spooky camping trip and told me I could come along." Stacy adjusted her shorts, then socks, then shirt—each with a practiced slowness to see who was paying attention.

Travis stared at the actions of his latest conquest and, when his leering was caught by Renna, he smiled and nodded as if approving of Stacy's actions.

Jeff, however, remained oblivious and fixated on metering for a shot of the sign. A test pic fired off, then another. He scrutinized each on the LCD display, zooming in and thumbing across the image before preparing to take another shot.

"So, I was asking," Stacy said to Jeff.

Renna gently grasped her arm and shook her head. "Not now. Wait 'til he's between shots."

A visible pout appeared on the blonde's face.

"Jeff shoots just about everything," Renna said in a low voice. "People. Landscapes. Animals. You name it." Another click of the camera gave punctuation to her answer.

"Would you mind if I asked if he'd…you know."

"Shoot you?" Renna stressed the first word at Stacy.

"Yeah."

Click.

The two looked over to see the unblinking eye of the camera pointed at them.

Jeff grinned. "I'll call it 'Moon Over Discontent.'"

Stacy furrowed her brow. "It's too early to see the moon."

Renna thumbed back toward the pickup without looking. "Gonna get a sunburn on that pasty white thing one of these days, Trav."

A series of simian whoops and howls echoed as a reply.

Stacy looked back and burst into laughter. "How'd you know?"

"His ass sees enough open air that I think he breathes through that thing."

Jeff stood and walked back over to them. "We know he belches enough through it."

Another barrage of whoops drew everyone's attention back to the truck bed. Travis held his open pants with one hand and pointed emphatically with the other. "Jeffy! Up here man! This is where you want to be."

Camera in hand, Jeff climbed into the pickup's bed, studying the tree line on the drive-in's side of the road. Orange light sliced through the pines, illuminating the remains of an oversized billboard. Little else was visible. One click became five, which in turn drew into two dozen in under a minute.

"Jeff, we're here now," Renna called. "Why don't you tell us what makes this place so spooky?"

Stacy mumbled, "Aside from the obvious?"

"In my bag," was all Jeff said without even bothering to pull his eye away from the camera. Renna reached into the bag's main compartment and pulled a thick tabbed manilla folder out. Opening it revealed a printed blog listing cursed locations. The photo accompanying the text showed a crudely drawn demon wisping out of a car. She scanned the first page, thumbed to the second and ended on the third before finding reference to the Sky Maiden. Not much more than a blurb, the drive-in's reputation spanned over half a century, claims ranging from boogeymen waiting to pull the wary traveler down to the depths of hell to fairies wanting their land back. Not one reference fell back to Antoine. Further pages ranged from magazine articles scanned from the library to newspaper clippings.

"So, we're on cursed ground?"

Jeff finished the shot and hopped down. "Not so much cursed as unhealthy."

Stacy frowned with concern. "We're not going to get sick, are we?"

Travis looked down to hide the blustering laugh threatening to escape and Jeff chose that moment to clear his throat.

"No," Renna answered after fighting her own smile, "we're not going to get sick. He just meant this place isn't welcoming to people so they stay away." Her attention fell back to Jeff. "Why don't you just give us this part of the story before we go poking around?"

Jeff continued to stare at the tree line as he walked over to them, trailed by Travis. "In 1965, Bradford Willis bought part of Antoine's acreage from the county. It'd been vacant for over sixty years and he got it for a song. It's several miles out of town, but still on a paved road linking Parish Hill to his own Willshire. So, in his opinion the property's a good buy." He walked past everyone and went to the Sky Maiden's sign, disappearing behind it. "His entire inheritance goes into the venture…even the family house is mortgaged to the rafters. For three years workers from both towns construct the drive-in. Well. Septic. Power. Trees border the entire work site, leaving onlookers shit outta luck."

Boom!

The three jumped from the thunderous bang coming from the sign. A secondary screech of metal on metal pulled at their eardrums before two working bulbs, one red, the other yellow, flickered to life on the sign. Sockets for the other forty or so either were empty, had broken bulbs or simply remained dark.

Renna applauded. "You had the electricity turned on for this?"

He grinned. "Nope."

Travis stepped forward and reached out to the red bulb. "Could burn the whole place down."

Stacy moved beside Travis in an obvious effort for comfort. "This isn't what I expected."

"What's weird is the power's never really been turned off. They just flipped the master switch out here at the sign and called it a day."

Renna clasped her hands behind her back. "And you know this how?"

"A year and a half of research. Utility workers like it out here about as much as everyone else so the job never actually got done."

They followed Jeff around the sign and stared into the woods. Remnants of pavement were still recognizable. After that, only the dip in the tree line told of any access.

"June first of 1968 the Sky Maiden prepares to open its doors. Bradford hires from both towns in an effort to generate more interest." Jeff wiggles his hips, causing the camera to bounce back and forth. "Enter Ann Marie Wilcox."

Travis's hand dropped behind Stacy, eliciting a screech a second later. "Quite the name."

Jeff smiled. "Ann Marie needs the work. You see, she got a little too much loving a few months back and is in the motherly way. Now here," Jeff waved his arm in a great sweeping motion, "in the heartland of America that wasn't just unseemly, it was downright taboo." He stepped into the shadowed gloom of the trees, motioning for them to follow. "So June fifteenth rolls around and everyone's playing their parts. Chucky Dillon and Ann Marie are manning the concession counter and keeping everyone in hot dogs and hamburgers. A crew of eight, including Bradford who's running the projector, are ready for the opening night's events.

"Just a side note I nearly forgot about." Jeff cleared his throat. "Bradford made a special point of hiring Chucky and putting him somewhere highly visible. This is the summer of '68 and racial anger is still burning hot. The Chicago riots were less than two months old and he wanted to show everyone that he hired equally, but not too equal, if you get my drift. To Bradford, the best part about his new employee isn't that Chucky's black, it's that he's the size of a linebacker and that's good for business when patrons get too lippy. He hired Chucky away from the maintenance crew that worked this stretch of road."

Renna said, "Looks like they're still doing a fantastic job, too."

"Bradford puts Chucky on the grill figuring every man knows how to char food."

Jeff turned and trotted fifteen yards ahead of them and stopped beside a hulking mass of vines and undergrowth. As the other three approached, telltale features of a ticket booth peeked through nature's ongoing reclamation. Waist-high brickwork bordered the shack. An empty window frame, save a palm-sized sliver in the upper right corner, stared out at them. Inside, warped paneling lined the back wall, yet still held enough tension to bear the clock upright.

"Little Becky Corruthers sits out here in ninety-degree heat…. Ren, flip to her tab."

Renna thumbed through the multicolored tabs, taking notice that their uniformity seemed to give the collected documents teeth. She found B. CORRUTHERS written in pencil near the back. The black and white smiling face from a high school yearbook stared back, stiff brown or dark red hair framed a freckled face straining to look beyond her years.

"Don't turn the page," Jeff said. "Not yet." He had the same grin as when he talked her into skinny dipping in the river last year.

"Why?"

"All in due time."

"You might want to speed this up some, champ." Renna noticed even Travis's smart-assed comments had caved to the story Jeff told. Mister cowboy stood slack-jawed, staring at Jeff with rapt fascination…or boredom. She couldn't really tell which.

Jeff turned and led them down to the entrance of Sky Maiden's parking arena.

It was surprising that no garbage lined the entrance as was typical for any abandoned place. Only pine needles and scraggly weeds in extreme need of mowing littered the way. Three brick pillars bordered the twenty-foot-wide access. The one in the middle contained some type of glass dome, sporting jagged blades for any daring to touch.

Renna knelt at the center pillar and shifted a handful of brown pine needles and pulled out a piece of the dome. On it the outline of South America and just the lower edge of the United States could just be made out. A click and a bright flash brought her back to the moment. Jeff continued pointing the camera at her, popping off a second blinding shot. South America fell to the ground.

"Next time ask."

Jeff acted as if he didn't hear her. "Welcome…to The Sky Maiden." He stepped aside and, with a swoop of an arm, let them pass.

ACKNOWLEDGMENTS

First, hats off to my family (*for their unlimited patience offering input after hearing, "What about this draft?" enough times to make their ears bleed*), Fiction Foundry— *fictionfoundry.org*—(*the critique group who tore these stories apart and showed me how to rebuild them*), the Denver Horror Collective (*for their insight*), the Colorado Springs Fiction Writers Group (*for their encouragement to pursue publication on some of these early works*), Scott Leonard (*my high school English teacher who kicked my ass when it really needed kicking and remains a friend to this day*), and finally Bob Lewis (*who pushed for this collection to happen, and brought it to fruition*).

ABOUT THE AUTHOR

For over 30 years, Henry Snider has dedicated time to helping others tighten their writing through critique groups, classes, lectures, prison prose programs, and high school fiction contests. He co-founded Fiction Foundry (est. 2012) and the award-winning Colorado Springs Fiction Writer's Group (1996-2013). Henry lives in Colorado with his wife, fellow author and editor Hollie Snider, son—poet Josh Snider—and numerous neurotic animals.

Also available from Polymath Press

Ghost Girls and Rabbits
Cassondra Windwalker

Flush with the victory of winning the election as Alaska's first Athabaskan Senator, Noni Begay wakes to find herself buried alive. When her coffin lid opens, though, it's not to rescue but to six years of captivity, betrayed by the one person she trusted most. Escape will require not only all her strength but all the strength and stories of the ancestors she had until now imagined were only a useful device, an accessory she wore to win votes and social media followers.

Mary Nelson's only daughter, Ryska, went missing ten years ago, with no one but her mother to search for her. Having used up every favor and chit she has, Mary is willing to risk everything on one last ploy to save her daughter from the monsters...even if she has to become one herself.

A chilling psychological horror novel excoriating the epidemic of missing and murdered indigenous women and girls in North America, Ghost Girls and Rabbits is an unforgettable read perfect for fans of Scandinavian noir and literary horror, told by two fractured minds in the trappings of myths truer than mirrors.

Bright City, Shattered
Millie Abecassis

Reine just started her job as head of security at Clean Crystal Corporation (C3) when Isaline, a brilliant technician and the CEO's niece, is found dead in the crystal's Core Room. Chief Executive Max Caldwell and Detective Inspector Novau are convinced Isaline was murdered by another employee, dismissing theories of a safety accident. They claim the crystal, powering Bright City's clean energy, is harmless. But Reine, haunted by Isaline's fear when she warned her away from the crystal, suspects otherwise.

Isaline knew something, and Reine is determined to uncover the truth. The problem is: she needs her job at C3 to support her family, and Max Caldwell won't tolerate Reine's eagerness to investigate Isaline's death as a potential accident.

A retro-futurist vision of life in an isolated metropolis, Bright City, Shattered is a gripping mystery of lies, loyalty, and the relentless pursuit of truth.

In the Woods: A Fiction Foundry Anthology
Edited by Robert Lewis
Featuring the story "Olden's Wood" by Henry Snider

Strange things can happen in the woods.
Sometimes they're frightening.
Sometimes they're funny.
Sometimes they're just plain weird.

The authors of the Fiction Foundry writers' critique group have taken it upon themselves to explore all the strange things that happen in the often majestic and yet often harsh woodlands.

Fiction Foundry, established 2012, is a group of writers dedicated to helping prepare one another's work for professional publication. In this anthology, the group's authors show off their eclectic visions of life among the trees.

Featuring contributions by John H. Howard, Sangita Kalarickal, Josh Snider, Carolyn Kay, Robert Lewis, Charli Cowan, Henry Snider, Shiloh Silveira, Kari J. Wolfe, Christophe Maso, and Hollie Snider, this anthology brings us out of urban life and shows a world of forest spirits, haints, mental illness, parasitic spiders, werewolves, out of control plants, evil forces, reincarnation, humans with animal ears, witches, and Lovecraftian horrors.

And all of them can be found…In the Woods.

Arithmophobia: An Anthology of Mathematical Horror
Edited by Robert Lewis

"Arithmophobia," *n.*: The fear of numbers or mathematics.

Whether you love mathematics or find it terrifying, this anthology of original tales of terror is sure to send a chill down your spine. With an unlucky thirteen brand new horror stories and a bonus poem in case any readers suffer from triskaidekaphobia, these pages combine the talents of some of the genre's most experienced award-winning practitioners of terror and some of the literary world's most promising new voices.

These stories tell us of strange and horrifying new geometries, crazed and violent mathematicians, sentient and malevolent numbers, and even some new mathematical twists on some classic monsters. You needn't be a mathematician to experience these new forms of mathematical terror, though students of the discipline might recognize some familiar names and ideas lurking in the shadows.

So pull up a chair, dust off your abacus and slide rule, and prepare to experience…

Arithmophobia.

Get your copies of these and other Polymath Press titles online at
www.polymathpress.com
or wherever fine books are sold!